Lore

Steve K Peacock

For my parents.
They're all supportive and revolting.

CHAPTER 1

I was drinking whiskey. As drinks go, the stuff tastes like engine lubricant, but I wasn't drinking it for the taste. The important thing about it was that *she* couldn't stand the smell. An odd sort of memorial, I suppose, but then she'd always enjoyed my sense of humour. Besides, it's a good thing to drink in front of a roaring fire.

The fire station had been on fire when I arrived, but it hadn't truly gone up until about five minutes after I had perched myself on the bonnet of my car. From glowing windows to a flaming tower, it was quite a soothing sight. There's something dangerously hypnotic about a lot of flames. Or maybe that's just me.

I was getting closer. This was the fifteenth building the mystery arsonist had hit, and the first that I had managed to reach in time to catch the main showing. Most of the time I managed to arrive at a blackened husk of a building, smoke spirals and sobbing families being the best entertainment on offer by that point. But I'd gotten a handle on his pattern now, sussed out his signature. I was gaining ground.

I took another sip from my glass and scowled. The

distant sirens of the fire brigade were just creeping into earshot now, speeding hell-for-leather on their way back from whatever wild goose chase the arsonist had sent them on. They hadn't been gone long, I'd put money on that, but a pissed off wizard didn't need long. Better they not have to deal with something they couldn't comprehend, anyway. Trying to explain to a layman that the fire they were chasing was an evocation at the beckon call of some shadowy bastard-wizard would have been too much effort, and great pains had been taken to keep it that way.

With the last fourteen places, I hadn't been willing to say one way or the other whether magic had been involved. Fire is a pain in the arse when it comes to forensic techniques in the material realm, but it's ten times worse in the arcane. It eats magic, carves through it like it isn't even there, and that means any trace magic left by the arsonist tends to go up in smoke quite literally. But I'd made it to this one before that had happened. There wasn't much, nothing I could particularly use, but there was *something* there, and that was enough to confirm my suspicions.

My phone buzzed in my pocket and I whipped it out and flipped it open. Flip phones may be old-hat now, but they're still cool. 'Hello, dear.'

'Tell me you've got something this time, Parker.' The voice was a silky southern accent, echoes of Oxbridge and a spoiled childhood, and young. Charlie had sounded young five years ago, when she had first started doling out instructions to me via telephone, and her voice hadn't seemed to want to change. 'Whitehall are getting uppity.'

I sighed. 'Whitehall are always uppity, Charlie. Paranoia is their bread and butter.'

'True, but we still need to shut this down. Did you get to this one in time? Just give me something I can show them to get them to back off a little.'

'There are definite traces. Not enough that I can track it, but enough that I can confirm we've got a problem,' I said. There was a small lie in there, but she wouldn't know.

Charlie went quiet for a moment and hammered at her computer keyboard. Or possibly a typewriter. I can never really tell the two apart over the phone, and up at Whitehall it could really be either. They had been hesitant to embrace the information age. 'Any leads?'

'Nothing solid,' I said. 'I'm going to have a wander around, see what I can pick up. Maybe I'll stumble across his casting site, find something that the fire didn't consume. Of course, if you'd approve a little tracking spell...'

I'd been needling her about that little demand for weeks now, and each time she had become more exasperated. Now she was one step shy of full-blown annoyance. It did nice things to her voice. 'Oh for God's sake, Jameson! You *know* they'll never sign off on that!'

'No,' I shot back. 'They would never have signed off on that before I had proof that magic was involved. But now we know for sure, and if they want him caught I'm going to need to fight fire with fire.' There was a pause. 'If you see what I mean.'

'I'll see what I can do,' she said. She did not sound happy.

I wrestled for a charming, yet patronising, way of thanking her, then gave up and snapped the phone shut. Then I finished my whiskey and threw the glass back into the boot along with the half-empty bottle and various oddities that accumulate in the rear of a man's car. I swear most of them just come into being on their own. I certainly didn't put them there.

Now I was just procrastinating. What I wanted to do was wait until Whitehall signed off on some minor magics. It had been so long since I had last cast a spell. Sensing the residue of our arcane arsonist had been divine, and now I was grasping for a way to throw off the enforced abstinence of Whitehall, even if just for a moment.

The tracking spell was bullshit really, I had a fair idea where to find my next lead, but I wanted my *hit*. Abstinence is all well and good when you've got no temptation, but a brush with your old mistress and the longing suddenly erupts in force.

Realistically, however, I didn't have time to wait. There had been a sourness to the residue, one that spoke of power borrowed rather than the sweet tang of something innate. Back when I had been part of the scene, power brokers had been raking in the cash, although that was very much a product of the old way of doing things. What few magicians that were still free of Whitehall's clutches preferred to throw their own magical muscle around, rather than that of someone else, even if it *was* more potent. Whitehall may not have had as firm a grasp on the North as it liked to pretend it did, but it had changed the landscape considerably in the last five years. It's always easiest to grab the noisy ones, after all, and people selling their power were always going to be near the top of that particular list, and their top customers right below them. But, if I could get to *this* broker, I could get to the arsonist. Surely there couldn't be too many of them left to sift through?

That would mean, however, a trip to the underground, and I'm not exactly popular there. Not that I can blame them, before they'd gotten to me, I was suspicious of the Whitehall Warlocks too. Bastard turncoats, magic vacuums sent to enslave or destroy every free magician in the country, that's what I had thought. It turned out that that my prior assumptions was were mostly correct, but slavery did have its upsides nowadays, at least the way Whitehall did it, although I didn't expect my former peers to see that.

Finding them would be tricky. The knowledge that warlocks could come for you at any time had driven the free magicians underground, and I wasn't really equipped to find them. It wasn't as if the free magicians were going to advertise themselves so people like me could come and kick in their doors. They had other means of feeling each other out.

You need a wizard to catch a wizard, that's more or less Whitehall's entire reason for having warlocks. Unfortunately, the easiest way of *finding* a wizard is by feeling out the tremors of his power and tracking it back to the source, like ripples in a pond. Ripples that warlocks can't see because we are banned from using bloody magic. Whitehall, therefore, likes us to use our knowledge of the craft to find other solutions, since clearly that would be terribly easy to do. I prefer to cheat.

Before Whitehall brought me in, I had my fair share of connections. Most of them had shunned me the moment I'd been nabbed, but I had collected favours like kids collect the trading cards put out by whatever Japanese anime is big nowadays. Enough that cashing one in was no big deal.

I took one last look at the blaze and then climbed into my car. Ordinarily I would have called ahead, as is only polite, but I was quite looking forward to playing the warlock card for once. Humberside City was too far north of Whitehall to have really developed a strong and active cadre of warlocks, so most of my jobs were wild goose chases and token gestures to get our visibility up in preparation of the inevitable big push. It was a far cry from the well-regimented and stringently controlled nature of the south. But the name still had some weight to it, and after so long chasing ghosts it would be nice to swing it around a little. My ego enjoys a good stroking.

As I drove, I tried some other telephone numbers from the old days. If this idea didn't pan out, I would prefer to have a backup just in case. No one answered, which wasn't exactly a shock: when the warlocks come for you, people tend to hear about it. Doubly so when they came for me, I should imagine. I did not go gracefully, to which I'm sure a great many will attest. A few of the numbers I dialled didn't even ring, and I caught myself wondering how many people had been brought in since myself. More out of curiosity than worry, truth be told. I'd never liked them enough to worry.

At least I was in the North, so I had that on my side. Northerners are not particularly well disposed to people from the government rocking up and telling them what to do at the best of times, and as such things were going slowly for Whitehall in this neck of the woods. They had a firm stranglehold on the South, but the bred in the bone independence of the Northerners made them more brazen and less careful than they should be. This was why an underground existed at all.

And yet, as I pulled up outside the bar that Toirneach Craic called his home, I felt myself gearing up for a fight. I swear I'm not always like this when I have to talk to an Irishman. Just the ones I have to meet in bars. Which, I admit, is where I meet most of my Irishmen. But I promise that's just a coincidence. *It is.*

Anyway, look, let me get back on track. Part of the deal in becoming a warlock is that you can't do magic any more, not even the simplest of cantrips – that's what we call the easy peasy baby spells, for you uninitiated – but to try and even the playing field you are allowed to have things ensorcelled by the few enchanters Whitehall keeps on staff. I'd eschewed the traditional amulets and bracelets for rings and a jacket – they were more practical and less likely to draw attention. Everyone was looking for amulets and bracelets, fewer people were looking for rings and almost no one was looking for a fabric blazer to hold an enchantment of any kind.

Of course, this didn't stop the entire room staring at me when I walked through the door, but I tend to get that reaction in any place I enter. I have one of those sexy faces, you know.

To be fair, describing the place as a bar was a bit of a stretch. It was only a bar in the same way sticking a long table in front of your drinks cabinet makes your dining room a bar. So when I say the entire room turned to look at me, I'm really only talking about two or three people. But they were angry looking people, so I thought it fitting to make the thing sound a little more grandiose. I'm sure you understand.

'Well, that's a face I ain't seen in a while,' came a voice from the far end of the room.

'Oh, Brendy,' I said, using his real name. What, you thought his poor mother actually named him *Toirneach*? 'Surely you see my beautiful face when you close your eyes at night? Quite frankly, I'd be hurt if not.'

He had fashioned himself a little throne out of a wingback chair, a cheap plastic skull resting under one of his feet to give him a sort of bargain-basement Conan the Destroyer look. Well, if you substitute rippling muscles for poor posture in equal measure. He was going for the full slouch of villainy, but hadn't managed the villain part. 'You've got some nerve coming to see me Jimbo, as if I wouldn't know what side you're playing for now.'

Obviously, I knew he'd know. That was the point. 'Then let's keep things civil, shall we? No need for me to start flexing the bulging muscles of bureaucracy, right?'

'I'm always civil, pal. You know me,' he said, but his hands were gripping the arms of his little throne a smidge tighter than they had been. He'd always been good at masking his fear. 'What can I do to facilitate your fucking off sooner rather than later?'

I know it might not look it, but this was Brendy at his most civil. He'd come a long way from when I'd first met him – some would say he'd fallen rather than come – acting as an agent of the Lord of the North during the period Whitehall now called The Dark Time. I'll give you a greater run-down on that later, when it's a bit more appropriate. It's not something I like talking about for personal reasons.

Suffice to say, back when things were at their worst, Brendy was at his. His Toirneach name was an honourific at first, bestowed for his reputation as his Lord's clean-up man. He'd turn up after the slaughter, doll it all up so word would get out and people would know exactly who was the biggest bastard in toy town. The thunder that followed the lightning.

He also made it his business to know other peoples', which was why he had survived as long as he had and why I needed him now.

'We've got ourselves a rogue wizard burning down bits of the city, as I'm sure you know,' I said.

His eyes narrowed slightly. 'Are you here to accuse me?'

'Give me a break, Brendy. I'm not daft enough to take a run at you on my own, am I? I'd at least drag along a couple of meat-shields for that sort of thing.'

Part of the reason he had avoided the warlocks coming for him as long as he had was down to his reputation. It wouldn't save him forever, but as long as he believed it would it would also keep *me* safe. He wouldn't want to antagonise Whitehall by getting into a scrap with a warlock, but he'd have no qualms about ripping my soul out through my eye sockets if he thought himself threatened. He was a pleasant sod.

8

'Then what do you want?'

I took a few steps forward. His boys, or whatever you call henchmen these days, shifted in their seats. 'It seems our wayward mage is using someone else's power.'

'A broker?'

'Looks that way to me.'

'Interesting,' he said and shifted his slouch. 'Not many people left with the balls or the requisite debts to go into that game. Your lot have properly fucked up this neck of the woods, you know.'

'Now now, there's no need to start playing the blame game with me, Brendy. We both know we weren't exactly innocent in the whole thing.'

One of Brendy's boys leapt to his feet, shouting. 'Don't claim kinship with us, you blood-traitor fuck.'

Brendy held up a finger and the man sat back down, frowning but without complaint. 'If you would like to argue about politics, perhaps it would be best we have a few drinks first. Friends should never talk politics sober.'

'Is that what we are, friends?'

'We were once, as I recall. It suits my purposes to keep you as that for now, rather than an enemy.'

'Oh, mate,' I said and forced myself to blush. 'You say the sweetest things.'

'Do you want a drink or not?'

I shook my head. 'Already had one today, thanks. The information will do me fine.'

'Just so's we're clear, this is you calling in a favour, right? I'm not about to sell you one of my own out of the goodness of me heart, like.'

Seeing as he had started putting the accent on thick, I figured it only fair to do the same. Besides, I'm English. You come at us with some weird foreign way of talking, it is in our nature to mimic it like masochistic mynah birds. Why do you think we've had so many wars? 'Consider it me callin' in one of me favours te be sure, boyo.'

I admit, I'm not very good at accents. I also admit that that was perhaps not the most politically correct way to address him. Then again, as you will learn about me, I am naturally imbued with supernatural powers of diplomacy. Even when I'm being a dick, it works in my favour.

Brendy let out a tight chuckle, although his boys were less forgiving. 'Good, I've been wanting rid of that black mark. Although I can't give him to you directly.'

'That doesn't sound like something I'd want to hear.'

'I've not been blind to your lot spiriting brokers away in the dead of night. I figured it best to maintain some distance from them, in case Whitehall started casting a wider net. But that doesn't mean I don't know how you can find him.'

I fired out a theatrical sigh. 'You're not good at suspense, Brendy. Get to the point.'

'Keeping track of the clients is almost as good as keeping track of the dealer,' he said. He leant forward, the horrid little plastic skull squeaking an inch forward as he did so. 'There's a gathering of minor talents, the sort that didn't bother themselves with the politics way back when, so haven't really learned how the world is these days. Might want to ask around there. You'll find them at the University.'

I laughed. 'Of course.'

'You get the best and cheapest booze in a university bar. That's just a fact, pal. Doesn't matter if the place has been shut down, it's seeped into the walls by then.'

'God, I hope they're not drinking alcohol out of the drywall.'

'You never know with these types.'

Here's a thing you may not have known: fighting a secret war against your own magical citizens is not cheap, and yet you still have to pay for it. Governments tend to get more leeway with their overdrafts than your average wage-drone, but it isn't infinite. You start seeing black holes in the budget, excessive cutbacks, and you can probably link it to magicians somehow. We're not cheap to keep.

This government had chosen to siphon the cash from the education budget, and Humberside had not done well. Being as it had never been a particularly popular university, the income from students just wasn't enough to keep the entire thing open. They'd wasted millions on whole buildings, only to find that they were now surplus to requirement. At this point half the campus was shut down, mostly buildings that had never formally opened at all. Perfect place for the empowered to meet for a tête-à-tête.

I'm not the super-spy or information broker that Brendy is, but I have enough about me to know whether I'm being spun a lie or not. The information he had given me felt plausible, however, and despite my current occupation I still felt like I had earned enough good will to get some measure of truth out of the man. You can't end a friendship so easily, not with Toirneach Craic, in any case.

'You can consider your favour repaid, mate,' I said as I turned to leave. I was going for the whole dramatic exit, all loud footsteps and billowing coat, but he called after me.

'There's one more thing you might want to know. Consider it a freebie.'

I stopped but didn't turn around. This was sounding awfully like the start of a setup. I made sure my rings were ready, just in case things were about to get nasty. 'And what would that be?'

'Only that it might be in your best interests to let this drop.'

'And why is that?'

'I am not in a position to comment. Perhaps, as a favour to you –'

I interrupted. 'Goodbye, Brendy.' I wasn't about to let him lure me in with seductive little factoids like that. The man would use words like weapons if you'd let him, and I wasn't really keen on finding myself indebted to *him* this time.

I made my exit before he could stop me, giving the dramatic thing a second go. I'm pretty sure it worked. It was totally swoon-worthy. Alas, the endorphins from being so cool had largely worn off by the time I closed my car door.

Brendy's boys watched me from the windows as I pulled away from the last little embassy of the old ways.

CHAPTER 2

I pulled into the empty car park and girded myself for another fight.

This would be different from my meeting with Brendy. The minor talents were unpredictable. They were as likely to see a warlock as a challenge as they would regard him as a threat, unaccustomed as they were to thinking of the bigger picture. They were low on the list of targets for Whitehall, but had a habit of jumping themselves up the list by merit of being too stupid to know when to stop talking back to the man with the boot on their throat.

You also tended to find them in large groups, which led to even more stupidity and bravado. Brendy and his ilk would weigh up the pros and cons of the attack, but minor talents were just as likely to resort to pack mentality, to strike as soon as they felt threatened. This made them tricky to deal with.

I didn't look like a warlock, which I hoped would at least give me some protection from the wrath of the people inside. People *expected* them to rock up in long leather trench coats, standing well over six feet tall and wielding a silver sword. I was a respectable five foot eight, in well-worn jeans, hiking boots and a blazer that looked like it had been dragged through a thorn bush more than once. Which was true. The look was starting to lose its edge a little now that I had hit my mid twenties, but as long as I kept my tattoo covered up it would be hard for people to immediately peg me as a warlock. As I had tried to grow my hair over it, that should have been easy enough.

This was very much a case where subtlety was warranted, but I've never been very good at that. Don't get me wrong, I'd definitely be trying that approach, but I'm a modern man. I am fully aware of my flaws and have planned accordingly. As I said before, I tend to wear a lot of defences.

My blazer itself didn't offer much in the way of protection. You can't do much with jackets really, permanence is not in their nature, so the best the enchanters could manage was making it so that I wasn't about to get cut-down by an instant-death spell. They'd still hurt, and most likely even kill through the force of impact alone, but the spell itself couldn't kill me. In any case, that would only work for down-and-dirty combat magic, it offered no protection from ritual magic.

My assortment of rings, however, were much better. I hadn't been allowed to enchant them with any offensive magics, as much as I had petitioned them to let me wield the Mandarin's rings from Iron Man, so had been forced to settle for a number of shields that I could trigger as and when needed. Most were one-shot things, burnt out as soon as they absorbed whatever it was they were designed to stop, and those that weren't were not particularly powerful. Still, the important thing was that I at least had some protection, even if my offensive capabilities were currently limited to how fast I can swing my fists – we like our jewellery to have corners, even the rings, lots of lovely jagged bits to catch on flesh. And there are ways to improve your chances, if you're willing to bend the rules a little.

As I entered the building I found myself cursing the fact that I lived in the UK and not America. A gun would have been lovely at this point, much as I hate them. Or a sword. Can Americans carry swords? At the time I was fully convinced they could carry anything from pocket knives to RPGs if they wanted, and any one of those would have been welcomed by me as I stepped into the dark hallway inside.

It wasn't pitch black – at least one external wall was mostly windows, which let in what ambient light there was outside, the sun having disappeared midway through my search – but just dark enough to make every shadow seem threatening. I was playing a part, however, and going for the big bad stranger thing, so I resolved not to let any of the shadows goad me into revealing quite how shit scared I actually was. You never knew who could be watching.

Which, might I just add, is a stupid thing to tell yourself if you are trying to avoid jumping at your own shadow. Pro-tip.

Someone had painted fluorescent arrows on the walls. I followed them dutifully, ever the curious kitten. They betrayed just how piss-poor the talents at this place would be. Ordinarily, anyone connected with their magic should have been able to find their way through to the others just by feeling out for the gentle thrumming of their power. If they were so weak as to need actual directions through this place, it was no real wonder that a broker had made them his clientèle.

Before too long, I found myself in front of a pair of thick wooden double doors painted purple. Wizards like purple. I'm not sure why, but it's just one of those things that seem to latch onto us as we grow. We also like beards, cigarettes, moaning at people, and hobbits, if you're keeping score. Anyway, the arrows led to these doors, so it was reasonable to assume this was the bar I was looking for. I suspect the light bouncing under the doors was the real give-away, all neon lasers and whatnot.

This was confirmed when I reached out to open the door.

The hallway was silent as a tomb, but as soon as I crossed the threshold I was smacked in the face by a wall of pure noise. Someone had set up one hell of a sound-proofing spell to keep that noise contained inside the bar, and considering what was playing, that was definitely for the best.

I couldn't place the music, largely because it was so loud I couldn't really hear it. What I was hearing was the sound of thousands of pounds worth of audio equipment tearing itself apart. At least fifty people had crammed themselves into the room to witness this event, most of them in their early twenties – or at least that's how it appeared – although one or two "classical" wizards were among the group too, all white hair and beards. So much of magic is perception, even today.

Free magicians these days – that is, anyone in the empowered community who hasn't been bagged by Whitehall and made to spy and capture their own as a warlock – are a bit overly keen on looking the part. Most of them have little in the way of natural talent, or have only come into it recently, so they're still trying to find their place in the world. Kids, basically.

Thankfully, they hadn't seemed to notice me, which was a godsend. If I could get in and out quickly, the chances were good that I wouldn't run into someone who knew me and get trapped in a ruck. In truth, I wasn't sure if they were the type to risk descending on a warlock like a herd of crazed jackals, but I wasn't willing to find out. To that end, I found a seat at the bar. You can always count on a barman to guide you, and they tend to prefer remaining non-partisan.

The code of the barman is a wonderful thing.

It was a barmaid today, actually. Beautiful in the way that made you want to drink beer, that depressing realisation that you can never get the time of day from someone that gorgeous unless you were willing to tip generously. I don't tip serving staff, so I don't think we got off on the right foot. She gave me a look as I summoned her over with what had once been a tenner, but was now a self-sufficient collection of creases.

'Yes?' she shouted over the din.

'I'm looking for someone –' I shouted back.

She scowled at me for a moment and flicked her wrist at the nearest speaker. The music vanished, although judging from the continued dancing on the far side of the room, only for the barmaid and myself. 'Can't even whip up a simple sound screen? Are you sure you're supposed to be here?'

My eye twitched as I swallowed my anger at that patronising statement. 'Hey, you drew those arrows for some people. We can't all be Gandalf, can we? Want to see some ID?' I said with a sly wink.

That earned me an impolite gesture before she quickly stormed off down the bar to serve a pair of goths who had merged their faces into one giant pair of slobbering lips. Thankfully she had left me with the sound screen, at least.

I gave the room a proper look. They weren't having a good time, they were dancing to forget. It's something you notice after years of being the one guy at the club who doesn't dance. You watch people, you see how they change when the drink takes them. You watch *which* drink takes them. This was a room of people who were looking to escape from the fear for just one evening.

Understandable, not that it would do them any good. It was only a matter of time before Whitehall's reach properly extended this far.

Eventually, the barmaid returned with a beer that was mostly head, slammed it down in front of me and glared at me until I paid her. I considered telling her that she hadn't actually let me order anything, but something told me it would be smarter not to. The hand on my shoulder a moment later reinforced that notion.

I turned around into a beautiful face with ancient eyes. Like many of the others there, he looked young, but only if you ignored what was quite literally staring you in the face. Perfect skin, hair, teeth, everything that said he was twenty, but keen eyes that saw more than they should; tired and old. He was worryingly attractive, and even with my magical senses atrophied as they were, I could recognise his kind instantly.

When you're young, sex magic sounds amazing. Get together with a group of sexy teens, bone into the dead of night, and use all that energy to whip up a spell or two. What they don't tell you, of course, is how dangerous it is. Opening your heart up like that, through such an intimate and primal thing as sex, is not a one-way conduit. It can lead to bad things I'd rather not go into right now, especially if you aren't even aware that bad things *can* happen. Suffice to say, a sex magician as old as this fellow was one step down from an incubus – a master manipulator and an expert at exploiting the young and the sexually charged for his own ends. He was most likely the only person there with any real magical muscle.

I'd never gotten on with sex magicians. Even discounting the creepy rapist vibe they gave off and knowing that they were exploitative arseholes, they were far too tactile. Always touching you, stroking bits of you, completely incapable of keeping their hands to themselves. The vermin of the magical world, as far as I'm concerned.

The only good thing about them is the derogatory nickname they picked up along the way. Vagicians. Well, it made me laugh.

He lowered himself onto the stool next to mine, his hand sliding gently down my arm and to my own. For a moment he tried to interlace his fingers with mine, but I pulled my hand back sharpish and he let out a girlish giggle.

'I haven't seen you around before, have I?' he said.

'Not as far as I'm aware,' I replied. Avoid eye contact and the creeps will go away, guaranteed.

'I figured you were new. A regular would have known that Lucy doesn't get on well with the charming types. She finds it... insulting,' he pointed at the barmaid.

'She seems to tolerate you well enough,' I said, barely thinking.

'Ah, well, she's not as immune to charm as she likes to think,' he said and winked. 'And you're not blending in as well as you think you are, Warlock.'

Shit.

CHAPTER 3

Not to repeat myself, but as I have said, I'd never been one for subtlety before Whitehall had taken me in, and of all the things I had learnt since then, it was this which I just could not grasp. There is a certain way to walk that conveys a sort of bombastic arrogance, a declaration to those around you that you are not a man with whom it would be wise to fuck. Having mastered *that* a long time ago, it had seemingly become impossible to turn it off.

Often it was useful to appear this way nowadays. Warlocks have little in the way of direct power, and everyone in the magical world is aware of this, but can bring down one hell of a shitstorm if given the need, even in the relatively wild North. They have an intangible army at their back, a force so vast that no one save the Warlock himself is ever really sure of how much chaos they can call at any one time. One-on-one, this can be a fine way to defuse even the most ardent of empowered people.

Things get a little dicier when a single warlock is going up against a group, however. The group can wind up getting confident and aggressive, and that sort of inferred power becomes a challenge rather than a threat. There were enough people in the makeshift bar to push them more towards this line of reasoning, if the sex magician chose to exploit it.

He was waiting for me to react. The sleek, predatory face had settled into a self-satisfied attempt at a grin, eyebrows slightly raised and lips firmly pressed together. They were all so very good at that particular face. It was their trademark.

'You're more observant than the others here, I'll give you that,' I said.

'Some of them suspect, I should think. They don't know you. None of them are really sure. Apart from me. But then, likewise, I can also tell you're not here to shut us down,' he rolled his shoulders back and something in his chest popped quietly. They were just incapable of shutting off, it seemed. Always trying to draw the eye to their best features. 'You didn't make enough of a scene for that.'

'What makes you think I would have made a scene?'

'It's what your kind does. Tyrants have to be seen. That you have at least tried to avoid detection, albeit incredibly badly, tells me you're after something else.'

I've heard people describe someone as having "honeyed" words as though it's a good thing. I can only assume that the people who do this enjoy honey, because whenever they use it I get quite the opposite impression to what they mean. To me, honeyed words are cloying, sickly and leave a generally unpleasant taste. By this definition, the sex magician was using extremely honeyed words.

And yet, he hadn't played his hand.

If I was going to play this properly, putting aside my prejudice and thinking about the whole thing completely rationally, this would have been an absolute gift. You'll find most people assume that the effluence of society are not to be trusted, when in truth you'll find they very rarely outright lie to you. They may bend the truth, or embellish the odd thing, but it will all be built around a core truth. I wonder if perhaps they just see the world a little more clearly than the sort of people who see them as filth.

But, you know, I don't want to get all class-conflict on you. Especially as I *wasn't* about to play this properly and I was, in fact, going to let my prejudices tell me that this man was a sly little rat-mutant wearing human skin and trying to get one over on me. We all have our little foibles.

He leant in close, his eyebrows dropped in a conspiratorial gesture. 'I could out you right here, you know. How long do you think you'd last against a room full of scared and angry magicians?'

'Long enough,' I said carefully. 'But how long will *they* survive once I'm dead?' I flicked my head in the direction of the group at large. Most of them were legitimately young and most likely hadn't fully grasped the precarious nature of their existence yet.

'True enough,' he said. 'But that won't stop them.'

'I'm not here to cause trouble with them. You said it yourself.'

'And that's the only reason I haven't announced to them who you are. I want you gone without incident, with no cause for your jackbooted masters to take notice in this little group.'

I laughed. I couldn't help it. 'You talk as if you're innocent. You *feed* on people. If you're going to try and shoo me away, at least credit me with a modicum of intellect and tell it like it is. You're protecting your food source.'

His face darkened.

And there it was, the monster underneath the skin. The demon behind the eyes.

The first time I encountered a sex magician was my seventeenth birthday. I walked in on him up to his dangly-bits in my fifteen year old sister, on my bed. I slammed him through the wall. It was the only reasonable response.

When he managed to get up from underneath the debris, in the road a good twenty feet from my house, I saw the same face then as I did now. Even when he had been caught in the act with my sister he had maintained that disarmingly smug grin as though everything he did was perfectly normal, but as he pulled himself back to his feet that was gone. The charming veneer had cracked and pure, primal rage had replaced it. Animalistic, terrifying and burning malice. It was a face of a demon sculpted out of human flesh.

A little hyperbolic, perhaps, but true nonetheless. Beneath the surface of every sex magician beats the black heart of a monster, slaves as they were to their own powers. It's one of the more tempting things to be enslaved to, admittedly, but I couldn't say it was worth the price.

The man before me caught himself in time, reining in the rage and reapplying his false charm. It was a waste of time now, he looked older somehow and more gaunt. Perhaps he had weakened his glamour a little, or maybe I was just seeing him for what he was now. What he had always been.

'Your words sting,' he said slowly. 'But I suppose I can be the bigger man here. You'll not bait me into a fight.'

'I thought a fight would be exactly what you wanted,' I said. It was pure bravado at that point and there was nothing I wanted less at that moment that a fight with a small army of magicians.

He clasped his hands together, the knuckles white. 'Just... how can I get rid of you without incident?'

'I'm looking for a broker...'

'And I am looking for a virgin. I do believe that neither are likely to frequent this sort of gathering.'

I cringed. 'I have been informed differently. We can certainly go through this whole rigmarole if you'd prefer, but we both know that it'll just lead to you telling me everything anyway. You've already said as much. Can we just get it done before your cologne gives me a migraine?'

'You're not very respectful for a government man.'

'Why on earth would you think the government would be respectful?'

That was a mistake. It made him smile and my innards churned. 'Perhaps there's hope for you warlocks after all. I like a man with a bit of... *fight* in him.'

'No. No no no,' I said, almost retching. 'We're not going down that road either. Just point me to the broker, please, before I politely vomit all over this fine establishment. He's been doling out power to our local arsonist, I'm sure you've seen the stories about him.'

'Her,' he corrected me.

'Pardon?'

'The arsonist is a woman.'

I grabbed his wrist. 'You know who it is?'

His glamour reasserted itself as he flashed a toothy smile my way, smoothing out his features. It was eerie. 'Not exactly, but I can infer it's a woman.'

'Bollocks.'

The smile went wider. 'Perhaps I am cheating a little. It would be more correct to say that I know the most likely broker, and I know the sort of clients he deals with. If I'm right, it would be very *unlikely* for your arsonist to be male.'

'Tell me where this broker is and I'll be gone.'

'I'm not sure I should. You put me in a difficult decision. After all, I wouldn't want people to think me a traitor to my kind. If news were to get out... There's no shortage of witnesses.'

It was getting harder to stay patient. The old ways were popping back into my mind, unbidden but I couldn't say they were unwelcome. I could make him talk if I wanted, with such a simple application of power. Power that I couldn't use any more, of course, but still it was so tempting. My fingers were tingling, anticipating me calling on my power to break the man. What was even the likelihood that anyone would care? Sex magicians were scum, surely Whitehall would forgive me one little transgression just to deal with a human cockroach. I took a couple of well-disguised deep breaths and the sensation passed.

'I could promise you complete discretion, if it would help.'

He shrugged. 'If you were discrete then I would never have spotted you, and the other people here would never have picked you out as someone to worry about. I think they're starting to work you out, you know.'

'Then tell me what I want to know before things kick off. Neither of us wants a fight to break out.'

'True enough,' he said with a sigh. 'But I must admit that I'm partial to a little *youthful exuberance* from time to time.'

I'd never seen someone cast a spell with a wink before, but somehow the sex magician managed it. Perhaps it was simple misdirection, but the important thing is that he ended his sentence with a wink, and something followed that wink in the direction of my face.

I threw up my arm in the hope the poorly enchanted sleeve of my blazer would dispel whatever it was he launched at me, although I did so too quickly and fell backwards off my stool and onto the floor. I had the wherewithal to roll backwards as I landed, however, and came up on my feet with enough grace to avoid looking the fool.

The barest shimmer of the darkness was there on the man's face, and during my fall he had been flanked by the barmaid and one other person, a rake of a lad with an obtrusive fringe and arms that would snap in a strong wind. I suspected I may have seen him dancing amongst the throng when I had arrived, but it was hard to be sure.

I made a show of straightening out my collar and brushing down my sleeves. I ran my hand over the spot the spell struck me in the hopes of getting some understanding from the residue, but it was too fine a working for me to read. It could have been anything from a full psychic attack to the magical equivalent of a peck on the cheek. Either way, it was unwelcome.

'Very nimble, mister Warlock,' the sex magician said. He was smiling again and it was starting to make me feel nauseous. One of his hands disappeared behind the boy's back. 'Still, not nimble enough. I don't think I want to give you any information. It'll only spoil.'

'Spoil?'

'I am merely weighing up the pros and cons. I can taste the mood of the room. It's delectable. I can taste the blood in the water, government boy. I think they might be working you out, and therefore things are in danger of becoming terribly, terribly ugly. In such a case, it is in my interests to side with my, as you say, food source.'

He wasn't wrong, unfortunately. The atmosphere *was* shifting. People were still dancing, but now that I was looking I could see the odd eye cast my way, the shifty glances and the hushed words – as much as you *could* hush a word in this place – directed towards me. They wouldn't be too hard to provoke if they kept up this trend, if I wasn't careful.

'It doesn't have to be this way,' I said. King of diplomacy. 'I know it's incredibly hard for you to be civil, but I'm pretty sure we can manage it.'

'I am not so certain. Best to run with the stampede than against it.'

Oh good, we'd reached the part of our conversation where vague threats started to pop up in conversation. This tended to happen sooner rather than later for me. I'd been on dates where, midway through the main course, the beauty across from me would loudly declare her intent to stab me in the eye with one of the weird little forks you only find in those special kinds of posh restaurant. Over the years I have developed the perfect counter-argument to all such threats, though I admit it is a method of last resort when on a date.

I tilted my head to one side and placed a hand on the sex magician's shoulder. He gave me a quizzical look, and I head-butted him.

He went down like a perfumed sack of shit, tumbling backwards over his own stool with considerably less grace than I had done. He hit the ground hard. The boy gazed wide-eyed, flicking his head from my direction to that of the sex magician, trying to work out exactly what had happened. The barmaid was brighter, however, and leapt over the bar in one smooth motion, flicking a wrist to silence the music as she did so.

The room fell quiet and all eyes turned on me.

Glorious.

CHAPTER 4

To be fair, you can hardly argue that the snide little shit didn't have it coming. Right?

If I had said that to the horde amassing before my eyes, it might even have worked as a mitigating factor, but I hesitated too long and the barmaid spoke up first. She addressed me, but the volume at which she spoke betrayed her intended audience all to well.

'I knew it,' she almost shrieked. 'I had you pegged as trouble the moment you walked in, all cocksure and fucking sly.'

I don't think I'd ever been called cocksure before. A *cock?* Sure. But never *cocksure*. I wouldn't dispute sly, however. There are worse things to be than a wee bit sly at the right time. Now, of course, was not the right time. Shame it's such a difficult thing to turn off.

The boy lunged at me, all fists and fringe, but I shoved him back firmly. There was no weight to him and he stumbled. The barmaid grabbed him and pulled him back to a vertical base. The crowd was watching silently, still a little too afraid to move in closer. Perhaps I could play to that.

'Your *friend* there,' I said, pointing at the groggy and bleeding sex magician, 'directly threatened the life of a Warlock of Her Majesty's government. He brought this on himself.'

Get in early. Grab the crowd by the balls. Don't squeeze. They'll fight back if you squeeze. Make them fear the squeeze yet to come.

'You're... You're a Warlock?' the barmaid asked. She was faltering, which was good. The longer I could avoid them seeing my perceived threat as a challenge the better, and without a strong leader it would take some time to trigger.

I crossed my arms. 'I'm not here for you. There's no need to make this into something that it's not.' I turned to the crowd and raised my voice a little, mimicking the barmaid's tone somewhat. 'All I want is information on a broker. They're rare, I know, but I'm sure some of you will have happened across one in your travels. This fellow has,' I said, indicating to the sex magician once more.

The crowd said nothing, which wasn't exactly unexpected. Honestly, you don't find many people willing to volunteer information at the drop of a hat, and never amongst a group of silent, shit-scared peers.

The sex magician shook the cobwebs out of his head and pulled himself up, using the barmaid as leverage. It brought a smile to my face to see I had broken his nose, and no amount of glamour was going to hide that fully.

His words were slightly slurred as he spoke, nor did it help that he practically spat them through his teeth. 'It wasn't a threat. It was a warning. Whitehall is going to burn by daybreak.'

I punched him. Look, before you start, I know it was unwise. I didn't know it was at the time because, quite frankly, he just needed a good punching, but later I would come to wonder whether I should have heard him out first. Not to mention the wonders it did for the horde.

No way to avoid it now, that last little outburst of completely legitimate violence had forced the mob to see me as a challenge. Exactly what I had hoped to avoid. The storm of spells the crowd sent my way immediately following the punch certainly heralded my failure as a diplomat.

A squealing bolt of pure force slammed into the bar next to me, stamping out a jagged hole of splintered wood the size of my head. Naturally, I responded as any battle-hardened warlock would have and leapt backwards like a startled cat. Though I did so in a manly fashion.

I had expected more bolts to follow me, but nothing happened. There was a strange silence in the bar, and it took me a moment to realise that, for all their bravado, they hadn't been thinking ahead when they had lashed out. They hadn't considered what would happen if they didn't kill me outright, and as they hadn't they were wrestling with their preconceptions of my kind.

Now, I'll tell you a secret. Warlocks are, *technically,* allowed to use magic in self-defence, it is just in their best interests not to do so. What the reasonable man would call self-defence does not equate with the preferred meaning in force in Whitehall, and that's a headache you don't want to blunder into if you can help it. They are not pre-disposed to listen to explanations, and are just as likely to act without being in possession of all the facts, just the ones they think they need.

The world at large, however, doesn't know this. They know that warlocks are usually forbidden from using their power, but an ordinary man will assume self-defence trumps all, and it is in the nature of the common man to assume all their enemies are working in perfect harmony. It doesn't cross their minds for a moment, for instance, quite how much Whitehall hates its own warlocks. That, I believe, is why I was still alive.

It's easy to play the big bad when the chains are off, or are at least perceived to be. The rookie mistake is to start out large and loud, a great booming monster. You'll get some measure of shock from your targets, sure enough, but they'll recover quickly. Also, and perhaps more importantly, if you fire off every salvo at once, there's an increased chance of a misfire; if your voice breaks for example, or wavers even a little, the entire thing is scuppered. Best to start small and quiet, and build to a crescendo.

I popped my collar, always a good way to start. 'Which one of you threw that?' I said, quiet enough to qualify for whisper status. No one replied, though a fair few of the younger members of the group growled quietly, too young to know that now was not the time to be making themselves into a target. 'I only ask because I feel you should all know who to blame for what is about to happen. Those of you that survive are going to have grievances, and I want to make sure that the person responsible can't weasel out of this by getting incinerated in the roaring rampage of revenge I have brewing. So, yeah, you might want to fess up.'

The sex magician, holding what was left of his nose onto his face with a bloodstained hand, spoke up. 'You can't–'

'Sit. Down.'

He sat down. It was an odd movement, in fact. He lowered himself onto his stool, as you do, and then almost fell to his feet again, as though he had experienced an epiphany the moment his arse hit the seat. Apparently he was clever enough to test me, and even with my dulled senses I could feel him draw in some power. So I responded by doing something very stupid.

I drew in some power of my own and channelled it to

my eyes, giving them a reddish glow. That shut him right down. It's very hard to argue with a man in possession of glowing red eyes and one monster of a frown.

Technically, I didn't cast any spells, so Whitehall couldn't touch me, but there is a reason I hadn't even messed about with this sort of childish trickery, and that is simply temptation. As I stood there with my eyes aflame, the feeling of that power flowing through my veins again bordered on orgasmic. No, it was beyond that. It felt like I had woken up from a very long, tedious dream, whole again at last.

I wanted to draw on more of it, Whitehall be damned. I couldn't even remember why I had let them shackle me. It burned inside me, power unimaginable in its potency, pure and vibrant and deadly, and I had let it go to waste. The flames in my eyes flared as I continued to siphon more and more magic into my muscles. At that moment, my bluff was rapidly turning into a very real possibility. Just like the old days.

There was no longer any thought guiding me, it was instinctual. My left hand curled into a three-fingered claw, motes of power dancing from my fingertips. Channelling the power was harder than I had remembered it being, but what consciousness was still functioning put that down to inactivity. I could remember all the rituals, all the incantations and the basic sensations of every spell locked away in my head, but there was a slight disconnect between these memories and their practical applications.

The crowd had started screaming and bolting for the door, as had the barmaid and the sex magician, though their attempt to flee barely registered in my mind. They could run, but it would do them no good. I wouldn't even need to chase them. If I could just open myself a little more, I could kill them all with a single thought.

My hand was getting warm and numb, but I couldn't quite get the spell to take shape. Something was distracting me. This wasn't right, but I couldn't remember why. I had to clear my head, think about this, just for a moment. I let my hand hang loose and, somehow, blinked away the power. Suddenly, my body felt like lead. I couldn't move, I couldn't stand, and I could barely even breathe. My knees buckled and I slumped to the ground. It was dusty and cold, but I wasn't in a complaining mood.

Consciousness crept back in, accompanied by a banging headache. My eyes refused to focus on anything, and as I struggled to regain control of my faculties I caught the sound of my telephone at the edges of my perception, the acoustics of the empty room amplifying it just enough to push through the mental fog. I had just enough wherewithal to answer the thing.

'Hmm?' was all I could muster by way of a greeting.

'What the *fuck* are you doing, Parker?!' came Charlie's dulcet tones. 'They're in the vault! If you hadn't stopped when you did...'

I tried to sit up but my head weighed a thousand stone. 'Calm down.'

'Calm down? *Calm down?* You... you utter idiot! Do you realise what you nearly did there, what could have happened? Thank God you came to your bloody senses.'

'Don't be so melodramatic. Or loud. Can you be neither, please?'

There are certain women who can silently and distantly convey an expression. Charlie was very good at that, and the expression I couldn't see was telling me I was in quite a lot of trouble, with her if no one else.

'They opened the vault for you, moron,' she said. The words came slowly and deliberately so she could make sure I took them all in. '*Don't do that again.*'

'Couldn't even if I wanted to. Ow.'

'Don't go looking for sympathy from me. What's going on over there?'

I managed to hoist myself up to a sitting position, although every fibre of my being called me rude names for doing so. 'Went for a drink, ran into a sex magician... The usual, you know.'

She sighed. 'Whatever. They want you to come in. Now. Apparently they have to make sure you're contained. Can we trust you to come in on your own?'

'Yeah, yeah. I can make it to the local branch at least, will that do?'

She whispered to someone on the other end of the phone for a second. 'They say that's acceptable. Just don't mess them around, Parker.'

'I'll be the height of professionalism. Can I have a hug? I'm in pain.'

She laughed. That was nice. 'I'll phone ahead, see if I can set one up for you. Idiot.'

'Kiss, kiss,' I said and hung up.

I flopped backwards onto the floor. It is important that you understand quite how much everything hurt. The slightest thought of movement hurt, let alone the act itself, and I wanted to just lie there until I blacked out, something which I was pretty sure would happen sooner rather than later.

The emptiness had returned, made all the worse for having felt whole again moments before. The mindlessness, however, had been new and entirely unwelcome. My power had never controlled me before, and I was not about to let it start now. Granted, I had never starved myself of it before, but still: I had a reputation to consider. I was not about to accept that Jameson Parker had become a slave to his own magic, so long ignored and cast aside. It lacked dignity.

There was nothing dignified about lying on the sticky floor either, but one indignity at a time. It was more comfortable than moving, which was what was important, and it felt pretty safe. It made for a nice nice bed upon which to relax for a few minutes as the feeling returned to my legs. When that was done, I peeled myself off the floor and stumbled back outside.

I grimaced instinctively as I stepped out, expecting a brain-rending flash of light from the street lamps, but thankfully they weren't feeling malicious and had switched themselves off. That or the stampede of terrified magicians and their wayward energies had fried the electrics. Either way, my head throbbed with gratitude at both the lack of harsh lighting and the absence of people.

The cool breeze helped, of course. That and the comforting background noise of civilisation, that hadn't managed to bleed through into the empty bar. There truly is such a thing as *too quiet*, and it is the sort of dearth of noise that allows you to *hear* each and every throb of pain. The sound of a car or two in the distance, the susurrous chatter of a great many people off towards the horizon, it could drown that out.

What I needed most at that point was rest. I wanted to lie down and go to sleep in the middle of the car park, just soak up the moonlight and heal, but that was hardly safe. Besides, the brain can do terrible things when it is exhausted, such as presenting bad advice like sleeping in car parks.

Driving was perhaps a worse idea in my current state, but it would get me to a bed, which was preferable to asphalt. I hoisted myself to my feet and trudged towards the fuzzy block that I vaguely remembered to be my car. I rerouted some energy from somewhere else in my body and willed it into my eyes, bringing everything back into focus.

Oh car. Glorious car. If worst came to worst, I could sleep in the back seat. It was an appealing notion, which, given the condition of my back seat, should say more about my condition than anything else I have mentioned.

I hadn't spotted the woman sat on the bonnet, which was quite embarrassing. In fact, I somehow refused to acknowledge her existence at all until she called out to me.

'Hello, warlock,' she said. Original greeting, I know, but I wasn't in the mood to call her out on it. Besides, her voice was confusing – a silky Scouse accent shouldn't be possible, but somehow she had managed it. I didn't want to detract from her achievement by trying to be snide. 'Been having fun, have we?'

I winced. 'I've had better days. Please get off my car.'

She slid off my car, and I'm sorry but my eyes were drawn to her arse. Don't judge me, I was incredibly tired and the safety locks that stop a man from being a terrible, leering pervert don't function properly when you're tired. I'm going to blame her outfit anyway.

There was nothing seductive about it, you understand, which is perhaps what made it so appealing. She wore black combat trousers and a navy blue blouse, all under a leather jacket that seemed to shimmer like gasoline, making it hard to properly determine its colour. Her hair was a thick, dark red that disappeared under the collar of her jacket, and all in all she was quite a striking sight. It wasn't a carefully considered look, but it did its job. It conveyed a lot of strength.

Her boots crunched on the ground as she walked towards me, smiling. That was when the illusion broke. I'd seen that sort of smile before: it was the entrancing smile of someone trying to hide their true face. You can do wonderful things to a face with a smile, if you know how to do it. The key is to hide the threats behind the joviality, and she had not managed that at all. It was a hungry grin, all teeth and bad intentions.

'This is a courtesy call,' she said, holding her arms

wide in an attempt to further deflect her intentions. 'Wouldn't want it to get ugly, especially not in your current state.'

'Everyone's always so polite before they start threatening me,' I said. 'Can you just threaten me and fuck off, please? I want to go to bed.'

She snorted and smiled properly for a moment. It was nicer. 'I can respect a man who gets to the point. Very well. I'm looking into the arsonist and I don't work well with others. After that little display in there, I gather you are looking too. Won't take long for the information to get out, so it is probably in your interest to let it go.'

'Why is everyone so bloody keen to get me to drop this investigation? You're just making it more interesting, you know?'

She frowned. 'Like I said, this is a courtesy call.'

'And who, pray tell, is providing me with such great courtesy this time?'

She crossed her arms and the leather creaked. 'Oh. Sorry, I thought my reputation would have preceded me. I'm the Bane of Whitehall, nice to meet you.'

CHAPTER 5

Every warlock knew of the Bane of Whitehall, although none of them was willing to refer to her by such a grandiose term. We called her by her name, Kaitlyn van Ives, when we deigned to talk about her at all.

Kaitlyn was an idealist, a radical fighting for the rights of the empowered. Ordinarily she would have been branded a terrorist and taken down by Whitehall in much the same way they take in any warlock, but she was a special case. She fought magician and mundane alike; anyone who would damage the credibility of those with power was fair game. She'd been moving her way around the country cutting down anyone who oppressed or enslaved the empowered, and anyone who would bring disrepute on their name, which had sown confusion amongst the Whitehall elite.

It wasn't really a secret that Whitehall saw the warlocks as a short-term thing. They didn't really trust us, but they had to do *something* to deal with all that uncontrolled power out there, so they snatched up who they could and turned them on their own until they could come up with something more long term. As far as they were concerned, Kaitlyn was pretty much doing the job of a warlock half the time anyway, and her terrorist activities, while not insignificant, were mostly minor setbacks at best. She was a useful problem.

On the other hand, her ultimate goal wasn't making her many friends in government. She wanted complete equality and autonomy for magicians, which is about as noble a goal as you can get, and in my younger days I might even have agreed with her. But then, I wanted a lot of things in my younger days that were perhaps ill advised. Any way you cut it, however, I was pretty sure I didn't want to piss her off if I could help it.

In my addled state, I didn't really have a response to follow her introduction. I just stared at her agog until she slipped back into that unpleasant smile and broke the silence.

'Oh, did I break you? Sorry. I know it's all a bit of a shock, running into your bogeyman in the dead of night, but I'm not really a monster. I just want you to know that you don't have to be my enemy.'

She stepped forward and laid a hand on my cheek. I would have recoiled but, honestly, what would have been the point? If she had meant me harm, it wasn't as though moving my head a few inches backwards would have been enough to stop that.

Her hand was warm and I couldn't help but let out a sigh of relaxation as she touched me. I reached up and put my hand against hers, then grabbed it and pulled it from my face.

'Keep your magic to yourself, witch,' I snarled. I wasn't even sure she had been trying a spell of some kind on me, but whenever a moderately attractive woman reaches for my face, that tends to be the reasoning behind it.

She nodded in agreement and turned to walk back towards my car. 'Fair enough, I won't force you to listen.

If you want to go blind into this whole thing, be my guest.'

I growled. 'Just, for once, can people stop talking in circles and just tell me what the fuck they are trying to say?'

'Very well,' she said and perched herself back on my car bonnet. 'You don't know what you're doing and it's going to get you killed. It looked as though you hadn't noticed that, and I felt you ought to know. Professional courtesy.'

Well, she had summed me up quite succinctly. But when had not knowing what you were doing ever stopped anyone? 'I'm tracking down an arsonist. That's what I'm doing. See, I do know.'

'You're treating a symptom as the disease, fool,' she said.

I was running low on patience. And consciousness, I think. 'Fucking Christ, speak plainly. I can't do mental gymnastics right now, all my squishy brain meats hurt and it's making me sad.'

She pinched the bridge of her nose, which I have learned is one step below a full-on facepalm. I love having that effect on the ladies. 'The arsonist isn't a big deal.'

'I beg to differ.'

'Who I suspect the arsonist is *working for* is the person that you should really be tracking down, if you were capable of doing your job without whining like a bloody child.' She looked disappointed which, again, is something I'm used to.

'I whine like an adolescent, actually.'

She threw up her hands.

'But,' I said. 'Let's say you're right. Who is it you think is holding this arsonist's lead?'

'If I'm right,' she said. 'It's The Rider.'

I think I might have laughed so much I actually

choked. 'Are you sure it's not zombie Robin Hood, firing arrows made out of Lord Lucan's flaming chest hair?'

'Believe what you want,' she said. I don't think she liked my joke. 'Just know that I warned you.'

And with that she leapt onto the bonnet of my car, made a quick gesture with her hands, and vanished in a puff of smoke.

Yeah, I know.

And I suppose I should explain my joke to you. It's easy to forget you don't know some of this stuff. These are the things that are just so obvious to magicians that it can be hard to remember to explain, but I'll try and do my best.

This will all make a bit more sense when I can properly go into detail on the Dark Times, but I'm still hesitant to do that just yet. I need something to contextualise it, so you can properly understand, and I'll get there, but for now I'll give you the short version. Just be patient with me.

The Rider, as a single person, is one of those myths that crop up from time to time. Back in the Dark Times, when the secret war essentially divided the country into a thousand different feudal wizard lords all vying for power, Yorkshire had The Rider. It was an elected position, as I understand it, with all the local lords coming together to create an alliance that would keep Whitehall away. The Rider was their mouthpiece, so named because he stood for all the ridings of Yorkshire.

Which seems all well and good, except for the fact some dunce got it into his head towards the end of the Dark Times to start spinning tales about him as though he was an actual person rather than a title. I was elsewhere, so I can't really tell you how such a dozy myth even happens, but not one person I've met since peace broke out has been able to confirm it as truth. That hasn't stopped him from becoming a local folk hero though, it seems.

Admittedly, lurking behind the scenes and steering everything with a subtle hand would live up to the myth but, quite frankly, I wasn't about to start believing any old ghost story. Now, someone *claiming* to be The Rider, that I could get behind. Maybe, just maybe, there was a baby despot guiding whoever was setting these fires, but it wouldn't be *the* Rider.

Frankly, I wouldn't have put it past Kaitlyn van Ives to have been playing with me, trying to throw me off the trail. If I had just assumed she was the arsonist, I could bring her in and just have done with the whole thing. From what I knew of her activities, arson wasn't necessarily out of the question as long as she could justify it, but none of the burnt out buildings had any ties to Whitehall or the empowered as far as I could tell. I admit that I hadn't looked particularly hard for any links, however, so it was still possible.

Unfortunately, as much as I despise having any sort of work ethic, I *did* have one. The story didn't fit with her whole warning me off thing. Unless my investigation into the broker was finally kicking some dirt loose.

But if she had been in Humberside long enough to be the arsonist, why had she only revealed herself now? It wasn't as though she was afraid of the warlocks, and having come to me directly with her strangely non-threatening threat implied that she would have come forward sooner if she had been present.

Then there was the matter of the borrowed magic used to set the fires. From what I'd heard, Kaitlyn van Ives was not short on power herself, which meant that she would hardly have need of a broker. It was perhaps conceivable that she would borrow power to mask her own trail, but again that didn't seem right for someone who was trying to trade off her reputation. A random arsonist is a problem, true, but the Bane of Whitehall is a whole different kettle of fish. A kettle of piranhas maybe.

What I should have done was to call Charlie to check in, to report a sighting of Kaitlyn van Ives so they could send another ill-fated squad of warlocks to try and bring her in. I didn't do that. There were too many women in my day, and I was fed up. It was nothing to do with being far too knackered to even reach the phone in my pocket.

Instead, I climbed into the back seat of my car. It was comfy, but then anything would have been at that point. I rarely had passengers in the back, which meant a thousand stampeding pairs of buttocks hadn't squished and farted into the cushions, leaving them firm and clean enough for a decent enough snooze.

I dropped my barriers and let the tiredness in. I needed it to wash away the pain that had been dwelling under my muscles from my little outburst. I yelled as the exhaustion peeled it away from my insides, leaving a dull aching scar of its former presence.

With the pain gone, the tiredness lingered, and now I couldn't control it. I wanted to sleep, but I was too tired for any facet of control now, even one as natural as letting go of reality for a while. Too tired, even, to guard my thoughts. They began to wander, which is a terrible thing for thoughts to do, and began to settle on the face of that one girl, the one who disliked the smell of whiskey.

Ordinarily, I did my best to avoid thinking about her. I kept busy, ensured my mind was occupied, and in return I maintained my cheery disposition and sanity. Once forced to wind down, however, the barrier falls and *she* creeps in.

She looked nothing like Kaitlyn – a short, cute blonde rather than a tall and striking redhead – and yet somehow she was invading my memory of the conversation with Kaitlyn, overriding everything. Now it was her giving me the warning, the serious expression on her face not quite meshing with her diminutive figure.

But then, as it always did, her expression changed to how it had been the last time I saw her. The look of pain, the betrayal she had felt, and the fear. I forced the barrier back up and drove her from my mind. Even after all these years, I wasn't ready to deal with that yet. It wasn't the sort of thing I could ever conceive of dealing with.

And besides, I had much more important matters, what with all the buildings bursting into flames and a magical terrorist rocking up to say hello. Now was no time for dredging up the past, stupid brain.

I willed myself to sleep, which is an unpleasant way to rest. It's the equivalent of forcing a square peg through a round hole – often mistaken as an impossibility by people who have yet to gain a full understanding of hammers and hammer-like objects. In truth, it is fully possible to get a square peg through a round hole, though neither peg nor hole will be the same afterwards. It doesn't give you the most refreshing of sleeps, but it's serviceable.

When the sun crept through my streaky car windows a few hours later, I felt vengeful and groggy, but alive. The pain had wound itself down to a dull ache, which was manageable at least, and movement no longer seemed like something that would require a team of specially trained engineers to accomplish.

I considered foraging under the car seats for breakfast but decided against it. I'm a manly man and far too busy to do something as pedestrian as sustain my body. Instead, I awkwardly clambered my way between the seats and into the driver's position. I caught myself on the gear stick. Pretty sure you can work out how unpleasant that was.

As to where I intended to go, I had no earthly idea. A

small part of me wanted to see about tracking down Kaitlyn as a purely juvenile gesture – she'd told me to leave her alone, let's see what she thinks of me rubbing myself on all her stuff – but the more adult and non-suicidal part of me wasn't about to let that happen.

I could go searching for more parties to crash and interrogate, see if I could get a lead on the broker. Not a tempting avenue after the last time, admittedly, but there was still a chance it would work. Word travels quite slowly amongst the empowered community for the most part, at least when it comes to describing danger. Magic makes you selfish, and while it tends to suit people to know danger is coming, those that know in what form it travels like to make sure they have the upper hand on their supposed friends, just in case.

You don't have to outrun the dragon...

Charlie would no doubt be willing to give me some pointers on the finer aspects of investigation and detection, but I wasn't in the mood. We'd have to banter, and as skilled as I am at such things, it takes up a lot of time that I could more properly spend brooding and being a grump. I was very much of the mind that today was a day for brooding and grumping. Sleeping in a car does that to you.

Naturally, it was at this point that my phone rang. In truth, it had been ringing for most of the night, judging by the amount of missed calls I had, but you don't last long in this job if you can't learn to ignore your own ringtone. I refused to answer, because of said brooding grump, although seeing Charlie's name flash up on the screen unlocked a possibility – I *could* track the magic.

I had asked for permission for a simple tracking spell without expecting it to be granted. It was the sort of thing you do when you hate your bosses: ask them for stupid things just to make them fill in the paperwork to deny your request. I was going to have to call them back, make an actual case to be allowed to cast a simple spell. It was the only lead I had left, and one I'd quite possibly locked myself out of with my little *incident* the night before.

Not my finest hour, but –

Then I remembered.

Actually, no, I tell a lie. I didn't quite remember at that moment. What truly reminded me of my promise to drop by the Whitehall branch office in Humberside was my car flipping onto its roof. Being mostly cheap metal and plastic, the roof caved in under the weight of the chassis, squashing me down between faux-leather seats and the stained felt roof lining. The steering wheel lodged itself in my chest and drove the wind out of me, and my immediate response to all of the above was, in my opinion, perfectly justified.

'Fuck me!' I may have screamed. I emphasise *may have*. Manly man, remember.

I tried to negotiate my body into a position where I could breathe if nothing else, but the steering wheel and the roof had conspired to keep me pinned. It was uncomfortable, but nothing was broken. Small mercies, eh?

Two pairs of stylish loafers stepped into view. Shining black, of the sort that only the most ardent of office workers bother with. They were joined by the hems of charcoal grey trousers, complete with an ironed-in crease down the front, and without having to see the rest of them I could tell exactly how the inevitable conversation would go.

There was a tingling sensation – one distinct from the general tingling sensations resulting from the assault on my car – and one of the men to whom the loafers belonged knelt down to what was left of the driver's side window.

He was younger than me, which was annoying. That

was really the only memorable thing about him, he was perfectly put together to not only wear a suit, but to have the suit wear him. The supremely faceless office boy. As a rule, Whitehall tends to employ stuffy older men with white hair and a charming line in pipe-tobacco scented cologne. You get the youngsters in the warlocks themselves, and their support crews. Or graduates, who were their own breed.

The kid was clearly a graduate. The fresh face, the barely-concealed arrogant grin, the frankly offensive suit, it all added up. That he wasn't wearing half-rim sunglasses was frankly a surprise.

'You're late, Mr Parker,' he said. To give him his due, he had an adult's voice, which can't be said of a lot of people who graduate into Whitehall.

'I'm going to be even later now you've destroyed my car.'

'Let me help you with that.'

There was the sound of metal crying, which sounds worse when you're *inside* it, and the bulk of my car peeled itself away from the roof, taking the steering wheel with it. Before I had time to move, strong arms seized me and pulled me free of the wreckage. They pulled me to my feet and let me go.

I looked at my car before I looked at the men, because I'm vindictive and petty, and found not much to see. A destroyed car always looks the same. I could *feel* my insurance premiums rising.

Although I had already seen one of the two men, they looked so similar I lost interest in distinguishing which was which. They were wearing ties, for God's sake. You can't trust a man in a tie. Only one of them seemed willing to talk, anyway, which made things easier for me.

'As we understand it, you were supposed to drop by last night. Whitehall called us and told us to be ready for you,' he said. He was very matter-of-fact, which worried me. People with ties like to use matter-of-fact as a starting point for their rages.

I winced, purely for show. 'You can't hold a man to the promises he makes of an evening. It only leads to disappointment.'

'I think you'll find we can,' the matter-of-fact tone was starting to slip. Slowly, gently, bring in the righteous indignation.

'Do you know what the word *warlock* even means? It *means* oath breaker. Frankly, you should take everything I say with a pinch of salt. I wonder why Whitehall hasn't worked this out by now.'

Baiting people is fun. Stupid, but fun. It became a little less fun when the kid grabbed me by my throat and hoisted me into the air, typical goon style, but at least it was informative. This guy was definitely on the Whitehall fast-track scheme.

There's a lot about Whitehall I haven't told you yet, and I'm sure I'll get around to it when it's prudent, but the fast-track scheme does warrant a little in the way of explanation. Not all graduates get onto the fast-track, although the ones that you tend to see out and about are the fast-track candidates. They take them straight out of university and train them to hunt magicians in a similar way to warlocks, except with more trust. They get to actually use magic, for instance. We're under no illusions that, eventually, the fast-trackers are going to replace us.

It's not their own magic, of course. Whitehall would never trust someone who had power of their own, but having magic and wielding it are not necessarily connected skills. One can learn to weave spells on a purely theoretical level, and that's how the fast-track starts off.

How they get people to bequeath them magic, I don't know, but they know how to use it. Sort of. Of course, knowing and *feeling* are two completely different things, and fast-track candidates are rarely as accomplished as natural spellcasters, but nor are they as reliant on the craft. In truth, they can be pretty scary, which is why they are tasked with guarding the vault at Whitehall.

And dealing with people like me when we go a bit wonky.

'You've made your point,' I spluttered. 'Can't interrogate me if I pass out, can you?'

'You'd be surprised,' the kid said, but he put me down anyway. 'Are you going to behave now? Come along quietly?'

'I'll be the perfect model prisoner,' I said, accompanied by an exaggerated bow. I don't think he appreciated it.

The pair of them led me to a black Jaguar parked just around the corner. They opened the back door for me and I climbed in, although I slapped one of their hands away when they tried to guide my head in. I've seen police do that before, and I wasn't about to accept this as an arrest. For all intents and purposes, an arrest it may have been, but as long as I didn't *accept* it, I was free and clear.

I sank into the leather and considered my options. I hadn't actually *done* anything wrong, so the worst I'd get was a severe telling off, but it was going to eat into time I didn't have. But then again, I had to talk to them anyway if I was going to get permission to whip up a little tracking spell, which I was pretty sure I needed at this point.

And I wanted a sandwich.

It wasn't a long drive, but it was in total silence which somehow made it feel like an eternity. I didn't want to talk to them, you understand, but being a passenger in a car is terribly boring, even if only for a short time. At least they were driving deeper into the city, which meant they probably were on the level and not a kill squad sent to finish me off for being a nuisance. Still, when we pulled up outside the field office, all tinted windows and sixties concrete, I was actually a little relieved. They were almost certainly not going to kill me now but, if worst came to worst, there would be other warlocks inside that uninspiring cube of alienation, so at least I'd be guaranteed a friendly face.

More or less.

Probably less.

Still, it's better than nothing. Right?

The younger of the two opened the door for me, polite as regulations demanded, and decided against helping me *out* of the vehicle. Maybe I'd hurt his feelings. It would have been preferable.

It was time to set the mood. Brooding and grumpy, all the way.

CHAPTER 6

Offices are rarely designed to look nice. Owing to bombastic American prime time dramas, I had always assumed that they'd be full of stylish marble-topped desks pointed at a giant neon command screen with a map of the world emblazoned across it. There would, of course, be strange wobbly lines all over it too, detailing the erratic orbit of some shadowy satellite or another. Every time I visited a new field office, I secretly hoped it would look like this.

Again, I was disappointed. I should have seen it coming, really; the key term in field office is, after all, *office*. This one appeared to have gained the title in the mid seventies, despite its external appearance, and had staunchly refused to change, so loyal it was to that particular decade. Weird brown and orange wallpaper, tacky chipboard desks, yellowed plastic telephones, it was all here. Even the concessions they had made to the modern day – computers and photocopiers and the like – were out-dated. Although, to be fair, as a group, we're not particularly keen on staying modern. When your key defining-feature is the ability to wield a power older than civilisation, you tend to be quite forgiving of trends and fads.

I'd been working Humberside for long enough that I should have visited the field office before, it's true, but the whole *Northern Wilderness* thing had meant that until recently there hadn't actually been an office to visit. They hadn't seen much point in putting something together just for the locals to burn it down. Operations had been run from York until the time had come to look at Humberside properly, and enough bodies were freed up to establish a beach head of spreadsheets and Windsor knots.

The fast-trackers that had dragged me in seemed a lot more relaxed now, as though they had been expecting me to bolt up until we had entered the building. As they led me between the desks, ignored by the men and women tapping away at their black and orange keyboards, doing whatever it was this sort of person did, I spotted where they were leading me and winced.

There was a desk at the far end of the room that faced inwards, an overseer's desk perhaps. It gave the whole room a sort of classroom feel, and the woman sat behind it did nothing to undo that image.

She was stern looking and older than me, perhaps early forties but with a face that wanted to look older. Everything about her was crisp: her make-up and hair looked like it had come prefabricated, lifeless but functional enough. There was a general impression that she was ready, willing and able to slice you into tiny bits with a liberal application of her tongue.

But I was committed to being broody and grumpy, and I wasn't about to let one of nature's headmistresses get to me when I had more important things to worry about.

The fast-trackers pushed me into a waiting chair and I did my best to make it look natural. It didn't work, but you can't blame me for trying. It garnered a raised eyebrow from the headmistress at least, but other than that there was no grand indication that she had noticed I was there. Her veiny eyes peered at me over her steepled hands, and yet seemed to be looking through me rather than at me.

I took a moment to stretch noisily, taking exquisite pleasure in cracking my neck, then locked my face into a frown and slumped back in my chair. It creaked noisily. Right on, my furniture ally: let's fight the power.

I wasn't sure which of us was going to speak first. I could tell she was trying to make me nervous, and she was certainly built to engender that feeling in people what with the eyebrows that could score glass, but she was relying on internal guilt eating me up to truly get that response. Seeing as I wasn't feeling guilty about anything, it just made the situation quite laughable. I chose to break the silence anyway, however.

'Hello,' I said. I am a word god.

Her eyes narrowed and she broke her hand steeple to flick through a folder on her desk. 'Mr Parker, I understand,' she said, her voice deep with age and contempt. 'Are you aware of why you are here?'

'Are *you* aware why I'm here?' I replied. Childish but who cares? I knew how this was going to go.

'You are here to be assessed on your competency to continue your role as a warlock and for us to determine whether you have the requisite sanity to hold such a position.'

The smart move would have been to play it calm, but I was already committed to being in a bad mood today. I'm also not very smart. 'You can certainly run me through all the damn tests you like, but considering we've got a magical arsonist and a known terrorist rocking around Humberside right now, you might want to make it snappy. Tick tock.'

One of the fast-trackers – the kid again, I think – slapped me round the back of the head for that. I shot him a glare. Being angry is fun.

'That may be the case,' the headmistress continued. 'But after your little contretemps last night, we can't just have you swanning about unchecked. You're a menace. You all are.'

It wasn't as though I hadn't expected that. Warlocks have never been popular, but we are necessary which is perhaps what makes us so annoying to people like the headmistress. People are allowed to hate us, but political mandate keeps them from actively persecuting us, which is lovely. It means we get to be incredibly bolshy. I wasn't about to start letting the side down now.

I sprang from the chair and kicked it over backwards as I did so. Moving forwards, I slammed my hands down on her desk and stared right into her eyes. To her credit, she didn't even flinch. I waited for the fast-trackers to do something about me, to drag me back or something, but they didn't. I risked a glance aside to check on them.

They had their backs to me, hands outstretched and charged, a shimmering blue shield of pure force being projected in front of them. Through the shields I saw four men and a woman – two men behind one shield and a man and a woman behind the other – standing perfectly calmly and serenely, staring at us all. I hadn't noticed them when we came in, but I recognised the concealed contempt in their eyes. Warlocks. Evidently the rest of the office staff had clocked this too, though they were trying very hard to make it look as though they hadn't – the tiptapping of the keyboards had slowed but otherwise no-one had moved from their desk.

I hadn't really made friends with any of the other warlocks in Humberside. Owing to the special circumstances of my recruitment, I wasn't often allowed to mix with the other kids, and even if I had been I would have chosen to keep my distance anyway. Apparently I still had a reputation, however. For whatever reason, the fast-trackers were more worried about my outburst setting off the other warlocks than whatever it was I was about to do to their boss.

Interesting.

The warlocks said nothing. They weren't about to betray their intentions, as apparent as they might be. They were playing the solidarity card, letting the brass know that whatever happened here and now would be disseminated to the rest of our ilk. They wouldn't interfere, but they would see.

I looked back to the headmistress. 'You know as well as I do that if they thought I was a threat I would be dead already.'

She didn't miss a beat, her predatory eyes gleaming. 'They were in the vault. You very nearly were dead.'

'And yet I'm not. Do you know why? It's because I'm needed. There's a man out there setting fire to buildings and you lot don't have the nouse or the contacts to find out who they are and stop them. Hell, you probably aren't even aware we've got Kaitlyn van Ives wandering around Humberside looking to pick a fight. So perhaps you should just back off and let me do my job.'

She had missed my comment about the terrorist before, apparently, as dropping Kaitlyn's name got a definite response. A flick of her eyes summoned one of the fast-trackers to her side, apparently the shield was no longer important, and she whispered a few words into his ear. He nodded and marched out of the room.

'That doesn't excuse you from acting like Humberside is your own personal playground, Parker,' she said to me once he was done stomping into the hall. 'Your file says you've served predominantly in the North?'

The chair creaked as I tried to fold myself into a position that would make me seem more dynamic.

'They're not keen on me being in the South, apparently. They reckon it's full of bad influences.'

'And yet, despite your experience up here, you haven't been able to notice how precarious our situation is? All it will take is one real push and the magicians up here will go feral. That they haven't already is thanks only to the fact people still remember the bloody war.'

'I'm sure my file will have my GCSE results in it. You'll notice I did poorly at history,' I said. Putting on my best shit-eating grin was probably overkill, but it felt natural at the time. Might as well play to my strengths, even if they are in frustrating older women.

She lent over her desk, looking like she was ready to pounce on me. 'Whitehall keeps telling me there's nothing to worry about, that the North is so apathetic that y the time it realises what we're doing we'll have already civilised it. But they're not here, I am, and I am telling you to stop getting them riled. Especially if van Ives is here. Just do your job and make as few enemies as possible, if you can manage that.'

I put on my croakiest old man voice. 'Fear will keep the local systems in line! Fear of this battlestation!'

Her eye twitched. I swear to god. I didn't think that was a thing people actually did outside of old comedies. 'Your humour does nothing to make you any less of a degenerate. Make yourself useful and get this done.'

'You are a very mean old lady.'

The headmistress flicked through the file on her desk some more and plucked out a loose document. She slid it across the table to me. 'Here's your authorisation for a single, one-time, non-sustained tracking spell. Get out.'

I cracked a smile and slowly picked up the paper from the desk, refusing to break eye contact. Then I nodded my head in understanding and turned to leave. The remaining fast-tracker tried to block my way, but one of my friendly neighbourhood warlocks took a step towards him and he relented. I made my way out into the street and put a bit of distance between myself and the office as fast as I could.

The office, as they tend to do, followed me.

I came to a stop a little way down the road, by the side of a collection of terraced houses that looked to have been hewn out of a cliff face rather than built. The warlocks were less than a minute behind me. They didn't really seem to conform to a unified fashion – which I suppose is a perk of the job – but they were all confident enough in themselves not to cover up their tattoos. The spot where the neck meets the skull, just below the left ear, is not a place you tend to screen when giving someone the once over, not unless you have or have had power.

I was still feeling confrontational. I'm always feeling confrontational. You'll have noticed, I'm sure. 'Hello, cupcakes. And what can I do for you?'

The girl in the group stepped forward. The face looked familiar, but I wasn't sure why. I'd probably smiled at her in passing. 'Try not to worry about the old bat, warlock. She's a worrier.'

'Well aren't you sweet. No offence, but I'm a bit busy making most of the magical community want to crucify me. I wouldn't want to fall behind schedule.'

She smirked. It made my brooding and grumpy shell crack a little, but I am a man of commitment. Most of the time. 'I won't keep you. We just want you to know you have friends here. We've been too submissive to Whitehall, maybe because we've been too divided. Just felt you ought to know that if you have a problem with them, you've got support, that's all.'

'Thanks. I guess,' I said. I've never been good with displays of solidarity. People don't tend to direct them my way, and when they do it's usually to trick me into doing something with a load of comrades-in-arms rhetoric. I removed myself from the group before they started knitting me a friendship bracelet or handing me a home-laminated membership card or something.

But despite the polite language, that was a dangerous message to be handing out. It had a seditious undercurrent. Making things better in the workplace? Shock horror, I know, but there are ways and means of dealing with people who think you are one bad day short of a nuclear explosion. I wasn't sure forming this weird *union* was the best way to go about it.

I hadn't realised warlock tensions were so high. Admittedly, I wasn't really part of the warlock community, and I didn't tend to keep up with the internal gossip, but it was the edginess of the fast-trackers that worried me most of all. Maybe they were just even more green than I had thought, brought up on tales of how warlocks are sinister monsters shackled by the state, keen to go rabid at a moment's notice, but I wasn't so sure. They didn't seem to be reacting on fear so much as expectation. But then, what do I know?

The vault is a lovely piece of Whitehall propaganda to keep the empowered in line, but by its very nature it only works at deterring the use of magic. The whole point is that both sides stick to the rules. They needed the system to appear legitimate, to play on the self-loathing inside every warlock. The method of last-resort had to stay a method of last-resort or else it would become a rallying cry. Your standard mano-a-mano fisticuffs aren't going to get them bursting into the vault, at least not in time to stop you, and some warlocks are keen fighters.

I wasn't, of course. I had always relied on my magic to get me out of tight spots, but in the years since I had been forced to give it up I had learned a few things. Guns were always useful nowadays, but getting your hands on one in this country is arduous. Whitehall even issues warlocks with permits for them, seeing as they are a much more direct and easily countered threat than an errant spell, but the rigmarole of getting one means that only the most hardcore of warlocks bothers. I wondered how many warlocks in the field office had them.

Personally, I owned a couple, though I almost never carried them. It is difficult and uncomfortable to properly conceal handguns under a blazer, although technically possible if you know how. I wasn't trained in them, however, and so owned them more as a security blanket than as actual weapons. I was better at punching, which says a lot.

I was starting to wish I was carrying them, however. I hadn't run into any danger requiring them yet, but it's the fear of running into that danger that makes you want them. I could have avoided a lot of trouble at the bar by pulling a piece rather than drawing on the arcane, and avoided the headache of dealing with the headmistress too, yet still gotten the same result overall.

My phone buzzed insistently against my thigh and I stopped to take a look at it. A simple text message from Charlie that read "You're welcome :)". The day was taking a turn for the better.

The tracking spell would be simple enough to sort out; I just needed a decent place to work it. Ideally I would want somewhere with a trace of the magic used, some residue I could weave into the spell to make it easier to detail exactly what I was looking for, but the fire would have burned up most of that. I was going to have to guide the spell by memory for the most part, which was tricky at best.

Using a memory to focus a tracking spell is like using an e-fit to track a criminal: it's possible, but there's a lot of margin for error. Even a blurry photograph tends to trump an e-fit, but with a bit of legwork you can get there in the end. I had gotten a definite taste of the magic

I was after at the fire station, and it was something I could vividly recall, but that wouldn't be as good as if the magic was still fresh. Hazard of the job, I'm afraid.

That said, it couldn't hurt to run the spell from the fire station anyway. I may not be able to grab hold of any residue, but at least the ambiance would help keep the memory fresh. It would be quite a walk to get there, however, thanks to the destruction of my car.

At least I could finally get that sandwich.

CHAPTER 7

The sandwich was delicious, in the way breakfast can only be if you take it at lunchtime. I wasn't entirely sure what the time was, but I assumed it was around lunchtime because of the amount of people in the shop I had ducked into. Keen detective skills at work, there.

I was just polishing off the last bite when I arrived at the fire station. The building had survived the fire, with only superficial exterior damage from what I could see and that was confined largely to the upper floors. The inside was almost untouched on the ground floor, scorch marks and smoke damage, but nothing a good scrubbing couldn't bring out.

They had still shut the building down, however. I'm sure they have a better understanding of how fire screws things up than I do, so I wasn't going to question the decision, especially as it made things much easier for me. Very rarely will you find a guard at an abandoned building, and fire damaged doors are easier to kick in, which in turn provides a lovely ego boost.

I made my way inside easily, and wasted no time preparing the spell.

A tracking spell is one of the first things you'll learn, assuming you are getting proper magical tuition. It's incredibly simple, easy to whip up, hard to *screw* up, and uses pretty much a little bit of every magical skill you'll need. There were a few varieties, as there always is, but the restrictions placed upon me meant I had to go with the easiest and simplest of them all: your typical map burner.

Ordinarily, you want your tracking spell to constantly direct you to your target, like a magical GPS, but Whitehall's unwillingness to grant me a sustained spell put the kibosh on that. Instead I would have to settle for a snapshot of the target's movements. If I could accurately pinpoint his magical signature, I could burn the locations of anywhere he lingered for a prolonged period onto any paper map of the city. It was the sort of spell any empowered parent would use to keep an eye on their wayward kids, and was damn near impossible to defend against.

There were two downsides, of course. Firstly, you needed the magical signature of whatever you were seeking, and using just the memory of the signature would mean a lot of false positives and a lot of leg work to track down the, in this case, person you were after. Secondly, it only showed you where they had been, not where they currently were. Yet more leg work, but at least it would give you an idea of their haunts.

I dropped to one knee and started my preparations. I'd picked up a pack of cheap highlighter pens from the same shop I had bought my sandwich. I uncapped the pink one and drew a pentagram on the floor in the centre of the room, or as near to the centre as I could manage.

There's a lot of misconceptions about pentagrams, I'm sure you can name them yourself without me going on about it, but the important thing to know about them is that they focus magical energy. It draws in small amounts of local power and channels it around and around itself, like a magical circuit. They're very useful for novices and people out of practice, like myself, because they take a lot of the effort out of spellcasting. The negatives to this are that you are effectively rooted to the spot, but for ritualistic castings such as this, that's rarely an issue.

I let the pentagram draw in the energy on its own, deciding against giving it a small magical jump-start in case that got Whitehall all jittery again. It wouldn't take long to absorb enough energy to get itself going anyway. I unfolded my newly purchased Ordnance Survey map of Humberside and placed it in the centre of the star and waited.

I used the time to reconstruct in my mind the magic I had sensed the day before. It had an arresting, powerful cadence, tinged with the atrophy associated with all borrowed power. Newly borrowed, freshly harvested from its original owner, but there was nothing detectable from the person to whom it was bequeathed. The best I'd get was a line on the broker, but that would be sufficient. Whoever they were, they were above average on the scale.

The smell of burned wood and melted plastic was helping to bring the signature together. I could see the fire inside the magic now, dancing among the probabilities of what it could have been, consuming every other possibility hungrily and viciously. It was as close to perfect as I could get it. It would have to do.

I reached out with my senses to check on the pentagram. It had siphoned enough ambient magic to do the job, now it was all on me. Even basic spells can't work themselves, they need some magical input from the caster, even if it's little more than a spark. The pentagram would do the heavy lifting, but I had to input the search criteria and tell it exactly what I wanted done, and that would mean drawing in some power of my own.

I'm not going to lie, I was a little trepidatious after the incident at the bar. I had let the addiction take me over then, and while I was still buzzing from it I had no desire to repeat that loss of control. Not least because the next time I made Whitehall open the vault, they wouldn't stop until I was dead, but also because it showed a weakness in me I thought I had overcome. Magic itself isn't addictive, but the power you wield can be if you do with it what I did, and despite what I may indicate a lot of the time, I'm glad to be rid of it. Becoming a warlock helped me control that part of myself, and while I miss the magic, I don't miss *him*.

I did it slowly this time, a gentle inhalation of power. The sensation was the same as before, but more manageable. It flowed easier this time, without the unbridled rush of emotion and longing that it had brought with it at the bar. I could shape it this time, control it.

I willed the reconstructed notion of the broker's magical signature into the spell, sending with it the instruction to find the owner. It melted into the power effortlessly and then I reached out and touched the nearest corner of the pentagram, releasing my magic as I did so.

I watched as my magic shot through the vertices of the star, mixing with the neutral magic it had drawn in itself. It bounced its way through the shape, gaining in speed and clarity until the pink pentagram was burning white with constrained magic. Small wisps of smoke started forming on the map at this point, pinpricks of light seeming to be the cause. They flared up suddenly, tiny licks of flame rising up a few inches from the surface of the page, and then died out just as fast. The pentagram turned black.

I wiped away the blackened star – which was

remarkably easy, all things considered – and picked up the map.

There were more places marked than I had expected. Either I hadn't been as precise with the signature as I had thought, or the broker had some serious speed. There were at least twenty buildings all across town that had lit up, and a few smaller scorch marks indicated one or two other places that might just be becoming haunts. It wasn't as precise as I had hoped.

At least there were a couple of front-runners I could start with. There were a couple of burns that were larger than the others, which indicated a larger concentration of magic, so the safe money was on the broker hanging out more often in those places. It wasn't a sure thing that I'd catch them there, of course, but it saved me having to traipse around the entire damn city.

The phone came out again and I hit Charlie's speed dial. It barely rang before she answered; apparently I was expected.

'Parker,' she said.

'You can get them out of the vault, Charlie, I've got something.'

'Please say it's something we can use. I've got bean counters lurking behind me while they wait for you to screw up, you know that right?'

It was easy to forget that Charlie had to go to bat for me whenever I did something stupid. I like to think it's a testament to her skill that I feel I can take her for granted like that. 'The tracking spell was just what I needed, you little diamond. I think I've got a workable lead.'

She turned her head away from the phone – must have, judging by the dip in volume – and shouted something. I couldn't make out what was said, but whatever it was resulted in a large metallic clang from somewhere in the distance. 'I think they're relieved. Especially after how you handled the check in at the field office.' She was trying to sound stern, but there was an element of amusement there nonetheless.

'What's going on, Charlie?' I said. 'They seemed especially on edge at that place. I know I'm an historic bad ass, but seriously.'

Her voice dropped again, still audible but I suspect drowned out to those around her by the general din of Whitehall. 'We've had troubles here. Whitehall is trying to blame van Ives, but as far as I can tell she's just a convenient excuse. Truth is, more and more warlocks are rattling their cages, and one or two have broken free.'

'How many?'

'They've had to go to the vault for six in the last month alone – seven if we include you, but you came out of it better than they did. Most of the Whitehall staff are keeping a lid on things, but the satellite offices are not doing so well.'

'That doesn't sound good...'

'Not really, no,' she said and sighed. 'We've kept it as quiet as we can, but not all warlocks are as antisocial as you. Word gets around. The wheels of gossip may grind slowly, but they're moving, Jameson.'

Oh dear. First name: things must be bad. 'Just don't let them do me in before I catch this guy, will you? And thank you for stopping them yesterday.'

'You're welcome. Don't rely on me being able to do that again, though. You've had your free pass, everyone's too edgy to give you another one.'

'Understood.' I snapped the phone shut.

Well, that was worrying.

CHAPTER 8

I checked four different buildings, all of them functioning as squats for people trying to stay off Whitehall's radar, before I got lucky. I'd run into a few people who had claimed ignorance of the broker, mostly kids about the same age the people in the bar, and though they were bad liars I didn't want to push my luck. They were minor talents, barely enough power between them to light a candle, but they didn't have the skittish nature of the ones I had run into in the bar. They wouldn't give me anything accept lip if I pushed them.

This building felt different, however. My withered magical senses, given a fresh lease of life from what little magic I had used in the last twenty four hours, were alive enough to feel the gentle hum of a practitioner at work. It had a similar cadence to what I knew of the broker's, although it was mixed with another, unknown flavour.

I wanted to call the building a factory or a warehouse, but only because whoever designed Humberside was not endowed with a sterling imagination. They were very keen on functionality over form, and a building can be functional as long as it has walls and a roof. Perhaps I'm a little harsher than I should be, but the fact remains it was difficult to place the purpose of the building. I think it might have been a youth centre at one point, if that helps. Possibly one of those inner city designer churches, the ones that try to look all modern so people don't start worrying about the god squad moving into the neighbourhood.

It was in pretty good nick though, so at least I didn't have to wander around another abandoned wreck.

It wasn't deserted either, which was another pleasant surprise. The place wasn't heaving, but there was a definite thoroughfare of foot traffic from room to room. A sign above a softwood reception desk declared the place to be a youth centre run by the church of Saint Judy of the Immaculate Complexion, another point for my detective skills I should think.

A drowsy receptionist gawked at me as I wandered past her, and though she started to call after me she must have decided against it. She clearly wasn't getting paid enough to care about people blindly wandering around the building – that's the usual excuse, right? I had no idea where I was going or what I was looking for, but the faint hum of magic could draw me in now. Tracing the ripples back to the source, relatively simple. This is made easier when said source is flaring all over the shop like a, well, signal flare.

That should have been a warning sign, all things considered. Flaring is a tell tale sign of magic in use, spells being cast or rituals being performed, and you should always be careful about interrupting such things. Best-case scenario is you find someone practising their cantrips, but worst case is you stumble upon someone opening a portal to the underworld. There's not very many positive ways out of that situation.

You may think that sounds like a pretty vast range of

things you could stumble upon in such a situation. You might quite rightly believe that things pretty much always fall somewhere in the middle, between the best and worst cases. Of course you would think that, because it makes perfect sense in the mundane world. The arcane sorts of screws that up a little when you realise that the best-case scenario includes things such as, for example, the ability to fire lasers from your eyes. Seriously, that's a really easy thing to do. It rather makes danger assessments pointless.

Somewhere in the back of my head I had remembered this, but hadn't quite managed to relay the information to the conscious part of my mind. Even once you've experienced it, the lethality of magic can start to dim in the mind's eye when you're not around it as much as you were. Why do you think the world at large ignores us? But anyway, as a result, I was oblivious enough to blunder into the room without looking, but astute enough to dodge the spell that flew at my head.

An azure bolt of energy whipped past me as I rolled to my right, landing in a crouch. It hit the wall and dissipated soundlessly.

I scanned the room quickly. It was a dance studio, all mirrors and lacquered wood floors, high windows, and only one entrance. Across from me, pressed into one of the mirrored corners, was a boy of maybe seventeen, scared out of his mind and gleaming like a glow stick. He was panicking and drawing on all the power he could muster, which was arcing across his body.

His eyes locked on me, watery and fearful, and he shot another azure bolt my way, followed closely by a third. Another combat roll got me out of the way of the first, but he had anticipated that and the second slammed into my right shoulder, sending me flying. I spun backwards and crashed into the mirror behind me, cracking it.

My blazer's enchantments had done their best to cushion the blow, but it hadn't been enough. I couldn't rely on my blazer to protect me from another blow like that. The last shot had winded me, and I didn't have it in me to dodge again, not that there was anywhere to go – the room was devoid of cover of any kind.

On the plus side, the boy was too scared to think, and I was pretty sure he was casting on instinct. I triggered one of the rings on my right hand and created a translucent half-sphere of shimmering energy, a shield designed to absorb the sort of energy I assumed the azure bolts to be: pure kinetic force rather than anything elemental. It wouldn't hold for long, but it would buy me some time to think.

The boy shrieked and hurled another barrage of bolts my way. They thumped into the shield and disappeared, absorbed by the barrier. There are few times I have been happier to have been right. I just wished I could move.

'Who are you? What do you want?' he roared. Spittle flew from his mouth and a vein in his temple was pulsing like a jack-hammer. He was storing too much power and didn't know what to do with it.

Talking was hard, what with the whole being winded thing, and being heard over his tirade was even harder. 'I'm a Warlock. I just want a word, nothing serious.'

'Bullshit! You're here to kill me!'

I dragged myself to a standing position. 'Kid, if I was here to kill you I would have put up a better fight than this, right?'

The boy frowned but he didn't relax. 'But they told me... They told me a Warlock would come to kill me!'

'Well it's not me. Just calm down. We'll talk about things.'

'I *can't* calm down,' he screamed. His eyes were bloodshot now and his face was bright red. The glow stick effect was slowly shifting its way up to a floodlight-level glare, and the arcing power was getting more aggressive, sparking off of him and scorching the floor nearby. He was going nuclear. If this kid was the broker, that he had survived this long was a miracle. 'I can't stop!'

This is not a problem most empowered people have to face, but the seriously gifted ones do. Your average spell-slinger can't draw in enough juice to overload their internal safeguards – think of it as how most people can't use the full strength afforded to them by their muscles because their brain knows it would cause permanent damage to the rest of the body. The potential is there, but they can't tap into it unless it's a serious life or death situation. Even then, they can usually shut themselves down in the end without major incident.

Your proper heavyweight spellcasters, however, don't have this safeguard in place, and that is what lets them bring out the big guns. They have to learn how to control this surge or a time will come when they just can't shut down. This tends to happen most when you're casting out of instinct or emotion – fear for your life is a very good motivator, after all – when you're not fully aware of what you're doing. If you haven't had someone teach you combat casting, or had time to teach yourself, it's only natural you'd get a bit carried away.

The thing is, and it is important I stress this, it sort of makes my statement about him going nuclear more apt than you know. Magic doesn't like being contained, which is why using it to cast a spell is so easy, you're really just letting it go. Bottling it up with no release can lead to a very real explosion. It's why some unscrupulous bastards liked to have a small group of young, untrained idiots in their employ during the Dark Times. Not so much suicide bombers as dead man's switches.

There were only two options in this situation. I could try and talk him down, walk him through the process of shutting down his magic, but that would take time I wasn't sure I had. I had to do this quickly and I had to do it now.

'Kid, listen to me very carefully. I'm going to help you, but you have to promise not to freak out when I do, right?' I said, placing my left hand against the cracked mirror behind me. The shield was getting heavy and I wouldn't be able to hold it much longer.

'Okay... just, please!'

'When I say, throw everything you have at me. Everything.'

'What? What are you talking about?'

'It'll be fine. I'm going to catch you.'

I prepared myself. This was dangerous and stupid, but it was that or watch a kid burst a blood vessel right in front of my eyes and, quite possibly, obliterate a small part of the city while he did so. I wasn't about to deal with that; I couldn't just stand there and watch it happen. I like living. If it makes you feel better, I can say I did it for the information on the arsonist, but be aware that that would be at least partially a lie. Sometimes you can't help but *care*. Disgusting, I know.

I siphoned some power from one of my other rings – one for deflecting ice attacks, I believe – and started to weave it into something new, something I could use. My shield was already buckling, trying to draw on emergency reserves from me that I didn't have, but it had to hold, just a little longer. The energy cracked and groaned and squealed as it sucked at my veins for something to fuel it, but it held.

Until I let it drop.

'Now!' I shouted.

A white-hot wave of crackling energy burst from the kids hands and shot towards me. It was untempered and, from what I could tell from that brief moment, unnatural. It bucked and weaved exactly like magic shouldn't, whipping itself at me like some arresting serpent. But I was ready. I flung forward my left hand as the energy slammed into it, and I watched as it engulfed my arm.

You might remember that I said his earlier attacks had dispersed soundlessly as I dodged them like the superb physical specimen I am often mistaken for. More magic 101 for you: mirrors are great if you want to not get exploded by magic. There's a whole metaphysical thing going on with them that I don't really understand, but the main thing is that they are very easily turned into windows when given the right nudge. Ever looked into a mirror and just felt something was off about your reflection? Consider the window.

Anyway, the key thing is that magic gets confused when slamming into mirrors. It's less likely to destroy it, instead passing through it into *somewhere else*. Now that's all well and good for your standard spells, but with the kid dumping his entire stockpile of power at me, I needed something I could control. You don't just lob a uranium rod into the sea, do you? No you don't, you lock it away in a lead-lined barrel and lob *that* into the sea.

Oh, fuck it. Look, put simply, I sort of turned my hand into a mirror. A bit. It's more that I borrowed its sort of reflective, *mirroryness.* I was still working on weaving it into something more stable, but it would do to hold his energy still while I properly worked out what I was doing.

It hurt every bit as much as you would have expected, though. Like gripping a tiny sun, which sounds like it should be awesome but really, really isn't. All I'm saying is it really hurt. But this was all part of the plan, and although the thing felt like it was burning its way through my hand, it wasn't. Yet. The weaving wasn't exactly robust.

I hadn't wanted to exploit a loop-hole in the warlock charter so soon after having that conversation with

Charlie, but I didn't feel I had a choice. Besides, I wasn't really doing anything wrong. It wasn't as if I was *casting* anything, doing a bit of weaving. Weaving was totally, maybe, sort of, a bit, not entirely against the rules. It didn't use any of my own magic. Besides, it wasn't as if I had much choice. I needed to get his energy out of him in a controlled way, and having him just throw it into the mirrors themselves, while sounding like a good idea, was too random for such a purge. For all I knew, it would overwhelm the damn things and explode anyway.

Which, you might be interested to know, is a thought I had largely tried to ignore, seeing as I felt it was bright to have him pour his power into my mirror ball hand. But that at least helped me take out some of the randomness.

'What do I do?' the kid screamed at me. 'I can't stop!'

I did my best to look like I wasn't terrified. Magic is all about appearances. 'You do nothing. This is on me now. Just keep going.'

With the beam burning into me, all I had to do now was dissipate the energy. I could release it slower and more efficiently than he could, but I didn't want to leave the entire room a glowing bunker of magical fallout. I staggered back and risked looking away at the wall behind me. It wasn't hard to find where my back had cracked the mirror, good old spidery veins. I moved closer and pulled a loose shard out from the impact zone.

Now came the hard bit.

I've heard that when people get electrocuted, they actually burn inside. The path the electricity takes through the body leaves a scorched wake behind it, and that's the real threat when it comes to electrocution. I'm not sure if that is true, but judging from how it feels to shunt so much magic up one arm, across your shoulders, down the other and into the palm of the opposite hand, I have no trouble believing it.

I didn't grip the shard; I wouldn't need to. It just lay flat on my right palm as I rerouted the kid's power through my body, feeding it into the glass slowly and gently. Keeping the momentum constant but restrained was important – maintaining control as you release such unbound pressure is incredibly difficult, all you want to do is let it go, which is exactly what the kid had done on command – but with every second, this became harder and harder to do.

It felt like an eternity, and I was certain I was going to black out, but then the final motes of power blinked out and the kid slumped to the floor. He was still red, but at least he had stopped glowing; that was something. My left hand also dimmed and I let the mirror weaving unravel, taking the time to have a little swear as I did so. I slipped the charged shard of mirror into a pocket. Nothing like a cavalcade of curse words to deal with a burning, searing pain in your dominant hand.

Well, I say that, but it was somewhat cathartic to stroll across the room, grab the boy by the scruff of his neck and slap him so hard his eyes spun.

That was lovely.

He blinked a couple of times before his eyes could focus on me. I waited until I was sure he was conscious. 'Now then, you little shit, we're going to have a chat about why you were trying to blast me into a thousand pieces just then. All right?'

He nodded. Smart kid.

CHAPTER 9

He didn't have any resistance left in him, which was very helpful. Trying to crack through even the egg shell defences of your typical coward can be arduous – they are just as likely to share unimportant things as the important stuff, leaving you to sift through the shit – but seeing as the kid had damn near killed himself with his magical outburst, he didn't even have the energy to gabble.

'I thought you were here to kill me,' he said. He was refusing to meet my eyes, which was probably for the best. I doubt I was wearing a friendly face at the time.

'That part I gathered. Why did you think I was out to kill you?'

'She told me Whitehall might send a warlock to get me. She warned me! Said that what we were doing was dangerous and that they'd send someone to shut us down before long!'

I loosened my grip on him a little, a gentle gesture that he was going the right way. 'Tell me about this woman. Her name, a description, anything I can use.'

The kid frowned. 'I don't know her name. She was

pretty though, I guess. Always wearing a hood and wanting to meet in dark places so I never really got a good look at her. I don't ask questions, it's not good for business.'

That seemed believable. Asking too many questions was a good way to get yourself shot with the gun you'd just sold, or in this case blasted into thousands of pieces by the arcane forces you'd just bequeathed.

'You said she was pretty,' I said. 'You must have seen something worth commenting on.'

He blushed and before he spoke I knew where this was going. 'Well I couldn't see her face... But her figure...'

'I get the idea.'

'*Are* you going to kill me?'

There was an interesting question. I'm not sure I had even decided myself. 'I didn't come here to kill you, but I'm considering changing my mind thanks to the welcome you gave me,' I said and pinched the top of my nose. The pain had travelled up to my head now. 'Listen, a word of advice: before too long they *are* going to come for you. It's what they... *we* do. Right now you're just a small fish, but we're running out of bigger ones fast. When we do, don't pull the same shit you just did, all right? It won't end well.'

He blinked. 'But won't they kill me?'

'Yes. But some ways are better than others.'

I could see he didn't understand, but then that was sort of the point. If I told him the truth, that they'd coerce him into a life of ratting on his peers while denying him the one thing that made him special, he'd freak out when the time came. There's something about the threat of having your liberty removed that makes people suicidal, not realising that if they fight it they *will* lose. The smart move is to endure it and fight it from within.

That had been my plan at the start, and I'm sure most

warlocks had thought that way too. Then the system gets inside you and, before you know it, you're just doing your job. Apparently my job involved making future prospects a little compliant. That should have shocked me, but at least he was less likely to throw his life away. I'd been responsible for enough death. Better they be miserable and alive.

I let him go and took a few steps back. 'When are you meeting her next?'

'I can't...'

I slammed my fist into the wall next to his head. You'll have seen people do this in films when they want to intimidate someone, but what they don't tell you is how much it hurts. Logically, punching a wall is a bad move at the best of times, but doing it to intimidate someone is actually, rationally, even worse. If you don't scare them enough to acquiesce, you've just taken one hand out of the game should it come to fisticuffs. And yet, I did it anyway, because a nice bit of showmanship never hurts.

Except it does, and trying to keep the pain off my face was quite an achievement.

In any case, it did the job. 'I don't know! She texts me whenever she needs a top-up, tells me where to meet her. It's done on her schedule, not mine!'

I snapped my fingers at him. 'Phone. Now.'

He fumbled around in his pockets for a moment and pulled out a smartphone of some description. One of those sleek obsidian tablets that would likely snap in half if you put it down too quickly on a table. 'Here! She's in the address book as "Babe".'

I took the phone off of him and frowned. 'Seriously, kid, grow up.'

I tucked the phone into a pocket, straightened my collar because that's what people do after interrogations like these, and left the room. On the other side of the door, a small crowd of nervous-looking people were trying to work out whether they should risk seeing what all the commotion was about.

I don't think they were expecting a dapper young man in a stylish blazer to stride confidently through the doors. Any chatter stopped dead, and they looked to me for some indication of what the hell had happened. I considered throwing them a witty line or something, a dismissive joke to really ramp up the confusion, but I couldn't be bothered. Instead, I just smiled at them and walked out. They didn't even try to stop me.

Despite my best efforts, I was starting to like Kaitlyn for this. It didn't fit what I knew of her motives, true, but it was just too much of a coincidence that she turn up now, just as I was starting to get a lead on the arsonist. That the arsonist was a woman was hardly conclusive proof that it was Kaitlyn, but it was a step in the right direction. I suppose, technically, it was possible that she had decided to use brokered magic rather than her own, although it was a roundabout way of doing things.

There was still a long way to go before I could finger her for this, but it was a start. It would be worth brushing up on my knowledge of the Bane of Whitehall, at least. Whether she was the arsonist or not, having all the available information on a terrorist was just the smart move. Eventually she was going to do something, even if she was innocent of this particular crime.

For a moment I considered just taking out the kid's phone and dialling the number anyway, or sending a text message. There was no way to tell exactly when she'd need her magic topping up, she might be able to manage a couple more attacks if she was careful and efficient with her spells. Yet doing that might blow my one chance to find out her identity. If she felt something was wrong...

No, the best course of action would be to wait for her

to contact me and try to stop her in the mean time. If worst came to the worst, I would have *a* way to track her down eventually, even if it meant sacrificing a few buildings.

For now, I would work on the assumption Kaitlyn *was* involved, and gather what information on her I could. I could do it in person, go back to the field office and have a chat with one of the archivists or fast trackers, but I would rather carve out my own eyes than talk to them unless I absolutely had to. A computer with an internet connection would suffice.

I made for the city library, it was the only one to which I had a membership card. While I possess a computer at home, using it for this task was not palatable – Whitehall has a habit of screening the hard drives of every computer that connects to their system, that should tell you enough. Besides, the library was closer, quieter and most likely safer.

The people of Humberside are, to their credit, big readers. Or rather I assume them to be, owing to the state of the library. It was huge and modern, a glass ceiling letting natural light spill over the shelves and reading areas. Pretty soothing, all told. The computers were in a room away from the books, to keep the tip-tapping of keys away from those who were content with the dead-tree delivery method.

In contrast to the library at large, the computer room was dimly lit and poor ventilated. Not that I cared, it meant less people trying to read over my shoulder. I sat down, logged into the Whitehall servers, and accessed the files on Kaitlyn.

There was little new information in the files. Huge documents had her pinned as a definite threat, from her propensity to lash out at Whitehall personnel, to the possibility that she was building an army of mages with which to instigate a revolution. All of the reports seemed far-fetched. All but one.

After perusing the others, reading one without a flair for the dramatic and an overuse of hyperbole was strange. Measured, reserved language detailed the pros and cons of letting Kaitlyn run free, ultimately deciding that her willingness to shut down any rogue spell-slinger outweighed the damage she could do to Whitehall at any one time. Every operative she iced and every building she raided could be replaced easily enough, but every rogue person of power she took out would be gone for good. Acceptable losses.

I promised you that I'd give you some more information on the Dark Times, and seeing as you won't see much mention of it in any official file, I figure now would be the best time.

As far as Whitehall is concerned, they themselves have always been there, monitoring the empowered crazies that crop up across the country from time to time and dealing with them as need be. But, up until about five years ago, they barely had an inkling that magic was a real thing. Obviously, they had heard of magic in the abstract way you most likely have – as a thing that shows up in books written by men with beards and as a smarmy way of talking about historic spiritualists and suchlike – but until the Dark Times they hadn't had a notion that it was something that truly existed.

We had kept it hidden for centuries. Bits had slipped out here and there, the result of people like John Dee and Aleister Crowley letting fame get the better of them, but for the most part we'd tried to remain below the radar. Which is kind of difficult when you can warp creation whenever you like.

It breeds hubris, and I'm sure that will come as no surprise. The longer you remain a secret, the more you start to believe your own bullshit. You spin ideas around in a closed space, bouncing them off the walls of similar minded people, and they ferment, they grow, and they take hold. Someone idly asking *so why don't we make ourselves known to the mundane* finds themselves being lauded as a great mind of a revolution, and suddenly it's not a query; it's a rallying cry.

Magic does not make you a better human being than the mundane. The fact that we call those without magic *mundane* should have been a clue that we weren't all we thought we were. The bigger clue should have been the moment things boiled over.

It always starts with one man. Or woman. It was a man this time, but we don't hold the monopoly on stupid ideas. In any case, an individual with a grievance lets it go to their head and things kick off. One angry magician, made redundant from some boring shit hole of a job in central London, slams a spell through the north face of Big Ben and everyone else gets ideas.

Why blend in? We're not like the mundane, we are *powerful.* We've already got the might, why shouldn't we have the political power? Same old questions. Same old problem: when everyone wants to rule, no-one can.

The fiefdoms probably hadn't been an intentional thing. Territory just sort of expands around your personality in times like these. Before anyone really knew it, certain magicians had risen to the top in their locality and they started calling themselves lords. Then the war wasn't with the mundane any more, it was with each other. Solidarity doesn't last long; you need an enemy you can enjoy killing.

I can't tell you how many fiefdoms there were. Some were very interested in the conflict, but others like myself were more interested in the craft and being left alone. Most of the conflict was in the South though, clustered around the money. I could present you any number of reasons as to why the North preferred isolation to open warfare, but I wasn't there. I can't comment. What I do know is that, in the South, things were bad.

Even as removed as I was, you don't get to hold dominion over a place as sizeable as Hampshire without having to get involved from time to time, and it was bloody. At the time, I revelled in these little diversions. There's a certain buzz to magical duels that you just don't get with fisticuffs or whatever.

Anyway, a lot of people died while we stupidly squabbled over territory that wasn't even ours, mundane and arcane alike. And yet, I don't know of a single magician that actually declared himself Overlord of the mundane. For everything we stated we fought for, we still kept ourselves largely in the shadows, ruling over other arcane souls and leaving the mundane to itself.

Which really just left Whitehall the opening it needed to fuck us right up. We had ignored the mundane government, and it had used that freedom to build up a force to remind us why they have ruled for those hundreds of years we have been in the background.

The first warlocks were volunteers.

But I'm sorry, I didn't mean to resort to a history lecture. You're very patient to put up with me. It's just that I feel it might be important you at least have a better understanding of how things were than Whitehall's official record allows. It is important someone remembers why things went as badly as they did.

I could talk to you for hours about the Dark Times, lecture you at length, and it wouldn't really get across just how it felt for those who lived through it. But you need a basic grounding from which, if you are intelligent, you can draw some understanding of how it feels to read Whitehall's summation of the whole period.

The Dark Times: Isolated upheaval of negligible interest.

I don't even know what that means.

It was strange to think that the conflict had only been a few years long, and yet the fallout was still ongoing. The warlock initiative had been the most visible response, but the collecting of data about every magician of worth had been just as important.

Which neatly brings us back on topic. Kaitlyn not showing up before the end of the conflict was weird for someone of her talents. It didn't sit right that she could have sat out of the conflict, and even if she had tried I would have expected someone to drag her into it. But then, I think like a villain. It's hard to parse the mind of a good person.

In any case, what they had on her from after the Dark Times certainly indicated that she had the stones for arson, if she had reason to go down that road. The records corroborated what I had heard about her in passing, that she was driven and idealistic and committed, and hated Whitehall enough to do anything to hurt it.

But that was the problem. Everything, even the bombastic documents that pegged her as the anti-Christ, was of the opinion that she was fighting for the belief that magic was not inherently evil. She wanted those in the know to see that the empowered community was not a nuclear bomb waiting to explode, and a string of magical arsons across the city was antithetical to that goal, especially when the buildings had nothing to do with Whitehall.

I wasn't going to rule her out completely, but I was sufficiently convinced she wasn't the girl I was looking for, which was very annoying. Things would have been easy if I could have just accepted it was her. Hell, maybe the *real* arsonist would have taken the opportunity to go into hiding. It wasn't as if Kaitlyn wasn't guilty of something, and I could probably track her a lot easier than this mystery woman. *A great body* is hardly a cast-iron description, especially when it comes from a hormone-addled youth.

There had to be a way to find this woman before she struck again and without having to rely on her texting me. I could have the number traced, but it would be a cheap pre-paid burner phone no doubt. I could call it, but that would tip her off and she'd vanish until she could find another broker. I needed more I could draw on, maybe something I could use to power another tracking spell. I needed a goddamned lead.

I unfolded my scorched ordnance survey map and laid it over the keyboard. I'd investigated all the likely hiding spots and potentially cased buildings as far as I could see, and the less likely places were far too numerous to check them all. Dead end.

I snapped my phone open and fired a text message off to Charlie. Libraries are quiet places. It would have been rude to call her despite the lack of people in the room. Besides, I wanted to avoid the telling off I would get for what went down with the broker. The amount of unread text messages I had from her indicated that she wanted to tell me off about something, and considering that was the only thing I had done worthy of a bollocking, I reasoned that the two were connected. I didn't read them. She would repeat herself whenever I next spoke to her anyway.

Trying to trace the phone was a long shot, but I had no other cards to play at the moment. If I was lucky then maybe, just maybe, the girl would have been stupid enough to use a contract phone and then we'd have her. Not likely, but possible.

Putting my phone away, I slumped forward and bashed my head into the keyboard. Magic just makes everything so much bloody harder. If she'd been starting the fires the old fashioned way, with matches and an accelerant, we could have tracked her down inside a week. But then it wouldn't be us tracking her down, because there wouldn't have been any magic. But shut-up, we're talking hypotheticals here. Besides, having the mundane authorities on this case instead of me would still be preferable.

I needed a better tracking spell. If I could just get permission for a sustained spell, something a little more powerful than the fire and forget one they had allowed me before, I could pinpoint every instance of the broker's magic currently floating around the city and track them down one by one until I found the girl I was after.

I sent Charlie another text message asking for clearance, but I knew what the answer would be. They were hesitant enough to give me permission for the damn cantrip, let alone a full-blown channelled working. I was too high risk, and the only way I was going to get that spell done was if I got someone else to work it for me.

This is where it comes in handy to have friends. Which I don't.

The only person I knew who I could perhaps trick into helping me was the broker himself, and he'd be burned out for at least a week following his magical near-meltdown. No-one else in the community was liable to help me, not after how things had gone down at the bar.

Curse my unique brand of charm that keeps people at a distance.

I could always have called on the friendly neighbourhood warlocks and their union of solidarity against The Man, but I still wasn't sure about them. It was a hard sell, owing a favour to such a group when I wasn't really sure I trusted them.

I peeled my head off the keyboard and folded up my map, took a few deep breaths and went to stand up to leave. As I turned I found myself staring right at the cargo-panted thighs of an angel. From a certain point of view. A few minutes earlier and that angel would have been a demon, but you know how things are.

'You need to learn to leave these things well enough alone, Parker.' Kaitlyn said.

CHAPTER 10

I like to think I have decent spatial awareness. I don't walk into walls very often, rarely spook myself by imagining a dark figure slinking past the doorway when I'm starting to doze off, and I'm not particularly easy to sneak-up on. Granted, I've been sneaked-up on before, but never from the side. As far as I was concerned, Kaitlyn had just appeared there, perched on the edge of the desk like some strange flame-haired bird.

What I would have liked to have done was tilt my head to the side quizzically, thus successfully hiding my surprise behind an expression of intrigue, and suavely welcomed her.

What I *did* was recoil in a comical fashion, throwing my centre of gravity out of whack and causing the chair to topple off balance.

Don't judge me. She was right in my face. I'd like to see you remain composed in such a situation.

I tried to catch myself on the desk, failed, and braced myself for a less than endearing impact with the floor, but it didn't come. My chair hovered at a weird angle for a moment and then righted itself. Kaitlyn had caught it with her foot. She smiled at me. The bitch.

'Quiet,' she said, softly. 'Don't you know this is a library?'

'Ha bloody ha. You've got some nerve showing your face to me again. It's expected of me to bring you in, you know.'

'You're supposed to be scared of me, *you know*. I've read the files you've just been nosing through, I know what they say about me.'

I tried to regain some manliness by leaning back in my chair. I'm not sure it worked, but it made me feel better. 'They say you're all business, but I don't think that quite matches up with the need for these little chats. Besides, you wouldn't have it out with me here. This is a public place; it wouldn't fit with your ideology to endanger the poor little civvies.'

'But you think I'm burning down huge bits of the city. How does that sit ideologically?'

'It doesn't,' I admitted. 'But it's a little coincidental that you happen to show up while this is all going on.'

She jumped to her feet. It was quite graceful. Not that I was paying attention or anything. 'I warned you to steer clear of this, Parker. I don't like repeating myself.'

'And yet you're doing it anyway.'

'Despite what those files might say, I'm not a monster. You're hardly innocent, but you're not an active threat to my agenda either. And I'd rather you didn't become one. I don't want to have to kill you.'

'Madam, please,' I said, placing my hands behind my head. 'You couldn't even if you wanted to.'

It was empty bravado, designed to elicit a reaction. Not that I'm a social super-scientist or anything, but it pays to know just how confident someone is in their ability to kill you. I was reasonably certain she wouldn't try it here, but as I had no intent of stepping away from this, I would force her to take the shot sooner or later.

Her confidence would give me a clue as to how she would try it, and how best to defend against it.

'Once, perhaps,' she said. 'Back before Whitehall neutered you. I've heard tales about those days. They are perhaps chief amongst my many reasons for wanting you to let this drop.'

'The tales don't do me justice.'

She turned her back on me. 'I don't know. The one about Robin seemed to sum up everything *I* needed to know.'

I must admit, I hadn't been prepared for her to go there, and my immediate response might have been more revealing than I had wanted. I didn't shout or scream, my reply was very quiet. 'We're not talking about her.'

'Still a little sore, is it? I would expect so, if what I've heard is even remotely true. They say the warlocks found you just kneeling over her, barely even aware of what was going on.'

'We're not talking about this.'

'Although I admit, I'd be a little shell-shocked too, considering the mess.'

I stood up slowly and took a few deep breaths. I wasn't going to let this get to me, get a rise out of me. I was going to stay calm and in control. This was the past, the past I had more than paid for, and I wasn't going to let her drag me back there just to make a point.

'We're not...'

'Did you enjoy it?' She turned around to face me again, her face one of serious contemplation. 'I suppose you must have. I wouldn't suspect it's possible to do *that* without enjoying it.'

I grabbed her by the throat and pulled her face close to mine. She didn't even resist. Then I caught myself and let her go. The anger had taken control for just a second, but it had been enough. I *had* to do better, keep myself in line. I took a few steps backwards.

'Don't talk to me about her. We're not doing this. Not here, not today. Just say what you came here to say and piss off.'

She was smiling. An honest-to-God beaming smile. It faded quickly, replaced by a serious glare. 'You've done some bad things, Parker.'

'Noted. Piss off.'

'I'm not done,' she said, spinning my vacated chair around and lowering herself into it. 'You've done bad things, but I honestly believe you are trying to atone for them. I just don't believe you are very good at it.'

'You don't know me.'

'No, that is true. I know what you've done, that's a matter of record. But I also know more about this case of yours than you do, and I'm starting to get a working understanding of the sort of man you are.'

My jaw was clenched so hard my back teeth were going numb with the pain. 'I am a good man. I have worked hard to be a *good* man.'

'I know. It's pretty obvious to anyone willing to look,' she said. There was genuine tenderness there. 'But I was at the bar, I saw how you reacted.'

'I had that under control.'

'Listen, Parker. You *are* a good man. You're on the path I want for every magician in this country, but your progress is more delicate than you are willing to admit. If I'm right about this case, it could break you. And I am sorry for bringing her up, but I needed to be sure.'

The anger flared again. 'What gives you the right to test me?'

'You know I'm right. If you keep pursuing this and it turns out too much, then I'm the one that will have to stop you. I'd rather not have to. I like being able to believe people can change. It's sort of my thing.'

I took a breath. Two breaths. 'Whitehall have systems in place to deal with that, should it happen. As you well know.'

'And as you well know, I'm not one to believe in the government.'

Which was true. I could well believe that, of the two of them, Kaitlyn would be more likely to do me in than Whitehall. Even with the way the vault worked, I'd still give her the edge in any race for my life. She had a hungry look about her, lean and vicious, that only seemed to come out when she needed to make a point. She had made her point very well.

And the worst thing was, I found myself believing it.

Now, again, I wasn't on board with the whole conspiracy theory that The Rider was behind this nonsense. It was going to take a lot to make me even consider taking that seriously, but she wasn't wrong in how I had reacted recently. Until you've been a proper bastard, as I have, and walked a bloody mile in my shoes, it's probably difficult to comprehend how hard every step is away from that.

As a warlock, your entire purpose is to fight magic. Everything you do is in line with the goal that, ultimately, there should be no uncontrolled magician out there, and you accept this or die. This was a simple case, minimal danger and stress, and still I had found a way to almost let my past get the better of me. It's a daily struggle to keep those thoughts out, to keep my magic contained, even knowing what letting it loose would do to me.

Because I want to be a good man, apparently.

Maybe Kaitlyn did know more about the arson than I did. Maybe she was right, and there was something about the whole thing that would kick those daily temptations just a little too much. All it would take, I suppose, is one truly bad day to fall off the wagon. It wasn't like I hadn't thought about how I would do it, if I was going to. Idle fantasising, nothing more. Everyone does it.

But, no. Fuck her, and fuck her pompous holier-than-thou attitude. She was no saint; nothing about her gave her the legitimacy to pass judgement on me. I wasn't going to slip up. That was not a prediction she could make because she was working on faulty assumptions. She thought I was a good man.

But I'm a villain.

'Your concern is touching, it truly is,' I said. It doesn't take long for your composure to return if you take the time to think things through. I think my calmness caught her off-balance. 'But all you had to say was that you found me irresistible. You're an attractive lass, I'm sure I could find a space for you in my diary.'

It's a lovely moment, switching gears so fast that you can lock a person between emotions with sheer confusion. Try it sometime, the muscles do this weird thing and the whole face seizes for a split second. 'I beg your pardon?'

'I just assumed, as you were so worried about my well-being, that you doth protested too much, m'lady,' I said as the anger slowly washed out of me. Being a dick purges anger really easily. Science fact. 'But if a date is too much to ask, I suppose I could find a spot for you in my little black book instead.'

'Are you deliberately being vile?'

'Yes, actually. Well spotted.'

Her lip curled. People don't actually do that very often. 'I'm trying to help you, you infuriating bastard.'

'Well, and I say this with all due respect: I'm a big boy. I can tie my own shoes and everything. I don't need protecting, from myself or anyone else, thank you very much. I'm going to do my job and finish this case, regardless of your little assessment of my mental state. So kindly fuck off now.'

'Fine,' she said. 'You know what? You want to throw

your life away by ignoring my advice, fine. You're right, it's not my place to stop you. Not yet. But I just hope you remember this when you force me to kill you. You remember that I gave you a chance to avoid this.'

'I remember everything. It's sort of *my* thing.'

Yes, that's a bit of a rubbish comeback, I know. It's the delivery that matters though, and I pumped so much slime into that line that I think it did the job well enough.

There was a flash of magic in her eyes for just a second. It seemed the self-professed queen of the temperance movement wasn't as clean as she liked to make out. But then, these people never are. There's always a skeleton or two in the closet. Or perhaps I'm just getting cynical in my old age.

She took a deep breath this time. 'Fine. Be that way. If you're dead set on doing this, then let me at least speed you on your way.'

'No thanks, I'm good.'

'Just... Stop being an arse hole for a moment and take *some* advice. Let me tell you where the arsonist is going to strike next.'

Well, that was certainly a pretty sharp about-face.

There was clearly a trap here. There were documented cases of Kaitlyn van Ives working with Whitehall warlocks when their goals happened to coincide, but very few warlocks lived through the experience, and those that did were usually subject to the business end of the vault. As far as Whitehall was concerned, they were tainted beyond repair from the experience.

Then again, any help would be welcome at this point, even if it was the equivalent of a deal with the devil. Plus, until I got a call from the arsonist herself, there wasn't much for me to do. I couldn't ignore a possible lead, just in case. It wasn't as if Whitehall particularly loved me anyway, so I didn't have too much to lose.

Except my life. As usual.

'Well aren't you a sly dog. Why would you tell me that? You just told me to back off, and now you're offering the location of the next target.'

'I *do* want you to back off, but that doesn't mean I want the arsonist to torch another building. I've got other avenues to work which, frankly, are more important than stopping the next attack. But that doesn't involve letting innocent bystanders roast alive in a magical war if I've got a difficult bastard who is dead set on getting involved.'

'War? What war?'

She crossed her arms. 'You don't know? Christ, how Whitehall functions *at all* any more is astounding. I don't have time to educate you right now, so you'll just have to work it out for yourself for the moment. Just save some lives, if you wouldn't mind, and *then* back off. Okay?'

I wasn't about to commit to dropping the investigation altogether, but then if she was willing to give me the next target, perhaps I could intercept the arsonist anyway. Beat her to the punch, as it were. Kaitlyn had either not considered that option, or didn't have faith in me to pull it off. I had money on the latter. Insulting, ego-damaging money.

'Deal,' I said. Can you spot the lie? 'Where's the next target?'

'An apartment building on Dog Street. An odd choice, I know, but that's where they're hitting,' she said and checked her watch. 'You've not got long, by the way. Half an hour, perhaps?'

I didn't waste time. Dog Street wasn't too far away as the crow flies, but as the beleaguered human runs it was a right pain in the arse to reach. I sprinted for the door to the computer room. 'I lied about the deal, you know,' I said as I turned the knob.

'I know,' she said, a crooked, sad smile on her

attractive face. 'But I had to give you the option.'

I slammed the door behind me and sped off for Dog Street.

CHAPTER 11

My legs were unhappy with the pace I was forcing upon them, but they are my legs and they'll do what I damn well tell them.

I'd spent most of the day running around, and it was starting to take its toll. Pure pig-headed stubbornness was doing a decent job at overcoming that for now, but I wasn't sure it would hold until I hit Dog Street. Even if it did, I'd likely be too tired to do anything about the impending attack.

One thing at a time, I thought. *Worry about getting the first.*

I pelted through Humberside like a man possessed, my feet heavy on the pavement and my shoulders heavier on pedestrians. I'm not built for shoulder-barging, but then most people aren't really expecting someone to smash into them in the middle of the day, so it evens out. If you keep an eye out for the big, burly bastards and avoid them, you tend to do okay. In a city, it tends to be faster than trying to fit into the gaps between them anyway. Make your own road.

There was the odd stumble, and I fell a few times, but

for the most part I kept a steady pace. Half an hour to stop the attack, and it should take just shy of that to get there. Perfect.

Humberside is an old city, and as a result its streets weren't so much planned as evolved. The very kernel of the city is easy enough to manoeuvre through, as old as it is, but then there's a ring of awkward asphalt arteries clogged with people and cars and weird buildings that can only crop up by accident. They looked for the paths stomped into the earth by the constant footfalls of travellers and merely paved over them. When you get to the outskirts you'll find sanity reasserts itself and it becomes easier to get around. But, unfortunately for me, I was moving deeper into the spiral of madness that was the inner city.

Locals, naturally, didn't have a problem negotiating the streets, but I wasn't a local boy. I knew where I was, and where I wanted to be, but the only way I would get there was by stubbornly charging the only route I knew.

But being stubborn wasn't going to be enough to keep my body going – sprinting flat out for thirty minutes is hard enough for an athlete, and I am certainly no athlete. Without having magic to tap into to keep everything going, I'd have to do my best with good, old-fashioned denial and distraction.

Kaitlyn's words to me at the library were still ringing in my head, and as much as I didn't want to think about them, I wanted to think about the burning pain in my lungs even less.

She had asked me if I had enjoyed it. That had been what had broken through the wall. Worst still, it hadn't been the carefully worded insult that had pissed me off, it had been that I *couldn't remember* whether I had liked it or not. The fear that I did what I did because, deep down, I had wanted to...

Before the warlocks caught me, I was a pretty

powerful wizard. I think I've inferred as much previously. What I might have omitted from my story, is that I wasn't a particularly pleasant one. I was a bit of a bastard actually, right on up there with the darkest of the dark mages. I was dangerous. Seriously dangerous.

I want to tell you that it wasn't my fault. Hell, I've already told you about how the magic took me at that bar, how I barely managed to contain the massive arcane explosion of death. You might even believe me now, if I said it was a sickness or an addiction. I tricked myself into believing that for a while in an attempt to clear my conscience. *I couldn't help it,* I would say, *it wasn't me.*

But it was, and that is what you have to understand. Everything I did during that time, I did *because I could.* It wasn't a sickness or an addiction, it was weakness of character, plain and simple. I wasn't alone either. The Dark Times were filled with people like me, all of us fuelled by arrogance and weak characters, lusting for power to fill that void inside. We sought power for the sake of power, fought with each other over it, and tried to carve up the country between us. We were monsters, for no other reason than we had the options to choose to be.

And it wasn't until Robin that I realised that.

She was truly stunning, a girl so attractive that I couldn't even talk to her. I would try, but everything would shut down as a sort of defence mechanism, as though anything I said to her would be far too stupid with which to waste her time. Eventually I managed to graduate from that to her beauty merely making me want to burn out my own eyes, for they had fulfilled their usefulness – they would never see anything to top her. And then, finally, I reached the level where I could both talk to, and look at, her without any major problems and so asked her out. This is a gross simplification, I know, but I can't do the details. I just can't.

Things went well, and as they do in these things, I introduced her to my interests, and before I knew it she was my apprentice. I hadn't even been aware I wanted one, nor that I was even training her at first, and I didn't so much notice that it was happening as much as it just became the norm. She just *was* my apprentice and always had been, and she was good.

Her attenuation to magic was formidable, and she learned quickly. Together we had a sort of Bonnie and Clyde thing going on, and it was glorious. And then I got carried away and fucked it all up.

Robin had never really enjoyed the killing, she liked the thrill of it well enough but had never really come to accept the actual act itself. I did the bulk of it, all the duels and whatnot, that was my realm, and she made do with the contact high. The Harley Quinn to my Joker. It had all been in service of a greater plan, of course, and most of the people I'd done in were warlocks trying to bring me in if that helps. Most, but not all. I had my fair share of innocent blood on my hands.

I'd been after more power. Everyone knows the phrase "power corrupts", so it should come as no surprise that, my own powers not insignificant, I had wanted more. Finding a spell to boost my own potential was difficult, and finding one that would do it with only a minimal chance of cranial explosion was even harder, and the one I had settled on was one of the darkest workings I had ever attempted. Which is saying something, seeing as one of my workings had killed an entire squad of warlocks the moment they kicked in the door of my current safe house. Ripped the life right out of them before they had a moment to react.

But this was something else: a ritual to take the power of the dead and weave it into my own. That was the idea. In practice, I don't know what happened. Something snapped in me, if that's even the right word. I don't know, I can't remember. During the ritual, I blacked out, and when I woke up she was dead. I'd screwed up the working somehow, although I'm not sure where, and she just wasn't there any more.

Just a loose sack of crushed bones and watery flesh.

A group of warlocks had been sent to stop me augmenting my already formidable power, but they turned up late. I heard them come in, shouting at me to surrender the whole time, but I just didn't care. It's strange how quickly things can change meaning with one little mistake, how clarity can be bestowed upon you so suddenly.

I fought back later of course. Briefly. But the thrill was gone. Why bother?

So I gave up, joined the establishment, played my part and hoped to forget about her. Some days I even managed it, and then Kaitlyn van Ives comes along with her stupid beautiful hair and face and rips open old wounds with a single sentence.

Wounds that had kept me distracted long enough to ignore my body's screaming agony at such Herculean exertion. As I remembered this my vision snapped back into full focus. I enjoy this moment, when you come back to reality and realise how much of what you've been doing up until that point has been purely automatic.

Or rather, I *usually* enjoy it.

Along with the improved focus came the pain. The burning, stabbing, twisting, all-consuming pain in my legs and my lungs, roaring back into my brain like a neutron bomb. It's a curious sensation, feeling your limbs shut down underneath you, and not one I would recommend you seek out. My legs turned to jelly mid-step, and I fell, catching myself on the road sign for Dog Street.

Well, I guess that had worked then. Good job, me. Now all I had to do was work out which apartment building was at stake. And get enough energy back into my body to actually move to try and stop it.

Dog Street was ugly, even by inner city standards. The road itself seemed to have been constructed purely by accident, as though the rest of the city had been created by pouring asphalt into a giant mould and all the run-off was swept into one place: Dog Street. The road was patchy and uneven, riddled with potholes and indentations where lazy council workers had stepped in the asphalt as it had been drying. The pavement that flanked this mess was not much better, loose and cracked slabs becoming intimately acquainted with weeds and the odd sapling.

And yet, despite all this, the buildings were highly sought after. In contrast to the traditional ugliness of the street itself, the buildings had gone for *artistic* hideousness, the sort that can only be achieved by giving an artist millions of pounds and no oversight whatsoever. One was a concrete monstrosity that looked like a cross between a giant tombstone and a wedding cake, another a glass and steel beast that could probably blow over in a strong wind. There was no theme to the area, and people seemed to love that.

To be fair, this schizoid approach to town planning didn't leave too many buildings that *could* catch fire to any significant degree. A great deal of the architects had been too committed to one medium to allow anything else inside, from what I knew, so I could rule out a few of the concrete buildings and one or two of the glass and steel beasts. There was still too many to choose from.

Sounding an evacuation would be the best course of action, if I had it open to me, but I didn't. I had neglected to call the police on the journey, both for means of energy conservation and because the last thing I needed was them stomping all over the place and getting in the way. Even if I had, getting them to evacuate the entire street would take more time than we had anyway. The only way was to find the arsonist while she was busy preparing her spell and interrupt her. And she had to be on site to cast this spell.

I reached out with my senses, looking for her particular flavour of magic. You don't need to use magic to sense it, which makes a warlock's job considerably easier if they can maintain their connection to the power, but trying to track down something by senses alone is a close-range skill. Given the choice, most people would still prefer a tracking spell of some kind, but you work with what you've got.

There was nothing reaching the mouth of the street, where I was, so I began to limp my way down the street as fast as I could. My legs had gone numb now, which was worse than the pain, and every step required more concentration than I would have liked, but at least I could take solace in the fact that they would work properly once the feeling came back. That tended to be how things went.

I made it halfway down the street, perplexed pedestrians giving me worried looks but none offering to help, before I felt anything. The faintest whiff of power, distant but unmistakeable, tickled the very periphery of my senses.

'Got you, you bitch,' I said aloud. A passing old man gave me an odd look, but I ignored him.

I picked up speed as best I could, following the magic as it got more potent, more powerful. It led me to one of the older buildings, one that still resembled an actual apartment building and not an elaborate architectural wet dream.

She'd be working the spell from inside, same as at the fire station. I wished I had my gun. The untapped rings on my hands and the enchantments on my blazer felt insignificant somehow. It wasn't as though I was a novice when it came to taking down magicians the old fashioned way, but you learn to rely on your gut too, and mine was telling me I was probably over my head. Or maybe that was just the searing agony in my extremities. I took some comfort in the knowledge that she was using the broker's magic, and I had already defeated that once today. Small comfort, admittedly, but it was better than nothing.

I could smell the smoke as soon as I opened the door. It led me as much as the magic did, from that point, and it didn't take long to track it to its source. The building had a large lobby for an apartment block, complete with numerous little rooms tacked onto it. Perhaps it had been a hotel or some sort of guest house before it became what it was now. Pretty much all of the rooms connected to the lobby were empty.

She had taken up residence in the biggest room at the very back of the lobby, what I guessed used to be an office or security station. What furniture there was had been pushed up against the walls to clear a space on the floor, although that wouldn't have taken particularly long. Two desks and a chair, all covered in cobwebs, was as far as the room's contents went. In the centre of the cleared space, surrounded by swirling motes of fireless smoke, knelt the arsonist, a pentagram throbbing in front of her.

I had time, which was nice. Her back was to the door, and although I didn't recognise the spell, the throbbing of her pentagram told me it would likely take another minute or two to finish it off. Time to work out a plan of attack. It needed to be a quick assault, one that would put her out before she had a chance to fight back. She may have been using the broker's magic, but I could feel her own roiling beneath the surface. I didn't have it in me to pull another trick like with the broker himself, and no mirrors to siphon the magic into even if I did. Cramming anything else into the shard in my pocket was just asking for it to go nova. That left me with one option. I had to shut her down fast.

Every dusty room, no matter its original purpose, will have a loose length of piping in it somewhere. It's just a fact of the universe; even if one is never placed in the room, one will materialise there. Sure enough, this room was no different – in the far corner, leaning against the wall, sat a rusty length of pipe about as long as a baseball bat. Just what I needed and completely out of reach.

It was time for plan B, then.

I crept closer, step by step, gently placing my heel down first and rolling pressure forwards onto my toes. Walking silently is surprisingly difficult, and with my legs as knackered as they were it introduced me to a glorious new flavour of pain, but it was that or lose the element of surprise, and again my stubborn nature prevailed. I got to within arm's reach of the chanting woman, shook my left hand a little, made a fist and held it up to the back of her head.

In truth, I wasn't really sure what I was going to do. The only thing I could think of was just dumping the enchantments of the various rings out as raw magic, hope it would hit her as a concussive force and knock her spark out. It was as good a plan as any, spoiled by one little hiccup.

'You need better shoes, Mister Parker,' she said, and I saw the brief flash of a magical shield wash over her. 'Very noisy. I could hear the dust grains popping under your feet.'

There was a noise behind me. I tried to turn but I was too slow, my head turning into the blow before I was ready. I spun back the other way, pirouetting like the best of them, tripping over my own feet and crashing to the floor. Pretty sure I landed on my nose.

A right royal sucker punch. I think it was a punch, anyway. Whatever it was, it made my head spin and my vision blur, and my brain had bounced around inside my head enough to mean I wasn't getting up any time soon. I did try, hero that I am, and got a boot to the face for my trouble. I saw it coming, so *that* was definitely a boot.

Regaling you with these tales makes me think I really need to take up some sort of martial art.

'Should I kill him?,' said the owner of the boot with what sounded like hesitation. From what I could make out it was a man. Yep, that's all. I was barely conscious, don't judge.

The arsonist didn't move. 'I'm not... I'd rather we didn't.'

'He's doing his job too well. If we let him go he might ruin everything we've worked so hard for.'

'I know but... I don't want his blood on my hands. *That* would undermine everything.'

The man snorted. 'My hands, technically.'

'You know what I mean. Let the fire do it. It's not our fault then.'

'Are you sure that's wise?'

'It's how van Ives would do it, right?' There was more than a little uncertainty in the question.

'I suppose.'

'Then that's what we're doing.'

I spat out some blood. Manners be damned. 'You work for Kaitlyn?'

Another boot to the head shut me up. The man said something as he kicked me, but in all honesty I was in no position to hear it. The kick shattered what little consciousness I had left, and I blacked out.

The last thing I remember is cursing myself for falling right into her damn trap. You can do a lot of cursing in the last few milliseconds of consciousness.

CHAPTER 12

Even though I was unconscious, I still felt the flames.

Have you ever been dreaming and had the real world creep in? A ringing phone in the real world becomes an alarm in the dream for instance, or a breeze creeping in through an open window becomes a gale in the dream world? More often than not, these are the things that let you take control of a dream, make it lucid and even wake yourself up.

Doesn't work that way when you've just had your face kicked in.

I couldn't wake up, even knowing as I did that I was slowly roasting to death in a burning building. Every lick of flame, every singed hair, every millimetre of burned skin happened in slow motion and in crystal clarity, and I couldn't even scream.

Apart from the pain, everything was black. I had expected some sort of dream, even a simple looping nightmare of the kick that had put me under, but not *nothingness*. I pushed against it, kicked and punched and scratched at my own mind, just trying to force myself to wake up and drag myself clear of the flames. The screaming in the darkness was me.

I could feel my flesh split and crack and char.

Then, suddenly, I woke up. My eyes snapped open and with them the scream, the one that had been echoing around my mind, burst free. I tried to get up, to run, to get clear, but I couldn't. As I shot up I felt strong hands grab me and push me back down. I tried to struggle but I didn't have the energy.

'Hold him still,' someone said.

'I'm trying!' came another voice.

'Dammit, Parker, calm down,' came the first again. It sounded familiar.

I stopped and actually *looked* at what I was seeing. Dull, painted drywall underneath peeling wallpaper, polystyrene ceiling tiles, seventies-style telephones. I was back at the field office.

A face jutted into view, angry and coated in wrinkles brought on by excessive frowning. 'Are you quite finished?' she said.

'I'm sure you don't get this very often,' I said back to her. 'But I'm glad to see you.'

The headmistress' lips did a strange dance while trying to hold back a smile. Her frown never wavered. 'Welcome back to the land of the living. Let him up, gentlemen.'

The strong hand released me, and I sat up and winced. I could tell I was alive from the pounding maelstrom of agony that was swirling and smashing its way around the back of my skull. Sitting up had been a mistake; the pain had been masked somehow while I was lying down, but now it rolled forward and became much more prominent.

There were less people in the room than I had expected. The two gorillas holding me down had been fast-trackers, which came as no small surprise, the same two that had picked me up from my house. Neither were showing any real love for me, although the younger of the pair was hiding some concern. Human after all.

Apart from that dynamic duo, there was the headmistress and, behind her, leaning on her desk no less, was a man I didn't recognise. He had a trimmed goatee, unkempt greying hair, and a suit that clearly cost more than it needed to. He didn't seem to be paying much attention to proceedings, flicking through a paperback novel and generally trying to look nonchalant. This probably meant he was making careful mental notes of everything that was going on. I hate office people.

I was lying on one of the desks near the one the headmistress called her own, the rest of the office having been cleared out. This did not fill me with confidence, but at least I was alive and relatively uncooked.

The fire. I had forgotten about the fire. Checking myself over I found that, aside from a few singed hairs, I was undamaged. Perhaps the burning sensation in the dream had been reality seeping in after all, just not in the way I had expected.

I swung my legs down off the desk and considered standing up. The unruly freshman party in my brain piped up again and I decided it best to stay off my feet a little while longer. Today had been, by all accounts, pretty shit.

'How did I get here?' I said.

'You might think we are uncaring monsters, Parker, but the truth is that we like to play things safe. Make sure every threat is carefully considered, contained, ' the headmistress said. 'We had a fast-track candidate follow you from the moment you left here this morning.'

'I would have appreciated it if he had piped up *while* I was getting my head kicked in.'

The older of the two fast-trackers near me adjusted his tie awkwardly. 'We thought...'

'We thought,' the headmistress interrupted. 'That you

were working with van Ives.'

'What?'

'You were seen talking to her at the library, and then, what, you just miraculously know where to go to bump into the arsonist?'

I cradled my head. 'She gave me a lead. It was too good to pass up.'

'And you just took that lead as read, did you? A terrorist pops up next to you, drips some obvious poison in your ear, and then you just follow it blindly. That's what you expect *us* to believe, is it?'

'I make do with what I've got! I'm not Basil the Great Mouse Detective, I can't whip this shit up out of thin air. Kaitlyn van Ives has a documented history of, on occasion, helping out Whitehall –'

'And then killing off those she helped! If you trusted her you are either a traitor or a bigger fool than I've given you credit for.'

'I had no –'

'Enough,' said the man behind the headmistress. 'This bickering is getting us nowhere. Hardly a surprise you haven't had much luck bringing a stop to these attacks if this is how you run Humberside, Miss Eames.'

So that was her name. 'She's not the best boss I've ever had,' I said.

'I wasn't talking to you, warlock,' he said. The paperback disappeared into a pocket. 'Quite frankly, that Eames can get anything done at all with a staff of warlocks as large as hers is impressive, but as that's the hand she's been dealt she could stand to be more efficient. There are appearances that need to be maintained, after all.'

I stood up slowly. Less of a mistake than I had thought it would be, but still not without drawbacks. 'I am doing the best I can to bring this arsonist in, and I nearly died today, twice, if that had escaped your notice.'

'It hadn't, actually. Considering I'm the one that stopped them vaulting you after your little scrap with the broker, I would think you'd be more pleased.'

'But I –'

'*Don't* try to lie to me, warlock. You unlawfully modified a Whitehall supplied enchantment. In popular parlance, you weaved it into something different. Don't try to deny it, we both know you did this. Thinking they wouldn't notice it amongst all the power flying everywhere was smart, yet it also betrays an ignorance as to how exactly we work. You're only breathing now because we don't have a fast-tracker to spare on this.'

'Forgive my impending rudeness, sir,' I said, rubbing one of the bruises on my head. 'But that's bullshit and you know it. You've got a whole army of fast-trackers.'

He peeled himself off the desk and crossed his arms. 'Again, ignorance. The amount we have with field experience is minimal, and those are all far too busy at Whitehall and keeping the South in line. It's why we have field offices, warlock, and why we don't just kill you all outright. *Do your job.*'

'Fuck you.'

Now, in my defence, I'm not great with authority, but this guy was something else. The way he spoke conveyed not just contempt – anyone in authority has overwhelming contempt for their underlings, it's bred in the bone – but also loathing, the kind backed up by fear. When properly harnessed, there is nothing more motivating than fear, and as his was motivating him to hate me purely for what I am I wasn't feeling the need to be polite.

'I can't help but feel, warlock, that you have forgotten your place. Have we not been good to you? We've given you a second chance at life, a third and a fourth even, and yet you still can't find it within you to show even a little respect?'

It was at about that point where I started to wonder if I had bitten off a little more than I could chew. He was building up to something, and I hate it when people do that. They can't just come right out and say that they're going to kick your arse. They have to work their way up to it. It's tiresome.

'Yes, my life is lovely. Give me another reason.'

'You're right, I haven't introduced myself. Charles Bennett, at your service.'

I frowned. 'Am I supposed to know that name?'

The young fast-tracker leant in to whisper in my ear. 'He's an under-secretary.'

'A what?'

'Wizard sheriff.'

And that was when I *knew* I had bitten off more than I could chew.

'Bollocks.'

I didn't know much about the sheriffs, as may have been apparent from the fact I didn't know their correct nomenclature, but anyone that gets *called* a sheriff by other people is no-one to piss around with. What I did know tended to revolve around them being arbitrary and pretty deadly, and just as many stories said they were empowered as not, although all were agreed that they were territorial. Too far up the chain for your average warlock to meet, however. They were for Whitehall cronies only, not for us.

Usually.

Bennett smiled. It was disgusting. 'Don't call me a *wizard sheriff* please. It makes me feel ill. What I *am* is above your pay grade; angry and capricious. Now, kindly show me some fucking respect!'

I'm not often cowed by authority, but messing with a sheriff was a sure-fire way to get myself killed, and I'm not suicidal. I am, however, thick as two short planks made out of pig-shit when I'm angry, and Bennett was not appealing to my better nature. I wanted to give it all up, throw away everything and draw on my power, show him that I truly *was* something to fear.

But you can get those sorts of feelings after a bad day, right?

I've never been good at showing respect, and to be quite frank I wasn't sure how. Do you bow? Kneel maybe? He was an office person, so perhaps he just wanted to be called *sir*? Respect is not a thing that makes sense to me, it's just fear by another name. Fear of losing your job, getting beaten up, or being inferior to someone and having them point it out. People who ask for respect are asking you to admit you are inferior to them.

I would do one of those weird head-bob bows, the ones that are basically a nod but with a slight tilt of the head. That was the best I could do, especially with him *watching* me like that. I was genuinely worried that he'd draw a gun the moment I took my eyes off him, that he'd shoot me dead in an instant. My headache was bad enough as it was, thank you very much.

And then Stan Bush joined the conversation.

'You've got the touch! You've got the powerrrrrrrrr!'

I'm not going to lie, it did a lot to defuse the situation. It's been a long time since I've seen five people, most of which at least dislike if not hate one another, all shift their faces into the same expression of amused bewilderment.

'And you never get hit when your back's to the wall...'

'What the hell is that?' said Eames.

'Gonna fight to the end and you're taking it all!'

'I think,' I said, groping at my pocket. 'That it's my phone.'

'Your phone?' said Bennett

'Well, the broker's. He gave it to me after he tried to atomise me. We're best buds now.

'When all hell's breaking loose you'll be riding the eye of the storrrrrm!'

Bennett's eyes lit up. 'Then answer the damn thing already!'

'Are you sure? I wouldn't want to interrupt this fine bit of bickering we've got going on.'

Everyone glared at me. There's not really much else you can say when an entire room of people are giving you the evil eye, other than to accept the bewilderment was over and so was the fun. I took out the phone.

'You've got the touch!'

I answered it and did my best impression of the broker's voice. 'Hello?'

'I'm coming to your house, you had best be in,' said the woman on the other end. It was the woman from the apartment building, the slight hint of an accent gave it away. Trying to remember it following the beating was difficult, but it made an impression. I wanted to say it was Eastern European, but I'm not particularly au fait with the continentals. It wasn't local, that was the best I could do.

'I'm out right now,' I said. 'But I can be back before you get there.'

'Good. I'm paying you for a timely service, Kenny. Have you had any trouble from the warlocks yet?'

'Not yet.'

'Good. Keep your eyes open. You don't want them to catch up with you, not in your state.'

His state? Had she seen him since my run in with the kid? 'Understood.'

'See you soon. Be ready,' she said and rung off.

I slipped the phone back into my pocket. 'Well, she was more pleasant that I expected her to be. You know, considering the fact she had me beaten to a pulp and all.'

'That was the arsonist?' said Eames.

'Pretty sure it was. The voice sounded the same at any

rate. She's heading to the broker's house to get a top-up.'

Bennett scratched at his goatee. 'Burning down an entire street must take a lot out of you. No wonder she needs another hit.'

'Excuse me?'

'Dog Street,' he said, looking away. 'The fire might have started in that apartment building, but it spread damn quick. By the time the authorities got there, half the street was up in flames. They couldn't stop it. Whoever she is, she's upping her game.'

'How many dead?'

'I didn't figure you for one who would care about that sort of thing, warlock.'

'How many dead?!' I roared back at him.

The room went quiet for a moment.

'Less than you'd expect,' Bennett finally said. 'A score, maybe more. Most of them saw it coming and got out in time.'

Something had changed. The arsonist had always been very precise before, hitting just the one building. There had been deaths, but few, as if she'd taken care to clear out as many as she could before she lit the fires, or waited for the time when the least number of people would be in. It had always been about the spectacle, not the death count.

So why the sudden escalation? I wasn't about to believe that this was anything but planned, not after the last few attacks. Perhaps it was a response to nearly being caught out, or her anger had overloaded the spell. Or a message, maybe? She could have been telling us that she could be more dangerous still, and that we should back off.

I was getting fed up with the amount of people telling me to back off.

Desperation or anger or whatever, it didn't matter. What mattered was that I had had the chance to stop her and screwed it up. As much as I wanted to blame it on Whitehall and their draconian oppression of my magic, the fact was I was ill-prepared to deal with her. I'd been more than a little blasé, and now a lot of people had paid for it.

Not that I was too bitter about it. It wasn't my fault they were dead – that still lay with the arsonist, despite my actions – but it did give me a little kick up the arse. I'd never get that nagging feeling out of the back of my mind now if I didn't bring her in. That willingness to destroy on such a scale, it sparked bad memories. Some well-needed motivation to do what had to be done and to be a little more serious.

It wouldn't last. This sort of thing never did. I'd be back to my usual self by the time I left the building, but it would serve to stop me from underestimating her next time. That much usually stays with you. You know, that and the memory of the work boots colliding with your skull.

'I need to go now if I'm going to beat her there,' I said. 'She's already on the way to his house, and I need to be there when she arrives if I'm going to stop her.'

'No,' Bennett said calmly.

'Excuse me?'

'You're not going. We'll send someone else to deal with her, you can't be trusted.'

'Like hell I can't! This is my job. I've been working on this for weeks. I *know* her.'

'You know shit,' he bellowed. 'All you've done for the last month and a half is turn up after the fact, watch the flames and drink cheap, nasty whiskey while the buildings burned. That you managed to get any lead at all is frankly amazing, and to do that you had to consort with a known terrorist. You're tainted.'

'If you honestly thought that, I'd be dead already.'

'You're a small fish, warlock, and there are concerns

bigger than you. I have to look at the big picture, and right now that's what's keeping you alive. Don't push it.'

I got right up in his face, close enough to smell his aftershave. I can't tell a cheap one from an expensive one by smell, but I can tell you he was wearing enough to make my eyes water. Thankfully it also made me squint a bit, which covered for that. 'You have no right.'

'I have every right!' He pushed me back and I stumbled into the arms of the fast-trackers. They held me firm, punching me once in the gut when I tried to shake them loose, winding me. 'Keep him here, Eames. I'll take some of the more trustworthy scum and bring this little ditty to an end.'

'Yes sir,' she said, turning her stern gaze on me again.

'But you don't even know where you're going,' I said.

'Not true,' Bennett shot back. 'We brought your little broker in for a chat. We've got him in a cell downstairs. Very forthcoming, that one. I'm sure we can find a place for him.'

'There are cells downstairs?'

Bennett let out a humourless grin. 'A couple. I'm sure you'll see them before too long.'

And with that he left, leaving me with a very unpleasant group of people for company and a set of bruised ribs to go with my probable concussion. What a good day I was having.

The distinctly uncharismatic fast-trackers dumped me back onto the desk so I could catch my breath. I'll give them their due, they didn't fall into the realms of brutality with their assault, this time. If I was important enough to earn a stay of execution from the arbitrary sheriff, they weren't about to risk messing that up just for a little game of beat the warlock.

I could have just left them to it, really. In fact, had it been someone else who had taken me off the job and gone to do the hard bit for me, I might have actually been relieved. But Bennett had come across as an industrial grade, gold-standard, die-cast arseface, and as such it was hard to just accept his word as law. I would even have been more amenable to Eames telling me to sit down and shut up than him.

Plus he was wrong. I *did* know her. I knew every wayward rogue to some degree, especially if they were the sort to throw magic around, but I knew the proper nasties best of all. It's no surprise that the best warlocks are the ones who fell the farthest during the Dark Times. We know how to think like a villain because we *are* villains. Bennett was a bastard, yes, but not a villain. He could never get into the head-space he'd need to truly *know* our arsonist.

He'd never know how sweet it is to wreak havoc without the bitterness of *a justification* upsetting one's palate. I did. It was something I could use to bring the arsonist down, I was sure of it, and if it humbled Bennett a little too, all the better.

As it was, I was filled with the overwhelming desire to beat him to the punch and wipe the smug little sneer off his face. I suppose making someone hate you is an easy way to motivate them into outperforming you, although I don't think that was his intention. In any case, I needed a way out. I've had my share of incarceration, and I wasn't willing to give the fast-trackers that much power over me. Not again.

Although there were now three people keeping me in the room, it was only the fast-trackers I cared about. Eames had the look of a scrappy fighter about her, but she was older than me and weighed considerably less. Without magic to back her up – which she didn't have – I could overpower her if I had to. But the fast-trackers were strong even without the aid of magic, and with it I wouldn't stand a chance. I was going to have to be creative if I wanted to slip past them.

My mind went back to my last visit to the field office. The way they had reacted to the other warlocks, who had done nothing but stand and stare at them, that was something I could do with about now. If what I had been told about the rise in vaultings was true, no wonder they were so skittish. It must be bad enough to work around a time bomb every day, but to be reminded of just how deadly that bomb could be must amplify that to no end.

Perhaps that was something I could use.

I turned to the younger fast-tracker. 'I bet right now you're wishing he'd vaulted me, aren't you?'

'Um,' he tripped over his words for a second. 'No?'

'Don't talk to him,' Eames said. 'He's just trying to bait you.'

I turned to her. 'Well how about you, Ma'am? I'm sure you were hoping he'd make the call. You made it clear earlier that you have no love lost for me.' She turned away and ignored me. 'Oh, very classy.'

'Shut up,' the kid said.

'I don't suppose they really tell you much about the vault on the fast-track scheme, do they? You're probably not subject to it, being as *trusted* as you are.'

'They tell us enough. It's a safeguard to keep you dangerous fanatics in line.'

'*Don't* talk to him,' Eames said again.

'They don't even tell you how it works, do they?' I said. 'It's really quite simple. When you agree to be a warlock, the alternative being execution I might add, and surrender your magic, they take one of your teeth and lock it away in a vault in Whitehall.'

'A tooth?' the kid said. He was intrigued now. As a rule the less savoury parts of Whitehall weren't taught to the fast-trackers until they reached the end of the programme, as I understood it, although they weren't directly withheld. Things like the vault were an open secret, but very easy to avoid if you wanted to, and most people did. It was enough to know that it worked, not *how* it worked.

'Well obviously, you need a part of someone if you want to work some thaumaturgy. Any part of the body will work – hair, fingernails, a few drops of blood – but I think Whitehall prefers teeth because they are so much easier to store. Fingernails and hair are too small and easy to misplace, and a vial of blood makes a hell of a mess if you spill it or drop it. Teeth are quite resilient and not particularly messy, so they are the preferred talisman.'

'I don't understand.'

I sighed. 'They really don't teach you how to use that power you're rocking around with, do they?' He frowned. 'Okay, thaumaturgy 101. Magic runs through every cell of a real magicians body, be it connected to the whole or not. As long as the source lives, the link is intact. A removed tooth or a stray hair is still magically linked to its owner, and as such there is a sort of conduit between the two.

'You can do a lot of things with this connection. Most of the time, the worst you'll do is track someone down with it, or maybe implant the compulsion to call home. A lot of empowered parents do this to their kids when they're out for too long, just to keep an eye on them. It probably wouldn't occur to them that it can be used in the manner Whitehall does. As a leash.

'They keep the teeth wired up to some magitech, as I understand it. That's how they know when a warlock tries to cast a spell. Not that I understand the technology myself, but I guess the link goes two ways. In any case, they spy a warlock casting spells, and they whip up a working of their own. Bounce the spell off one of the teeth in the vault, and it's essentially laser-guided to the owner. Boom. Dead. A magical kill switch.'

'That seems... extreme,' the kid said. I was getting to him. He was the weaker of the pair, the one most likely to crack. If I could just apply a little more pressure.

'Extreme is the only way to keep them in line,' Eames said. 'Don't try pretending you're an innocent in all this, Parker. I was there when they brought you in. I was there in the years before they even conceived of the vault. I've seen the damage an unchecked mage can do. You need regulation.'

'All of us? I've seen Whitehall bring in people who had barely any more power than a street magician, couldn't even do a card trick properly. And then you drag them in, rip out a tooth and send them back out onto the street to rat on their own friends.'

'We stop them from becoming people like you.'

'Bullshit.'

She was bordering on raving now, apparently I had touched a nerve. As I've said, I hadn't really taken it upon myself to really involve myself in the conflict during the Dark Times. I was self-interested and concerned largely with my own magical research. Whitehall, in turn, left me alone for the majority of the conflict. They had bigger problems, mages working in unison to actively overthrow the government. It wasn't until that was dealt with that they could commit their finest cadre of voluntary warlocks in earnest to try and take me down. Most of the atrocities – and despite popular opinion, of which I was responsible for only a small amount – didn't really register at the time.

'You may be neutered and muzzled, Parker, but you're still rabid. That's not an illness you recover from, it's seeped into your marrow.'

'Well aren't you poetic?'

'We don't even know how many people you killed. And then there was that girl.'

I hadn't handled this topic well when Kaitlyn had

brought it up earlier, and I didn't think I would do much better this time. I had to change track. 'It's true, I *was* a monster, but that puts me in a unique position, don't you think?' I turned back to the kid. 'Do you know what it's like to die via thaumaturgy?'

'I...no,' he said.

'It's not pleasant. Some people think it's like a heart attack, and it can certainly be made to look like that, but they're wrong. It's like having your entire body turn against you. Your blood boils in your veins, your heart slams against your ribcage, your eyes bleed. You feel like you're being turned inside out, like you're going to vomit up your insides all at once. And then, when the pain is at its peak, your heart just explodes. Pop. Now tell me: is that *regulation?*'

I had exaggerated a little for effect. For the most part, when Whitehall vaulted someone they simply shut the heart down. No explosion, just switched it off. They preferred not to make a spectacle if they could help it. It was quick, efficient, and while not instant it was debilitating enough that the target wouldn't have time to snap off a last second spell.

On the other hand, you can do an awful lot with thaumaturgy. Given the inclination and the imagination, you can do just about anything. The bloodier stuff is easier to do, as is usually the case, and tends to be much quicker to work. Mind magic is possible, but you can only really plant suggestions, never full on commands. If you want to rip out someone's heart or make their head explode, though, you can do that with a snap of a finger.

Whitehall didn't do that, but they had the capability to do so, and that was all that mattered. For most people, the abstract possibility is too distant to truly spook them. You want to get them on side, or off balance in this case, you go straight for the jugular. You pick out the worst, most heinously vile outcome that you can and you drive it home. Slam it right into their imagination so they have no choice but to see where this was going.

For the kid, what he saw now was hearts exploding everywhere. Crimson geysers going off at a moments notice. It was hard not to smile, watching him try to process that.

'It's a deterrent,' Eames said, trying to win the kid back on side. 'It has to scare people enough that they understand. We don't vault people often, just when necessary. It's not nearly as sinister as you made it sound.'

I was winning, I could see it in his face. I only needed one of the fast-trackers on my side, long enough to occupy the other. 'No, that's true. You just dangle the damn sword over our heads and send us out to take on other magic users. Unarmed. You don't *need* to vault people very often, the mortality rate is high enough as is.'

'Unarmed? Now who's spouting bullshit, Parker? We send every warlock out with some of the finest multi-purpose enchantments,' she said, stepping closer. 'Those rings, that blazer, that's your equipment. If you can't adjust to make do, it's your own fault.'

Wait, change of plan. I could work with this. Just a little closer. 'These rings? Have you ever tried to use these against a proper spell-slinger? Have you ever even *seen* what use they are?'

'They are tools,' she said, stepping closer. 'You make your strategies around them, not the other way around. You know your limitations and you act accordingly. This is the problem with you damn warlocks, you think the world revolves around you!'

'Doesn't it?'

'No, god dammit!' she said, her face turning red. Winding people up is so *easy.* 'And no, smart arse, I've never actually seen what the rings can do, but having seen what a wizard on a rampage is liable to pull out, I have no issues with them being limited in scope.'

And of course once you've properly wound someone up, they won't realise their defences are down until you strike. 'Oh, well allow me to demonstrate for you.'

I whipped my arms out to the sides and released all the magic stored in the enchantments upon the rings. The force roared out like a pair of cannons, striking both fast-trackers in their chests and sending them flying. The younger one took the full force of the attack and slammed into the far wall, but his partner managed to quickly cast some form of shield. It dulled the blow but didn't stop it completely.

In the confusion I pounced, seizing Eames by the neck and hiding behind her, a frail human shield to protect me from the incoming wrath. The fast-trackers got up – although the kid took a little longer than his partner, and was considerably less confident about the whole situation, it appeared – and took note of the scenario. Then they both powered up shields with one hand and readied a spell in the other.

I am a tactical genius.

CHAPTER 13

This was not part of the original plan, but you make do with what you can. Apparently what I do is take a tense situation and stuff it into a pressure cooker and crank it up until one errant twitch could cause a nuclear meltdown. I also mix my metaphors.

She'd made it too enticing, too tempting, and considering how much I disliked her she should have seen this coming. To their credit, the fast-trackers recovered pretty sharpish, on their feet with spells at the ready within seconds of me grabbing Eames, but there wasn't much they could do. She should never have gotten so close to me.

The thing is, there's not much you can do with a hostage. Taking a hostage is playing for a stalemate, and that rarely gets you anywhere. It buys you time to think, sure, but if you haven't got an exit strategy cooked up, a hostage is going to do little to change that. The best thing it does is stops you getting gunned down a few minutes earlier than you do. But if you end up playing for a stalemate, when the game is over you're going to end up with the other player looking to really kick your teeth in anyway. I learned this at chess club.

Then again, I knew something they didn't. We were playing different games, them and I. As far as they were concerned, this was me going off the deep-end, showing them that I was everything they thought I was. Out comes the monster, bright eyed and bushy tailed, claws and all.

Of course, if they had thought about it for a moment, they would have realised that this wouldn't have made much sense. I'd been loyal – for a given value of loyalty at least – for too long to throw it all away for a quick one-liner and an admittedly cool gesture of independence. If they had enough about them they would have seen this for what it was: a lesson.

It was a little heavy-handed, I admit. I doubt this sort of teaching technique would be something you'd get in most classrooms, but then they were used to the cushy life down south. I figured a short sharp shock would be the best way to make it clear to them that if I had wanted to bust out, I could do so.

Having Eames as a hostage meant I had some freedom of movement, at least while their nerve held. They wouldn't risk opening fire on me for threat of hitting her, and until Bennett and his boys were done trying to bring in the arsonist they didn't have the manpower to out-think me. That kept the dynamic simple – I keep her between myself and the fast-trackers and they would let me go wherever I wanted. This is how a villain thinks, and he can do it all on the fly without a plan.

They needed to see this, if I was going to persuade them to just let me walk out of here.

I moved.

Two hands shot out at me, power crackling between the fingertips. 'Halt!' the fast-trackers shouted in unison.

Slow and steady. I stopped moving. Time to explain

things and defuse the situation. 'Ok, boys, so here's how it is –'

'Ignore him,' Eames rasped. 'Put him down! Don't worry about –' I tightened my grip on her throat a little, just enough to shut her up. Couldn't have her ruining this.

'Now now, we don't want you getting them all excited. There's no need for any violence here,' I said. 'I'm just trying to make a point.'

The younger fast-tracker started to lower his casting arm, but the older shot him a look and he brought it back up. Then the elder's eyes fell on me. 'Let her go, warlock.'

'I have a name, you know.'

'Let. Her. Go.'

Things weren't exactly going as well as I had planned. This is probably why I was rejected for that teacher-training course. I felt it best to hedge my bets, just in case. I took another step. The door was on the far side of the room – despite its size the office was furnished with only one door, which seemed unsafe to me, but then at least it made this easier – although it wouldn't take long to reach so long as they didn't keep stopping me. Or started shooting.

They didn't stop me. I kept moving.

'Look, the whole point of this was to show you something,' I said.

'That you're truly the monster I said you were?' Eames replied.

I winced. 'There's sort of an *element* of that,' I said hesitantly. 'But what I was going for was that I know how to think like a villain. Bennett and his boys don't. This was supposed to be sort of a proof of concept.'

The younger fast-tracker's hand dropped again. 'I can't tell if you've done a really good job or cocked it up royally...'

Eames shifted in my grasp. 'We've got her. Bennett has got her. He doesn't need your help, if that assertion of yours is even sincere. Sounds more like a coward trying to talk his way out of trouble, to me.'

'Will you just listen to me, for a minute, *please!'* I shot back and pulled her closer to the door. The fast-trackers were following but keeping their distance. 'There is a high likelihood that I have indeed cocked up what I was trying to do, yes –'

'You're not talking your way out of this, warlock,' Eames said. 'Any way you try to spin it, as I see it you just forgot yourself for a moment. You let your true colours slip through. I'm going to see you burn for this.'

So yeah, it had sort of turned into what we in the trade like to call a *monarchistic penis elevation.* It's like a right royal cock up but more so. I think. I made it up, but I thought it sounded like it had a bit more gravitas.

Before we get right down to how much I had shot myself in the foot, I want to make it clear that, at the time, I thought I was doing the right thing. It made perfect sense to me that, once I showed them that I understood the criminal mind, they would just stand aside and let me go. No harm, no foul. It honestly never occurred to me that they might take it somewhat personally.

I'm holding my hands up here. Not my best idea, but I could have saved it. There was definitely a way to salvage the whole mess.

I couldn't see how, and I still don't, but it was totally there somewhere.

Was it really just pure, undiluted pride that was making me do this? Quite possibly. Pride comes before a fall, after all, and I was setting myself up for one hell of a fall if this was any indication. I wasn't about to blame it on arrogance or stupidity, that was for damn sure. Well, I might blame it on *Eames'* arrogance and stupidity. All she had to do was shut up and listen to me, and I would have walked out of there free and easy, probably even in time to help Bennett actually capture the bloody woman he was after.

But, while I still contend there was most definitely a way I could have saved face and avoided the oncoming shit storm into which I had blithely blundered, I couldn't see it. It was going to have to be plan B.

At that time, plan B consisted largely of running away. That should always be plan B. My predicament did afford me time to properly flesh this out, though, into something a little more considered.

As my whole idea of walking out with my ego stroked had started to crumble, it would be safe to say that Eames wasn't about to tell me where exactly Bennett had gone either. My original intention, before Bennett had kicked me to the curb, had been to have a quick nose through my map for anything that had a large enough concentration of his magic to be the broker's house.

I didn't have the time for that now. The argument with Bennett had delayed me, as had this little contretemps with Eames and her lackeys. My best bet now was to go straight to the horse's mouth. I had to have a word with Kenny the broker.

Out the door, down the stairs, and down to the basement – that would be where the cells were. They couldn't be anywhere else in the building or else I would have seen them, and besides, you have to keep your dungeons underground. It's the rules. Shouldn't be too difficult to reach, only a couple of flights of stairs while dragging a struggling old woman by the throat and trying to keep enough of myself hidden behind her to keep the suits from opening up on me.

Worst still, I was completely without magic now, having dumped all my enchantments in my blitz to seize Eames. I'd been banking on a resupply once my genius had been accepted, but c'est la vie. No point in dwelling on the matter. An actual practitioner of the art would have known about my predicament of course, making my hostage completely useless, but seeing as the fast-trackers didn't need to learn the theory they were oblivious. That wouldn't last. The longer I went without displaying how dangerous I could be, the more bold they would become.

We reached the door and I risked bringing my hand away from her head to clumsily whip it open. If only the damn thing had had a lock on it.

'Where can you possibly go, warlock?' the elder fast-tracker said. The power arcing off his fingers was growing in intensity. He would be the one to break the ceasefire, if I let him.

'I'll think of something,' I said, nipping through the door. I backed up to the top of the stairs by the time they sprinted their way through the doors to follow me. 'Please just go away. I'm not going to hurt her.'

'Just. Kill. Him.' Eames was hardly helping matters now. I squeezed a little tighter. I had no intention of killing her, but likewise things were now skewiff enough without her fanning the flames.

The elder fast-tracker took point. 'If you take one more step, warlock...'

'You'll what?' I said, all full of false bravado. 'You'll shoot me? You'd hit her; we both know it. Stop pretending you've got a plan.'

I may have directed that last bit at myself. I'm not sure.

I find the best way to defuse a confrontation is the liberal application of hypocrisy, don't you? Considering the full depth of my plan at this moment in time was "go downstairs", I was doing well on the whole hypocrisy front.

And then I took a step.

I didn't see him cast the spell, nor did I really feel it when it struck the wall by my head. What I *did* feel was the chips of brick kicked up from the impact as they scratched across my face. I recoiled and my foot slipped, which is all that saved both of us from the second spell. I looked up in time to see him flick his wrist to reel off the third, and most likely lethal, spell.

It was indigo. I'd not seen much indigo magic, most people seemed to go for blues and pinks and reds. Even greens. There's no reason a spell couldn't be indigo though – unless you're casting a fireball or something, I suppose – but I guess most people just never think that way. At least I'd die an uncommon death.

I didn't even try to move. I thought I was being manly, facing death with dignity and whatnot – let's ignore the fact that I knew there was nowhere I could go anyway – and this was why I survived. As the spell left his fingers, that was when the kid chose to tackle him.

I've been calling him a kid as though that meant he was weedy and short, which is perhaps misleading. He looked young, but he was strong, although not as strong as his older partner, but with the element of surprise he didn't need to be. The elder wasn't ready for someone to rugby tackle him from behind, and he went down in one of those ultra-embarrassing sprawls people do when they are caught unawares. None of the graceful, Hollywood movie tumbles you see on screen, but something that you just *know* hurt.

The cry of pain as he hit the ground may have been a tip off, mind.

I scrambled to my feet, dragging Eames up with me and stumbled down the stairs as best I could. When I glanced back, I saw the kid standing over his partner.

'You could have killed her!' he was screaming into his face. He wasn't sure what he had done, the confusion and shock was making his voice crack, which made him look even younger. 'What the hell were you thinking?'

There was a flash of indigo and a bestial roar and the kid was launched into the air, slamming the back of his head off the ceiling. He fell back to earth limp and unconscious. 'I'm doing my job,' the elder bellowed as he hauled himself up.

I took that as a sign to bloody well move.

A couple more indigo bolts flew at me, but I was on a roll now, I had momentum on my side. They struck the walls behind me impotently as I barrelled down to the basement, old woman still in hand. Today really had been more eventful than I would have liked, all things considered.

We fell down the last few steps. I tweaked my ankle as we rounded the corner onto the last flight of stairs and my leg gave way. We slid rather than rolled, which was a godsend, but it still brought some more unwanted pain. We slammed into the door of the cell block, knocking it open, and landed on the concrete floor behind it. I dragged Eames out of the way and kicked the thing shut.

Eames was out cold, or dead. I was pretty sure she was just unconscious, but I wasn't really in a position to check. Things needed to be done fast; I had only seconds before the fast-tracker caught up with me. I needed to bar the door.

The door was iron, a couple of inches thick, and complete with a deadbolt. Unfortunately the frame was wooden, and the deadbolt slotted into a fixture on this frame, so it wouldn't hold long. Still, it was better that nothing, and I slammed the deadbolt across and ran down the lines of cells in search of the broker.

The cells clearly didn't get much use. The entire floor was dimly lit, the yellow strip-light blinking off for a millisecond at random intervals, and most of the cells hadn't been cleaned in a while if the smell was any indication. The broker was in the very last one. They had a decent read of him; stick him at the end of the hallway and every footstep would sink in, get him properly worked up by the time the questions were asked. I could only hope that would work in my favour.

He was curled up in the far corner, looking pretty pathetic, but then he'd had one hell of a shit day. No-one seemed to be enjoying today, as far as I could tell. I drummed on the bars and he raised a tired face. 'Oh not you again,' he whined.

'Me again,' I said with a manic smile. I was going for soothing, but all things considered I think I did well nonetheless. 'Listen, I don't have time to chat, I just need you to tell me where you live.'

'What?'

'Your address. Sooner rather than later, if you don't mind.'

'Piss off. Let me sleep.'

The fast-tracker was throwing himself into the door. The tell tale sounds of shoulder on steel and wood cracking were making their way down the corridor. 'Please? Just tell me your address and I'll leave you alone.'

His head dropped back down. 'Get me out and I'll tell you.'

'I don't have time!'

'Bye then.'

It never ceases to amaze me how much of a pain in the arse even the most meek of people can become when tired. 'You've already told them, why can't you show me the same courtesy?'

'Quid pro quo.'

'Oh please, don't throw Latin at me. It makes my brain itch. What could they possibly have done for you?'

He ran both hands through his hair slowly and sighed. 'As the bossy guy in the suit put it, the favour they did me was not killing me on the spot,' he said grimly. 'They want to rehabilitate me.'

'They want to drain you to fuel their toy soldiers,' I said.

'I know. They told me that too,' he said. He got up slowly and walked to the bars. They hadn't tortured him, not that I had expected them to – Whitehall were scum, but they didn't truck with your traditional forms of torture – but he was doing a damn good job of making it look like they had. Most likely it was fallout from the magic he had pumped out at me earlier, but whatever they'd done to bring him in couldn't have helped. 'I'll make you a deal. You get me out of here, and I'll take you to my place, seeing as you want to go there so badly.'

'Are you serious?'

'I don't think you have much time to question me about this, not if that noise is anything to go by.'

The fast-tracker was really putting his all into the door now. Why he hadn't just blasted the thing off its hinges, I wasn't sure. Perhaps he'd regained some of his composure, remembered that he was trying to rescue Eames from my evil clutches and not just murder everything in sight. Or perhaps he was just saving up one massive hell-fire death blast to launch my way when he had a clear shot and was saving every last bit of energy for that. I'd find out soon enough.

'Fine, you've got a deal,' I said. 'But I don't know how I'm going to get you out of here.'

His lips curled into an exhausted smile. 'Could do with a bit of magic.'

'Do it yourself.'

'Can't. Far too tired. It's all I can do to stand up.'

'Well I suppose that explains why you haven't blasted your cell door off.'

'Partly. They said the bars are enchanted, that they reflect any spell cast on them back into the cell. Didn't want to end up cooking myself by accident. But maybe you could –'

'No,' I snapped. 'Warlocks can't do magic. It's forbidden.'

'They can't use their own magic,' he said as he pushed his hand through the bars towards me. 'But there are other ways.'

He had a point. The arsonist was using borrowed magic to make herself harder to track down, so perhaps the same principle would work on me. It was a risk, but there was every chance whatever weird magitech they used in Whitehall to track magic use wouldn't be triggered by borrowed magic. Necessity is the mother of invention, however, and it wasn't like I had much choice but to try this. The door would buckle any second, and then one very pissed off suit would start hurling death made manifest my way, and the only way I was going to prove to these people that my indiscretion hadn't been me going all dark side would be to get out of here alive and help bring in the arsonist.

I took his hand.

'Are you sure you've got enough juice to give me?' I said.

'No,' he replied. 'But what's the worst that could happen?'

I could have my heart explode in my chest via remote control, I thought to myself. He didn't need to know that though, and it would at least give me one last measure of joy – if that's the right word – to see the shock on his face when my heart exploded. Gotcha!

I wasn't ready for the sensation. I had expected it to be similar to the event at the bar, electricity roaring through me, everything burning white hot and deadly, confidence surging, but it was almost the exact opposite. A chill rolled up my arm slowly, melting around me, almost painting over me in a way. I could feel it searching for my own magic, dowsing through me for whatever magical conduits I had, wrapping around them rather than pumping through them.

I waited for the overconfidence to come, the thirst for power that had tagged along when I last tasted my own power, but it never came. I was in control.

'Is it always like this?' I said. I had pins and needles in my fingers, but the rest of me had warmed up now, as though it had absorbed the magic. It was a strange sensation, I'm not sure I can even properly describe it. 'This feels *weird*.'

'I don't know,' he said, pulling his hand away. 'People don't tend to try and describe the experience to me, you know. Did it work?'

'I think so.'

'Then get me out!'

Easier said than done. There are certain skills you don't forget – riding a bike being the most well publicised one – but magic is more than just a skill, it's a part of you. Using his power was weird and clumsy, like trying to write with the wrong hand. I knew the motions, the words, even the correct way to hold my will together, but there was a block there that made it awkward. Getting the cell open with finesse would be difficult, and I didn't want to risk blunt force in case the enchantment on the bars wasn't particularly picky about where it redistributed the energy.

I could blow the lock out. That was my best chance. Slam a bit of power into the pins and, more likely than not, the thing would vibrate itself apart. Assuming that happened, it would be simple to just kick the door open at that point, the lock itself being held together by belief more than anything else. Of course if I got it wrong it would just weld the door closed forever, but it was still my best option.

Start out small, that was what I needed to do. That

was my mistake at the bar, trying to take on too much too quickly. I willed the tiniest speck of power into the lock, a green-blue spark leaping from my hand. The lock rattled gently and I waited for my heart to explode.

It didn't.

Unfortunately, neither did the lock. I ramped up the power, slowly but surely. The lock rattled more and more as I did so, the pins clicking noisily inside the metal shell. Then there was a crunch and the rattling stopped. Then, further up the hall, a cracking sound as the fast-tracker broke through.

He shouted at me, but my heart was pounding too much for me to understand what I heard. I felt my body move, an instinctive response, and turned in time to see him leap over the unconscious form of Eames like a well-dressed panther. No time for thought, it was all down to the hind-brain to save me. Instant response.

I brought up a hand as he landed, muttered a word and blanketed the corridor before me with energy. It stretched out wall to wall, a perfect barrier, just as he whipped off another indigo bolt. It thrummed into my shield and crackled across the surface, and I felt the feedback jolt up my arm.

This was *delicious*. It had been so long since I had been able to feel this, the world had been so drab and I hadn't even realised. So much power coursing through me, all of it at my command once again. But it was fleeting, temporary, and I could already feel it start to ebb away. As he threw more bolts at the shield, I could feel the magic start to drain from my body. The refreshing chill of this foreign power was lessening, each bolt bringing with it a new wave of fatigue. And yet, somehow, even this was thrilling.

He let off one last salvo and then stopped, panting about halfway down the corridor. I let the barrier drop, I didn't have much left with which to maintain it anyway.

It cracked and shattered into a colourful mist, gently dissipating in the moment of calm.

'They will kill you for this,' he said eventually.

I shrugged. 'Honestly, I'm surprised they haven't already. I think I might be going off the deep end, buddy.'

He cracked his knuckles. He was really trying to hide how drained he was behind his bravado, but it wasn't working. I wondered how long it had been since he last recharged his borrowed power. 'All your kind do, eventually. I knew we were right about you and van Ives. The woman's a cancer.'

'Oh, please, enough of the rhetoric,' I said. 'I'm so bloody *tired* of it. I'm giving you a chance to just listen to what I was trying to say before. Please?'

'They *will* kill you, no matter how this ends.'

'Hey, as far as the fellows down in Whitehall know, I'm still the model inmate.'

'And how long will that last once people get back here and see what you've done?'

I winced. He had a point, annoyingly. It didn't look good, and it would probably read worse. 'I'll just have to do what I can before they get back then. Prove I'm not consorting with the enemy, and that this whole thing was just a misunderstanding.'

On reflection, if I had just played nice, sat in the office and been the dutiful little warlock until Bennett got back from his sting, I would have probably been okay. There would have been hearings, sure, but they didn't have any evidence that I was working with Kaitlyn van Ives. I'd run into her a couple of times, admittedly that might look suspicious to an outside observer, but I hadn't actually *done* anything.

But that didn't sit right. It was relying on the good will of people who had professed to hate me from the moment I met them, people who were genuinely terrified of some phantom threat I *might* become. I couldn't help but think they would use this as a way of rubbing me out, if I let them. And besides, I *knew* her. I'd done the legwork and I wanted to look the arsonist in the eye when she was taken down, see her dreams collapse around her ears. To see what villains get for their troubles.

To keep myself grounded. Besides, I still needed to balance the scales any way I could to make up for who I had once been. That sort of guilt makes you do stupid things.

That said, I think I also enjoy making my life difficult, sometimes.

I ran a hand over my face and rubbed my eyes. The magic was nearly gone, it was practically dripping off me now and I wasn't sure why. Being expelled like a foreign body, perhaps? It would explain why the arsonist needed to top-up so often maybe. More likely I was just rusty, that I'd forgotten how to hold onto magic. The fast-tracker must have been able to sense that.

There was a moment of understanding. You get these in most fights, the second or so when you look on your opponent and you can almost tell what he's thinking, and he you, and what he's thinking is exactly how hard he's going to hit you. Everything stops, as though for that brief moment the entire universe is watching you. Then with an almighty crash, everything happens at once.

'You won't get the chance –'

He had opted for a taunt, one last *fuck you* before he killed me. As though it would have made a difference to me whether he had said it or not, either way I would have been dead. But it *did* make a difference in the end, that simple sentence was enough to let me strike first.

The human mind loves projectiles. We understand the idea of lobbing one thing at another thing to smash the latter into tiny bits, or make lots of little holes in it.

Most spell-slingers work the same way, they work their combat spells into bolts because that's what they know. But, at the end of the day, it's the magical equivalent of a punch; deadly enough, but the bottom of the martial chain as it were.

I knew better.

I spat a word under my breath and reached out with both hands. The last bit of power I had shot forth as a colourless sheet of pure force, wrapping itself around the fast-tracker before he had time to move and cutting his sentence short. His eyes went wide as his body went taut, trying to scream out one final curse at me.

I clapped my hands together and he died. He did not die well.

The sheet of force I had thrown at him contracted suddenly and without resistance, as though he wasn't even there. I heard the bones snap all at once, like a lorry-load of celery smashing into a cliff, and the ghost of a scream finding its way out of his mouth before he became a sack of watery meat. One last gesture threw him aside with a wet smack, and that was that.

Where the *fuck* had that come from?

Magic is all about the will. There are incantations and hand gestures and all that, but they are there purely to help shape the will. The incantations and the words are supposed to put you in the correct mindset to let you shape the working in your head, which is why it can take a long time to truly learn how to properly handle your power.

And yet, even knowing this, I had no idea where that spell had come from.

No, better not to dwell on it. If I started thinking about why I chose to turn the man into paste rather than anything else – the very same paste Robin had become all those years ago – I might not like the answer. Introspection was not for me, just accept it as a heat of the moment thing and move on, that was what I had to do. That was the *sane* thing to do.

I barely registered the sound of the cell door being kicked open. To be fair it was a clumsy attempt, taking a couple of kicks and one final run up to break the shattered lock, a far cry from the sort of sudden crash that would have put me on edge. Not that anything could have put me on edge at that particular moment; I'd just crushed a man to death, I was golden.

'You look like hell,' the broker said, placing a hand on my shoulder. The gentle thrum of his magic snapped me back to reality.

'I *am* hell,' I said. I was going for a sort of insincere, jokey boast, but I missed and hit menacing instead. I tried to recover. 'You never told me your name.'

'Um... I don't really give out my name...'

'I was trying to be polite. I already know your name, Kenny.'

He looked uncomfortable. Hard to believe a broker could get by on word of mouth if his own name made him so uncomfortable. 'Call me K.'

'K? One letter, are you serious?'

'If you wouldn't mind...'

'You know what? I don't even care. Whatever. Let's just go and crash the party at your house, okay?' I had a headache forming. I could feel it clouding up in my skull.

He nodded and we made our way outside. I took the time on the way out to throw Eames in one of her own cells and lock her in, after taking the liberty of relieving her of her phone. I doubted she'd wake up in time to warn them – assuming she *was* alive – but I could do without word of my *escape* spreading before I had some way to undo the damage. Plus she had a car, and I was through running everywhere.

I found said car through the time honoured tradition

of waving the fob around and hammering on the unlock button until something beeped. The pair of us got in and I turned to my new-found navigator.

'Right then,' I said. 'Let's go blunder into a sting, shall we?'

CHAPTER 14

K, as I was still learning to call him, had told me a little about his house on the drive. He'd said it wasn't so much a house as a squat, a single room in what had used to be a club long ago, usually shared with up to five other guys, usually junkies. They left him alone for the most part, sensing that there was something about him that made him too dangerous to fuck with or rob, and he left them to themselves because you don't want to corner a junkie if you can avoid it.

The junkies had given him an even wider berth as of late. Apparently they hadn't wanted to run into the arsonist. K wasn't sure what their problem was with her, as far as he was concerned she was hot and pleasant enough to talk to, and not particularly scary at all. A bit brusque at times, but not menacing. Shows what he knew.

All this cooked up a picture in my head, one oddly similar to a student flat but slightly less bleak. Perhaps a few more needles and a few less textbooks, but on the whole pretty similar. The same number of bongs. I wasn't quite prepared to find it looking like a battlefield.

I was half an hour behind them, no more, and yet whatever they had done when the arsonist had turned up had happened quickly. The entire front of the building was just gone. A couple of bricks, slowly working their way loose from the few bits of ageing mortar that were holding them steady, were the only indication that the building hadn't always been open facing. Bennett and his team were gone, and there were definite signs of a struggle.

I know, *no shit*, right?

'Wait in the car,' I said to K. 'Something happened here.'

'You think?'

'Something that wasn't supposed to, I mean. This isn't your typical black bagging operation. Something went wrong.'

'Fine,' he said. 'Just don't be too long.'

I nodded and got out of the car. Something crunched under my foot, glass from a broken brake light, but for the most part it seemed like little was actually damaged. You know, apart from the wall. There was no blood, no twisted wreckage or splintered timber or general debris of any kind. That didn't leave a whole lot of options.

The street was eerily quiet, but then it was out of the way. People didn't tend to come out this far unless they had a reason, just another casualty of the rise and fall of the local economy. The cash-rich student population were too lazy to travel this far out nowadays, as the club was too far to stumble back from in a drunken stupor. It was no wonder the club had gone bust and been filled with the social detritus. Even if someone had called in a commotion, the police would be in no rush to get down here. It was firmly planted in that economic dead zone between the inner and outer city. The council's biggest regret.

I had to hand it to the down-and-outs though, they'd

made a decent home for themselves inside the building. It was dark inside – I suspect whatever force removed the wall also blew out all the lights, if they had ever worked to begin with – but quite well furnished for a squat. Not your finest quality Swedish flat-pack goods, but serviceable. There was a pair of sofas, one cracked crimson leather and the other a patchwork of varying fabrics; stained wooden drawers; a plastic garden table covered in soggy pizza boxes; and a load of other things strewn about that I couldn't really place; things with drawers and doors and knobbly bits that didn't seem to fit any specific role. The place actually looked quite decent.

No beds, of course. Rancid sleeping bags were laid out in the spaces between the furniture, although only the one on the leather sofa seemed to have been used at all recently. I had joked before about comparing the place to a student flat but, in all honesty, I'd seen worse student flats than this. Apart from the whole, you know, having a front wall.

There were clear signs of conflict in here, however, much more recognisable than the eerie cleanliness of the street outside. What looked like bullet holes littered the walls, and blade marks were clearly visible on some of the furniture once I got close enough. I needed more light, so I went back to the car in the hope that Eames was one of those anal people who is fully prepared for any sort of vehicular eventuality. She was, and I found a sturdy torch tucked away in the boot behind the spare tyre and the first aid kit.

With light, the place looked much less pleasant. Things tend to look better in the dark, but it also helps when you can't see the blood. I hadn't even noticed it before, probably even written it off as just part of the unusually torrid aesthetic you tend to get in dives like this, but there was no hiding from it now. The bullet holes were framed by the stuff, the blade marks on the furniture too, enough to let me know that the carnage had not been as bloodless as I had thought.

I stepped out into the hall, all cracked floorboards and dust, and followed the blood. The fight hadn't been over quickly, a lot of blood had been spilled as it moved through the rest of the building. As I went deeper I found less bullet holes and more blade marks, and then scorch marks and pure force damage started to show themselves. They hadn't started throwing spells around until they were well out of sight of the road, or backed into a corner. It was hard to tell who had been throwing their weight around back here, but I would have put money on it being more than one person.

The blades would have been Bennett's cadre of warlocks, that much I could place. I doubt he'd have taken many with him given his prejudice, but he would have had to take some even if just to serve as a meat shield. They would have had guns too, but give us a blade and we'd find a way to use it. We're jury-rigged to run on the rule of cool; it helps us make up for the gnawing temptation to break out the magic again. One of many coping mechanisms.

The signs of magic were harder to place. Most of it seemed wild and unfocused, the calling card of a fast-tracker, but then that could have been true of someone rocking borrowed power too. My own experience a few moments ago had told me that it felt different, and that even an experienced practitioner would have had trouble wielding it with any finesse, so I couldn't rule out the arsonist or her boyfriend throwing the odd spell around either.

I kept moving deeper. The building was bigger than it looked, deeper than it was wide. Eventually the corridor opened out into what had been the main room of the club, where the dance floor and the bar had been, and technically still were. Apparently I had taken the scenic route.

The brunt of the fighting had happened here. I want to describe the place as looking as though a bomb went off in it, but it would be more apt to say a lot of little bombs had airburst over it. The ceiling was peppered with holes, the debris from the damage spread across the dance floor. Huge chunks of cement, the odd steel girder poking out, were embedded in the floor, and from the look of it, had caused considerable casualties. There were *bits* of bodies near them, and I dreaded to think exactly how many.

Bennett had pushed her back here, out of the confined spaces and into this perfect playpen. She would have been too careful to risk any powerful spells in the corridors, but as soon as she was in here she would have seen the potential. I still looked at rooms this way. Small spaces were not to be fought in, too limiting, but a big room like this would let you make *it* the weapon. You didn't need accuracy when you could drop the ceiling on your foes. Frankly, that she'd done it without bringing the entire building down was an achievement in and of itself. The fast-trackers wouldn't have stood a chance.

I tiptoed across the room, doing my best not to step in a puddle of squished person or trip over a bit of ceiling. I doubted there would be any survivors, and if there had been they probably wouldn't still be here, but I had to know who won. I had to know whether there was still a chance I could save my own skin and be the hero.

There were a lot of dead, more than I had expected. Bennett had cleared out the office, but most of those had been clerical staff, not suitable for fieldwork. The warlocks he took would have been trusted – or as trusted as he could get – so small in number. It didn't add up, not unless he had brought a lot of people with him from Whitehall, and there can't have been that many available by his own admission.

The far wall had been where the arsonist had made her last stand. A semi-circle of bodies lay in front of a pile of rubble where part of the wall had fallen in on itself. They had not died well, faces frozen in agony for the most part, corpses gently steaming. One or two had fist-sized holes in their chests, through and through. They'd done well to get this far, and not a single one of them had been a warlock. Not that we carry cards or anything, but we tend not to wear ties.

There was a noise behind me, the grinding of stone sliding over stone, and I spun around to see what it was. K stood a little way behind me, kicking a piece of debris out of his way. His hands shot up defensively when I shone my torch on him.

'It's me! Hey!' he said. 'Don't shoot!'

I turned away and went back to examining the last stand. 'I don't have a gun, genius.'

'But in the car you said...'

'I do *have* a gun,' I snapped. 'But I don't have it with me.' It had been a mistake to talk to him in the car on the way over. I had thought it might calm him down a little, but all it had done was made him worse. He was doing a decent job of hiding it, but there was a twitchiness in him that was irritating me. 'I told you to wait in the car.'

'I got bored,' he said as he kicked another stone. 'And scared. I didn't like just sitting in the middle of a ghost town while you wandered off. What if you didn't come back?'

'A ghost town? This is where you *live.*'

'I know, but normally I can hide behind my walls. Most of my walls are gone now.'

I tried to feel sorry for him, honest, but I was busy being intrigued. There was something about the collapsed section of wall that was drawing my eye. 'You can get another squat, K. I can't imagine it's too difficult to find an empty shit-hole in the rotten core of Humberside.'

'But all my stuff was here...'

'I didn't see much worth keeping,' I said, poking at the wall. Something was off about this, but what the hell was it?

'I did say *was.*'

And then an arm shot out of the wall.

CHAPTER 15

I'll let you guess how the pair of us reacted to that. Go on. Yes, we screamed like little girls and fell over as we recoiled in horror. Now, to be fair, you don't expect a full arm to climb out of the wreckage of a wall, and it doing so in the dark just makes the whole thing worse. When it was joined by a shoulder, and then a head, things just went from worse to terrifying.

I had dropped my torch as I fell, so I was looking at the form with my imagination in full-on fear mode, trying to fill in the gaps for my eyes. It was thin, humanoid, with dank, snake-like hair on its head. It moved slowly, as though it was acclimatising to our world, dragging its way through the ether as well as the wall.

Something had to be done. Whatever foul beast of the arcane this was – no doubt dragged into our world by the confluence of magical energy in the recent battle – it would be nothing good. There are dimensions beyond ours, and nothing good has ever come from interacting with them. The things from beyond the veil don't regard us with much respect. If we allowed this monstrosity to adjust to our world, who knows what horrors it could bring.

It had a leg free now, slender and terrifying. I had no option, I had to stop it before it was loosed upon our world but I had no weapons, nothing to fight with. There was no time to try and drag the last few drops of K's power. I had to improvise, and I had to do it quickly.

So I threw a stone at it.

There wasn't much else I could do, okay? There were a lot of loose stones; it made sense to use them.

It sailed through the air, steady and true, and caught the beast in the side of the head with a joyous thunk.

'Ow! What the *fuck*?' said the beast in a familiar voice. It couldn't be. 'A fucking rock? Why would you throw a rock at me?'

It was. Bugger.

'Kaitlyn?' I said. 'Is that you?' And then my imagination shut off and my night vision kicked in. I really wish it had done that earlier.

Kaitlyn van Ives looked the worse for wear, and my rock to the head had not improved matters. The dank, snake-like hair I had seen before was just *her* hair, matted with blood and brick dust. She was filthy – as you'd expect of a woman pulling herself out from under some rubble – and her clothes were torn and scorched in places.

'You're a smart one, you,' she said as she pulled her other leg free. 'Bit of a hand?'

I tracked down my torch and went over to help her. Never let it be said that Jameson Parker is no gentleman. By now it was just one arm left in the rubble, but she was having a hard time pulling it free. I called K over to hold the light and lent her my considerable strength. We gained some traction and the arm came free, and with it another head and pair of shoulders. I gave Kaitlyn a quizzical look but she waved away my questions until after the other body was free of the wall.

It was a girl in her early twenties, wearing a hoodie and jeans. She was unconscious, but breathing, and seemed to be undamaged. Her hair looked grey from the rubble, but underneath there was the odd hint of raven. She looked quite peaceful, all things considered. And familiar.

'How many more people are in the wall?' K said. 'Not to be insensitive or anything, but you know...'

Kaitlyn let out a breathless chuckle. 'Just the two of us. It was a bit of a squeeze.'

'They don't build wall cavities like they used to,' I said. 'Time was you could fit a whole family in the drywall.'

'Time was you didn't have to blast yourself through the bricks, either,' she said. 'Times change.'

I took the torch back from K and shone it in the face of the unconscious girl. She didn't react, not that I expected her to. 'I've seen her before. I know that face.'

'Yes,' Kaitlyn said. 'Allow me to introduce you to Ania Petrova, your little arsonist.'

And then it came back to me. This was the girl that had led that little warlock union the day before. Was my arsonist really this little warlock, so eager to offer her support in matters of grievances with the management? I couldn't say it didn't sound plausible.

Then there was the accent. It had been pretty noticeable the first time she had spoken to me, but I hadn't really picked up on it during the whole nearly getting roasted alive incident. Not that it was hard to put on a fake accent, foreign or otherwise.

Nothing but questions, but at least this gave me a chance to clear my name.

'I'm sensing there's a story here, Kaitlyn,' I said. I could also sense I was on a precipice here, one into which I could very easily be pushed if I pressed Kaitlyn too hard. Yet I needed to know how she was involved in this, and to what degree. 'Care to fill me in?'

'I told you not to get involved,' she said.

'And I ignored you. I do that. K, is this the girl?'

K bent down to get a look at her face. 'Yeah, that's her. She was prettier when she was awake.'

I sniffed. The dust in the air was clogging my sinuses and making it hard to breathe. 'Have you been playing me, Kaitlyn?'

'What do you mean?'

'I know you're not a saint, but my instincts told me you weren't responsible for this. You weren't in town for most of the attacks, then when you did show up you tried to warn me off, then tried to help me. Was all that a ploy to keep me distracted while you and your girl here torched the rest of my city?'

She sighed and landed herself on one of the larger bits of debris nearby. 'I know as much about this as you do, Parker. If I let you take her in, or had Bennett and his goons succeeded in doing so, I'd never get to the bottom of this. You'll understand if I don't have much faith in Whitehall.'

'It's not your job to police the magical underworld, Kaitlyn. Apparently, it's mine.'

'My job is what I *say* it is,' she said, pulling a crumpled cigarette out of one of the pockets on her trousers. She clicked her fingers and it lit itself. 'Anyone brings magic into disrepute, I take notice. This is between Ania and myself, I told you not to get involved.'

'You told me not to get involved or you'd kill me.'

'Drama queen. That's not what I said and you know it. I said this case could tip you over the delicate edge into someone I would have to kill.' She took a drag of the cigarette. 'And I still believe that.'

'You honestly mean to tell me you still believe the Rider is involved in this?'

The red dot of the cigarette floated in the darkness for a moment then flared as she took another drag. 'Yes.'

'And yet, everything I've seen says that this girl is working alone,' I said, carefully leaving out her boyfriend. I had no idea who he might have been, but I was willing to bet he wasn't going to be the Rider. I didn't need to give Kaitlyn any more ammunition for that theory.

She let out a sigh of frustration. 'Look, you want answers, so do I, but now is not the time. The sheriff and his posse will be back before too long. My decoy seems to have drawn them away, but it won't keep them distracted forever. I need to get Ania out of here.'

'Good one,' I said with a laugh. 'I'm taking her in.'

'No. You're not. Not until I've talked to her at the very least.'

'She's been systematically burning down my bloody city, Kaitlyn! And I *need* to bring her in. There have been *complications*. I get to be the hero here, not you.'

She finished her cigarette and flicked it into the darkness. 'You don't even recognise her, do you?'

'Should I?'

'She's a damned warlock, Parker.'

I had hoped Kaitlyn wouldn't have known that. I mean, of course she was going to work that out from the whole borrowed magic thing, but I had really wanted her to take a little longer to reach that conclusion. Her being just your standard wayward wizard would have made it much easier to try and convince Kaitlyn that Whitehall would have gotten information out of her if she was brought in. Flip that round, however, and her being a warlock meant that they were just as likely to kill her as question her, and Kaitlyn was apparently not willing to take that chance.

At least this solved the question of the borrowed magic. Using her own would get her vaulted. It was about more than just covering her tracks, it was about survival. Although there was still the question as to why she was doing this at all.

'That changes nothing,' I said. 'She's been burning buildings, killing people. It has to end here. I need the win.'

Slowly, Kaitlyn stood up and placed herself between me and Ania. 'I might be hurting, Parker, but I've still got enough in me to stop you. Please, don't make me.'

'Guys,' K interrupted. 'If you want to argue about this, more power to you and all that but can we do it later? If Bennett is going to come back like this lady says, I'm pretty sure none of us wants to be here when he does. The whole escaped prisoner thing isn't going to work in either of our favours.'

The kid had a point. 'Fine.'

'Fine,' Kaitlyn said, and nodded.

'What even happened here?' I asked.

'The sheriff happened,' Kaitlyn said, pulling out another cigarette, staring at it for a second and then tucking it behind her ear. 'I'm not sure how it started, but when I got here Ania was trying to fight off an army of Whitehall scum all on her own, and she was losing. A lot of power was flying, a lot more lead, and they had her cornered.'

'How was she holding them all off?'

'Defensive casting, mostly. She had a pretty impressive shield set up, fuelled by a trio of pentagrams I think.'

I scanned the room again. 'I don't see any pentagrams.'

'They're buried under the debris,' K said. 'I had them set up as a sort of magic panic room in case something like this happened. I don't know how she knew about them though. I never mentioned them to her.'

'I don't think she chose to end up back here,' Kaitlyn

said. 'I think they just pushed her back and she made the best of a bad situation. It was some decent working, but when I got here it was starting to collapse. If Bennett's warlocks hadn't broken contact, I doubt she would have lasted long enough for me to get there.'

'What?'

'They were on the way out as I was going in. Took out a couple of them before I realised they weren't attacking me,' she said. I didn't want to think about what she meant by *took out*. 'My guess is they realised they were being sent after one of their own and objected. Solidarity: something you seem to lack.'

So Ms Petrova's little warlock union had enough reach to sway even the most loyal warlocks in Humberside. Admirable. In fact, I'd go as far as to say impressive. I still wasn't convinced it was worth all the hassle, but at least it had some teeth.

There was that bloody word again though, *solidarity*. That damn thing was starting to feel like a blunt knife in the ribs every time someone said it, as though the bloody word was meant to *mean* something.

In the interest of avoiding another argument, I managed to overlook it this time. 'So how did you end up in the wall?'

'Magic, naturally. I kept to the shadows and worked my way round most of the group, leapt in when the shield fell and obliterated them. I used the chaos to make it look like Ania had opened a portal and made a run for it. The sheriff is tracking the signature now, I imagine.'

'A portal? You can do that?'

'Sometimes. I prefer short-range teleportation, but portals are doable in a pinch. Just don't ask me to make them safe.'

Teleportation is tricky enough in and of itself – trying to pull your entire body from one place to another takes a lot of skill if you want to avoid finding bits of you embedded in a wall – but portals are the height of stupidity. I won't go into too much detail here as it would take a while to explain, but for the moment imagine it as trying to hopscotch through dreamspace. It's hard, and cocking it up means you're trapped for eternity inside the dimension where all your nightmares live. So there you go.

Theoretically, however, they're a decent way to cover a lot of ground very quickly, assuming you can pull it off. The amount of power you have to pump into it makes it very easy to track, but you'll likely be so far away that it doesn't matter. Theoretically, of course.

'Please, guys,' K said. 'Enough chat, okay? We really need to go.'

Kaitlyn grabbed Ania by the hood and started to drag her. The girl's limp body slid over the debris, occasionally catching on the odd bit of it. If she'd been awake, I doubt it would have been comfortable. The girl was going to wake up with a lot of bruises. 'Very well.'

I fell into step beside her. 'We're coming with you. I'm not letting the girl out of my sight until she's locked up and unlikely to burn down any more of my city.'

'I figured as much,' she said. 'But you might change your mind once you hear what she has to say.'

I scowled. *Not bloody likely,* I thought to myself. It was warlocks like her that made my life more difficult. I was a nuisance to the higher ups, but I did my job, and with a minimum of danger – today's *mistake* doesn't count. Yes, the whole warlock thing is oppressive and constricting, but I need that, the framework. I needed to know there was something there to stop me slipping back into old habits, to scare me straight. Admittedly I'd spent the last few years trying to prove that theory wrong, that we're not monsters – if for no other reason than to make myself believe it – but until I felt we had reached that point, it was hard to argue against the

Whitehall belief that *some* of us *couldn't* be trusted if left alone.

Now, you might take issue with assuming guilt in those who have shown no interest in power and glory and whatnot, and that's fine. But us villains, we know the score. When one of us, like Ania, starts to break away, we feel the old ways gnawing inside. It gives the darkness hope that we can escape, continue our previous work, and we can actually feel our resolve start to erode.

When she had been just a faceless, nameless magician on the loose, I had wanted to bring her in and give her a chance at a life. Bennett and his cronies hadn't been concerned with her survival if Kaitlyn was to be believed, shooting first and saving the questions for the autopsy. It was the worst of Whitehall, and she had given them the perfect justification by being a damned warlock. And yet now I knew that, even *I* hated her more, for the conflict she set stirring in my gut.

But that was something I didn't have the time to deal with. K had the right of it none of us would be welcomed by Bennett right now. Ania's position as a warlock would only make things worse for me. Perhaps I could have written my actions off as a prideful indiscretion before – which I'm pretty sure is what they were – but with her being like me it would make it difficult to disprove I had gone rogue for her benefit. Idiotic attempt to prove I was the real man for the job, or nervous comrade trying to warn his partner? I was pretty sure which story they would go for.

I wondered if I should take that as a sign, try to go on the run and see how far I could get. Whitehall was so riddled with bureaucracy that they couldn't vault me without my casting a spell without authorisation, no matter how far I ran. It was the rules that gave them their mandate over us, after all. The rules were what separated them from us – order versus chaos. If they gave into temptation and started bursting our tickers for any old bout of misbehaviour, word would get out. Opposition was fractured and confused right now, sure enough, but that would give them something to rally behind.

No. If I tried to run, they'd have to send someone after me. That was how it was done. A warlock or two, tracking me to the ends of the Earth and either bringing me home in chains or in a box, depending on how annoyed they were with me by the time they caught up. And they *would* catch up, I had no doubt of that. Even at my darkest, when I actively prepared to outrun the warlocks, they had found me. If I ran now, I'd be running on fumes with not even the most basic of preparations. Daft, Jameson, very daft.

The only way I would stand a chance would be to run somewhere that would give them pause to follow, like America, but...

The wishful thinking of a stressed-out mind, that's all that was. Tempting, but impossible. The grass is always greener on the other side and all that, but when you came right down to it, I needed my job. I felt useful and it helped me atone. Ultimately, if I ran away from it, there would always be that little question chewing through the synapses at the back of my mind: how long until I relapse?

Kaitlyn led us out of the building with more grace than you would expect of a woman dragging an unconscious person behind them. She was not careful with or kind to Ania, making no effort to avoid dragging her over some of the worst of the debris, or to particularly avoid any corners. The poor girl bounced her way out of the building like a rag doll thrown down some stairs. Still, she didn't complain.

K did, though. The kid was softer on her than I had expected, and he offered to carry her so that Kaitlyn would stop dragging her. She was hesitant, but ultimately agreed.

We were led on a merry chase in perfect silence. Apparently Kaitlyn didn't want to fall into another argument with me, something I was happy to avoid as well, and K was too busy muttering to himself. He may have been a twitchy little guy, but he did occasionally speak some sense. I'd rather he didn't do it while muttering under this breath, but you can't have everything.

It wasn't until we got outside, and the sunlight hit her face, that Ania showed some signs of life. She let out a quiet moan and for a moment everything stopped, as we prepared for her waking up. Kaitlyn had the kid put her down, no doubt hoping the girl would be able to continue the journey herself, although that didn't pan out. Ania went right back to silent unconsciousness, and again K hoisted her onto his thin shoulders.

I opened one of the rear doors on Eames' car. 'Okay, load her in and we can go somewhere out of the way to hash this out. Deal?'

'No,' she said, heading in another direction. 'It would be safer to walk. They'll no doubt be able to track the car.'

'Are you sure?'

'Trust me.'

I had to stifle a laugh of derision, and I'm not sure I did a good job. She didn't think it necessary to reply, so that was something at least. I really needed to avoid baiting her; the longer I was around her without her actively taking a dislike to me, the more information I could extract. Safe houses, motives, anything of that kind would be helpful in getting back in Whitehall's good books. Not that I care about being a model employee, but I do want to stay alive.

'Fine, lead the way,' I said.

And she did. I don't want to harp on about the whole

dragging thing, but I was glad K stepped up to carry Ania. She was only a slip of a thing, but she was heavy enough for him to suffer a little by carrying her. He did well to keep up with Kaitlyn's pace, to be fair, and wasn't vocal in his complaints. There was a slight growl to his breathing, but that was all. Not that I've had cause to carry much dead weight in my time, but K was a natural at it.

As we walked, I looked for a weakness I could exploit. Despite what Kaitlyn may have thought, I had no interest in listening to her *explanations* or excuses. I had to bring in Ania, but she did have the right of it: there was no way I could overpower her. Even if I hadn't drained all my enchantments – sans blazer, which was not something I was going to mess with – and hadn't tapped out K's reserves, she was still untouchable. If she had been the one to cause that massacre at the last stand location, as she had claimed, that was power to rival my own at my darkest point. I wasn't going to be able to bash her on the head and just make off with Ania.

Best to play it cool, wait for an opening, and disappear without detection. The events at the office had me thinking that perhaps discretion was the better part of valour after all. The subtle knife cuts deepest, or something like that. Although doing any of that with K around might be somewhat tricky.

This was all supposition. There was the very real possibility that Whitehall would hear of my actions at the field office and immediately write me off the books, and it wasn't as if they wouldn't have reason to. I could feel the doubt creeping in. I needed to be sure bringing Ania in wouldn't just get me killed on the spot.

I had to risk a conversation with Charlie. I wasn't going to be much good if I was fretting all over the place.

'What are you doing?' Kaitlyn said as I hit the dial

button.

'Checking in. Maybe I can get a heads-up on where Bennett is heading. Stay one step ahead of him until this is all sorted out.'

There was a pause. 'Fine. But don't try and rat me out.'

I rolled my eyes at her. I wasn't about to place *loyalty* over my own life. What had that ever gotten me? But I also wasn't about to jeopardise my one chance at redemption.

The phone rang a little longer than usual before Charlie answered. 'Hello, Parker. How's the investigation going?'

'About as well as could be expected,' I said. 'I got set on fire earlier, that was fun.'

'I was expecting some sort of joke about how *hot* you are, then. You're slipping.'

I laughed. 'It's been a long day. Listen, can you give me the run-down on a few things?'

'I hate it when you ask me for things, Parker. You always want to know about restricted stuff, and then I have to go and talk to the supervisor, who hates me by the way, just to get clearance...'

'It's important, Charlie. I need a bit of information on the arsonist subject before I can be sure.' Kaitlyn shot me a look but I ignored her.

A good detective double checks. It's that simple. I'm not a good detective, but I aspire to be so I might as well try acting like one once in a while. Besides, maybe Whitehall would know something about Ania's past that could help me in working out her motives. Or ways to keep her in check once I found a chance to spirit her away from Kaitlyn.

I know villains, but it always pays to *know* them. That's the sort of doublespeak you pick up when you hang around suits all day.

'You've got a suspect?' Charlie was on the brink of sounding excited. It was a weird thing to hear. '*Finally*. I knew an under-secretary showing up would motivate you.'

'*You* sent Bennett?'

'No, I don't have that kind of clout. But I heard about it. Their presence tends to make everyone a little aware of their work ethic.'

'Vader on the Death Star,' I said under my breath.

'Nerd,' Charlie shot back. 'Anyway, what did you need information on?'

Kaitlyn was staring daggers at me now, but I hadn't done anything to risk giving away her location, so there wasn't much she could do. I was enjoying that. Always pushing people. 'A local warlock called Ania Petrova. I'd like to know her history, see if anything makes her look good for the arsons.'

'A warlock? You sure you want to go down that road?'

'Why not?'

'I told you about the... *tensions*,' she said. 'If some of the more politically astute warlocks got to hear about one of their own turning on them...'

'How has all this politicking suddenly become so important without me hearing about it? Why does it even matter? If a warlock did it, a warlock did it.'

'Firstly,' Charlie said matter-of-factly. 'The reason you don't hear about this stuff is because you're an anti-social and difficult person. Secondly, it matters because they'll see it as treason.'

'I really don't care. I just want to do my job and go home without getting killed.'

'Without getting killed? What have you done now?'

'Your concern is touching. I'm sure you'll hear about it soon, but for now can I just get my information?'

'I worry about you, Parker. I really do,' she said. I

heard her fingers hammering on a keyboard for a few moments. 'Okay, Ania Petrova. What did you want to know?'

'Let's start with the basics. Her background?'

There were a few more taps at her keyboard. 'Right. We don't have all her details from before she came over here, but we reckon she was born in a former Soviet bloc country.'

'Did the name give it away?'

'Shut up. We first have record of her arriving here when she was about twelve, then she immediately vanishes for about six years.'

'Does that happen often?' I said. 'I thought you lot kept pretty in-depth records of my lot.'

'More often than you'd think,' she said. 'The sort of people that become warlocks are usually quite good at going off the grid, as you well know, but this was before the conflict so records of that time are spotty at best. We've got a few ideas what she was up to, but no solids. By the time she showed up again at eighteen, Ms Petrova was a thrall to a sex magician.'

'Those bastards really get around.' You can almost always trace a childhood tragedy back to a sex magician if you look hard enough.

'Yeah,' Charlie said, her tone darker. 'We're not entirely sure what he did to her, or *with* her, but when he was taken down she helped defend him. Whoever it was that brought her in thought there was a determination in there worth saving, according to the file. That's why he didn't kill her outright. Took a year of deprogramming to make her useful, but she's a pretty decent warlock according to this.'

'How decent?'

'She's worked in York, Reading, Cardiff, brought down a werewolf in Leamington Spa, took out a few rogue magicians in Kent. Solid work, few complaints from whoever she was working under. An unusually high rate of approvals on her requests to use magic, but also a high trust rating. Basically, she's on the path to super-stardom, unlike you.'

'Hey, I take my work very seriously,' I said. The pain was only partially faked. 'She seriously took down a werewolf? I thought they were just myths.'

'You live in a world of magic, Parker. You can't start playing the sceptic. And yes, a big one too, old. More wolf than were, apparently. Feral, and especially dangerous. Then again, *she* wrote the report, maybe she bigged herself up a little.'

Things weren't adding up. A future superstar warlock didn't sound the type to start setting fires all over the place. 'What about the sex magician who had her enthralled, what was his name?'

Charlie's keyboard was seriously too loud. I wondered if she had it attached to the damn phone. 'Lucian De Sade.'

'De Sade? Really?'

'That's the name he went by. It probably wasn't his real name, but we couldn't find any other ID for him. He died in the sting.'

'Definitely? I hate to ask, but you hear about this sort of thing from time to time. They found the body, I'm assuming?'

'Yes, you cynic. Knife to the eye socket, very much definitely dead. Body was burned once a positive ID was made.'

Being a sex magician's thrall is orders of magnitude worse than just being his plaything. For the most part they just use you for their rituals, but prolonged exposure can break a mind, and that's when they start getting really sinister. They'll turn you into whoever they want you to be, and you won't even notice. They'll put booby-traps in your head, run your thoughts in zigzags through what you perceive to be reality, and make you little more than an automaton. It's degrading, disgusting and, even in my darkest days, not once did even I consider doing such things.

Maybe De Sade had left a little mental bomb in there somewhere, embedded so deep the deprogrammers couldn't find it. That could explain her apparently out of character behaviour perhaps, if she was some sort of sleeper agent. Given how thorough the deprogrammers could be, however, it was a long shot.

Or maybe someone new was pulling the strings.

'And the guy who brought her in?'

'A warlock out of Kent again, that's where they found her. Paul Renner. Hasn't had any contact with her really since he brought her in, they sent him off on assignment while she was working Kent. Curious.'

'Thanks for the information. Doesn't tell me much of use right now, but you never know. Could you do one more thing?'

'Is it going to get me into trouble? You haven't asked me to do anything that would get me into trouble yet and I'm scared.'

'Only a tiny bit, maybe a slap on the wrist,' I said, nodding at Kaitlyn. Had to play my part a little longer.

'Fine, let's hear it.'

'It would really help me to know what Charles Bennett is up to right now. You know, his current location, entourage, that sort of thing.'

I could feel Charlie scowl at me. I could *hear* it. 'I would ask why you wanted that information, but I'm not sure I want to know.'

'You definitely don't.'

'Last time he checked in he was at the Humberside field office, with an entourage of fifteen fast-track candidates and ten Whitehall warlocks. Your standard under-secretary entourage really.'

That was damn near an army, as far as I was concerned. That much magical muscle at his command would make him quite formidable if he caught up with us, although it hadn't done him much good so far. I caught Kaitlyn looking and I mouthed over what Charlie had just said.

'He's sourced locals then,' she said quietly. 'There was a lot more than that when I got there.'

That didn't seem possible. There's no shortage of fast-trackers down in Whitehall, but up here in the proverbial sticks – which to a Whitehall fellow is anywhere outside London – you'd be lucky to find enough to rub together and start a fire. Admittedly, they all blended into one arrogant, entitled whole when I saw them usually, so I couldn't give you direct numbers, but I doubted it would be enough to make a notable difference to his entourage.

And if he brought Whitehall warlocks, would they really have abandoned their posts when they found out who they were after? It was a cushy job, nothing bad ever happened in London any more, and they were rarely called up to go into the field. Why risk all that for one girl? It didn't make sense. I was sick of things not making sense.

'Okay, thanks Charlie. You're a little life saver,' I said.

'Little?'

'Well, I imagine you as little. Like a gnome. A computer research gnome, with the pointy hat and everything.'

'Thanks...'

The click of her hanging up made me smile. Talking to her always made me smile, regardless of my mood beforehand. Even when nothing made sense, winding her up was my one true constant. Good old Charlie.

I'd lost track of where we were walking while I was talking, trusting in my natural autopilot to keep me in step behind Kaitlyn. I couldn't even recognise where we were now, although it did still look like the same sort of abandoned misery that pervaded the area around K's squat.

Wherever we were, however, it was close enough to hear Bennett swearing.

CHAPTER 16

It was an incoherent curse, trapped in the wind and thrust over the rooftops from far away, but you only needed to hear the tone to know that it was one. It floated on the breeze like sour music, and for the first time since she'd pulled herself out of the wall, Kaitlyn smiled a full smile.

'Come on,' she said. 'We've still got ground to cover.'

We stuck to the main road for most of the journey, which was weird considering she had made it very clear she wanted to go unseen. Not that anyone *had* seen us yet, but surely it was more likely if we stayed out in the open. I tried suggesting we get off the road, but all that earned me was a rather stern shushing.

She knew where she was going, though, I couldn't argue that. Every now and then she'd swerve into a side street for a moment, then straight back onto the main road, in a weird sort of pac-man style. There was no obvious reasoning to it that I could see, yet still she did it, Ania bouncing over K's shoulder like an overgrown ragdoll.

And that was another thing, Ania had been unconscious for too long. She seemed otherwise unhurt, but something clearly wasn't right if she had been out this long. That a good deal of her clothes were now in tatters from being dragged out of the wall didn't help either. Someone was going to spot us, it was only a matter of time, and that news would eventually get back to Bennett. We were hardly very inconspicuous.

K, on the other hand, seemed to be getting stronger the more we walked despite his burden. I could tell what was happening just from the look on his face; his magic was returning to him. It's not a truly rejuvenating sensation, but its damn close. As your magic starts to come back, all your aches and pains no longer matter. It's a fleeting feeling, but real enough. At least if we got jumped, two of our number would be ready with the spells.

If K could even be trusted with his own magic. I hadn't forgotten his unsettling position when we first met, and though I hadn't had the time to mention it to him I was very much keeping a close eye on him. He'd clearly not been trained, and I very much didn't want to end up being the one to train him, or worse, force him into a life of servitude. If I could catch it early, get him to realise how much discipline he would have to embrace to keep himself and others safe, maybe he could survive without the gilded cage.

For the moment, I could rest safe in the knowledge that Kaitlyn could control him if need be. Hell, if my last minute moment of inspiration had been enough to stop him, someone with power *and* training should have no trouble. But I'm not afraid to say, I was formulating ways of approaching him for more of his power. Purely to keep him safe, of course. Stop him overcharging his circuits.

The allure of power makes bad liars of us all, I know. And I wasn't about to try these approaches, but I was still working on them in my head. The key to managing addiction is not to ignore the schemes and plots that form with a purpose to kick you off the wagon, but to let them take form and then simply not do them. Sounds simple, but it serves as a nice reminder of how desperate you are and, in my situation, keeps the brain alert for those life or death situations. Not that I had any trouble with that, considering the last few hours.

Eventually, just as I was about to lose my patience with the whole follow the leader thing Kaitlyn had going on, she ducked into yet another alley and stopped. She shot a glance at K, which the kid returned with surprising grit, and started tapping at one of the walls. She worked her way up the wall slowly, and tapping the whole time. I'd seen people do this on television, looking for hollow walls or something that could be identified by the sound, but I hadn't thought that would work on bricks. Even if it did, this was her secret hidey hole, surely she would know where the damn thing was?

After a minute of tapping, in which myself and K stayed perfectly silent as we watched in confused fascination, Kaitlyn found what she was looking for. I had expected a secret door or some extravagant mechanism to slide a section of wall away, but then I had overlooked her flair for the dramatic. She waved a hand, muttered a word, and just walked through the wall.

It was impressive on a technical level. Well, not that impressive, relatively simple really, but it *looked* impressive and that seemed fitting for her. All spectacle, that one. K was entranced, however. I guess that without proper training the spectacle can work on even the empowered. I found myself wondering just how many of my ilk would have been as awestruck as K was, although perhaps I was a little in awe myself. Everything becomes a little more magical, for want of a better word, when you're not subjected to it often.

Kaitlyn's head appeared from inside the wall. I had

seen her climb out of walls quite enough for one day. 'Are you coming?'

K immediately jumped to attention and walked up to the wall, having put Ania down to properly investigate Kaitlyn's working. He dawdled, and Kaitlyn grabbed him by the scruff of the neck and pulled him through with a muffled yelp. Poor kid, you never get used to walking through something that by rights *should* be solid, although it's never as bad as the first time. At least I hoped so, seeing as this would be only my second.

I lifted Ania. I must admit, for the few feet she would have to travel, I was tempted just to drag her. It's easier on the knees. But, I like to imagine myself as a gentleman, from time to time, and I think the poor lass had suffered enough bruises. It wasn't as though she was heavy either, or perhaps I'm just a finely crafted example of manliness and muscularity. In either case, I took her to the wall.

Truth told, I had trouble walking through it.

The last – and to this point only – time I had done this was when I had been on the run during one of my escape attempts. When they'd come to take my tooth for the vault the first time, my fight or flight instinct came down heavily in favour of flight, and I'd led them on a merry chase around London before they finally brought me down. I'd whipped up the permeable membrane spell before I knew what I was doing, and was through it even faster.

This time I didn't have adrenaline and manly cowardice driving me. Now every single fibre of my being was telling me not to walk into the wall – this is something drilled into you from the moment you take your first step and I now realised it was not something easily overcome. I decided to test the waters with Ania. I'm a gentleman but not to a fault.

I swung her legs at the wall slowly, just to make sure.

They phased through without resistance, the wall rippling gently. Bricks shouldn't ripple. I pushed her in up to her knees as that was as far as she could go before I would have to touch the damn thing myself. Watching the bricks ripple helped to knock down a layer or two of mental conditioning, although it wasn't much easier. Bloody K and his free ride through the damn wall. No thinking, just being dragged through. I wanted that.

But instead I took a deep breath, just in case I started to drown in wobbly liquid bricks, and threw myself into the wall. I didn't remember seeing the inside of the wall the first time I had done this, but I remembered it this time. Yes, it was pitch black so it wasn't like there was much to see, but the mind knows what's going on and it still freaks the fuck out. When I flopped through the other side there was one hell of a scream caught in my throat.

That I was looking right into the eyes of Kaitlyn van Ives made me swallow said scream, however. It's never polite to scream right in someone's face.

'Look at me,' she said, her voice soothing for once. The aggressive edge had gone, although I doubted it would stay gone for long. 'Good, your mind is still in one piece. Sorry about that. It takes some practice, but it's the only way I know to avoid snoopers. Even if you know the door is there, takes a bit of time to work up the courage to walk through it.'

'You're telling me,' I choked back. Not going to lie, not my manliest moment.

K was leaning against a wrought iron support beam, sweating like a fat tourist. I found a dusty but comfortable chair onto which to deposit Ania and then tried to regain some composure. Kaitlyn was busying herself doing *something* as she wandered around the place.

I'm not even sure I can adequately describe the

building. I wanted to call it a disused factory, but I had always envisioned those as having huge smokestacks and a roof that looked like a cubist had tried to draw waves on the black sea. The building didn't fit that profile from the outside, and inside it was actually quite homey. The floor may have been patched concrete, but there was furniture and plants and whatnot. Room dividers had been taped between some of the iron supports, although not many, breaking the space up a little.

It was quite nice for a safe house. I wondered if perhaps Kaitlyn and her posse had set up a number of these around the country for just such eventualities, or if her underlings had been working Humberside before she showed up. Sleeper cells maybe? No doubt once I had worn out my welcome, this safe house would be abandoned. That was a shame – Kaitlyn really knew how to make a safe house feel like a home.

She was still pacing. 'What are you doing?' I said.

She stopped. 'Turning the wards back on. I don't think they've got anything they case use to track me or Ania, but you and the kid are another story. This should give us some time alone before any tracking spells can zero in on us.'

'That's not possible. You can't block tracking spells, they're linked to your very being.'

'I didn't say block, did I?' she said. There was a disappointment in her words that cut deeply. My poor, poor pride. 'The wards sort of refract the spell. It makes it much harder to get a specific lock, but like you say it can't block it completely. Gives us time, not a shelter.'

'Time for what?'

'Time for us to learn a little more about what's really going on here. Sit down. You too, kid.'

She indicated towards a glass-topped dining table on the same side of the room as Ania now lay. The chairs looked uncomfortable, with wicker seats and weird wooden backrests, but then I never feel comfortable at a dining table. People are always *watching* you. Still, we sat down like good little boys. It wasn't like I had anywhere else to be at that moment.

Kaitlyn walked over to Ania and knelt down next to her. It was weird seeing her try to be gentle and affectionate after the quite brusque way she had treated the unconscious girl until now, but I saw her features lighten as she stared at the girl for a moment. There was a sadness in her face just then, like she didn't want to wake the girl up, and I would guess because she hoped that Ania was somewhere better, somewhere safer. She was going to break the girl out of her dream, drag her back to reality, and she was envious of the dream the girl had escaped into.

She lay a hand softly on the girl's head.

'No sudden moves when she wakes up,' she said. 'This isn't going to be pleasant for her, and she's not as weak as she looks.'

'She's not going to kick off, is she?' I said.

Kaitlyn closed her eyes. 'She might. I'm not sure. If you stay still, she should be all right. Just give her time to acclimatise.'

K scooted his chair slightly further away. 'O... okay.'

There was no spectacle this time. Kaitlyn uttered a few words and the hairs on my arms stood up. Her hands glowed gently for a fraction of a second, and then Ania's eyes opened. They darted around wildly for a second and then she screamed and vaulted over the back of the chair.

'Ania, it's okay –' Kaitlyn said but was cut short when a bolt of golden flame shot over the back of the chair and barely zipped over her head. 'Ania! Calm down!'

For a moment there was silence and then, slowly, the girl's face appeared over the back of the chair. She looked even younger than I remembered, fear having a way of doing that to the already young. 'Where am I?'

'You're safe, for now. Come out from there.'

'I'm safe?' Ania said, her accent slightly harder than I remembered it being, perhaps as a result of the confusion. 'But, the raid...'

'Taken care of,' Kaitlyn said, offering a hand to the girl. 'But I want an explanation, and I'm not the only one.'

Ania saw me for the first time. 'What's he doing here?'

'To be honest, kid, I'm wondering that myself,' I said. 'But hey, I was never too good at planning ahead.'

'He's here to learn, despite what he may think,' Kaitlyn said with a lovely thick layer of disdain. 'And he's not doing a very good job of it. Perhaps you could fill him in as to why you're doing what you're doing.'

'The fires?'

'Exactly.'

The girl winced. Whatever Kaitlyn had done to her had apparently not been refreshing and she looked as though she hadn't slept for days, despite the fact she had just woken up. Then again, you're not likely to sleep well when getting dragged around the city like a dead dog. She rubbed her eyes and found herself a seat at the table. K was hiding under his chair as a result of her brief outburst, but she smiled at him and he came back out.

I remembered her being more brutal than this, but then my brief experience with her did end with a bludgeoning and near immolation, so I suppose my memory was somewhat biased. But as she sat before us then she looked weak and tired and sort of *soft*. Weakness isn't always, well, a weakness. But I had expected more vitriol from this arsonist, this woman that had set fire to a score of buildings without much care for if anyone was inside. Being so bloody cute didn't get her out of that.

It didn't get her off the hook for what she had done, for what she represented. I couldn't allow that.

'I'm so *tired*,' she said once K had reseated himself. 'I've spent the best years of my young life doing what I was told, first by De Sade and then by Whitehall. I thought if I lost myself in the work, I could get something back, you know?'

'I understand that,' I said. 'Whitehall doesn't exactly take on warlocks without baggage.'

'No, you don't understand. We all thought you would, but you just don't get it at all.'

'What?'

'We all know the stories about you, about your past. The self-styled Dark Lord of Hampshire. I wasn't exactly coherent for most of your reign of terror, but the others remember your declaration of independence and the response. The way they tell it, the world might as well have ended at the moment you sent out that letter.'

'It wasn't like that.'

She pinched the bridge of her nose. 'We don't judge you. If you bothered to talk to any of us you would know that none of us is free from guilt of some kind or another. You're an example.'

It's never good when people start saying you're an example. It starts at school, when the head of year starts telling you of your need to set an example for the younger years, and it never stops. It's just a way for people to place the blame on someone else under the guise of flattery. They never need to become their own person, they can just follow you forever and you'll take the blame for all their fuck ups.

I resisted the urge to slam my fist down on the table. The last thing I needed was a hand full of glass. 'How am I an example for anyone? Everything I've done since then was to forget what I am, to keep that controlled.'

'We see how you've changed. From the great evil to a good guy. Not once have you apologised for being what you are.'

I did slam my fist down that time. Thankfully the table held. 'There's no-one left to apologise to. I could apologise to the graves if you'd prefer. I doubt they'd hear it, but who else would I apologise to?'

'You misunderstand,' she said carefully. 'That is apologising for what you did, not what you are: empowered. Whitehall wants you to hate yourself for how you were born, twist you to their whims as nothing but a puppet. We all know this, we've seen them try to break the spirits of every warlock. But you, you never waver. We have watched you, and we think you are right.'

'What? What are you talking about?'

She reached out a delicate hand and took mine into it. 'Your insubordination is legendary amongst the other warlocks. Even your unwillingness to mix tells us that you care not for this gilded cage Whitehall built for us. Your very existence is a symbol of disobedience, and people have started to listen. You are the spirit of the revolution.'

Oh. Fuck. Me.

I don't recall ever wanting a revolution. Nothing I have done since becoming a warlock has been as some part of a master plan to get my own little personality cult going. I'm a dick. I do and say dickish things to my bosses because I like to wind them up. I've never been a smash the state sort of guy – except in my dark times, I grant you, but even that was due to hubris rather than idealism – and I wasn't sure how she'd managed to read this much into my actions.

There was a wild-eyed fanaticism about her now. 'We knew you weren't interesting in joining us, that you might even oppose us, but your message would live on.

Your message of freedom.'

'She's got a point,' Kaitlyn said. 'Your whole redemption thing does give what I've been saying some credence. Magic isn't innately good or evil, only how you use it.'

'No, she doesn't,' I shot back. 'The only reason I'm not cutting a bloody swathe through most of the country is because I was forced to swear off magic altogether. Whitehall's tactics are barbaric, but they're not necessarily unfounded. I've given them plenty of evidence to the contrary.'

'That wasn't the magic, that was you,' Ania said. 'The magic didn't make you kill.'

'Don't you fucking dare presume to tell me about my motivations,' I roared. 'You weren't there. You know nothing of what I did or why I did it. I am not some messiah to hold up to your little club to justify your crimes.'

'But –'

'No, you shut-up and you listen to me.' I was cooking on brimstone now. Kaitlyn had hit this button before, but not this hard. She had known the facts of the matter, but not once had she tried to impart some understanding of the situation. 'Everything I did, I did for the power, for the magic. It made me kill to get more, to make myself stronger, and then, at my ultimate peak, it *betrayed* me. I would never have killed her, I would never have made that choice. She was the one thing that kept me tethered to this world. Don't even pretend you understand that. I am a symbol of fear, not rebellion.'

The edge returned to her voice and her cute, tired little face regained some of the harshness that I had expected. 'Have you ever had someone break your mind with magic?'

I took a breath. I knew where this was about to go. 'No. Not to my recollection.'

'You are aware, though, that I have?'

'I've skimmed your file. I know about De Sade.'

'Do you? Do you know what it feels like to have a man, a considerably older one at that, play with your mind like a child's toy? The sensation when it starts to snap under his ministrations, and the realisation that he's been doing it for so long that you *like* it?' She made a steeple with her fingers and rested her lips against them. 'When you can see through your own eyes, see the depraved and disgusting things you are doing, and find yourself physically and mentally incapable of doing anything to stop it, then you can cry that magic made you do it. When your very thoughts themselves come from the mind of another, then you can blame magic for your actions.'

'That's what –'

'No, Parker,' Kaitlyn interrupted. 'We both know that's not how it was with you. You had the choice, you just didn't care.'

'How could you possibly know what I felt?'

'Because I struggle with that same allure every day,' she said. 'You're not exactly unique, you know.'

There wasn't much I could say in response to that. Any attempt at a retort was going to do little but prolong the row and turn it into an exercise in he-said-she-said. The room dipped into an awkward silence.

'Look,' I said, eventually. 'I think we've gone slightly off topic here.'

'Maybe,' Kaitlyn said. Ania nodded in agreement.

'The important thing is she is burning down buildings,' I pointed at Ania. 'And I have to stop her.'

'It was for the greater good!' The hardness I had glimpsed on our first meeting was coming back now in full force. 'I made sure the buildings were as empty as they could be!'

'Apart from the one you left me in.'

180

'I wasn't too happy about that either, but I'm not idealistic enough to think you'd understand at the time. Given time, maybe you would come around, but we didn't have it then. You were going to get in the way.'

I got right in her face. This was an argument I could win. 'Of course I was going to get in the way. These weren't Whitehall properties you were torching, they were full of unambiguously innocent people. People who think magic extends as far as card tricks and slight of hand.'

'You don't understand!'

'I don't need to. I just need you to come in before Bennett and his guys think I've gone rogue and sided with you. Maybe they'll care for the explanation, but I don't give a shit.'

'Guys...' K said. I barely registered him.

'I need you to understand, please,' Ania continued. 'Just think about things for a second. Consider my position!'

'You set fire to half the city. As far as I'm concerned, your position is bat shit crazy.'

'Guys!' K tried again.

Ania waved a hand at him without looking, a sort of shut up gesture. 'I was just trying to get *her* attention!' The hand shot out in Kaitlyn's direction.

'Wait, what?' Kaitlyn and myself said in perfect unison.

'Jesus Christ, guys!' K practically screamed.

All three of us turned to look at him at once. 'What?!'

'I believe he's trying to warn you about me,' came a voice from behind us.

CHAPTER 17

Ania and Kaitlyn fell immediately into a combat stance, K disappeared under his chair again, and I did my best to look threatening considering there was very little I could do at this point if it came to a magical throw down. The key is to try and look taller than you are. Like a cat.

The mystery man was standing at the door and looking a little worse for wear. He had his shoulder against the frame and blood-matted hair was hanging down over his face, his head hanging limp. He was wearing a ripped suit covered in grey dust and generally looked like he'd been given a bit of a kicking.

'I would have knocked,' he said, lifting his head. 'But my knuckles hurt.'

I knew that face.

Apparently so did Ania. 'Greg!' she squealed and ran over to him. She gave him a shoulder to lean on, but he politely pushed her away.

Greg, or the kid as I had been calling him when he had just been a nameless fast-tracker to me, pushed himself upright and off the door frame and snapped his fingers. Most of the blood vanished into a wisp of red smoke, a few of the more obvious bruises too, and suddenly he didn't look nearly as beaten up as before.

'Sorry, needed the guys back at the office to think you'd given me a proper beating when you'd escaped,' he said. His suit was still dusty and torn, his eyes sullen and dark, but without the blood he was much more recognisable.

'Nice illusion,' I said. 'I didn't think you types would have the finesse to pull that off.'

'Because we're all *RARGH FAST-TRACKER SMASH?*' he said, pulling a pantomime monster face. 'Some of us do our homework, warlock.'

He found himself a seat and lowered himself into it, Ania fluttering about behind him wanting to help. 'What happened to you?'

He winced. 'Got slammed into a ceiling during this guy's escape attempt.'

Ania gave me one hell of an evil look.

'Hey now! First of all,' I said quickly. 'It wasn't me that punted him into the wall. Secondly, don't go calling it an *attempt*, that implies I failed. Thirdly, *what the hell is going on?*'

'Kind of wondering that myself,' Kaitlyn said.

'Greg is my lover. He's on our side.'

'Lover? Who says *lover* any more?' K said, but no-one was listening.

For my part, I was feeling all self-righteous again. 'It's not *our* side, it's *your* side. I'm not with you, remember?'

'Not yet,' Greg said with a pained smile as he rubbed his temples. 'But I listened to your speech at the office, you're well on the way. You're no fan of Whitehall, you just need a little push over the edge. Oh, and before I forget, here.' He reached inside his stained jacket and pulled out a pistol. *My* pistol. 'Swung by your house on the way here, figured you'd need it.'

I took it off him and gave it the once over. Fully loaded. I hadn't used the thing for a while and, in all honesty, I wasn't even sure where I had put it. The best I could guess was that it had been *somewhere* inside my flat, but its exact location had been a mystery to me. I'd always found that guns do more to escalate violence than to combat it, but then I'm English, I don't have to deal with gunfire as a real danger of my job.

Still, with things as they were, it was nice to have it. Everything was spiralling out of control around me, so having an equaliser on hand was a small but tangible comfort against the threats that were starting to pile up. I found a space for it in my blazer.

'What's to stop me just shooting you all right now?' I asked. Always pays to be direct.

Greg shrugged. 'Just hear us out, please. Ania and I have a plan, one that will sort things out.'

'He's not going to listen, Greg,' Ania said. 'I tried talking to him but he's too roped up in his own guilt to understand.'

'No, he's not. If you'd heard his little speech earlier you'd see how much he wants to believe us. Please, warlock, just hear us out. All we want to do is give warlocks their lives back.'

'Oh, I see,' Kaitlyn muttered beside me.

'See what?'

'I know what they have planned. It's not going to work.'

'Yes, it will,' Greg shot back. 'Whitehall would never expect it, they think they've got everyone cowed and submissive.'

'Excuse me,' K said putting up his hand. 'What won't they be expecting?'

'We're going to burn down the vault,' Ania said as if it was the most natural thing in the world.

I burst out laughing.

I had to hand it to them, it was one hell of a plan. Destroy the vault and sure, every warlock in the country is suddenly free to live his or her own life how he chooses once again, no danger of dropping down dead all of a sudden just from doing something the suits down in Whitehall find a little bit scary.

I'd never seriously considered the possibility of being free again. The notion of freedom scared me even when I thought it impossible, the chance that I could go off the rails again with nothing to stop me, but now that people were promising me that freedom I couldn't help but find it a little appealing. Had I been holding onto the fear of what I was capable of as a way to avoid the hopelessness of my situation?

Of course, their wanting to burn down the vault didn't mean they could actually pull that off. There were a few flaws in their plan.

'How could they possibly not be expecting an attack on the vault?' I said. 'The one thing keeping scores of dangerous magic users in line, and you think they won't be ready for an attack on it?'

'Not the way we're going to do it,' Greg said. The whole wet behind the ears, fresh out of university thing was an act, I could see that now. There was a cold and calculating mind behind those eyes. I wondered what had flipped him over from Whitehall to Ania's camp. Other than the sex. 'They're all set up for a warlock assault, but they aren't really prepared for a strike orchestrated by active magic users.'

'That's not going to work,' I said.

Kaitlyn waved me down. 'We've tried it before. A couple of times. Whitehall is monstrously well defended. The place is a fortress. I've lost countless men and woman to plans like this before we wrote them off altogether.'

'Yes, I know,' Greg said. 'We get to hear about them a

lot around the office. People used to take bets on how many terrorists would smash themselves into the defences that week. You know, until you stopped.'

'Charming people,' Kaitlyn scowled.

'You would have done much better, of course, if you'd had an inside man,' Greg said and threw up his hands. I'm surprised he didn't follow it up with a 'ta-da'.

'Oh, I get it. They set the fires to lure me here,' Kaitlyn said. 'They knew I would hear about a practitioner burning down buildings and set out to shut them down before they sullied the good name of magic.'

'And who thought up this bright idea?' I asked?

'I did,' Greg replied. 'I approached Ania with it and we developed the thing together. It didn't take us long to realise we needed the help of someone who knew what they were doing.'

'Exactly,' Ania said, smiling. 'The fires were the quickest way to contact her, and we would need her expertise to pull this off.'

'You couldn't just look her up in the phone book?' I said.

'Yeah,' Kaitlyn said, her voice thick with sarcasm. 'I'm in there under T for terrorist.'

'You know what I mean, smart arse,' I shot back. 'There must have been easier ways to reach out to her, ones that didn't require lots and lots of burning death.'

Ania went to reply, but Greg spoke over her. 'There are ways, but they take time. Miss van Ives is very conscious of how much Whitehall wants to bring her in. By the time we managed to make contact the traditional way, it would be too late.'

'There's a time limit on this plan of yours?' Kaitlyn said. 'I don't do well with time-sensitive offers. They reek of betrayal and traps, in my experience.'

I couldn't help myself. I might not have been happy to be there, but that wasn't about to stop me twisting the knife if given the opening. It's one of my things. 'I think you're looking for the word *trappish*.'

'Shut-up, you.'

'Sorry,' I said. I wasn't. 'Why is it so important to get things done sooner rather than later? It's not like the vault is going anywhere.'

'Whitehall likes to shunt its fast-track candidates around the country, give them a taste of how things are in the various districts,' Greg said. He was looking at Ania as he spoke, a loving gaze or near enough. 'I've got maybe a couple more months before they send me to the Hebrides or something and Kaitlyn loses her inside man.'

'But why her? Why not just do it yourself, or get one of the other grumpy wizards to do it for you?'

Ania scoffed. 'Yeah, because there's like an agency for disgruntled mages. You can order them off a menu.'

'Point taken,' I said.

Kaitlyn leant back in her chair. 'I suppose it helps that I've been in the vault before, too.'

'Excuse me?'

'When they were still putting it together, I broke in and snooped around. Got detected before I could do any damage, but I got a good lay of the land. That was always the lynch pin in my own plans. Unfortunately, security has made it impossible for me to get back in.'

Greg clasped his hands behind his head, the cocky little shit. 'That's where I come in. No-one's going to look twice at a fast-tracker roaming around Whitehall. We're invisible to everyone down there until we're needed for something, and we all have clearance to get deep enough in to find the vault no worries. The problems start once I do.'

'He doesn't know where he's going,' Ania interrupted. 'And he's not actually allowed *in* the vault. If he tried to blunder around down there they'd catch him for sure and we'd be no better off.'

Kaitlyn chuckled. 'That's it? You're stymied for want of a map?'

'Pretty much,' Greg said. 'But even if we had the map, I'm not equipped to pull off a job like this. I couldn't get the door open, and I certainly couldn't defend myself from the sort of trouble that would fall on me even if I could. I'm muscle for the suits, not a real soldier. We could never pull this off just the two of us, but you and your resources... Maybe you would stand a chance.'

There was a moment, a very short and very scary moment, where I thought Kaitlyn was going to snap. I could see the question working its way through her mind, trying to determine whether these two were on the level and, if they were, whether it was worth the damage they had caused just to get her attention. How idealistic was she? This was a chance to deal her biggest blow ever to Whitehall, and yet it would come about from the actions of an arsonist and, apparently, a traitor. A true idealist would kick them to the curb, but I was willing to bet she'd go through with it.

An idealist would have taken the time to question their little story about the Bonnie and Clyde of magic whipping up this plan all on their todd. Especially after her words to me about the Rider. Again, not that *I* believed he was out there, but she seemed to have a reason to believe that, and that she was taking this so well, made me wonder just how committed she was to her ideals.

As I understood it, a true idealist wouldn't have taken a deal with one devil just to bloody the nose of another, much larger one.

There are no true idealists.

'It's not as simple as just getting inside the vault,' Kaitlyn said with a frown.

'Forget simplicity,' Ania said quickly. 'We just want you on board. You'll give the movement more credence, get the last few naysayers to come round to our way of thinking, and then we'll have enough muscle to pull this off one way or the other. Ideal case, you and your guys help us pull off a sucker punch blow to Whitehall, and worst case, you at least give us the gravitas to rush a few people together to do it ourselves.'

They kept talking about the plan, about how one would even go about getting the vault open without triggering every alarm in the place, but I had stopped listening. It all seemed too good to be true. Something about the way the other warlocks were getting unruly didn't mesh with this proposed stealth mission. Why bother getting *them* on side at all?

Whitehall would never trust a warlock with tracking down anyone who attacked the vault, they'd send a sheriff to do that, and probably cull half the warlocks anyway just to make an example of them. Maybe they were a contingency plan for if things went awry? It wasn't inconceivable that the force Ania and Greg proposed to build as a contingency could have been formed of warlocks. That said, I can't speak for my contemporaries, but I'd be in a lynching mood if I found out the latest crackdown was as a result of the Bonnie and Clyde of magic getting caught doing something daft.

But then, that was a very real possibility if news of their romantic relationship got out anyway. The whole Romeo and Juliet scenario never ends well, especially when the Montagues have been kicking the Capulets in the balls for a good few years.

And whose idea was this anyway? Ania was a bright up-and-comer, no doubt about that, and she certainly had the nose to work this out for herself. The vault was hardly a secret to the warlocks, and if she'd taken the time to explain it to this Greg guy it was perfectly possible he'd turn on Whitehall. Love does tend to bring out the two-faced traitor in us all. But then, seeing his mercurial nature, I wasn't so sure.

Greg had openly said it was his idea, but then he would, wouldn't he? Getting the empowered sort to trust a government stooge, even one claiming support, was always going to be a tough sell. It would be easier if he could have you believe that it was all his idea, of course it would be. Helpfully clears away quite a bit of the distrust. That's the sort of thing a villain would do.

Beware of Greeks bearing gifts, old people and racists say, and while I don't necessarily think its fair to tar all Greeks with the Trojan brush, the message still rings true. I had no proof that what they were promising was anything other than what it seemed – a grotesquely over-confident plan – but there were too many questions and too many holes.

It changed nothing. I still had to bring the girl in.

I glanced at K. While the other three were conspiring, he had taken himself to the far side of the room and was pacing nervously. I decided to join him.

'What do you think of all this, K?' I said. 'You've been very quiet.'

Evidently he hadn't seen me approach, he had to blink a couple of times before his eyes would focus on me. 'Oh, that. It's all a bit beyond me. I just want to go back to the estate and sell what I sell, you know?'

'I can understand that.'

'The whole vault thing, I don't get it.'

'It doesn't concern you anyway,' I said, putting my hands in my pockets. 'Not until they properly bring you in. If they keep you as a broker for their fast-trackers, you might never have to deal with it.'

'And if they don't.'

'They get everyone eventually. They might give priority to the strong and the dangerous in these parts, but eventually they'll come for the weak and the quiet too. That's just how it is.'

He nodded. 'I don't trust the suit. He was one of the guys that brought me in.'

'I can't tell if he was playing a role then or doing so now,' I said. 'But in any case, I'm not happy with this.'

'I never thought I'd get to see like a proper revolutionary meeting, you know?'

'This isn't a revolution in the planning,' I said. 'It's a mistake. You need the baying masses cheering for you to lead them, that's a revolution. I don't even know what this is.'

'But wouldn't it be nice, to not have to worry about Whitehall?'

'That's how they get you,' I said quietly. 'It's the simple promises that hook you best. You don't have to think about the simple ones. They don't warn you about what else could happen. All they'll show you is the idyllic outcome, the Disney ending.'

K looked defeated. 'I don't understand.'

'Good. It's better that you don't. You might start believing, and that'll get you into real trouble. All that matters is that this right here, it's not going to be as simple as they make it seem.'

K threw up his hands in desperation and let his head fall to his chest. I felt it best to leave him to his thoughts. As much as Ania had railed on about how this whole business was for the good of empowered people and all that jazz, we didn't factor into their little conversation. It was all about them now.

I wasn't sure what to do. Now that there was the slightest glimmer of hope, I wanted nothing more than to be free. I wanted to be complete again, not to have the great gaping hole in the centre of my body that constantly reminded me of everything I was missing out on. But then, at the same time, I knew I could never have that. Not now.

Everything was so much bigger than it needed to be.

First, it had been about an arsonist, that was it. Then, the arsonist had been a warlock. Suddenly she had become a warlock with pretensions toward revolution. Now she was a warlock with pretensions towards revolution, aided by a turncoat Whitehall operative. This was spy movie bullshit.

It was all too big.

I needed to find some firm ground and clear my head. Something I could trust.

I flipped open my phone and sent a text to Charlie. The little revolutionary cadre was too busy talking among themselves to pay me much mind, and K didn't have a clue what to do. Neither did I, to be fair. But, unlike him, I could see what they were doing.

Maybe they didn't know they were doing it, or perhaps hoping I wouldn't notice, but they were trying to get me to turn on Whitehall through necessity. I wasn't about to get swept up in something, not unless I definitely meant to. I'd had my stab at politics and my hubris had nearly destroyed me, quite literally. Fuck freedom, that was just a pipe dream, a quiet life was the best I could hope for. I knew on which side my bread was buttered.

The text message was short and to the point. I needed a word with Charlie, off the record. The place would be protected to some degree, but I was mostly sure the phone would work. I'd seen the wards when we came in, scratched into the walls so gently as to be nearly indistinguishable from the various nicks and notches that had been there before. Unless you knew to look for them, and I did even before Kaitlyn had mentioned their presence.

It was classic magician overconfidence. So focused was Kaitlyn and her crew on keeping the place hidden from magic, they had totally overlooked electronics. They could blot out or divert tracking spells, or whatever they were doing to them, but they hadn't done anything to stop a simple text message from potentially cocking up everything they had planned.

This wasn't loyalty, this was self-preservation. Greg was right, I had no love for Whitehall, but he was wrong in thinking I was on the razor's edge. I could recognise desperation, and their plan reeked of it. You can't just stroll into the centre of Whitehall, bold as brass, and blow up the vault, or whatever. I wasn't about to let myself get associated with such idiocy.

And even if they did succeed, then what? A war most likely. A war fought largely by people who had no interest in fighting, all of them dragged into it by the actions of three people sat around a table right now. Whitehall wouldn't just sit idly by while thousands of bottled up magicians started relearning their craft, they'd try to cut them down as fast as possible. I'd be one of the first targets, so I'd have no choice but to embrace my magic quickly, get back to my fighting weight. And if Ania was right, if I was the symbol or the spirit of this little revolution of theirs, how long before I had people falling in line behind me without asking? I couldn't stay clean, not that way. I was already making the rationalisations for every potential kill, just so they were ready for the inevitable.

Maybe I *could* run, emigrate to America or the continent. Not the best idea, but better than getting caught up in a decidedly uncivil war. America belongs to the vampires, and they wouldn't be pleased to see an Old World magic user showing up, and the continent has its own issues. But they'd still be better than a mage war.

Again, pipe dreams.

The best thing to do was to simply prevent the war in the first place.

My phone buzzed in my hand. Charlie had replied. *Five Minutes*, it said.

CHAPTER 18

I excused myself from the group and asked them to open up the wall for me so I could have a minute to think things through. As transparent a lie as anyone as ever told, but they were far too busy scheming and plotting to care, and they knew I couldn't leave without Ania. Greg hit me with a masking spell as I left, ostensibly to hide me from any divination, but I wouldn't have put it past him to have slipped something else in there. A tether maybe, to stop me running off, or some sort of eavesdropping spell. I'd have to take the risk.

A cigarette would have been nice. Standing around waiting for a phone call is boring, as I'm sure you all know, and is the reason for which cigarettes and other smokeables were invented. Waiting for phone calls and for moments of victory. I should have bummed one from Kaitlyn on the way out, but as I didn't I would have to make do with musing.

The old me was resurfacing a little. Not the mass-murdering magic-junky me, but the overly cautious and slightly paranoid version of me that was there before the murdering took over. The version of me that liked to have an exit strategy at all times, just in case. America was looking more and more tempting, despite the whole vampire problem.

They weren't really a problem anyway, the danger was whether they would think I was. They all naffed off to the new world specifically to avoid people like me – back then the majority of magicians were drawn from the sort of people who could lay their hands on a lot of weird books: university professors. University professors and vampires don't have the best of histories. But things were different now, and vampires were very keen on the whole secret underworld deal, which you can't pull off if you're draining people dry on a regular basis.

But Whitehall would never dare step foot in America to try and track me down, and I doubt the little revolutionary cabal would be any braver. Then again, they might not have to. The locals might do the job for them.

I checked the phone. Two minutes left. It had only taken three minutes for my mind to plan out the worst possible scenario and an escape plan that hinged on making it worse. Hide from your mortal enemies in the realm of your immortal ones. Good job!

This was why I needed to talk to Charlie, to stop myself overreacting. For all I knew, this sort of idle scheming happened all the time. There's any number of threats to Whitehall and the warlocks that we never hear about because it's stamped out before it becomes an issue, and this might just be another one of them. I could do without them holding me up as an ideal just because I was an evil scumbag for a bit, though.

One minute.

You don't have a choice in this, Jameson, you've got to rat them out, I kept telling myself. I had wanted to bring Ania in from the beginning, and her twisted attempt at conveying some sort of honourable motivation hadn't swayed me. True, I now understood what she was after – sort of – but I wasn't buying it. But this was delicate, and a lot more was at stake than I had considered.

I remembered that the warlocks had walked out of the assault on K's safe house. It didn't seem like a particularly important detail, one that Kaitlyn and Ania had basically glossed over, but with context it was starting to make sense to me. You don't get civil disobedience from people who aren't, on some level, gearing themselves up towards being *uncivil.*

The increase in vaultings, the walk-outs, Ania's professed support from the other warlocks, none of this was so much part of this great plan for freedom as a dead man's switch. Ania and Greg needed Kaitlyn for their under-the-radar sabotage plan, fine, but they didn't need an army of oppressed magic users. They weren't looking to storm the building. At best, fear of a warlock uprising following the attack would lead to Whitehall capitulation, but that fear would have been there regardless and it was unlikely to work.

But if things go wrong, suddenly there's an awful lot of very angry and very insubordinate warlocks all over the country that might not be too keen on staying quiet. Ania and Greg and Kaitlyn would become martyrs. It's never a good thing to have martyrs. Yet another thing I wouldn't want to get caught up in.

My phone rang, *exactly* five minutes after receiving the text. It made me smile.

I snapped the phone open. 'You kept me waiting.'

'Shut-up. I was perfectly punctual as you well know. What's the deal, need your life saving again?'

'Something like that,' I said. 'I'm with Kaitlyn van Ives, Ania Petrova and their inside man. They're planning to take down the vault.'

Charlie hardly missed a beat. 'Way to ease me into

that information there, pal.'

'Sorry. It was either get it all out now or start having a mini freak-out.'

'No, I understand,' she said and I heard her tapping away at her keyboard. 'So what's the play?'

'I don't have an earthly idea. I was hoping you'd be able to give me some insight or advice or something.'

She paused. 'That's your serious voice. Is this a serious voice situation?'

'I'm starting to think so. Ideas?'

She tapped away at her keyboard some more. It was nervous tapping, a distinction you can only deduce after extensive phone conversations with a person permanently grafted to a computer. It's an acquired skill. 'Ordinarily I would recommend you just let Bennett know where you are and let him mop things up.'

'I was considering that...'

'But he has just spent the last half hour screaming into a radio that when he finds you he's going to tear off your head and boil it in pitch.'

'Pitch?'

'He's old school. Eames has been filling him in on your little escape.'

'That explains the pitch then,' I said and winced. Bennett was hardly a supporter of mine beforehand, but I still had confidence he'd hear me out if I could bring him Ania. It was either that, or just give up and swap sides right now.

'Which reminds me,' Charlie said. 'We're going to have to have a talk about that.'

'What, now?'

'Not *now*,' she snapped. 'But once this is sorted out. There are people here wanting a word with you about what happened to the fast-trackers guarding you. Especially the dead one.'

'Brilliant. Now I have two people who want to boil

me in pitch.'

'It's a few more than two at this end. Still, I'd worry more about Bennett.'

I was. Despite her ferocity and general hatred for me and my kind, Eames was manageable as best I could tell. She was middle management, beholden to bureaucracy and a terrifying web of red tape and guidelines that detailed exactly what she could do and when she could do it. She was a very limited threat, outside of having me harassed and bothered there was little she could do to actually *hurt* me. But Bennett was different.

Sheriffs were, despite the connotations of their name, the guys who made the rules. They were arbitrary and, as he had so eloquently put it himself, capricious. If he was out to get me, there was no way I could talk him down.

America was looking more and more appealing.

'So what are my options?' I said.

'You could bring them in yourself.'

I let slip a derisive laugh. 'There are three skilled magicians in there, Charlie. That's more than enough power to fuck-up an entire platoon, and all I have is a pistol.'

'Is it loaded?'

'Yes, but –'

'Then you've got an advantage.'

'Not really,' I said, fingering the grip of the pistol in my pocket. 'They know I've got it, your missing fast-tracker gave it to me when he showed up.'

'Huh?'

'You've got a proper traitor, like I said. The inside man.'

There was a sudden cacophony of noise from the phone, loud enough to make me recoil from the speaker. It was like an endless feedback loop, bouncing between unbearably loud and mind-meltingly shrill. It lasted for a few seconds and was then replaced by a couple of pops and a loud bang. Then silence for a few seconds.

Charlie eventually broke the silence. 'There, say that again.'

'Um...' I said. 'One of your fast-track candidates has gone rogue.'

'Which one?' Her voice was muffled slightly, a crackle on the line indicating she was outside in a strong breeze, the dull murmur of other office drones was now absent.

'I don't know. Ania called him Greg, looks pretty young. Seems to have a sharp mind.'

'Shit. Shit, shit, shit.' There was the sound of papers rustling.

'Charlie,' I said slowly. 'What are you doing?'

'Bear with me,' she said. 'One moment... There! There we go.'

'Charlie...'

'Fast-trackers aren't supposed to go rogue. They're screened. They have special, irrevocable clearances. They get magic for god's sake!'

'Well this one is having a chat with two wanted criminals about having a group of Kaitlyn's bad boys mess up the vault, so that's clearly backfired.'

Wherever she was, the wind was picking up. 'Are there any others?'

'Any other what? Treacherous fast-trackers? I don't know, I doubt it. Greg and Ania have a sort of Bonnie and Clyde vibe going on.'

'I'm going to have to tell Bennett.'

'But what about the whole head-boiling thing?'

Charlie groaned, barely audible over the wind-induced crackle. 'I'll tell him you uncovered the traitor, and his ties to the arsonist. That might get him to calm down. Maybe.'

'I hope you know what you're doing.'

There was another loud bang and the wind stopped.

'Me too. But hey, what's the worst that could happen?'

'Head. Pitch. Boiling.'

'Pessimist.'

I held the phone to my ear with my shoulder and took out my pistol. It was a revolver, of course, because if you're going to have something highly illegal it might as well look cool. Your typical semi-automatic may be more functional, but seeing as I wanted to avoid using the damn thing it was its looks that won out. Besides, six shots is more than enough to kill anything that moves. Or six anythings that move.

Kind of boned if there are seven, mind.

He'd given me my gun back. He'd gone to my house, nosed through all my stuff, and brought me my gun. Why? It was a nice thing to do, I supposed, in a really nonsensical way. Would have been nicer to have just let me go back at the office. He was inciting violence my way by giving me my gun back.

At least it was loaded. A little icon of trust, perhaps. A nod that he was trusting me not to use it on him, and that I could be trusted to join their little cadre. They hadn't given me much choice – I hadn't given myself much choice, come to think of it – but there you go. Or was there another reason?

I flicked off the safety.

'So what should I do? Hide out somewhere while Bennett raids the place?'

'No. Bennett won't buy it if you're not there when they break in. I can tell him you were holding them captive until he got there or something.'

I glanced back at the wall into the safe house. 'Think he'll believe that?'

'Hopefully. I'll put on my best Oxbridge voice, that's usually enough to sway the brass. If you could put on a show, that would really help sell it, though.'

I tapped the barrel of the gun against my temple.

People do it on TV when they're stressed, I suppose I must have acquired that little trait by cultural osmosis. 'I'm putting an awful lot of trust in you here, Charlie.'

'Oh good,' she said. 'I'm normally the one who has to say that. Nice to be on the receiving end for once.'

'Pitch. Head. *Boiling.*'

'Calm down,' she said. Her demeanour was relaxing now after having bordered on being uptight for the last few minutes. 'Just sell the story when he turns up and you'll be okay.'

'I shouldn't have to sell it, I haven't done anything wrong,' I said, and added to that quickly. 'This time.'

'Yes, well, Bennett's a dick. You either sell it or, well...'

'I guess. How long do I have?'

'Where are you?'

I looked around, as though there would be a helpful sign with the exact GPS co-ordinates on. 'I... don't exactly know. We're still in the less lovely part of town, not too far from K's squat.'

'Hang on, I'll track your phone. Should only take a minute.'

It was time to see if Greg's masking spell was just another instance of empowered hubris, or whether he had the nouse to think about the material world. I was betting on hubris, to be honest. Or arrogance. Suits are big on arrogance.

'Gotcha,' she said at last. 'You're not too far from Bennett actually, he's been combing the city looking for you all. I reckon maybe fifteen minutes to get to you, once he's been told.'

'Not long to think up a plan to sell the situation to him.'

'Oh that bit's easy!' she said. 'Just wait for them to smash the wall in and make sure your gun is trained on the terrorists when they come in. You can always put a bullet in one of them if you like. I suggest the fast-tracker.'

'That's awfully bloodthirsty of you, Charlie,' I said.

Her tone dipped for a moment. 'Well, to be frank, it's him or you. Like I said, there's a lot of people here who want a word with you about the other fast-tracker, putting down a traitor might buy you a lot of leeway, possibly even friends.'

'What do I need friends for when I've got you?'

'I can't tell if that was sweet or an insult.'

'Good.'

Neither of us said anything for a minute or two. You need to give the brain some breathing room after a masterful charm offensive on that scale, and I needed a minute to soak in the fresh air. One moment of clarity and calmness would hold me over for the rest of the day.

The sky was blue. I'd never really thought of the Humberside sky as being anything other than grey, but then I'd never really looked at it. It's always grey in my memory, just as how it's always raining. That's just the image Humberside conjures up.

But, in that one moment of peace, it was quite nice. I may have been surrounded by empty industrial buildings, asbestos riddled nightmares and an ant farm of squats, but it looked pretty nice when the sun was shining.

'Are you ready?' she said at last. 'I think I've worked out how best to tell him about all this.'

'No,' I said, slipping the gun's safety back on. 'I'm not going to kill anyone.'

'Fine then, but at least make it look like you would have done.'

I put the gun back into my blazer pocket. It sat there heavier now, as these things always do once you notice quite what they are. 'I'm very good at looking deadly. Chavs cross the street when they see me coming.'

'You make me quiver, dear,' she said as deadpan as possible.

'Make the call. I'll put on my trustworthy face.'

She hung up. I expected some sort of mocking retort, but there you go. She always finds new ways to surprise me, especially leaving such an easy insult unsaid.

I knocked on the wall and waited for it to shimmer open. There was still the possibility Greg had been listening in through some magical means, so I kept my gun close to hand. Violence was unlikely at this point – with such a short timetable before Bennett and his boys turned up, the trio would be better suited by running away – but Greg was starting to look like the sort of person who would take such a thing seriously.

As the bricks liquidised I shifted my balance, ready to jump aside just in case. I made it look casual rather than as preparation for an acrobatic dodging of arcane energy. I'm a talented guy. Fortunately, it was unnecessary.

I stepped through the wall, which was still as unpleasant as it had been the last time, and I was greeted by the three revolutionaries still chatting away about their plan. K had been the one to open the wall for me. He rolled his eyes at them as I stepped through and he closed the wall behind me.

I put an arm around his shoulder and led him to one of the corners of the room. Bennett wouldn't breach a corner. 'How did you do that?'

'Easy enough to do once you've seen it done once,' he said. 'Just needed to see which bits were the ones that wanted to move.'

'There's no magical lock on it or anything?'

'Don't be daft. It's a wall. People don't tend to go about *opening* a wall.'

'Good point.'

I sank into the corner and felt my gun clank against

the concrete floor while still in my pocket. Then my phone, in the other pocket. Two little things, suddenly so heavy.

I won't lie, I was scared. Not in a fight or flight way – my course of action was already set, there was no running from it – but the uncertainty of the outcome was troubling. This wasn't a case of getting something right and the correct result will be afforded to you, this all hinged on the mood Bennett was in when he kicked in the door. This was luck.

'What do you want, K?' I said.

'What?'

'Out of life. What do you want out of life?'

K scowled and rubbed his face. 'I'd rather not have a big personal chat right now, if it's all the same with you. Not really in the right frame of mind.'

It was a stupid thing to ask, but I had wanted something to tell me that this was the right decision. I had wanted K to say something like *just to go home and live* or something just as mundane. No grand plan, no distant ideal to uphold. Just to live. Yes, with what I was doing, he'd be living under the thumb of Whitehall, but it wasn't so bad.

But he hadn't obliged, and with nothing else to say, we sat there in silence and watched Ania, Kaitlyn and Greg discuss their plan.

Considering how simple and straight-forward it was, they were putting a lot of effort into making it appear complex. From what I gathered, their plan was simply to have Greg walk in and stick a bomb down there, in and out in about thirty seconds. But then they were trying to obfuscate this by using words like *redundancy* and *tertiary* and *contingency*. They weren't really using them correctly either, or at least not in a way that made tactical sense. They were excited, that was the important thing.

I wasn't sure how I expected them to be, not really. You always imagine a little conspiratorial meeting to be in a darkened room, possibly a cellar, yellow lamps hanging by their cables from a wood beam ceiling providing what limited light there is for the secretive cabal to read their wrinkled maps. They're probably all wearing berets too, the men possessing of pencil moustaches and the women with golden hair in perfect rings, talking in hushed whispers. Every now and then the leader of the group will slam a fist down on the table, gesticulating wildly as they discuss the plan, drawing the proposed movements onto the map with a white pencil.

Or maybe that's just me.

In any case, what you don't expect them to be doing is to be talking about the whole thing in the same sort of tone as a teenage girl might use when harping on about the guy who has asked her to prom. If you replaced every instance of the word *bomb* with *Johnny the quarterback* I doubt there would have been any tonal inconsistency. It was an oddly sobering thing to see.

It's easier to justify their upcoming incarceration and/or deaths if they *act* like terrorists. Knowing what they are doesn't help much with the sting of it all, however, if they still look like cuddly and excitable lovelies. If they'd just had the bloody berets...

I was being daft. I had to get control of myself, keep a straight face. They were the bad guys, despite how ridiculous they looked right now, and I'd known that from the beginning. Hell, bringing all three of them in would make me a hero, especially Kaitlyn. This was the sort of haul I was meant to strive for during my "career", if you could call it that, and I had been doing so in my own way. My own way, of course, being to pursue such a thing while being a total dick to my bosses, thus locking myself out of certain avenues of investigation. If anything, that would make this result even more impressive. *Look what I can do with barely any resources at all*, I would be able to crow.

Yet, I could feel myself wanting to sympathise with them, just a bit. It wasn't as if they were crazy or talking nonsense: there truly was a great deal wrong with the treatment of warlocks, but the difference was that I didn't care. What I truly didn't understand, I suppose, is why they did. Why not just keep your head down and make sure that *you* made it through okay? To hell with the rest of the "community", only you matter.

No, I had definitely made the right choice. Definitely. Right?

CHAPTER 19

I don't think I am very patient. I understand that most people believe that patience is something you can learn, and that it's a virtue and all that business, but I'm not sure those people can feel the pressure building as I do. A constant increasing compulsion to act now rather than later. Although it wouldn't be the first time I had displayed poor impulse control when compared to the populace at large, I suppose.

Here's the thing. What I had intended to do when I got back inside was to just sit quietly and wait for Bennett to come crashing through the wall with his little army. I'd draw my gun on the trio across from me, make sure I was seen to be doing my part, and ride the adequacy train all the way to safety. But it's just, the wait...

I couldn't get it to sit right.

If I was going to be serious about clearing my name and proving my worth all at once, which I certainly intended to be, then just hanging around until daddy came to my rescue seemed wrong. Realistically, things had to be comfortably wrapped up by the time the backup arrived. Or, you know, as wrapped up as I could make it so that I could legitimately claim to be the hero.

Lying is not outside my considerable skill set, as you may be aware, but if you can do the job without lying, it's probably worth doing it that way. Can't get caught out if you're actually honest for a change.

I took out my gun and looked at it. They were so caught up in what they were doing that I could have been waving it about and they wouldn't have noticed. K clocked it though, and shot me a confused look. I shook my head at him and stood up. If he stayed down, maybe I could keep him out of this.

I cleared my throat quietly. It wouldn't do to have my voice crack while I was being all authoritative. 'If I could have your attention.'

I saw Kaitlyn and Ania sigh and roll their eyes before they turned, though Greg managed to restrain himself. By the time they actually turned to look at me, it was pretty apparent they weren't actually registering what was going on.

'Don't be stupid, Parker,' Kaitlyn said. 'Really?'

'You're all nicked,' I said.

Greg raised an eyebrow. 'I told you he'd get in the way.'

'I thought we were making progress –' Ania began.

'You really aren't very good at all this cloak and dagger shit, are you?' I said. 'Did you think you were just going to turn me with a bit of rhetoric and charisma? Please.'

'Actually, they did.'

When Whitehall came for me at the height of my power, I wasn't in a position to remember much. What I do recall is that it was fast and brutal, but that memory was nothing compared to the reality of Bennett's attack.

I felt prepared. I knew it was coming, and the memory should have been enough to insulate me, but it wasn't. Shock and awe was their order of the day, it seemed, as bringing the wall down involved carving open the building at every face at once, as though some great hands had just ripped the bricks out in one fluid movement. It wasn't hard to piece together how they had affected entry to K's squat now.

It was surgically efficient, and even having been prepared for it the damn event was so spectacular that I would have been too mesmerised to act even if I had wanted to. Apparently the same was true of the trio, managing as they did to only take in the destruction rather than react to it in any meaningful way. K was the only one with the wherewithal to move, and that was just to scramble for cover.

'You're nicked!' I shouted again, trying to convince myself that I still mattered in this drama. Maybe, just maybe, that would also be enough to keep me out of the firing line. I shouted it loud enough to make my throat hurt, in the hope it would be heard over the din.

It felt like there was a lull. There couldn't possibly have been one, there really wasn't the time for it, and yet that moment after the walls fell felt like it lasted hours. I know that sounds terribly clichéd, but I can't help it, it did.

The three of them stood there, staring at me, staring at the chaos. No-one moved to fight me, no-one reacted in shock, they just stared. Blank, featureless faces staring right at me.

And then Greg cracked a smile.

Bennett and his fast-trackers fell into the room like a wave of dapper death, and for a moment I thought they would be able to take them by surprise. A bloodless, carnage-free arrest. But Kaitlyn had been more ready than she appeared. She made a gesture and the floor around them cracked and split, hurling a barrier of flame six feet high all around the three of them. Bennett's men skidded to a halt.

I heard Ania call to K, ordering him to lend her some power and quickly, and he moved. Give the boy his due, he had courage when it counted, even if it would have made rational sense to stay hidden. By the time I spotted him in my peripheral vision he was moving too fast to stop, peeling away from whatever intended hidey hole he had been heading towards. He moved towards the barrier, magic rolling off him as he charged, and I pulled back the hammer of my pistol.

I wasn't going to shoot him. I need you to know that. I could shoot *at* him, maybe, scare him into slowing down. Would that work? I couldn't kill him.

And then my pistol was gone.

I barely felt the force pull at it, though it yanked me off balance anyway. As I stumbled forward I tried to watch where the gun went, but seeing it soar through the wall of fire was not something I had anticipated. There were two gunshots before I even finished my ungainly trot forwards, and by the time I regained my balance the fire was gone.

Ania was down and bleeding, K too, and Greg had my gun trained on Kaitlyn. His little transformation was complete now. Gone was the naïve and young looking guy I had preached at, and in his place stood the hard-face, mercurial, bastard he had been hiding. Very little had actually changed, but you team up a slasher-smile with a pair of dead eyes and you might as well have a completely different face. Kaitlyn, for her part, was hiding her shock well.

Bennett's men moved, catching Kaitlyn in a moment of indecision. They came at her, arms outstretched and magic cracking between their fingers, and she whipped her head around madly trying to pick the one that was the most dangerous. It didn't seem to occur to her that the one with the gun was, at that moment, the most pressing threat.

Greg took a shot at her as well, although I'm surprised it took him as long as it did. Perhaps he was expecting her to whip up some voodoo to deflect his shots or something, I don't know. In any case, he waited for her to look away before he fired, catching her in her moment of indecision. The bullet took her in the chest and she went down. For a moment I thought he had killed her. She certainly dropped like a corpse.

As her shoulders hit the ground, however, she rolled with the force and came up again on her feet, her eyes glowing with rage and magic, ready to strike back. Bennett's men fell on her and held her down, brutally cracking her upside the head as they did so. The glow faded from her eyes and she went limp, alive at least. Greg took one last look at her, his head cocked to one side, then threw my gun back to me.

'Wasn't how I intended things to go down,' he said. 'But it could have been worse. A bit of warning would have been nice, you know. Don't worry, I'm not about to take all the credit.'

I had caught the gun by the still warm barrel and wasn't quite sure what to do with it. Part of me wanted to turn it on the smug son of a bitch, but where would that get me? Instead, I returned it to my pocket and did my best to play the dutiful employee, despite the various emotions burning through my head.

'Likewise,' I said. Nothing quite felt real, perhaps that's the point of this sort of attack, and I was having a hard time sounding anything but heavily bewildered. That was a lot of violence to deal with so quickly.

'I gave you your gun back. That should have been a clue, warlock.'

I heard feet crunching over gravel, and somehow I could tell it was the crunching of expensive loafers. It didn't really sound any different, but somehow there was an arrogance to the tread. I turned my misty gaze towards the sound and was greeted by Bennett's beaming, bearded face. The damned paperback was in his hands again.

'Well, this is certainly unexpected,' he said, gesturing at the girls and K with his book. 'Honestly, warlock, we thought you might have gone a little rogue there, what with the whole busting out of the office thing. Especially before my guy here had a chance to break you out.'

I blinked. My brain wasn't quite connected enough to my face to follow up with the obvious question, but Greg took it as read anyway and answered it. 'We were hoping you'd lead us to any stragglers. Never occurred to us that you might be, well, *loyal*. You did a wonderful job of appearing to the contrary.'

Bennett was surveying the scene, soaking up the ambience of the battlefield. His eyes were closed now and he just stood there, taking deep breath after deep breath, enjoying his victory. When he was done with that, he knelt over the bleeding Ania and laid a hand on her face. 'Is she dead?'

'I shouldn't think so,' Greg said. 'Not yet anyway. I got her pretty good, but I don't think the shot was immediately fatal. That can be remedied, if you'd prefer?'

'No,' Bennett said, stroking the girl's cheek. 'Might as well see what information we can get out of her. This level of discord in the North is unusual, maybe she can help explain why.'

'I don't think she knows anything she hasn't told me, boss.'

'That's as maybe, but it would be prudent to check nevertheless.' He turned to look at Kaitlyn. 'What about this one?'

Greg growled quietly. 'I *tried* to kill that one. Not sure what happened there.'

Bennett moved over to Kaitlyn and knelt by her this time. The book disappeared back into his jacket, and when his hand came back he slowly and meticulously slipped on a pair of purple latex gloves. He ran his gloved hands down her face and neck, over her chest, and stopped where the bullet struck. There was a spark and he whipped his hand away fast. 'Simple spell. Apparently she was ready for you.'

'I took too long with Ania and the other guy,' Greg said. 'Couldn't be helped, it wasn't like I was prepared. It was all rather spur of the moment. Frankly, if our pet warlock here hadn't tried to do his job, you might have had a fight on your hands.'

'Never mind. She's out of play, that's the important thing. Help the boys clean things up, would you? I need a word with our valiant warlock.'

Greg nodded and joined the other fast-trackers in tagging and bagging Kaitlyn, Ania and K. A pair of paramedics appeared from seemingly nowhere to tend to Ania. Poor girl had not had the best of days, although I was still hurting a little from the whole being left to cook thing. Still, I didn't need to see her bleeding all over the floor, I wasn't that vindictive.

Valiant was not a word that I felt fitted me particularly well at that moment. Even knowing it was the right thing to do, it left a sour taste. Bennett playing the big old friend card wasn't helping. His sly beaming grin was making me want to vomit, or to learn how to projectile vomit specifically so I could aim it at him without needing to be near him. He came closer, gloved hand outstretched, inviting me to shake it. In my addled state, it never occurred to me to refuse him.

He had a handshake like a vice. My knuckles popped under the pressure, but it wasn't a juvenile attempt at showing superiority like such handshakes can easily be. There was no malice in his face – outside of what was usually there at least – and no need to see me squirm. It was more indicative of a complete disregard for how I felt. He wasn't trying to hurt me, he just simply didn't care if he did. In response, I refused to shake the feeling back into my hand when he was done. It felt like the thing not to do at the time.

'Honestly, warlock, when that young lady back in Whitehall called me to relay your location, I had a hard time believing her.'

'What?' I was regaining some composure now, and along with that came a measure of defensiveness regarding Charlie's trustworthiness. I apparently managed to cram it all into a single word.

'Don't get me wrong,' Bennett said, holding his hands up. 'The young lady has a sterling record, no-one is questioning her honesty. But bonds form, relationships form, people start to get soft. You know how it is. In any case, you've got to accept that this is hardly the outcome anyone would have predicted.'

'Because I'm a warlock?'

'Well, yes. Why else?'

And that was that. The status quo reasserting itself ever so calmly. Not that I'd expected anything different, in fact I hadn't even *wanted* anything different, but it would have been nice to have at least an hour before the veiled insults started again. It was all I could do not to sigh and throw my hands up in the air in exasperation.

'Do you need me for anything else?' I said, instead. 'I have a powerful urge to be elsewhere right now.'

'In a minute,' Bennett replied, draping a giant arm around my shoulder. 'We need to have a chat about your future first. You did kill a valued colleague during your escape, after all. We can't just let that slide.'

'I really wish you would.'

'Would that I could, dear boy. But things aren't that simple.' He started to guide me through one of the holes in the wall and out into the street. 'While this whole thing is a very good way to get yourself back onside with the fellows down in Whitehall, we've still got another mess to clear up and, quite frankly, you're probably the only one to do it.'

I hung my head. '*Another* mess?'

'Same mess, different perspective, if you prefer. We know Ania has turned quite a few warlocks to her heretical cause, and we want to bring them in before they hear about this *mess*. No repercussions, nothing like that, we know how... *suggestible* your kind is. We just want you to track them down and assure them it's safe for them to come back. Consider it an amnesty.'

'Get one of your boys to do it,' I snapped. 'I've done enough for today.'

Bennett's grip tightened ever so slightly. 'If I send my guys, there is a likelihood your lot will kill them on sight. They'll be more inclined to listen to you. I'm not so blind as to have missed that tensions are rising between our camps. I'd like you to consider yourself our olive branch.'

'Excuse me?'

'We think you've earned yourself a promotion, what with helping to bring in two dangerous fugitives. Your motives might be a little off, but no-one can say you don't get results, or question your loyalty, *Warlock Supreme*.'

It was the most pretentious and downright ludicrous title I had ever heard. The sort of thing a committee would come up with when trying to decide how best to stroke someone's ego. It would be purely honorific, entirely pompous, and most likely it was something he'd invented in the last twenty seconds just to keep me sweet. No benefits, no perks, nothing but more responsibility and more problems.

But fuck it, it had *supreme* in it. It's hard not to get

excited by a job title with *supreme* in.

As far as I was aware, Whitehall had never taken the time to structure the warlock ranks. They left most of that to the warlocks themselves, figuring it was best to let the violent criminals work it all out prison-style or something. Most of the time, as I understood it, it boiled down to who had seniority and who had the biggest metaphorical penis – or, for those of you who are confused by this, the one with the best history of closed cases – and it seemed to work pretty well. Not that I ever had to engage in such things. Never have to worry about who's in charge if you're a self-styled lone wolf.

Whether having a *Warlock Supreme* was a smart thing to do, I don't know. It wasn't as if we'd needed one before. But then, we'd never had someone sowing dissent to such a level before. Things had been uneasy, but more or less stable. There had never been enough upset to form something you could describe as a faction. Maybe some oversight was necessary now. Or maybe Whitehall was just creating a new level of paranoia, more watchmen for the watchmen. If they could keep us busy fighting ourselves, there was no way we could fight them.

But at the time, I didn't care. I was still enamoured with having *supreme* in my name.

'They won't listen to me,' I said. 'No matter what my title apparently is. There's an undercurrent of individuality and resistance in every warlock, they're not going to be cowed by me just because you've told them to be.'

Bennett frowned. 'They've obeyed orders before.'

'Because they've had to, because the only alternative was death.' I pointed in the rough direction of Ania. 'She seems to have given them an alternative.'

'But not you?'

'I've... thought it through more than they have.'

'Then help them think it through, warlock.'

I am, it must be said, more tolerant of people than I might have portrayed myself as being. With the exception of myself, I do honestly try to see the good in people first and foremost. I'd just rather not interact with them if I can help it. To that end, it still leaves a sour taste when I spot a person playing on this optimism. Don't get me wrong, I'm not naïve – all it takes is one slip for me to see your true nature – but there's something decidedly reprehensible about a man who will paint a picture of you as a liberator when he's actually asking you to build a cage.

Bennett was far too good at that. It's not a skill that should come naturally, such vile manipulations, but it seemed so fluid that there didn't seem to be any way he could have learned it. He had threatened them, every warlock, by simply asking me to help them.

It wasn't as if I could turn that down now, could I?

Still, I waited until they had finished cleaning up the damage to the safe house. Everything had been so hectic for the last few hours that I needed time to reset. Watching faceless men in cheap suits drag away one corpse, one near-corpse and an unconscious body wasn't exactly soothing, but it was something I *didn't have to do,* which was enough. The smoke and dust took longer to clear than the bodies.

When I finally stepped outside, it was getting dark. I had completely lost track of the day, but I was sure it hadn't been so close to evening when they had breached the building. Had I slipped into some sort of torpor while I had been just stood there, watching? It would seem so.

I felt better, at least, more like myself again. I wouldn't have gone so far as to say the whole day had been traumatic, but at times it is easy to forget just how close to the line the default for my life is. I'd stepped over that line because of idiotic pride, nothing else, and had then been forced to scratch and claw my way back as fast as possible. Now I was back I felt better, more secure.

As long as I could avoid thinking about the things Ania had said.

CHAPTER 20

Bennett had left me a car, which at least saved me from having to wander around industrial estates in the dead of night. Humberside is not keen on street lights on its industrial estates, an expense the local government would rather reserve for the places people actually tend to want to go.

It was some new hybrid thing, the car. Bulkier than a car has any right to be, full of soft fabrics and cheap plastic trying to pass itself off as something much more upmarket. The perfect car for a government employee. All things considered, I would have rather my own car back.

And the radio didn't work.

I went home. Some of the sheen had worn off the *supreme* in my job title as I had regained some perspective, and suddenly I wasn't particularly keen on striding into a group of pissed off magic addicts and proclaiming myself to be their better, and how they should just come on back to their gilded cage. Those who didn't outright snap and start throwing spells my way would be just as likely to smash my face in for the sheer cheek of my declarations.

And honestly, I'd earned the evening off. Bennett may have intimated that he wanted me to track them down before they heard about Ania, but fuck him and his orders. If they were as well informed as he was afraid of, my turning up at all would be a symbol that something was different. Turning up *without* Ania would be just as good as hearing about her through the grapevine.

Or, whatever. I just wanted to go home and forget for an hour or two that I just got a young man killed and betrayed one of my own. Fuck you.

Whitehall really had no idea what was going on. They honestly believed that once you got your hooks into someone they would be loyal. But then there was the burning paranoia that threatened to undermine all that. It was impossible to understand their thought processes.

That's why I had Charlie. I didn't need to understand the politics of bullshit when I had her as my intermediary. She was a quite literal life-saver, and if you're going to have a jailer it might as well be a pleasant one. The Barney to my Hannibal Lecter, or something.

I got home relatively quickly. I had driven slightly slower than usual to give myself a little extra reaction time. I didn't feel tired, but considering my day, I wasn't going to take any chances. I knew I wasn't all there, at any rate. There was little traffic, so it was an unnecessary precaution in the end.

My car had been returned to my house, left upside down in front of my door like a crinkly obelisk, my meagre lawn looking worse for wear as a result of whatever perplexing method they had used to get it into place. The neighbours had never been fans of my lawn anyway, at least now they had good cause to dislike it. Not that it bothered me. I barely noticed having a lawn at the best of times, and I was daring them to pick today to try and have it out with me.

All in all, everything was the same as it was when I left it. For some reason I had expected it to look different, as if the knowledge that Greg had been rooting around inside my home would give it some sort of burglary-induced glow. Perhaps that was what the car was, a little message from the sinister fast-tracker that he knew where I lived. A little extravagant for my taste. Governments were supposed to be good at cover-ups, which I don't think is a term that includes dragging a wrecked car onto someone's lawn. I suppose they knew that no-one would really care what was going on in my life – I'd long theorised that if I died in my sleep my neighbours wouldn't notice until my house was so full of flies the windows would burst outwards – but it was the principle.

I tiptoed around the wreckage and up to my door. It was ajar. It was closed when I left, I was sure of that, as I'd heard the damn thing slam shut. I drew my gun. Perhaps Greg had just forgotten to close the door after he retrieved my gun, but with today's luck I wasn't willing to take any chances.

Pushing the door open, I slowly entered my house, muttering and swearing under my breath as I did so. I had considered the stealthy approach, but I wasn't in the mood for it. It had been a long day. Trading the element of surprise for pure British rage – the sort kept barely contained and liable to cause an embolism – seemed more prudent. I may even have started increasing in volume as I cleared each room, being just shy of shouting by the time I reached my bedroom.

There was a silhouette against the window across from my bed. These things are always silhouettes, it's like intruders just gravitate towards any source of light that can silhouette them for maximum dramatic effect. I was immune to such things at this point, however, my complete frustration at the day having taken over. I just wanted to rest for the night, to be allowed a couple of hours of downtime.

'What do you *want?*' I whined. I'm not too proud to admit it, I was whining. 'Can't I just get some sleep without some mysterious stranger breaking into my house?' I pulled back the hammer on my pistol. It's not a loud noise, but it has a way of cutting through all others and jumping right into the forefront of your mind. 'Go on, then. You might as well get your cryptic threat out the way so I can go to bed before it is officially tomorrow.'

'I've been driving for hours, you idiot. You're not the only one that's exhausted,' said the silhouette. 'Do you know how long it takes to drive from London to Humberside without a sat nav? Too bloody long, that's how long.'

'Charlie?' I said and I reached over to flick on the light.

'Hello.'

She was shorter than I had expected, but everything else seemed to fit with my mental collage, with some room for scientific error. Thin, dark hair that fell in line with her jaw, one of those upper class faces that has exactly the right amount of angles, the small and slightly upturned nose, nothing surprising. Her grey eyes were marred by the onset of black bags underneath, still in their infancy but noticeable, and her eyebrows were peaked as though trying to hold her eyes open.

I gently uncocked the gun and tucked it away in my blazer again. Charlie smiled at me and gingerly sat on the end of my bed. It had been freshly made, which was odd seeing as I hadn't had time to observe the correct bedroom etiquette when I had left that morning.

'Isn't this a massive break in protocol?' I said.

'What?'

'You being here. I thought you were supposed to stay in Whitehall, I was supposed to go wherever the stuffed shirts told me to go, and never the twain shall meet lest it disrupt the perfect efficiency of the British government.'

She laughed. It took away some of the tiredness. 'Ordinarily, but something is going on and I don't trust Whitehall to –'

'There's a shock, Whitehall being less than trustworthy.'

'Shut your face, you,' she said with a smile. 'Not everyone there is a baddie, you know.'

'No, it's just the system itself that I don't quite get on with. But I'm sorry, I shouldn't interrupt.'

'Why break the habit of a lifetime?'

I sat on the bed next to her and flopped back so I could stare at the ceiling. 'Because I am a mature, responsible adult and I am trying to grow as a person.'

I could feel the look that earned even though I couldn't see it. 'Oh, well, you've *totally* convinced me. *Anyway*, the important thing is that there's something going on in Whitehall that they're not telling me, and I don't like it.'

'Do they usually tell you everything?'

'No, of course not. But there are *ways* of not telling someone everything. It's very rare that I'm in a position where I can't learn something I'm not supposed to know, even if it takes me a while. There's always a way. But a few hours ago I hit a black hole.'

'A black hole? You mean something you can't get any information on?'

'Exactly. Normally all the hidden information is covered up and disguised as other things so people will only be able to find it if they know exactly what they are looking for. There's never been a noticeable void in the data before.'

'Well what is it?'

'*I don't know*, that's the point,' she said slowly and flicked the side of my head. I sat up.

'Well if you don't know,' I said, trying to work my head around it. 'How did you find it?'

'I was looking into that rogue fast-tracker of yours –'

'Not as rogue as I thought, apparently.'

'Apparently not,' she continued. 'But all we have on him in the file is his name. No recruitment data, no assignment history, nothing. Just the name Greg Wild.'

I hung my head. 'Does this mean he's a spy then?'

She made a look of disgust. 'A spy? Get real. You don't go deleting all the background information of a spy. You need to know everything you can about them just in case. By their very nature, you can't trust a spy.'

'So what *is* he then? Why scrub out all that data?'

Charlie rolled her eyes at me and clapped her hands to her face to muffle a scream. 'What part of *I don't know* are you finding so hard to understand, Parker? There is a *void* in the *data*.'

'But what does that *mean?*' I said, fighting back a smile.

She groaned, jumped to her feet and stormed to the far side of the room. Then she turned and stormed back towards me. 'Are you being this stupid on purpose?'

'A bit.'

I watched her face as I said this, and it was exquisite seeing her try not to laugh. She wanted to be annoyed, but she just couldn't hold onto the anger. She had been expecting an argument, gotten herself all geared up for it, and then I'd undercut her with a charming, boyish jape. The amusement bubbled through the rage and therefore did hilarious things with her face, like it was a zoetrope animation.

Eventually she couldn't fight it any longer and she practically sighed into a smile. 'I really bloody hate you.'

'No, you don't.'

'No, I don't.'

'Can I ask you a question?' I said, hoping it wouldn't bring the tired anger back.

'Is it a serious question or a stupid one?'

'Serious. I hope.'

'Then yes, you may.'

'The whole void thing doesn't really explain why you're here.'

She sat back down. 'It does if you have a bit more context. I guess you're used to dealing with Whitehall as a big mountain of suspicion and distrust, but I'm not. They're actually quite nice to people who aren't ticking time bombs of arcane horror, most of the time. They've never been *sinister* before.'

'We'll have to beg to differ there.'

'Listen to what I'm saying. They've not been sinister to the people they actually like, until recently. It's not just the warlocks that are getting the thin end of the wedge now, they've been canning operators like me for months. On a much slower rate than they've been vaulting warlocks, and not actually killing them, but anyone they can't trust completely is getting the sack.'

'They're up to something,' I said, worried.

'So it seems,' she said, echoing my worry. 'I don't know what it is, but when they find out I've stumbled into a the black hole in the files, I'm willing to bet I'll be right at the top of the redundancy list.'

'What loyalty and trust you have in your bosses.'

'Maybe you're rubbing off on me,' she said. There was a pause. 'Don't.'

'Don't what?'

'I could feel you thinking it. Don't try and turn that into a euphemism.'

'Would I do such a thing?'

'Yes!'

We laughed again. It seems that most of our interaction boils down to laughing – either at something or at each other – but what can I say, we're bloody hilarious. They are meant to team you up with a handler you can trust, and who you don't hate. Sometimes, it seems, they give you one you actually *like*. Things suddenly seem a lot less real when you've got someone you can laugh with.

'If I had to put money on it,' she said. 'I'd be inclined to think that Wild was up to something, and they wanted it kept hidden.'

'You mean, besides feeding Ania Petrova the perfect plan to topple the Whitehall regime?'

She blinked. 'I beg your pardon?'

'That's what he claimed, anyway. He said he'd approached Ania with a plan to take out the vault. Maybe he dripped a little more poison in her ear, I don't know, but that seems to have been the core of her rebellion. All the fires were just a means to an end, to draw Kaitlyn van Ives.'

'So Wild's, what, an *agent provocateur?'*

That would make a certain kind of sense. He played the part very well, and until he revealed himself, there was no way I would have believed it. So maybe not a spy, but something just as insidious. But if that was true, Whitehall was actively trying to entrap its warlocks now. That was a big accusation. Not something to let take hold in my head lightly.

'We can't know that, not yet,' I said. 'But it's a possibility, I guess.'

'I hate my job.'

We didn't talk for a while. I went back to staring at the ceiling and she sat next to me in silence, tapping away on a smart phone. It wasn't awkward, although such situations often are. There was no drive to rekindle the conversation immediately – both of us knew it would spoil the good mood we'd put ourselves in. So, for a while at least, we sat in silence and enjoyed the good mood, for as long as we could let it last.

'Bennett wants me to try and talk down the other warlocks,' I said at last.

'I know, I gave him the idea.'

I sat up. 'What?'

'I thought it was time to start cashing in on some of this trust I've earned over my years at Whitehall,' she said, not looking at me. 'And as you are the most level-headed warlock I know, I figured you could do with an opportunity to prove your worth to the higher-ups.'

'You think I'm level-headed?'

'I don't know many warlocks, it's a small pool. Besides, you're level-headed enough once people know to look past your crust of idiocy. For a start, you recognise how dangerous magic can be. You'd be surprised how few warlocks are able to do this.'

'Well you stopped most of them before they could see it first hand. Not very many went the whole anti-Christ route before you caught up with them, and even less survived long enough to be pressed into service.'

'I know. A lot of people don't realise how valuable your insight into that side of magic actually is. And you don't exactly make it easy for them to put up with you.'

I decided to take that as a compliment. I think you'll agree it says a lot of positive things about my character. 'My charm can be somewhat overwhelming to some, it's true.'

'If the last few weeks have taught me anything it's that some day soon, we're going to end up separated, and it's looking more likely that I'll get sacked before you get vaulted.' She rubbed her eyes. 'I've developed an odd attachment to you. I don't want to see you getting vaulted as soon as you don't have me to protect you.'

I puffed out my chest, all proud and cocksure.

'Madam, I hardly think I need protecting by you.'

'Don't be a dick, you know you do. If you knew how many times I'd stopped them vaulting you –'

'All right, don't go bringing facts into this. You'll tarnish my ego.'

'Please. Nothing's going to make a dent in that bloody thing.'

I chose to ignore her point because, as it stood, it wasn't something I was quite ready to accept. Granted, I knew that she had saved me from the bureaucratic menace of Whitehall more than once – she had hardly been shy in telling me – but it never really registered as an intervention on her part. It was just the status quo, the default setting for my life. I'd be annoying or overstep my boundaries and Charlie would clean up after me, no questions asked. *That's how things were.*

To have that suddenly taken away would be jarring to say the least. It was best to just pretend that wasn't a possibility for now, file it away as a joke or a quip, a dig at my playful exuberance.

'So, what? I play nice for a while, play up to the whole *Warlock Supreme* thing and get the others to come in quietly?' I said.

'That's the best idea I have,' she said as she laid a hand on my shoulder. 'The agitator isn't a threat any more, but her ideas are still floating around in their heads. They need to see reason. Especially if Whitehall is going down the agent provocateur route. They at least deserve a warning.'

'And what if reason is why they are doing this in the first place? Petrova might have been thinking a little too romantically about things, all revolution and smash the state, but it's not like she doesn't have a point about a few things. What if I can't talk them down?'

Her hand squeezed my shoulder. 'I have to believe you can.'

I reached up and placed my hand on hers. 'I *am* amazing, aren't I?'

She laughed and, slowly, we both lay down on the bed.

CHAPTER 21

Charlie was gone by the time I woke up, but she had been kind enough to leave me with some cold, un-buttered toast and a cup of tea with a weird skin forming on the top. I guess it's the thought that counts.

It was amazing how a bit of company can defuse a mood. I'd been bordering on misanthropy after the events of the day before, but just having someone there to chat to had straightened me out, or at least given me the mental energy to shut out the pain until I had the time to deal with it. Or maybe it had been the sleep that had done that.

It was hardly a full night's sleep, but it was enough to get me through the day. After the day before, every moment of rest was divine, so even without my full twelve hours, I was much more like my old self. Which meant I was thinking again.

I had agreed to everything so quickly that I hadn't actually thought about how I was going to do it. Oh, sure, I'll bring in a group of guys that have been whipped into near frenzy, who spent their lives trying to avoid being found, who are mad, bad and dangerous to know, as the saying goes. *Of course* I can do that. They don't call me Warlock Supreme for nothing, right?

Except no-one but Bennett calls me that, and only because he wants something. But, hey, it wasn't as if it *couldn't* be done – every single warlock had been caught before, after all – it just meant I'd actually have to *do* something.

What I didn't want to do, I realised as I was crunching on the toast, was sift through hundreds of bloody case files to try and find some common ground between god knows how many warlocks. It wasn't just laziness either – seriously, it wasn't – as leaving them alone for too long would just let Petrova's sedition build to a crescendo. Get enough scared and thoughtful people into one place and leave them to simmer and it won't be long before something gives. Mob mentality or whatever you want to call it. Most likely I was overreacting, but in this case it was better to be a pessimist.

They were loyal to Petrova, but they weren't stupid. You don't get stupid warlocks, they're the ones that turn down the offer of employment or blow themselves up before they even get that far. With that in mind, they wouldn't go far and any response to what went down yesterday would be subtle and swift and well thought out. At the very worst, they'd be planning it now, so I still had time.

I needed to chat with the conspirators, see if they'd organised any other safe houses or hideaways. I could have called the office and set up an interview, but it was still early, barely past seven. There would be someone there, and I certainly *could* have called them to organise the interviews, but I just wasn't feeling it. Besides, Kaitlyn would be locked down so tight that even if I *did* get to talk to her, she'd give me the cold shoulder out of spite and I wasn't even sure if Ania Petrova was still alive or not.

That left the inside man, who was in need of a little re-education when it came to our relationship. A man as comfortable with slipping into whatever social role required for his job as Greg Wild, was not someone you wanted thinking he had one up on you. So I did call the office, but only to find out where he lived.

The smart money would have been on giving him a wide berth. More likely than not, the whole agent provocateur thing was just myself and Charlie jumping to conclusions, but just in case it would perhaps be better not to kick the hornets' nest. If he was trying to goad warlocks into situations that would get them struck off, it wouldn't do to piss him off and make myself a target.

And yet, if you've learned anything about me over these last few hundred pages, it's that I am not a particularly smart person.

He had caught me unawares, tricked me, and in turn had made me look a fool. Hell, I'd been so bewildered that I had actually bordered on being genuinely subservient. While that hadn't really registered at the time, it was there in my head, blaring like a big old neon sign of self-disappointment.

Maybe I had just woken up in a bit of a difficult mood. Perhaps my night with Charlie had given me back some of my devil may care attitude that had been slowly draining after my last stupid decision, I don't know. The important thing is, to hell with being smart. I was going to storm right into that duplicitous little turd's house, stare him straight in the face, and make a goddamned mistake.

I took the car Bennett had left me, of course. It had a wonky, hastily installed sat nav system to try and guide me to Wild's place, which was still better than trying to puzzle out the way myself. Even with technology working against me, I still managed to get there early enough to be an annoyance.

Leaning on the doorbell, I checked to make sure my gun wasn't showing. Like I've said, I'm not keen on the thing, but considering what my business of the day was going to be – and the events of the day before – I was starting to get the feeling that it was a necessary evil. Better to have it and not need it, as they say. It also helped to keep me calm when the snarling man-beast finally opened the door.

Perhaps "snarling man-beast" is a little unkind, but that's what a hangover does to a person. Wild smelled like an up-town bar – the whiff of liquor somewhat masking cheap perfume that was meant to smell expensive, the sort worn by the kind of girls employed in such places to *entertain* VIPs – and his face wasn't quite sitting as snugly to his skull as it had the day before.

He looked me up and down with watery, bloodshot eyes and tried to make himself personable again. On anyone else, even attempting such a thing would have just made them look more pathetic, but Wild made a good show of it. He wasn't fooling anyone, but he came closer than I would have expected.

'Do you know what time it is?' he said, taking extra time to make sure his words didn't slur.

I shot him a huge grin. 'Of course I do, dear sir. It's *the morning*,' I said with great gusto.

I've found that most people don't know how to react when you are exuberant towards them so early in the day. They almost always want to punch you, but the brain isn't quite awake enough to convey that message to the limbs, and a sort of social redundancy kicks in where they are forced to replace anger with confusion and politeness. But then maybe that's just the people I run into.

In any case, as he grunted and ushered me inside, I found myself regretting having not worn brighter colours today. Wild was having a hard enough time dealing with the pinstripe on my blazer, but if I'd coupled it with an eye-gouging shirt his face would have been delightful. Hell, even my bling would have been nice, just for the childish glee of reflecting sunlight into his face, but I'd stashed that at home seeing as most of it was in need of a top-up from the friendly neighbourhood enchanter.

'What do you want, Parker?' He said. There was a drink of some kind gently steaming on a bureau just inside the door and he scooped it up and took a large swig. He kept walking as he did so, beckoning me to follow him.

'I just need to pick your brain about a few things. Bennett wants me to track down the other warlocks and get them to come in without incident. Seeing as you were doing what you were doing, I was wondering if you had any leads.'

He led me into the kitchen. It was huge, marble everywhere and those sleek cupboards that always looked unused, no matter how much cooking you do. Seemed fitting for a Whitehall employee. 'I don't know. Maybe. What sort of leads?'

'Safe houses, meeting points, anything that will give me somewhere to start looking.'

He groaned. 'Read the reports, man. I'm too tired to recite every damn thing to you. That's what reports are for.'

'Reports are dull. It's so much more fun to go straight to the source. Besides, I'm sure you saw a lot of things that didn't make it into the report, right?'

His face re-attached itself just a little. 'What's that supposed to mean?'

'Nothing suspicious or anything. I was just thinking, you know, that maybe there were some insignificant details that you may have omitted from the official record. Just in case.'

He stared at me as he finished what was left of his

drink. It was a gamble on my part, but one that stood to reason. I had no cause to believe he had kept anything hidden, other than the fact he was a professional spy and that, by definition, he dealt in secrets. Besides, I don't care how committed you are to your job, *everyone* leaves things out of reports. No-one wants to write them, no-one wants to read them, and as long as they are serviceable you won't get any blowback from leaving things out just so you can submit the thing.

On anyone else, you play the whole *I know you know something you don't want anyone else to know* card – or the IKYKSYDWAETK card, if you're feeling flash – to unsettle them and shake something loose. That wouldn't work with Wild, but then it wasn't supposed to. I wasn't trying to coerce him into anything, just to kick the foundations out of whatever understanding he had of me and to be a bit of a nuisance. Maybe he would think I was an idiot now, or a man getting in over his head, or perhaps I'd strike gold and actually scare him. Whatever he thought, he couldn't be sure now, which was the point. I don't like people having the measure of me, and the best way to avoid that is to act inconsistently around them.

Also, sometimes, it makes them tell you what you want just so you'll go away. Which is nice.

'I didn't interact much with the warlocks, Ania wasn't keen on us mixing,' he said when he was finally done drinking. 'She said that they wouldn't understand why she trusted me.'

'Fancy that.'

His expression warmed a little. 'She's a pretty girl, that one. Not quite as smart as she thinks, mind. If she'd listened to her advisers a little more, she wouldn't be in the hospital right now. You can't con an honest man.'

'Her advisers?'

He rubbed his hands over his face. 'Yeah, she sort of

tried to set the thing up like a pyramid scheme. I mean, she started setting all this up before I got involved but it was very grass roots stuff. Things got a little more real once I charmed my way in. I can't be sure on the specifics, but from what I saw, Ania only directly talked to maybe three warlocks. Those guys went and got the rest involved. At least that's what she told me.'

'Do you have names?'

'I did, never bothered to make a note of them. She was the ringleader; as far as I was concerned the rest of you would just fall in line once we took down the only one with backbone.' That wasn't delivered like an insult. It hit like one, but there was something else behind the words I couldn't place.

Either way, the politeness was wearing off. 'Wasn't worth the effort, right?'

'Exactly. You lot have always done what you're told, just so happens that Ania could play on her perceived esteem amongst the brass up in Whitehall and use that to skew the hierarchy a little. We don't need you to bring them in, they'll revert to type anyway like the good little pets they are. It's their nature, apparently.'

'I can't tell if you're full of shit or so scared at what they might do that you're trying to convince yourself you're right.'

He was properly awake now, his face firmly re-attached, and the arrogance was oozing from his pores again. He'd started holding himself like a politician, which hardly helped matters, and gave his voice the booming resonance of the professionally condescending. 'Or I'm right, and by this evening they'll have all come back to work. What else are they going to do, grow some balls and fight for a change?'

I knew that I shouldn't rise to it. I'd spent too much time recently dwelling on the darkness that lives in the heart of man and all that business, using it as a weapon to get people to shut up. It was running the risk of being devalued. But he was talking as though warlocks were harmless, which was hubris of the highest order.

I wanted to address that hubris head-on, to smash in his smug face with a mallet made of threats. But I'd been doing that too much lately. I had to stop using the memory of who I no longer wanted to be as a tool when people started to annoy me. It was opening doors, or it would open doors, in my head that I wanted kept firmly closed. It would be far too easy to start believing my own hype. Again.

Besides, I was here to rattle him, not be rattled. This was supposed to be me bringing my A-game, rattling his cage and frustrating him into giving me what I wanted. Fight the power, man! Yeah!

'Humour me,' I said, forcing down the venom. 'Worst that happens is you send me on a wild goose chase. I would have thought you'd jump at the chance to make me waste my entire day.'

He waved a hand at me dismissively. 'If you want to waste your time having a chat with these cretins, then fine. It's not as if you have anything better to do, is it?'

'Who, me? I just make the coffee, and it's not like anyone down at the office is going to be thirsty today.'

'You are a very irritating person, Parker,' he said with the sort of insight you tend to see reserved for psychics. I don't know how he did it.

I tried to slap him in the back, but he recoiled and slowly shuffled his chair away a little. Like a pro, I modified the aborted back slap into a joyful clap of understanding. 'Then give me something I can work with and I'll piss off for you.'

'You'd have to talk to Ania. I don't know anything.'

'She's still alive then?'

'Last I heard. But then, I was very drunk when I got the call, so I can't be sure. They've got her under guard at the hospital, I believe. Shut down an entire wing just for her. The local MP is kicking up a fuss, so all the guys at the office were having a right laugh.'

'Reckon they'll let me in?'

His laugh contained so much derision that I could feel a chunk of my self-worth trying to detach. It felt decidedly similar to getting a mouthful of something stuck in your throat. 'Good god, no! They're not letting anyone in but the under-secretary and myself. I was given special permission on account of my sterling work being the reason she was there in the first place. But, I suppose I can call ahead, have them let you in. I did say I wasn't going to take *all* the credit.'

'That *would* make me go away.'

'Fine. But not until you leave. I'm not having you hover over me.'

I gave him a crooked nod. 'As you wish.'

He escorted me to the door, trying as he might to resist the urge to take me by the arm and forcefully drag me out of the place. It was a near thing, I could see his hand twitching. When we got to the door, he waited for me to step out and then hurriedly closed it behind me. He managed to stop short of making it bang.

That wouldn't do at all. I knelt down and lifted the flap covering the letterbox. 'Thank you!' I shouted through the gap and slammed the flap down hard. My last little malicious act.

At least I wouldn't have to go into the office, so my reasoning hadn't been flawed. No sir. But then, I wasn't exactly keen on talking to Ania directly. Not that I had much experience in the matter, but it stood to reason that she wasn't going to be pleased to see me. At least I hadn't been the one to shoot her, that had to stand for something. It didn't make my gun feel any lighter, but that was because I was attuned to a melodramatic sense of guilt rather than any actual responsibility, as I saw it.

As I got back into the car, I considered calling Charlie to talk things out. The phone was in my hand before I thought better of it. Didn't want to start looking clingy. I didn't *need* to call her, but then I never did, just another strand in my web of addiction. Or something like that. I understand these are the sorts of things addiction counsellors say.

In any case, while Wild had told me that Whitehall had cleared out an entire hospital wing, I hadn't quite prepared myself for the actuality of the situation. For some reason, I had imagined it as being a couple of burly policemen outside one of those swing doors that hospitals have, all chins and chests, turning people away with a cockney grunt. No, I don't know how my imagination comes to these conclusions either.

What I was presented with was quite an intimidating scene. Enough men in suits to fill a bespoke army were milling around outside the hospital, and littered the hospital corridors like giant ants in ties. It was really disconcerting trying to navigate my way around them. At least when I reached the entrance to the wing they had appropriated, the actual guards sort of conformed to my expectations, although they were fast-trackers rather than cockney coppers.

They let me in without incident, and the other side of the door was somehow even worse despite having a distinct lack of suits. Perhaps that was what made it worse, the emptiness of the whole place. I could hear the echoes of the equipment from what I could only assume was Ania's room, doctor's voices tagging along too, but it was some ways inside the wing. It gave me time to put on my brave face.

There are two ways to handle a long walk down an empty, echoing hallway. The first is to be shit scared, which is the standard and most natural reaction. We as a species didn't create the notion of things being too quiet for nothing, and big empty spaces that should be full of people always come across as a trap. That heightened awareness can be helpful if you are actually *in* a trap, but can put you on the back-foot if you need to display some authority.

I was assuming I was going to need authority, because the right kind of arrogance is always necessary when dealing with doctors. This would mean I would have to adopt the other approach to such hallways: co-opt the fear.

That moment of footsteps slowly coming down the hallway, owner unseen, is ingrained into the subconscious as being just as terrifying as being in an empty room that shouldn't be. You see it used in films to build tension, and while it doesn't tend to work to quite the same level in the real world it still has its place. But to achieve this you have to own your echoes, to stride so confidently that your footsteps carry properly. They need to be regular, loud, powerful steps without any deviation. The moment you scuff a step, that mystique and tension is gone, which is why you can't do it if you're busy being terrified of all this unsuspecting *space* around you.

By the time I reached Ania's room, however, I was getting fed up with striding about confidently and was slipping back into my normal walk. They'd put her so far back in the wing that it took a couple of minutes to even pinpoint the sounds properly, let alone reach the room. My echoing footsteps hadn't managed to instil in me quite as much fake authority as I had wanted, but it served well enough to let me keep a straight face when I finally saw Ania.

I only knew that I was looking at Ania because no-one else in the building would have needed that many tubes. For a minute I was worried she was being cocooned by some hideously surgical spider, entombed in a web of gauze and bandages. She was unrecognisable, but then most people are when their mouth is stuffed full of pipes.

It had only been one bullet.

The doctor and nurse in the room were far too busy doing *something* to pay any attention to me. There were so many machines to deal with, all the various beeps and boops of whatever weird science was keeping Ania alive, that while they acknowledged me they didn't bother to challenge me in any way. The nurse took the time to indicate that I stay in the doorway, and I obliged. There was no arguing with that.

Ania *was* alive at least, I could determine that much. She wasn't exactly in any position to furnish me with the info that I needed, but it was nice to see her alive nonetheless. Not that I want to get all emotional and weepy about the whole thing, but it is nice to see someone not die, you know?

I'm not sure how long I watched them work on her and the machines. They didn't really seem to be doing anything, although they gave off the impression they were, but nothing seemed to be changing so it was hard to tell. Perhaps they were all about keeping her stable. I wouldn't want to second-guess them. Whatever they were, or *weren't,* doing, they were doing/not doing it with captivating efficiency.

There was the spectre of a shout from down the hall, and even though I heard it I didn't have it in me to react. It took the sound of footsteps to rouse me, and even then it was mostly from jealousy. These were good, old-fashioned, purposeful footfalls, slamming down on the squeaky hospital floor at a deliberate pace just shy of a run. They were followed by a pair of shouts, but they were dropping behind the footsteps.

He made an impression as he stormed past me. So much so that the nurse didn't feel the need to warn him to stay out of their way. He just zipped ably between the doctor and nurse as they flitted about, dropping to his knee beside Ania and taking her hand in his. As soon as his fingers wrapped around her, the fast-trackers that had been guarding the door caught up.

They stopped in the doorway and nervously ushered me out into the corridor. I politely indicated I would be staying where I was and they decided to do what most people do when I am in such a position. They talked over me.

'Sir, please,' one of them said. 'You're not authorised to be in here. We'll have to ask you to leave.'

'You've asked,' the man replied, his voice low with grief. 'I've declined.'

'We'll drag you out if we have to,' said the other fast-tracker, garnering a shocked look from the other.

'If that's what you have to do,' came the reply from the man.

'You're not giving us much of a choice, *warlock*,' the fast-tracker said, and again his partner gave him a look, this time followed by a swift slap on the arm.

'Be careful what connotations you put on that word, boy. I'm not in a tolerant mood right now.'

And then I felt it, the steady surge of power being summoned. Call me old fashioned, but I'm not one for a magical fracas in a place of healing. Especially not when I might get caught in the crossfire. So I played diplomat.

Stop laughing. I can hear you doing it.

'Fellows, can we just cool this down a little?' I said, stepping between the two parties and blocking the door. 'He's not doing any harm. Let him be, eh?'

'Shut it, Parker. This is none of your business,' snapped the fast-tracker that had proven he had a bigger ego than his brain could handle.

'Everything's my business; I'm nosy,' I said.

The griever's shoes squeaked as he stood up behind

me. 'Parker? You're Jameson Parker?'

I looked back at him over my shoulder. 'One argument at a time, okay, chap?'

He was on me the moment I turned away. 'I'LL KILL YOU, YOU SON OF A BITCH!'

The capital letters were justified.

CHAPTER 22

I wasn't sure what hit me harder: the man who launched himself at me or the marble floor smashing into the back of my skull. I do know it was the latter that filled my mouth with the metallic taste of blood, which was lovely.

The landing had knocked me silly, and there was little I could do as he bore down on me, his hands closing around my throat. Dark eyes, a rough beard, nicotine stained teeth, all of them right in my face as I gasped for breath. What the hell were the suits doing, just watching?

Maybe they had been stunned into silence, or were just cowards, but they did eventually involve themselves. They grabbed the man by the shoulders and tried to haul him off me, but his hands had clenched too tightly. I looped my arms inside his and tried to pry him loose, but even with the suits' help he wasn't about to let go.

'God *dammit*, Renner! Let him go!' one of the suits yelled.

'No!' the man screamed into my face, his eyes never

leaving mine.

'Hit him,' said the other suit. 'Knock him out or something!'

There was a thwack and the man blinked for a moment. His grip slackened a little and he turned away. My vision swam as I sucked in what air I could, but I could still hear perfectly fine. The growl the man gave at the suits, beyond rage, beyond wrath, and their footfalls in the corridor as they ran away, promising to return with reinforcements.

I couldn't move. Nothing worked. What the blow to the head hadn't shut down, the lack of oxygen had gotten to, and my body was a dead weight. It was all I could do not to let my eyes roll into my head and black out. And then his face was back, not as close as before, and it was less wrathful.

I felt a firm hand grab mine and start to hoist me up. 'How's your head?'

'What?' was my cutting, vicious retort.

He snapped his fingers in front of my eyes. 'Sorry about that. Didn't think I'd hit you quite so hard. Thought you'd be expecting it.'

'Who –' I tried, but my head was shutting off the bit of my brain that dealt with words so that it could shunt power to the bit that stopped me vomiting. It was touch and go.

'Paul Renner,' he said. His voice was still gruff without the rage in it, like Tom Waits with throat cancer, but it was preferable to his previous tone regardless. 'I'm guessing you've read about me.'

'You brought Ania in the first time.'

'Yeah. Now be quiet for a minute. I've got a few things you need to hear, and the kids will be back with competent people soon.'

I found the wall and tried to lean on it in a way that didn't betray my condition. The nurse and the doctor had vanished, probably during the scuffle, and the room seemed considerably larger without them skittering about. Or maybe that was just the concussion I was definitely self-diagnosing myself with.

'You're not going to kill me?'

Renner scratched his beard. 'No. The way I see it, this wasn't your doing. It's been building for a while. Ania trusting that stuffed shirt from Whitehall got her into this mess. But there are things going on in the North that laid the groundwork for this to happen at all, and it might help you to know about them.'

'That's charming, but could you not have done it in a way that didn't send me all loopy? I feel like I'm going to vomit out of my ears in a minute.'

He took me by the arm and gently led me to the side of Ania's bed. I perched on a corner of it, which was preferable to the wall. 'I need to know why you're here,' he said.

'Why?'

'Because I need to know whether to change my decision on not killing you. How hard-line are you?'

I winced. 'Enough that I want to find her soldiers, not so much that I want to see anyone else dead.'

'Her soldiers?'

'The other Humberside warlocks. I thought she might be willing to tell me where they're hiding.'

'She doesn't know,' he said with certainty.

'With respect,' I said, slowly and carefully. Didn't need more hands at my throat. 'But you've barely had contact with her since you brought her in. I'm not inclined to believe you are an authority on what she does or doesn't know.'

The dark eyes twinkled. 'It wasn't *all* an act just now, you know.'

'Excuse me?'

'If I haven't been in contact with the girl, explain to

246

me why I'm here. Explain to me why it's taking a herculean effort not to break down in tears right now. Hell, explain to me how I even heard she was hurt.'

He had a point. 'You have a point.'

He wiped a tear from his eye and I pretended I didn't notice. It's the polite thing to do for those who are trying not to grieve, and I knew that better than most. 'We've been in contact constantly. She needed my help with assimilating to the life, and I needed to be sure she was okay. What De Sade did to her...'

'De Sade was a monster. You'll get no argument from me.'

He produced a self-rolled cigarette from a pocket and started idly rolling it over his knuckles. 'It was worse than the files say. They're very... clinical. They don't go into the details. Just the cold hard facts, so the secretaries that have to file the things don't piss their knickers.'

'Charming.'

'Whatever. I needed to know she was surviving, getting better.'

'And the coup?'

'I wanted no part of it, but she kept pushing. The... freedom of the North was rubbing off on her, I guess. Before here, she'd only worked in the thoroughly controlled South and what bits of the North Whitehall had already instilled some semblance of order,' the cigarette flipped between his thumb and forefinger and he reached up to tuck it behind his ear. 'She said that she hadn't realised how much of a prisoner she still was until she reached Humberside. I told her that I wasn't going to help her, that she needed to take a step back and properly think about things. But she pushed. It's hard to say no to her. I set her up with a place for them to run off to if she got caught. She didn't want to know where. That way, they couldn't drag it out of her with a spell or something. I guess she figured Whitehall would go for the leader rather than the underlings.'

'Smart girl.'

'She was... *Is.*'

I recognised that pain in his eyes. It was Robin all over again, right down to the feeling of responsibility and the anger that had nowhere to go but deep down inside. It wasn't hard to imagine how close he was to shutting down completely, but how he had managed to keep going long enough to talk with me, I'll never know. The protection instinct, beating back the uncompromising rage, perhaps. He had to stay functional to make sure nothing else happened to her.

I could respect that.

'So where are they?'

'I can't tell you that. She wouldn't want me to.'

I stood up. The ringing in my head had started to subside a little, I was now pretty sure I could talk and stand at the same time without losing my breakfast. 'If you don't tell me, they're going to come back here and crack her mind open like an egg. You know they will.'

His voice dipped back into a growl. 'You won't get close enough to touch her.'

'Not me. *They.* I have no interest in seeing her hurt any more than she has been. I just want to stop this getting any more out of hand. If you fight them, all you'll achieve is giving them another corpse to bury.'

'I don't care. Not if it gives her some peace.'

I put a hand on his shoulder. It was a wary gesture, uncertain as I was as to whether he'd bite the thing off. 'You can't stop them all. No matter how long you hold them off, they'll get through eventually, and then she'll have to deal with what they'll do. Alone.'

Renner took a deep breath and tried to calm himself. 'Even if I wanted to, there's not much I could even *do* to help. The place is magically shielded, might not even be where I left it if you understand me.'

'You did that?'

He raised an eyebrow at me. 'I'm a warlock, mate. Same as you. You should know whipping up that kind of mumbo-jumbo would just get me vaulted. I can't even get permission to keep the rats out of my bedsit.'

'Ania managed fine with borrowed magic. Maybe you did the same.'

'*Borrowed*?' he nearly spat in disgust. 'What do you think I am, a kid? I'm not interested in playing fast and loose with the possibility of getting vaulted. I'm a lifer, not looking to get myself killed. I'll admit, I'm playing closer to the line with helping Ania than I would like, but I've been doing this a long time. There are some lines I just won't cross.'

'Then who shielded it?'

'She had her boyfriend do it,' he sneered. 'That Whitehall turncoat. I told her not to trust him, but she said that they'd never break him. I guess she figured he'd proved himself.'

'Oh come the fuck on,' I whined in a manly and entirely macho manner. 'He's the one that sent me over here to talk to her in the first place.'

'What?'

'I figured he'd know where the others would have run off to, so I went and had a word with him this morning. He said he didn't know a thing.'

Renner slammed his hand down on the bedside table. 'That little rat bastard. What is he up to?'

'Are you *positive* that he was the one that set up the defences? It couldn't have been anyone else?'

'I'm sure,' he said. 'Ania didn't want to know where the place was, and she didn't want the others knowing about it until it was ready. It had to have been him.'

'Or K,' I said, under my breath.

'What?'

'Her broker, K. He was part of the underground, so

it's feasible she asked him to put the stuff together.'

'Don't be daft. Would you trust *your* dealer with delicate information?'

'Probably not,' I said with a groan. 'It's Wild, isn't it? The bastard played me. *Again*. Jesus Christ!'

And I was out into the corridor, a storming soldier of bad intent, heading back through the hospital to my car. Renner was behind me, but that didn't matter. Wild had tricked me, sent me to the hospital to get me out of the way and buy himself some time no doubt. He was up to something, and I was sick of playing catch-up. I was halfway through the wing when Renner gave up on shouting at me to stop and grabbed my arm.

'God dammit, *what now?*' I roared.

'I need to know if she's safe. Answer that, and you can go.'

It took me a moment of awkward gesticulation to translate the roar I wanted to reply with into actual human words. 'I don't know. Maybe? Probably not, no. Wild is in deep with Bennett, so god knows what's going on here.'

He reached into the same pocket from which he had produced the cigarette and fumbled around for a second. The hand came out clad in a gleaming silver knuckle duster. 'Understood. Promise me that bastard will pay for this.'

'I'll see what I can do.'

'Good enough for me,' he said and let me go.

The fast-trackers were coming back through the door at the entrance to the wing as I was on my way out, a cavalcade of terrified young kids in suits they couldn't afford. Apparently Renner had sufficiently freaked out the two that had been guarding the door; they had rounded up everyone they could, and I couldn't exactly blame them. The older gentleman is better equipped to distribute his rage in a suitably terrifying manner.

The black-tie wave parted around me and vanished up the corridor. I didn't miss a step. Even if they hadn't moved aside to let me through, I was too pissed off to let them slow me down. I would have slammed through them and kept on trucking, so sure I was that Wild had earned himself a right royal face-punching.

I heard the commotion start behind me, and as I moved to the car I saw that even the suits guarding the rest of the hospital were starting to head towards Ania's ward. Renner was putting on a real show, tough old bastard.

What I should have done was taken the time to cool down, work out a way to interrogate the lying rat without showing my hand. Now more than ever, I needed a cool head. I should have just sat in the car for a few minutes, taken some deep breaths, gone to my happy place and reined it all in. That was the smart move. It should have been obvious that I was going to be heading right into a trap.

But, as we know, I'm not always that smart. I was angrier than I should have been, and it was limiting me. In the mood I was in, the only logical course of action was to gun it to Wild's house and interrogate him in the basest sense of the word. With lots of punching, most likely. Maybe I could catch him before he made his move, whatever his move was.

And before you say it, I know I was overreacting. He'd lied to me, but there was no reason to take it quite so personally. Well, other than the fact that he had done so because he hated me, and other warlocks like me, which was *kind of* personal, but still. I was an adult, and I should have been able to rise above it.

It was building inside me though; the rage was pushing at the barricades in my mind. I'd built them to try and keep the hubris and the arrogance contained, to help me stick to my enforced abstinence, but there was always going to be a weakness if I let my ego get involved.

Wild had lied *to my face* and I hadn't even sensed it. He had looked me in the eye and spun me some bullshit lie just to get rid of me, and that wasn't even the bad part. The worst thing was that I thought I had been so clever, that I could trick him into some little revelation. I thought I knew exactly how he ticked, exactly how he thought *I* ticked, and that that was that. I even invited him to send me on a wild goose chase, so sure was I that he wouldn't because of some childish notion of the class clown always getting his way.

Oh yes, I was so *fucking* clever.

My knuckles were white from how hard I was gripping the wheel. I didn't even remember getting in the car, nor starting the engine and actually driving. I was dragged back into the *now* thanks to a near miss at a junction, but then I was back in my head again, watching the barricades fall. I could already feel the thirst start to grow, trickling through the gaps in my resolve, tagging along with the drips of that dangerous arrogance.

The feeling was too fresh – the incident at the underground magicians' bar was still crystal clear in my mind – but that had been brought about by an actual, reckless working of power. That was simple compared to this. That was just the allure of power, an old feeling you could talk yourself away from if you caught yourself early enough, but this was darker. This was the *will* to power, the little voice in the head of every psychopath that tells you how superior you are, how right you are, how god damned enlightened you are compared to the mewling masses beneath you.

It was a construct built out of a special kind of rage, a self-righteous anger that burned through reason and flourished entirely on the notion that *I am always right.* The old thought processes that you can never really lock away. Vindictive, malicious, burning hate, directed at Greg Wild for something that was, in essence, nothing more than pulling the wool over my eyes.

But then, as we all know, you're always angrier at yourself for allowing yourself to be duped than the person who fooled you. In this case, that was why the feelings were so dangerous. It was how this all started in the first place, and I really thought I had it locked down.

He was up to something, sure enough. He'd had a reason for fooling me, outside of pure prejudice, but that was irrelevant. It shouldn't have been – that was the sort of thing I should have held at the forefront of everything – but it was regardless. There was no realm of reasons and rationale for me at that moment, it was all the *now*.

I should never have messed around with that power at the bar. It opened me up to the old me, a little peek through the crack in the door. Working to Whitehall's regulations about when I could use magic hadn't just kept my addiction at bay, it had regulated the way I thought about it altogether. I was starting to miss that.

I was speeding, that is the only clear memory I have of the drive outside the near collision at the junction. The car Bennett had lent me was louder than I had expected it to be, the engine growling under the bonnet as the gears ground themselves into paste somewhere in the depths of the thing. In true British fashion, I managed to pick a route that avoided every single observant copper in the city, which is not a feat I would dare to attempt when in sound mind, and would almost certainly fail to do so if I did.

The dramatic part of me, which always enjoyed chumming around with my vindictive side, was now joining in with the urgings. The thirst was building, and I wanted nothing more than to draw in my power and turn the car into a gambolling machine of flame and vengeance just so Wild would know what he had wrought by his actions. A roaring, fire-belching, four-wheeled avatar of death and destruction, the very thing a modern-day horseman of any apocalypse would have been proud to drive, and the very last thing Wild would see before I ripped what I needed out of his brain and crushed his head between my fingers.

I was nearing a crescendo as I pulled up to his house. I left the engine running and started drawing in power as I ran full-pelt up to his door. To hell with Whitehall. What were they going to do, vault me? I was one step shy of being a god when I had my power. By the time they had noticed what I was doing, I'd be too powerful to stop, even with thaumaturgy. As the warmth of the magic coursed through my veins and the hair on my arms stood erect, I drove my foot into his door, just below the lock.

CHAPTER 23

He wasn't there.

That was, without a doubt, the best result.

I fumed my way around the house, calculating spell after spell after spell that I would have used to rip and rend and tear the knowledge that I had wanted out of him. And then, when it truly set in that I'd missed him, I started *thinking* again and the wall went back up almost instantly.

It was more like an iron shutter slamming down, actually. The warming glow of the magic was gone instantly, leaving a vacuum under my skin and in my mind, one that wasted no time in filling itself with the realisation of what it was I had nearly done. I checked myself over frantically, a futile method to see if I'd gone far enough for Whitehall to vault me *this* time. There was no way I could have known from just a cursory examination of my body – it wasn't as if they etch *'oops'* onto your arm before they explode your heart – but somehow it helped me feel better.

My right leg ached, and my ankle felt tender and swollen. I was unsure how I had missed it at the time, but kicking in a solid wooden door is apparently not as easy as one would think. The magic or the adrenaline had hidden the pain, perhaps, but now it was back full force. I hobbled to Wild's kitchen and found somewhere to sit down.

I noticed my gun was in my hand as I sat down. When had I drawn it? Had I fired it? I was too afraid to check. I couldn't smell any gun smoke, and my arm didn't feel as though it had suffered the jolt of a gunshot, but then I wasn't sure what was real at that moment.

There is a profound and crushing guilt that follows in the wake of such a powerful rage, especially once you mix in the vindictive arrogance of my old lifestyle combating my current apologetic nature. It's a sensation that is hard to describe, a little like all eyes in a room turning on you at once with unspoken disappointment. Yet it is more than that, a deeper feeling that serves ultimately to sap any will to act at all, forcing you to take a moment to rethink your plans. Your inner parent for your inner child.

A rapid-fire montage of thoughts shot through my mind, and considering how gruesomely I was thinking before, I would rather not go into much detail on them. Suffice to say, I lingered on the whole head-crushing thing. I had to remember that, use it as a talisman for what I was trying to avoid becoming one more time. I was a dickhead, I had put a lot of effort into *being* a dickhead, but I wasn't a monster. Not any more.

I had to get back into the right frame of mind. The addiction would be even stronger now, but with it being back to the physical side alone it would be easier to manage. I had to remember that, and the one memory would be helpful in that regard. Even as I could feel my innards crave the magic once again, I was looking for a distraction.

Wild. I had to focus on Wild. He wasn't here, which

either meant he had been called into work, or my visit had spooked him into action. It most likely wouldn't be the work – there was nothing left for him to do with Ania, and Kaitlyn would be reserved for whoever had the job of breaking in new warlocks. Humberside was more or less locked down with regards to empowered people for the moment. No-one would kick up a fuss so soon after such a massive raid.

I considered entertaining the notion that I had scared him off altogether, but it didn't gain much traction. He assumed warlocks were largely benign, he'd shown as much himself, and even if that wasn't the case he was hardly defenceless. He'd taken down three magicians in less than a minute, all on his own. I was no threat.

So, as my keen detective skills started to wind back into action, I concluded that he definitely had to be up to something. This was good. This was a thing I could latch onto and pursue, all cat and mouse style, and keep the cravings in check. There had to be a clue here somewhere. Even if it was just a piece of card with a penis drawn on it and the words *Jameson Parker is rubbish* scribbled underneath. At least then I would know he was just messing me around.

I didn't want to be respectful to Wild's place, which is why I was. Ripping the place to shreds while looking for the clue would most definitely have been cathartic, but it's also something the "baddies" do, and it was worth avoiding that sort of thing. It's also a really crap way of searching a place. It's great at making a mess, but any useful stuff you find is just going to get lost in the debris. Best to be meticulous and efficient. If you just *happen* to drop a plate or snap a door handle while you do so, c'est la vie.

But I found nothing. Realistically, I hadn't expected to find much, but there was always the hope. Perhaps he could have left a message on his answering machine, or an open letter somewhere. Was it so much to ask for a post-it note with directions to his secret lair hurriedly scribbled upon it?

It would seem so.

There was still one route left open, of course. In truth, it would be more correct to say that there were a number of avenues I could have explored, but my brain leapt onto this particular one and refused to budge. You can always count on a tracking spell.

The more astute amongst you, by which I mean anyone who read the last chapter, will perhaps be wondering whether my using magic at this juncture would be an intelligent move. I confess, I did jump straight to magic as the solution without considering other options fully, and perhaps there were some noticeable reasons for that, but in my defence I was in a rush. And, honestly, magic is all about making things faster. As long as I held onto that memory, I *was sure* I could control it.

Time for another phone call.

'Have you found them yet, warlock?' Bennett said the instant he answered.

'Working on it,' I said. 'Things would go a little quicker if you could sign-off on something for me, mind.'

'After a spell, are we?'

'Just a little one.'

'You're supposed to make these requests through your handler, warlock, you know that. We have systems for this sort of thing.'

He had a point, and ordinarily I would have made this request through Charlie. Of course I knew something he didn't, namely that my handler wasn't actually in Whitehall. 'You know how things are down there, boss,' I said, bringing the charm like a pro. 'If I call Whitehall, it'll take a good few hours *at best* before they allow me to do anything.'

'The bureaucracy is slow, but it's never wrong.'

That was bullshit, but I wasn't about to call him on it. 'That's as maybe, but if you want the guys brought in by the end of the day...'

He mulled this over for a moment. 'What do you need?'

'Just another tracking spell, that's all. Got a suspect I think can lead me right to the wayward warlocks, just need to track him down.'

'All right. You have a go. But this better pan out, warlock. Don't go thinking you can jump the queue just because you have my direct line.'

I would rather stab myself in the ear with a rusty corkscrew. 'I wouldn't dream of it, sir.'

As I've said before, the flip-phone is a little outdated, but nothing is more satisfying than snapping one shut to end a call. Certainly helps with the sour taste that starts to form in your mouth after sucking up to the boss. Getting the approval wasn't bad either, of course.

I chose the kitchen for my working, seeing as it had a lot of easily cleared floor space and no carpets. It's hard to draw a pentagram on carpet when you don't have any paint. Chalk and marker pens just don't cut it.

Clearing the floor didn't take long. The chairs were simple to tuck away behind the main kitchen unit, and the table was helpfully one that was able to be folded into all kinds of shapes, most likely to facilitate the sort of swanky cocktail parties people such as Wild no doubt hosted. Office people do the whole *having guests for dinner* thing, right? In any case, hurling a few chairs over a marbled counter and kicking a table until it bent was the order of the moment. I'd done my search, no need to stand on the ceremony of not trashing the joint now.

When the floor was finally cleared, the table

irreparably dented and the chair splintering out of view, I daubed a pentagram on the floor and wandered off in search of the bedroom. I could leave the pentagram to draw in its own power from the surroundings, just as I had done when trying to trace K, but I was looking for a more accurate fix this time. Trying to track Wild by his magic wouldn't work, it would just lead me to the magician they had press-ganged into lending him the power in the first place. I needed a thaumaturgical link.

The vault works by taking a tooth, but anything with your DNA works just fine. I didn't expect I'd find a tooth just lying around, but everyone leaves a little bit of themselves in the bedroom, or the bathroom. Warlocks are good at keeping this stuff hidden or destroying it outright – a past hinged on using thaumaturgy for personal gain instils a certain level of paranoia – but fast-trackers never really develop these neuroses.

I was cruising for some hair, which is an odd sentence. A comb or hairbrush would have been ideal – Wild liked to look his best, so he definitely had one or both of these, and it's easy to forget that they will retain the odd strand. If I could find one, I'd have my spell catalyst. Which is why I couldn't find either, I suspect. He was demonstrably smarter than your usual fast-tracker after all.

My next port of call was, therefore, the bathroom. It's even easier to find DNA in here, considering all that goes on in such a room. There is a slight caveat in that, sometimes, you have to get your hands dirty. It's not exactly a palatable alternative to mooching through someone's dresser, but it is effective. With that in mind, however, I wasn't quite desperate enough to go spelunking in Wild's U-bend.

Okay, that's not strictly true because the sink has a U-bend too, but we both know what you thought of first. Digging around in the inner workings of a sink was considerably more preferable to *another* U-bend. As such I retrieved his tool set and got to work.

All men have tool sets, whether they bought them for themselves or they were gifted a set by a father desperate to get his bookish son to do some real work for once in his life. They are *always* under the stairs – if the house has any – or in the garden shed. Sometimes both. Wild had chosen under the stairs.

The U-bend detached easily enough and I tipped the contents out onto the floor. A great amorphous blob of bristles and sludge plopped out and sat there, looking like a thing that would fall out of a giant's nostril. It *looked* at me, in the way only a truly vile and inanimate *thing* can do. I longed for a pair of gloves, or a lackey I could order to do this job for me, but sometimes heroism means doing the jobs no-one else can.

I'm a bloody hero, mate.

The globule had the consistency of wallpaper paste, which was bad enough, but my stomach somersaulted every time I inadvertently caressed one of the mystery nodules within. There shouldn't be solid lumps of gristle in anything that is mostly some sort of plasm. It's not *right*. The only way I resisted vomiting was by reminding myself that the hideous blob was already bad enough, and being coated in my stomach juices would only make things worse.

Eventually I had carefully disassembled the blob into a sort of pancake of fear and putrescence. Then my work could begin in earnest. After all that, it would have been disappointing to find that Wild was the sort of man who shaved over a bin, or in the bath, or just straight onto the floor like some sort of mad man. Thankfully he shaved over the sink, like a proper gentleman should and there was a fair amount of hair trapped in the sludge. I scooped out a section that was more hair than slime and took it back to the pentagram in the kitchen.

Magic is *awesome*.

With my catalyst secure, and the pentagram sufficiently charged, I took out my map and performed the spell. A proper thaumaturgical spell feels different to the more abstract working I had performed to track down K. You have to use your power to reach through the connections between the part of the person you have and their main self, like threading a cable. Push too hard and you'll pierce the spell and send your energy out randomly into the wilderness, giving you a false reading and, potentially, one hell of a headache. Push too softly and you just won't make progress at all, your power stagnating in the conduits between the catalyst and the target.

But if you get it right, if you push enough through, you can feel the connection form. You reach through into their very selves, not simply their magic itself but to the very magic of nature that sustains it. Everyone runs on this sort of magic, whether you're a layman or a magician, and that's what makes thaumaturgy so powerful; there's always something to grab onto. With a tracking spell all you are doing is reaching out and stroking this natural magic, charming it into telling you what you need to know and bringing that knowledge back down the connection. If you wanted to vault someone, however, you'd grab that energy and squeeze.

And the target would have no idea whether you had done one or the other, or either, until it was too late.

Reaching out to Wild was difficult and slow, like swimming through treacle. The walls of the spell – for want of a better word – were strong at least, so I could risk pushing harder. The better the catalyst, the more stable the spell, and despite appearances the hair from the sink was good. The pentagram wasn't giving me the best battery of energy to use, but it was no slouch either, and as I channelled more and more of it into the spell I could feel the resistance begin to lessen until I burst through into Wild.

Incidentally, please don't read that as a euphemism. We're all adults here. Grow up.

Describing this feeling is difficult, as with most magical things, because it sort of defies translation. The best way I can put it is as if you had been born into the true darkness of a cave, not even the tiniest speck of ambient light, and then one day walked out into the sun. Suddenly you are using organs you didn't even realise you had, experiencing something that you had never even conceived of, and it is beautiful and painful all at once. You have no choice but to screw your eyes shut because you've never used them before, they can't deal with so much information slamming into them at once.

Thaumaturgy is a bit like that, except swap light for life. You think you know what life is, what with being alive and all, and yet you cannot comprehend how little you truly know until you tap into another's essence. And this feeling is something that you *never* get used to – it's as powerful and humbling the first time as the five hundredth. It took me a moment to remember why I was even there.

Reaching out, I carefully tied myself to his essence and let my will search for the part that knew his location. A single strand of truth in the roiling, burning, gleaming web of his existence, but no more difficult to find than any other. As long as you can visualise what you want of a person, the essence is more than happy to oblige – it has no concept of harm or deceit or anything like that. It provided the strand I was after, and I harnessed it gently, teasing it back towards the conduit.

All of this took a few seconds in real time, but in the mind it felt much longer. These things always do. Minds are malleable things, and they can give you all the time you need if you know how to ask properly. When I finally broke the spell, Wild's location was tied to the map until the bonds of the spell were cut. In layman's terms, I had until midnight.

Time is a human concept and all that, but so is magic to some degree. The general consciousness still accepts that with a new day you get a new start, and as such magic works the same way. As soon as today becomes tomorrow, spell-crafted bonds end. There are ways around this, as in all things, but you rarely need to use them. They're not hard, just more effort than is usually necessary, so I wasn't about to use them to lengthen this spell.

I watched the map and waited for his location to coalesce.

CHAPTER 24

Wild hadn't gone far. He clearly wasn't afraid of me catching up with him – perhaps he thought I was too dim to put all the pieces together – and he had set himself a decidedly leisurely pace. I didn't even need the car to catch up with him, a few minutes sprint got me close enough to track him safely.

He'd been moving through the streets with the lithe confidence only someone from a metropolis can muster, the utterly pompous certainty that other people will recognise your trip is more important than theirs and therefore make room for you to pass unmolested. It was harder going for me, what with the lack of any such skill, but he wasn't going to lose me. It helped that I could move in his wake.

A lot of this job seems to be following shifty looking people around one city or another, and they always seem to move in the same sort of way. Head down, shoulders up, hunched in on themselves and watching their steps very carefully. It's all an effort not to draw too much attention, but you couple this with the inbuilt need to check if they are being followed and what you get is something incredibly conspicuous. Seriously, the only way it could be more obvious is if they were wearing fedoras. Have you ever seen someone in a fedora that wasn't trying to convey they were being shifty?

Tinker, tailor, soldier, twat.

But, again, Wild was doing his whole sneaky confidence thing. He was walking around bold as brass, like a normal person, which meant he blended in completely and it was very annoying. Obviously, I could track him, but I had magic on my side and my enormous brain. If I wasn't actually a little bit good at my job, I might have lost him once or twice even with him moving at such a leisurely pace.

The problem with stalking someone who just looks like everyone else, however, is that it makes you look like the weirdo. You end up having to weave around people, poking your neck around corners like a caffeine-addled giraffe sniffing out a Starbucks. People start staring, which can tip off your target pretty easily.

But I'm brilliant, so it wasn't too hard to deal with. Besides, as he went further into the city towards wherever he was heading, we got closer to the cultural centre. All the weird people hang out there anyway. Artists, writers, actors; a whole bunch of people who are naturally a bit *off* when you let them out in public. They weren't going to notice Geoffrey the Great Giraffe Detective's pendulous head swinging into someone else's business amongst the general throng of peculiarity.

Before long, Wild had slipped through the crowd of *cultured* people and ducked down a side street, a slight boost in his speed telling me he was almost at his destination. He slipped around another corner and I quickened my pace so as not to lose him, rounding the corner myself to find a theatre nestled away in the little cobblestone maze.

I hadn't thought Humberside had any theatres left,

what with the rise of television and the general belief that treading the boards was reserved for poncey southerners. That said, I'm a poncey southerner, so perhaps I'm not giving the locals enough credit. That the theatre Wild approached looked like it had only recently closed sort of lent credence to both arguments, if I'm honest.

A sign above the door identified the place as the Royale, which told me a lot about the sort of place it had tried to be. You only stick an 'e' on the end of royal if you are trying to fabricate a sense of grandeur, or want to lure in a few social climbers. That the place was quite small – a double door for an entrance, and from what I could see a lobby that practically fell into the auditorium – served only to back that up. Not that it mattered, as I was hardly a connoisseur.

Wild skipped up to the main door and unlocked it. I didn't see him reach for a key, so I'm going to assume he did it with magic because he would have thought that was cool. To anyone who wasn't a suit-wearing poser, that was the magical equivalent of driving your car through the front of your house because you think you left the gas on – overkill and just downright laughably stupid. Okay, that's an exaggeration, but the point is just use a bloody key, mate.

It's difficult to tail someone into a building without them spotting you, especially if they control the place. Without anyone to hide behind or a crowd to melt into, you have to make the best with what you've got, so I pressed myself up against the outside of the door and peered in through the cloudy glass panels in the door itself. Slow movements, nothing to draw Wild's eye.

He had stopped in the lobby, apparently to talk to someone on the phone. I cursed myself for cutting the spell the moment I was sure I wouldn't lose him. Eavesdropping through a tracking spell wouldn't be too difficult, and probably wasn't too dissimilar to what workings I was currently allowed to perform that it would set off alarms in the vault. The problem is that the closer you are to your thaumaturgical target, the greater the risk of feedback if you leave the spell running. It's a really minor thing, so small that Wild probably wouldn't even detect it, but I hadn't thought it was worth the risk. I was regretting that now.

I gave lip-reading a try. I sucked at it, to put it mildly, but it was that or ask him to speak up. Not a single word stood out to me. It was very annoying. After a minute or so he hung up the phone, closed his eyes and took a deep breath. Then he changed.

The man I had seen walk in was the scheming, sharp-eyed bastard that had shown himself at the raid. With a simple deep breath, however, he had gone and been replaced by the soft-featured and kind-eyed young kid he had been when I first met him. It was chilling to see someone change so quickly and so noticeably just through holding themselves differently. Hell, I'd seen him do it before, and it still shocked me.

Now wearing his friendly face, Wild moved to the main doors to the auditorium and flung them both open. I tried to maintain distance from him as I moved up, and I did it well I'll have you know. Like a ninja. A handsome, well-dressed ninja.

It never occurred to me that the whole thing was a glamour.

He'd never opened the door. He'd never even moved from the spot where he had been on the phone. That was some pretty sophisticated magic to whip up so suddenly, that's my excuse at least. I'd always had a blind spot when it came to illusion spells and the like, a little too quick to believe what my eyes were telling me. The only reason I even worked out what he'd done was because no-one else could have put the cold metal of the blade next to my carotid.

'Hello again,' he hissed into my ear. 'Fancy meeting you here.'

'Jesus Christ,' I said. 'I'm really bad at this.'

The knife came away from my neck and I slowly turned around. The friendly face disguise hadn't been part of the glamour, it seemed. 'Truth be told, I didn't even know you were there. My superior felt it was worth checking to see if I was being followed. Better safe than sorry. Seems he was right.'

'Your superior? What are you up to, Wild? Are you and Whitehall trying to bump us off now, is that it?'

He laid a hand on my shoulder. 'You're really not the brightest kid in the class, are you? I suppose I shouldn't be too hard on you though. You're missing bits of the equation, that's your problem. Working on false assumptions. If I was you, I'd leave it to the big boys.'

'If I *were* you,' I said and slapped his hand away. Got to let a little of the childish pedant out every now and then. Puts people off balance.

'You really are determined to get in over your head, aren't you?'

'To be fair, I hadn't planned on it. I just wanted to do my job, go home and have a sandwich. But you had to go and give me false information on the other warlocks and now everything is getting complicated in my head again. *You knew* exactly where they were. You bloody sent them!'

'Yeah, they're in there. What of it?'

'In the auditorium?'

'Yes. Not exactly a comfy place to bed down for the night, but it's safe enough. Untraceable, I saw to that.'

'Why keep them from me, then?'

'Sorry, orders are orders,' he said.

'Orders? Bennett is the one that sent me here you idiot.'

He pulled a face like a confused puppy. 'I never said they were Bennett's orders,' he said and slammed his palm into my chest.

I had been expecting the blow from the moment I had met him, more or less. Not many people like me, so I've learned to prepare myself for violence, and I have a routine all lined up for this sort of thing. The first step is to deflect the blow, then I reach for whatever weapon I have upon my person – my gun in this case – and jam it painfully into the assailant's face. I got as far as raising my left arm to block his right before I spotted my mistake.

It was a stupid mistake, and one that showed why Whitehall was so enamoured with fast-trackers. Warlock's taking on magicians are still very much able to recall the destructive power on hand to their empowered opponents, but they still see fast-trackers as laymen. Wizard armies were always full of, well, wizards. They'd never had foot soldiers before, and the social consciousness of the empowered constantly forgets that the laymen are armed now.

So, as a result, the spell struck me right in the chest, although I'm not sure whether it was that or the crippling disappointment in myself that paralysed me. It could have gone either way really. Whatever the cause, however, I went down like a rotten tree. Wild caught me as I went and lowered me down gently. He stood over me and watched as I tried to will some movement back into my body, energy dancing over his palm, but only my eyes were willing to heed the call. He didn't look pleased with himself, strangely.

'I'm not a cackling super-villain, Parker,' he said as he grabbed my collar. 'I'm just a man doing his job. You're too competent for your own good. The Rider has noticed.'

He really didn't know me at all. And also, fuck. *The*

Rider?

You might have been willing to accept he was involved from the moment Kaitlyn brought him up. You've probably spent the last few hundred pages rolling your eyes every time I said it was nonsense, sucking your teeth and saying *of course he's involved, you tit.* Well, I hope you feel proud of yourselves.

But come on, it was like hearing the King of Thrace had uninvited you from his birthday. You try and get your head around that telegram. There were so many questions stampeding around inside my stupid brain that I wanted to ask through a bespoke language conveyed by blinking, but Wild was more concerned with dragging me out of the lobby.

It's no fun being dragged by your collar. Before you get all smarmy and start saying that getting dragged is never fun, you've clearly never played with a seven year old. They love getting dragged around by the feet or the arms. They also dislike being dragged by the collar, however. Funny that. Kids and adults alike can bond over their hatred of being choked with their own clothes.

I had thought he was going to drag me before the assembled warlocks, perhaps serve me to them as a traitor for them to carve up or something equally vile. Ania had said they revered me for some reason, and yet she had been willing to set fire to me so I doubted their worship would do much to keep me alive if they saw me as a threat. Wild dragged me straight past the door, however, and up a set of wrought iron steps in the far corner, a spiral roped off with a dusty cordon.

Once at the top – the ascension not nearly as painful as I had expected it to be – he dragged me into what looked like a VIP box and hoisted me up onto a seat. Positioning me wasn't easy thanks to the complete paralysis, but he managed it. I will say this for him: he did wonders for my posture.

'Can you see them down there?' he said. 'Milling about. It's too dark up here for them to see you, of course, but it is important you can see them. Orders are orders.'

These sorts of conversations never end well.

I *could* see them, though. Maybe twenty or so figures lurking in the gloom down below. They'd split off into little cliques from what I could see, each one containing no more than five people, occupying their own sections of the red velvet seating area. The boredom radiated off them in waves, so much so that some of them had even resorted to card games.

Wild's face slid into view. 'Right then, you just sit up here and have a listen. You might learn something, if you pay attention, eh?'

And with that he was gone. Then, thirty seconds later, he threw open the doors below me just as I had seen him do in his glamour, and he stumbled into the room. All heads turned to look at him, which is hardly surprising considering the entrance he made. In fact, considering the place was supposed to be a hidey-hole, I'm surprised a few of the warlocks didn't just put him down the moment the doors slammed open. Perhaps they had been expecting him.

'Okay guys, we've got a problem,' he said.

A warlock stepped forward, a tall and thin girl from what I could make out. 'We've been getting a lot of those lately,' she said in a soft Scottish brogue. 'We were kind of hoping you'd have some good news for a change, Greg.'

'It's not through choice, believe me. They've taken Ania. Kaitlyn too.'

The room erupted in confused, angry murmurs. It wasn't too loud, but there was a cadence to it that made it ring louder in the ears than it should have. It was a controlled fear rather than a controlling one, which meant the murmuring was about planning.

Another warlock stepped forward. Older and bearded, this one was a Scouser. 'How the fuck did this happen?'

'A traitor. Jameson Parker led Whitehall right to them.'

'Bullshit,' said the first warlock. 'Parker's the poster child for sticking it to the man.'

Sticking it to the man? Were we back in the nineties now? Still, at least I had someone on my side.

'I was there,' Wild said. 'He damn near led the charge himself. He's Whitehall through and through, we've suspected as much for a long time. Don't try to pretend you didn't see this coming.'

There was a chorus of debate from the various cliques, apparently about my trustworthiness and devotion to the cause. Watching people talk about you as though they know you is quite surreal when it's done on this scale, especially when you yourself have no idea what you think of a situation. The best I could hope for was that they would come out on the side of me not being an untrustworthy bastard, because no-one likes being thought of as that. It was a bit touch and go.

The Scouse warlock spoke up again. 'It doesn't matter who did what, just that they've got our people, right?' There was a murmur of agreement. 'What are we going to do?'

'What can we do?' The Scot said. 'This was never meant to be about actually doing anything. We can't *do* anything, they'll vault us.'

'They only vault people for magic, don't use that as an excuse for your cold feet,' the Scouser turned on her, his own clique slowly falling in behind him.

'Don't be an idiot, Romsey. You really think that they'll just watch as we kick in some doors and not flip their kill switch? The only reason they've shown any reservations so far is because they need us to tame the North.'

Romsey crossed his arms. 'And what would you rather we do? Sit in a fucking circle and sing kumbaya? We need to make a stand.'

'The entire point of this thing was non-violent resistance,' the Scot shot back. 'We refuse to work, show them how much they need us, and they start to respect that. It was supposed to be the first steps on the long road!'

Wild placed a hand on her shoulder. 'Sophie, he's right. Maybe non-violence was the goal, but we can't just sit back and let this happen. Whitehall has already showed their true colours, it's time to stop believing the best in people and live in the real world. We've got to do something.'

'We march on Whitehall,' Romsey said. 'We take back our freedom with a single, decisive stroke.'

'No, we'd never get close,' Wild said, moving away from Sophie and positioning himself between the two. 'That's an endgame scenario. We'd need to thin the defences, draw them out so we would have time to sneak in. Or drum up enough support to make an actual assault feasible. In either case, we would need more warlocks on side.'

Romsey cocked his head to one side. 'So what do you suggest?'

'We need a symbol to rally behind. Something that will tell the other warlocks around the country that it's possible to resist. If we can bust out Van Ives from her confinement too, get her cadre of terrorists on-side, all the better.'

He was laying it on thick. It wasn't hard to see his game now – he was still playing the agent provocateur. But why? If this was on the orders of The Rider, what was the point of it? He was using Wild as a double-agent, taking down the two figureheads of this little resistance, and while I could believe Whitehall would want excuses to take out as many warlocks as possible, this seemed too soon. Why even send me to bring them in if you had an inside man who could deliver them to you on a silver platter? If this was directly tied into whatever weird plan The Rider had, what little I knew of him from before the end of the Dark Times didn't seem to mesh with breaking a wave of warlocks on Whitehall's levy.

Trying to pick apart the motivations of a double-agent is just going to give you a headache. Mark my words.

'You're saying we hit the field office,' Sophie said. 'That's suicide. They've got a Sheriff!'

Even through the darkness and the distance, I could see Wild grin. 'It's not suicide, not unless they expect us. They'll be too busy patting themselves on the back for last night that they won't even see us coming.'

'This is ridiculous!' Sophie's movements were exaggerated, angry. 'They see us bearing arms, they pull the plug. It's as simple as that. I'm not going to be a party to this.'

Romsey stepped forward and pushed her out the way roughly. To her credit, she didn't even stumble. 'Then stay here and we'll fight for your freedom instead, coward. We'll risk our lives so you can have a platform on which you can wax lyrical about how violence is *bad* and that doing fuck all is the way to peace.'

This led to a row. I know, what a shock, right? I was tempted to tell you it was a debate, or even an argument, but there really was far too much swearing for me to do that with a straight face. Honestly, the only words I could actually pick out of the din were ones you wouldn't say around your parents. Even paralysed and helpless as I was, I still found it quite funny. A lot of people swearing at each other at the top of their lungs is unquestionably hilarious, it can't be anything else.

It wasn't a long row, perhaps five minutes, and when it was done all the little cliques had merged into two super-cliques. On the one side you had Romsey and his cabal of hardened bastards ready to *wreck Whitehall's shit* as they put it at one point during the row. On the other side you had Sophie's mob of lovey-dovey magical hippies who wanted to hold a bake sale for equality, and paint tiger stripes on kids' faces for 50p and a promise of an end to prejudice some time down the road.

I'm not even sure if either of those are an exaggeration.

The coalition of hardened bastards was, as you might expect, slightly larger than the love-in crowd. I would harp on a bit about how easy it is to whip up some righteous furore and prod both groups towards open conflict, but I don't want to get all heavy-handed here. You can draw those conclusions yourself if you like, and I might even agree with you. Watching the two groups stare at each other was, however, too much like a scene from a bad musical to make those points to myself at the time.

Wild still stood between both sides, ever the impartial mediator, arms outstretched to help keep the peace. What a talented snake he was. 'Sophie, please, think this through,' he said.

She surveyed her supporters. 'I think we're the only ones that *have*, Greg. Please don't do this. We're not going to win this by playing to their expectations.'

'It's the only way we will win this!' he was slipping into performance mode. 'I've been on the inside. I'm *from* the inside. I know how they think, and they're never going to relax their grip on you. Why would they? They are grooming people like me to replace you. The only way this grip gets lessened is if we break their fingers.'

Romsey and his coalition actually cheered. It was creepy, like watching a political rally where only a handful of radicals had bothered to turn up. 'No, this is wrong. This is the sort of thinking that got us into this mess in the first place,' Sophie said.

'Not all of us were into the Black, Sophie. Don't go lumping us in with your sort,' Romsey said. 'I was a fucking gardener. I used my magic to levitate coins to entertain the kids at the bloody park. We're not all genocidal maniacs in shackles, and I'm sick of being treated like one.'

Wild stepped in again. 'We're wasting time. Sophie, if you and yours want to stay here, that's fine. We won't judge you,' he shot a look at Romsey. '*We won't judge you.* But we are going to do this, and we're going to do it now.'

'Then go and do it, but don't expect our support.'

Romsey snorted. 'Frankly, I think we're better off without you anyway.'

Wild's head snapped towards the Scouser, but he said nothing. The pair held each other's gaze for a moment and then Wild turned to leave, Romsey and his fellows falling into step behind him. The last man out slammed the door shut.

Sophie slumped into a chair and one of her people knelt next to her. They talked, but it was too quiet for me to hear. I doubt it was a particularly upbeat conversation, though.

My fingers twitched. Wild's spell was starting to wear off. Was this intended? It was conceivable it was a proximity thing, the working getting weaker as he and Romsey stormed off to the field office. Or maybe he had actively released me now I had apparently seen what he had wanted me to see. He had successfully confused me, if that was his plan.

I knew Wild had been acting to gain their trust. I had

no doubts about that. The way he had turned on Ania and Kaitlyn and K so suddenly, so efficiently, did not ring true of a man of conflicted loyalties. But then, I couldn't see the underlying idea behind marching a group of angry warlocks up to the office. Was it just to smash them against the walls? A very small victory for prejudice and hate if it was. Well, small in the grand scheme of things, but it would make life hell for any Humberside warlock.

He was certainly provoking a reaction, but I couldn't see the purpose to it outside of pure brutality. There had to be an angle. Governments don't go for brutality for its own sake, they need some sort of justification that they can sell, and The Rider couldn't have just been crazy. Well, he *could* have been, but I wasn't going to get anywhere trying to deal with him as a problem if I treated him as an insane loony. He would need some sort of justification for whatever he was planning as much as Whitehall. A warlock uprising might work for both camps, but that would be messy and very bad for everyone involved, arcane and mundane alike.

It wasn't good, whatever it was, and the likelihood was that Bennett would be involved on at least one end. Wild was clever, but I didn't think he'd have anything up his sleeve that hadn't been mandated from one of his higher ups, and he had to play the dutiful employee long enough for Bennett to trust him. He was a climber, and he'd need his bosses on side for that, which meant at least playing along with some of Bennett's decrees.

Feeling in my neck came back next, which left me with a canyon of numbness between the two things I could move that somehow felt worse than it had before. When everything is numb it's still unpleasant, but you have no frame of reference, but as soon as some things have feeling you suddenly realise how horrible it is to feel nothing at all. I very much felt that I needed to test whether I was in a have-no-mouth-yet-must-scream situation, because that would have really been the last straw.

I couldn't scream. I could sort of hum in a higher pitch than one normally does, but a good powerful scream needs the mouth to co-operate and I wasn't quite there yet. I did my best, of course, to amplify the hum so that Sophie and her lot could hear me, but *I* could barely hear the noise and it was coming from inside my own throat. I would have to wait for the feeling to creep further up my neck.

And then the fire came. Of course it bloody well did.

The smoke got to me first, which was perhaps the way I would have preferred to have learned about the fire. The smell crept up from behind me, and as I relearned how my neck worked I turned to see it creeping under the door. Thin wisps of black smoke rather than the thick belches I had expected, but it was sufficient to shit me right up. I remembered Ania trying to cook me alive, and it was not something I was anxious to relive. Especially fully conscious.

I weighed up my options, because I am nothing if not thoughtful and brave in the face of danger. The people down in the auditorium apparently had no idea of the fire, still mumbling away to each other as they were, but with me in my current position I was going to need their help. Besides, the fire would spread downstairs soon, if it hadn't already, and I think that gave us something to bond over. They were also the lovey-doveys, so it wasn't like they would leave me to burn up here once they knew.

A good scream was all it would take, if I could get my throat to co-operate, which I couldn't. I considered tapping out SOS in morse code on the wooden panels of the box with my living hand, but two very real problems presented themselves with that: there was no way I could make it loud enough for them to hear, and I didn't know morse.

The smoke was starting to get thicker, and I was sure I could see the gentle flicker of the fire itself under the door. I still had plenty of time before the fire would even *start* to burn through the door, and the smoke wasn't going to choke me any time soon either, but the longer I let it burn the harder it would be to escape the building. There was no fire escape that I saw coming in, or any signage for one whilst inside. As far as I was aware, the only exit was the way I had come in, from which the fire would almost certainly cut me off.

I *needed* Sophie's help. I *needed* to scream. But how can you scream when your mouth doesn't work?

The answer was surprisingly simple.

CHAPTER 25

You've got the touch! You've got the powerrrrrrrrr!
YEAH!

Phones are awesome.

With my hand having come back to life, I could reach into my pocket and pull out K's phone. Why I was still carrying it around with me, I'm not entirely sure – must just have fallen under the purview of the wallet/phone/keys check all men do before they leave the house – but I wasn't about to complain. *My* phone was in my inside blazer pocket, but K's sat in my trousers, much easier to reach.

It's a simple thing to flick through the options and find the thing that kids on buses use to irritate everyone. And no-one on Earth is going to be able to ignore Stan Bush screaming at them from the shadows. Although, to be sure, I carefully dropped the phone off the edge of the box.

When all Hell's breaking loose, you'll be –CLONK– the storm!

Phones are bloody sturdy.

Sophie turned warily. I had expected a more

immediate response, considering the circumstances, but she was cautious. She ushered the others back and approached the phone slowly, squatted down by it and stared for a moment, and then followed the trajectory back up to me. I did my best to smile suavely, which didn't really work but the darkness up in my little box probably saved me from looking foolish.

Now she knew I was there, all she had to do was come up to investigate and I'd be fine. She'd see the fire on the way up and would be forced to do something about it to save her own skin. Sorted. I'd deal with the inevitable interrogation quite well once I knew I wasn't dangerously close to, well, danger.

The thing is, it can be quite hard to accurately determine how a person will react to any given situation. I had predicted the more likely route, it's true, on account of Sophie's unwillingness to get involved with Romsey and Wild's little crusade. I hadn't taken into account that she might react differently when *forced* to act.

She shifted in the squat, and first I thought she was dropping to a knee for ease. Then I saw the shimmer on her right hand as she slammed it into the floor between her legs, and the corona of power that billowed out around her as she launched, like a human rocket, up towards me. I would have fallen back, had I been able, but instead she shot up to my box and grabbed me by the throat with her left hand as she shot over the railing, knocking me down and landing on top of me.

I tried to speak, more out of habit than any belief I was able to yet, but another serpentine shift of her body meant I had her knee in my trachea. Apparently she wanted to talk first. 'Who the hell are you?'

This time, I didn't try to speak. Instead I raised my eyebrows and flicked my eyes down towards her knee, then back up to her face, and put on my best puppy-dog eyes. She frowned and moved her knee away, but brought her right hand up into a pose that threatened sudden violence if I acted up.

'Now answer the question,' she said.

I shook my head. There wasn't really a way to convey to her that I was unable to speak, so I took a chance on her noticing that I wasn't being the gloating villain she was likely expecting me to be. Judging from the resulting slap, luck was not with me.

It won't surprise you that I've been slapped before, but never by someone wearing rings. Maybe *a* ring, singular, but Sophie's right hand was coated in the things. No wonder she had been so blasé about magicking her way up to me, the girl had an entire armoury of enchantments on each finger. Had she been stockpiling them?

Oh, and it really bloody hurt. A lot. It doubly hurt, actually. Once for the slap itself, and the second time for the other side of my face bashing into the floor.

'Jesus, ow!' I shouted. 'God, did you need to –' And then I noticed. It's a cruel sort of man that plans a spell you can break by one hell of a slap. But then maybe he hadn't, and perhaps all the stored magic in her various rings had cocked up the spell. It was impossible to tell either way, but I could move again, which was nice.

Her slapping hand scratched at the underside of her chin. 'I know that voice. Jameson Parker?'

'Hello.'

'What the hell –'

I interrupted, because I am a man of action. And fear. 'The building's on fire.' And abruptness.

'Pardon?'

'There is a fire,' I said, pointing to the box's door. Because of how I was lying, this looked a little bit like I was stretching, and it took her a moment to follow my fingers. 'In the building. Quod erat demonstrandum, the building is on fire.'

She leapt off me and up to the door, placing a hand on the nob.

'Wait,' I said, flipping onto my front and awkwardly trying to remember how legs work. 'You can't just open the door!'

'Shh,' she spat back. 'I'm not opening the door, I'm checking.' Another glow from her right hand. Some people get all the best toys, and I wasn't pleased in knowing that I wasn't one of them.

I watched as she tapped into another ring. She was playing very fast and loose with the stored magic in those things. Granted, I had done similar with my own quite recently, but I had still used the magic for its intended purpose. Sort of. Combat magic for combat applications. I doubted that any of the magic in those rings had been earmarked for what she was using it for.

I watched her weave the spell in her mind, which sounds more difficult than it is. Her eyes shone with navy light, and when she was done it travelled down her arm and into the door. When she removed her hand, there was a faint afterglow on the door for a moment, like a camera flash on a human eye.

She turned to me. 'The building's on fire.'

I nodded. 'Yup.'

'It's very badly on fire.'

'It's not just the corridor?' I said, frowning. There hadn't been time for it to spread too far, surely.

'Pretty much all of it is on fire. The boxes and the auditorium are the only things not burning. What have you done?!'

'Me?!' I held up my hands. 'I had nothing to do with this. I'm just here to ask you all to come back peacefully so we can get back to work –'

'Let's argue this later,' she said, moving to the edge of the box and looking down to the others below. 'How about we get out of here first, and *then* we can discuss why you may or may not be responsible for this?'

'That's probably for the best, yes.'

'Good. Hold my hand.'

That would have been the perfect time for a disarmingly charming comment, but I was slightly off my game on account of the fire. Instead of a witticism, then, I just took her hand. She vaulted over the railing and dragged me with her, and we fell for a split-second before another cushion of power set us down gently on the floor below.

The other warlocks formed a circle around us, one or two idly tapping into their enchantments in preparation. They clearly weren't the brightest of the bunch – as if I was going to kick off in such a situation – but I couldn't fault them for their reaction speed. By the time I looked up from the landing, all of them were ready to throw something my way if they needed to. We're good at what we do, no denying that.

Sophie ripped her hand out of mine – or mine out of hers, I'm not sure which way around hand holding is – and tried to calm the others. 'No need for that,' she said. 'We've got more important things to worry about. Someone's set the building on fire.'

A young man stepped forward. 'What? What do we do?'

'We get out, simple as that,' Sophie replied, giving him a calm smile. 'It's not too difficult. It's a big fire, but it's got magic in it. That means we've got a way in. Any of you carry elemental charms or anything like that?'

Two girls, one barely out of her teens and the other much harder to place on the age spectrum, put their hands up and Sophie walked over to them. They each unfastened a charm from their necklaces – one of the many ways to carry your enchantments – and handed them over.

'What are you going to do?' I asked.

Sophie placed both charms into her left hand and closed her fist around them. 'Hmm. Wind and lightning. Not ideal choices, but they'll have to do.'

'Hey,' I said, grabbing her shoulder. 'What are you going to do?'

A good glare can make a woman look quite beautiful, at least to me. Sophie was certainly heading that way with the look she shot me. 'I'm going to try and short out the magic in the fire, create an opening we can dash through. If I can weave these elements together –'

'Won't work,' I said. 'The elements are stronger than the magic. If you're right about the fire being magic-based, it'll feed off any spell you send in there and grow. You send in wind and lightning magic, all you're going to do is fan the flames *and* electrify them. I think we've got enough problems right now without you doing that.'

'Bullshit, I know what I'm doing.'

So it was going to be like that, was it? Well, two can play at the arrogant know-it-all game, my dear. I brushed her off and turned to the rest of the warlocks. 'Hello everyone. I'm Jameson Parker, *Warlock Supreme.*'

'Excuse me?' Sophie said over my shoulder.

'Shush, you,' I muttered back. 'I can get us out of here but you have to do exactly what I say. Understand? That means no deviation, no bright ideas, and complete and total obedience. You should be good at that, we're all warlocks after all.'

The group mumbled a sort of agreement. They weren't leaders, as evidenced by the fact they were quite happily following Sophie, and the best way to get them on side was to just talk louder than her. Shock and awe. Works for the Americans. Or did, before the vampires went knocking.

'My plan is going to work,' Sophie said. 'Just shut-up and let me work.'

'Your plan, dear, is going to create a wall of crackling

Thorfire around the building and trap us in here until we roast to death. I'm not keen on that plan.'

'Thorfire isn't a word, you can't just do that.' Step one: confuse the current leader.

'It's better than lightning-flame though, right? I mean if you want to debate the names now we certainly can. We can die safe in the knowledge that we have a suitable name for the thing that killed us, at least.' Step two: position yourself as the decisive and not at all petty replacement.

'We're not going to die. I can take the magic from these charms and weave them into a spell that will repel the fire long enough for us to get through the gap. I can use the wind to force the flames apart and the lightning to strengthen that effect. Any residual magical energy will sap at the magic in the fire, weakening it enough. *It's a good plan.*'

I thrust my hands into my pockets. I've seen loads of detectives do this when they're about to deliver the deductive equivalent of the killing blow. I figured it would work for this too.

Step three: punch her in the face with your amazing plan of brilliance.

Without meaning to, I slipped into the poshest accent I could manage. It does help to sell something to an audience if you treat them like bored sixth formers at a Shakespeare play, but in this case I hadn't intended it, my natural showmanship and charisma took over. 'My dear, you need to stop thinking purely about the world in terms of magic.'

'Excuse me?'

'Your plan is contingent on balancing a thousand different variables, holding them all in your head and weaving a spell with stored magic that can contain this. You're making things terribly difficult for yourself, and to add to that you're creating new ways for it to go wrong.'

In a single minute, I could tell that I was turning this woman away from her non-violent resistance principles. I do tend to have that effect. 'It will work,' was all she said, through gritted teeth.

'My way is easier. Give me the charms.' I held out my hand.

I hadn't thought she would actually hand them over. The plan had been to draw it out a little longer so I could be sure I'd have the others so caught up in my pantomime that they wouldn't think too much about what it was I was going to do. When the charms dropped into my hands so soon, Sophie's face locked in a delightful snarl, I lost my way for a moment.

It wasn't a long moment, only a second or two, but it feels like an eternity when you have to rewrite a plan on the fly. But then, if you're stubborn, you come to the conclusion that the original plan was fine anyway. It will not astound you to learn this was the conclusion I reached.

I whirled around on my heel, really hamming up my performance now. 'You, girl,' I said, snapping my fingers at one of the assorted warlocks. 'Surely you have some chewing gum. Fork over a couple of sticks.'

The girl blinked and handed over a pair of gum sticks wrapped in foil. Luck was on my side. Actually, she was perhaps the youngest in the room – sixteen if she was a day – and had the dark make-up and aggressive hair of a girl that would chew gum in an angry way, for when her face just wasn't quite expressive enough to detail the amount of contempt she held you in. *Of course* that kind of girl would have some gum.

I bounded up towards the double doors. 'You see, the important thing about magic is to remember that it is not a *win button*. It's difficult and scary and complicated. So the best way to win is to cheat.' I popped a stick of gum in my mouth and started to chew, then the second. 'You can certainly try to build your spells to function a certain way and to – Jesus, how much aniseed is in this stuff? – and to try to work magic like some grand combination of rock paper scissors and chemistry, but *cheating is better*.'

The gum was burning my sinuses. It felt like I was snorting fire, which actually served to help my performance. You can't help but ramp up the gravitas when it feels like your eyes are dribbling down your face.

I pulled the gum out of my mouth and affixed a piece to each charm. Placing them in separate hands, I slammed them onto the doors – one on each door, at about shoulder height and more or less central – and kept my hands pressed to them. I began to weave the magic.

'Let other people do the difficult parts for you. Why make a spell that reflects fire, when you've got a pair of fire doors right here?'

Step four: make the simplest things look downright miraculous.

I let the spell go and, with a roar of exertion, I pushed the doors up and off their hinges. Lightning crackled around my fingertips as I did so, sheering the bolts that held the hinges together and wrapping around the doors like a luminescent net, keeping them firming glued to my hands. I sent the wind out ahead of me in an arc, hoping it would dull the flames directly outside the door for at least a moment. It did.

Now came the cool part. Honestly, I had planned this to look *ridiculously* cool. With the doors detached, I stepped forward, pushing them out of their frame, and stepped into the lobby. I could hear the flames crackling, but there wasn't time to care. I whipped my arms out to the sides, one last expulsion of power from the wind charm to push the flames back a little as I did so, and I was done.

There I stood, on the smouldering carpet of the lobby, arms held out at my sides with a large wooden door attached to each one, holding back the flaming tide as smoke rose up around me. I glanced back over my shoulder, letting some of the exertion leak into my face for dramatic effect.

'I had a nice one-liner prepared to hammer home the cheating thing a little better but, honestly, this is really hard to maintain. Out. *Now*.'

It took a moment for them to overcome their awe-induced paralysis, but then they started to file out, one by one. The fire was mostly contained behind the doors – which were getting hotter, I'll have you know – but the smoke was still bleeding round the sides. As each warlock passed under my arms and sprinted out into the street, it became harder and harder to hold the spell.

Sophie was the last out. 'You're a bit of a dickhead, aren't you?'

'Please. Get to know me better and you'll see,' I said and coughed. The smoke had replaced the aniseed as the reason my eyes were stinging now. 'I'm a *total* dickhead. Now get out.'

She dipped under my left shoulder and came up in front of me. 'In case we don't have time later, this is an impressive spell. Mine would have been better, but yours isn't half bad.'

I managed a smile. 'Keep telling yourself that. Outside. Tell it to yourself *outside*.'

She nodded and bounded out of the lobby and into the group of warlocks waiting outside. Now it was time for the difficult bit, getting myself out to join them.

The doors were actively smouldering now. I'm not particularly au fait with the science of a fire door, although I'm pretty sure they're not completely fire proof. I'd tried to get the lightning charm's power to shore them up a little anyway, but the magic in the fire had clearly chewed its way through that and into the doors. They weren't going to hold much longer.

There was really only one way out.

I steeled myself and took a deep breath. When I was done coughing up my lungs from that, I released what magic was left in the charms and the doors dropped from my hands. By the time they hit the ground I was already moving, the fire dragging itself around them and after me.

Three steps, then I hurled myself at the door to the street.

And the funny thing is, Sophie's plan would have worked just as well.

CHAPTER 26

Within the collective consciousness, a person jumping out of a burning building is always accompanied by one last great spurt of flame. It surrounds them with a perfect image as they fly through the air, the great hero, and they gracefully roll to a halt in front of the baying crowds. Perhaps the love interest kneels down to them, their faces covered in soot, and they embrace in a kiss long teased.

When I jumped out of a burning building, I bounced down the stairs like a rag doll made of rusted springs and swear words. By the time I reached the last step – there were five, I counted – I felt bruises forming in places I didn't even know I had. There were three *inside my kidneys*, I was sure of it. And I looked up not into the eyes of my potential love interest, but a scowling Scot with very little patience for me.

'How's your head?' she asked, more out of duty than any real care.

'I think I'm okay,' I said slowly. Everything tingled from the brief lick of fire that had caught me, but nothing felt burned. 'Stairs are owie.'

She nearly smiled. Very nearly. And then I saw her face change into one of shock. She said something, but I didn't hear it. That was the moment I felt the flames creep up past my ear.

My bloody hair was on fire!

In truth, it was just a small bit of fire, and it was more singed than actually *on fire*, but I defy you to maintain your composure in a similar situation. As human beings we know on a fundamental level that fire is not meant to be within touching distance of our faces, that's bred in the bone. So yes, I may have freaked out a little.

Sophie stomping on my face to put it out didn't help, either.

'Are you all right?' she muttered when she was finally done.

'Well, my face feels like it has corners in it now, but at least it's not on fire.'

'I'm really sorry. It was the best way I could think of to put you out,' she said, and I could see genuine remorse in her eyes even if it didn't make its way through to the voice.

I stood up slowly. It was getting to be a habit, all this violence. 'By the minute softening of your tone, am I to assume you don't blame me for this any more?' I waved a hand at the burning building. The fire hadn't quite poked itself through the windows and main doors yet, but you could see the shadows of the flames dancing within.

'Well, if you *are* behind it, you're insane. You'd have to be to set yourself on fire and put yourself at risk with that little escape plan. From what I've heard of you, your problem is that you're *too* sane. I'll give you the benefit of the doubt for now.' Her features lightened a little as she spoke. Not scowling can do wonders to a face.

'Thank you,' I said. 'I think. I'm too sane?'

'That's what they say.'

'What does that even mean?'

She shrugged. 'Not a clue.'

Another warlock stepped forward. A mid-twenties, fresh faced male, and attractive enough to make me want to tear his face off. You know people like that, the ones who look like they were hewn from frozen unicorn tears? He was one of those.

'Now that we're not all going to die, can I ask a question?' he said. His voice was velvety too, traces of Welsh in there perhaps. The bastard.

'Fire away,' I said, then caught myself smiling. 'If you'll pardon the pun.'

'I'm not really sure that's a –' he replied.

'Just... What's the question?'

'You said the fire had magic in it, right?' he looked at Sophie.

'Definitely,' she said. 'I could feel it accelerating the whole thing, swimming about inside the flames.'

He reached up and idly pushed at the glasses on his nose. I hadn't even noticed them until he touched them. The *bastard*. 'Forgive me if I'm being dense, but how is that even possible? Fire is antithetical to magic. How do you even get it to hold a magical charge?'

'It's possible,' I said, jumping at the chance to show the attractive little twerp that I was at least clever. 'But it's not something just anyone can do. It's like trying to push two positive ends of a magnet together – you can do it, but the moment you loosen your grip the whole thing is going to go out of whack.'

Sophie frowned. 'So, what, the guy who did this is a specialist in fire magic?'

'Well, he would have to be,' I said. 'Or have worked closely with one.'

I wanted to see how long it would take her to come to the obvious conclusion, that it was Wild who had set the fire. Their relationship clearly had a little strain in it, judging from what I had seen in the theatre at any rate, but I was going to need her to see him as an enemy. Even if she had suspected it privately, I needed her to voice it to the rest of the group.

'You're talking about Ania, aren't you?' she said. I nodded. 'So you think Greg... No, why would he do that?'

'Well,' I said and picked at the singed hair on the back of my head. 'I would like to blow my own trumpet and say that it was to get me out of the way, but there are less grandiose ways to do that. I think he was playing a 'two birds, one stone' situation. He cherry-picked the warlocks he could use and decided to deal with the rest of you, and me, in one go.'

'To be honest, I don't have much trouble believing that.' The beautiful bastard may have been a beautiful bastard, but he wasn't stupid.

Sophie crossed her arms and turned away for a moment, trying to find another solution in her head. 'Are you sure? There's no-one else?'

'No-one else that fits. You defied him, I annoyed him, and the fire started the moment he left. It all adds up.'

'Shit,' she had a way of saying the word that made it sound positively genial. 'He's going to storm the field office, him and the others!'

'Yeah, but that really doesn't make sense,' the guy chimed in. 'Even with the element of surprise, the moment they start anything, someone will call Whitehall and they'll vault everyone there.'

'Not just them,' I said. 'If they're not using magic, Whitehall isn't going to know for sure which warlocks need vaulting. They're just going to pull plugs randomly across the whole of Humberside.'

'They... they can't do that! The rules –'

'It's a cynical way to look at it,' Sophie said. 'But I can't say I disagree. I've been talking to my handler recently, and he's been feeding me information about how many warlocks are getting vaulted down south, all for seemingly minor things. They're already playing with the rules, it won't take much to push them to ignore them. They're scared of something.'

'And all the while, Wild will be safe because he's not in the system,' I said.

I may have taken a dislike to the man in front of me the moment I met him, but watching the bottom drop out of his world wasn't fun. I don't want to speak for him, but I think it would be fair to say that he had never actually considered this. For him, the world may have been unfair, but it was unfair because of the rules. No-one liked them, but it wasn't in the best interests of those who benefited from the rules to change them, and at least it laid down the framework for what would and wouldn't get him in further trouble.

You show someone like that that the rules only apply to the big bastards until they get scared or the red tape starts to chafe, and you essentially shatter his entire understanding of the universe. It's a really unpleasant thing to see. Sophie spotted it too and turned to me, leaving the guy alone to sort out his thoughts.

'So what do we do?'

I clasped my hands behind my head. They'd gotten me involved, damn them. 'Well, if we do nothing, the likelihood is that some of us will die and we have no way of knowing who or how many.'

'Assuming they actually do resort to the vault.'

'They'll hold off for a while. They've got a small force of fast-trackers there, they'll hold their own at first. But knowledge of the craft will overcome brute strength in the end, someone will get scared...'

'But Bennett –'

My neck clicked. 'Bennett will probably be the one to make the call. He's the only one with the sort of authority to make people take him seriously. They'll back him into a corner and he'll bite back at all of us.'

'Most of Romsey's lot aren't exactly arcane geniuses, Parker,' she said. Her face was stone now, the cogs whirring in her head, trying to think up a way to sort this out. 'They're just magicians that got a little too loud at the wrong time.'

'Aren't we all?'

'No,' she said. 'We really aren't. Not everyone turned to the black before Whitehall caught up with them. Some of them were just living inconsequential lives with the odd bit of magic to brighten it up.'

'That's ridiculous.'

'It's also true. Almost no-one in Romsey's little group practised the black when they were brought in. We had a long time to get to know each other in that theatre, not much else to do. I can remember all their stories.'

Even knowing where this was going, I couldn't stop talking. 'But *statistically* most warlocks have dabbled in the black. Right? Where are they at in this little contretemps?'

'You're looking at them,' she said and indicated to the group with a nod of her head. 'We're the ones who know the most about magic, after all.'

Not much you can argue with on that point. 'Any knowledge at all will give them an edge over the fast-trackers, even if they don't understand what they're fighting *for*.'

'Won't dispute that. So what do we do?'

There wasn't really much else for it. I very much would have liked to have stayed uninvolved, or at least limit my involvement to my actual mission brief of just getting them all to come home without fuss. If there was any way I could have just stepped back and let things sort themselves out, that would have been my preferred course of action. But my cynicism wouldn't let me.

There was a very real chance Whitehall would start randomly vaulting people, and I could have been one of them.

I didn't really feel too keen on having my heart burst inside my chest, especially before I knew what Wild was even doing. I wasn't about to believe he was out to trigger a cull, but it was hard to argue with that possibility when he was leading a bloody march.

'Oh for God's sake,' I spat. 'We're going to have to go and stop Wild and Romsey from doing something foolish.'

This woke up the young man from his existential stupor. 'Wait, what? We can't do that! We can't fight our own. We were supposed to be about getting Whitehall to ease up on us, solidarity and all that!'

'Well, solidarity at this point might just get you accidentally killed. It's not worth the risk. Besides, *not* acting will only set your cause back, as I see it.'

He fell silent, his eyes downcast. Just keep kicking him when he's down, me, that's the best way to treat a person in pain. I got a curt nod of agreement from Sophie though, which was something.

'We're under equipped, you know,' she said quietly. 'We've got the knowledge, but not much in the way of enchantments to burn. Romsey's lot have an active spell-slinger in Wild. We're going to need a proper plan.'

'Bollocks to that,' I said, pulling out my phone and dialling a number. 'We've got people on the inside. We just need a few pyrotechnics with which to make an entrance.'

'What are you –'

'Shh!' I said as the phone rang.

I hadn't wanted to call Charlie so soon after our night, but then despite all her warnings I hadn't expected a full on life-or-death situation either. She would probably understand. Not that there was anything that needed understanding. It was all perfectly fine. Probably. I was over-thinking things. I knew I was over-thinking it. *But I couldn't stop.*

Her crisp voice snapped me back to reality, however. 'Oh good, it's you.'

'Hello, dear,' I said slightly louder than was necessary, the lingering residue of my moment of trepidation at making the call no doubt bleeding through into my voice. 'How's the job?'

'Hanging in the balance,' she said. 'I have *spreadsheets* to do. Do you know how many people are going to read these spreadsheets?'

'Not off the top of my head.'

'No-one. No-one ever reads spreadsheets, but they have to be done and, apparently, I need to be seen to be working. How are you?'

'Oh, you know, about to lead an army of reformed black magic warlocks against a force led by a fast-tracker that is laying siege to the field office. Your typical day in the jewel of the north.'

There was a noise that sounded a little like someone falling off their chair and dragging the contents of their desk with them. '*Excuse me?*'

'As much as I would like to fill you in, I don't really have the time. I need a couple of favours though.'

'You're making a habit of asking for the impossible, you know,' she said, and again I could hear the smile in her voice. No matter how annoyed I made her, she couldn't help but smile. 'What do you need?'

'One sec,' I said and turned to Sophie. 'Oi, missus, how's your credit with Whitehall. Actually, scratch that. What's your surname? I'll have my woman look you up on the system.'

'Preston,' she replied.

'Your *woman?*' Charlie said. I think the smile had gone, but I can't be sure.

'You're like my man Friday, but a woman. You know what I mean?'

'Very rarely,' she said. 'I'm guessing that's Sophie Preston you've got with you there?'

I slapped my hand against my leg as a really odd-looking form of applause. 'I knew you were good.'

'Hardly. There's only one Preston working Humberside,' she said as the click-clack of keys picked up speed. 'Decent standing with the brass. Why, what have you got planned?'

'I need a couple of spells authorised. Might be a bit tricky, but I'm sure you can swing it. And, we're probably going to need a distraction before too long.'

'Oh Christ...'

'Can you keep them out of the vault without losing your job?'

There was a beat of silence. 'No.'

'Let me rephrase. Can you keep them out of the vault at all?'

There was a longer silence. 'Maybe. For a time, but not very long.'

'We shouldn't need long, hopefully.'

'Well, if I'm throwing my job away anyway,' she said with faux cheerfulness. You can always tell when it's fake, it's ever so slightly shriller than is necessary. 'Your spells won't be a problem. I'll put you both through as carte blanche. That will keep them out the vault while you kick up whatever fuss you're after. Your little army will have to go as is, though, I wouldn't want to risk them noticing such a huge authorisation of magic. They'll notice eventually, but I doubt it'll be today it it's just the two of you.'

'How do you reckon they'll react to that?' I asked.

I heard her inhale. 'Well, like I say, I'll be throwing my job away but the way things are going it's not like that's much of an issue. Can't say how they'll react to you and Preston, though. I doubt they'll crack open the vault so suddenly after all that time, but it wouldn't be out of the question. There's not really a system in place for this sort of thing.'

'We'll deal with that later. The ticking of the cosmic time bomb will just distract us from today's peril.'

'And what exactly will *today's* peril entail?'

I told her the plan. Admittedly, as in most cases, the word *plan* was awfully optimistic for what I intended to do. I think *scheme* might have worked better. I was aiming for *plot* but I don't think I got there. *Scheme* was good enough though, and Charlie listened to it in silence, not questioning or picking apart any of it, which I like to take as a good sign.

'How do you come up with this shit?' she asked when I was done.

'My brain is powered by Sublimium.'

There was a nervous, exasperated giggle from the other end of the phone. 'Please don't get killed. You're going to need to set me up with a new job when this is all done, and I don't want it to be as your pall bearer.'

'Firstly, what makes you think I can set you up with a job?' I said. 'Secondly, you couldn't be my pall bearer. Not with those twiggy arms of yours. I am a mountain of sinew and chiselled masculinity, you ain't prepared to hoist that onto your shoulders, sister.'

'Fuck you,' she said, and the smile was back. 'Just... promise me you'll be careful.'

I descended into seriousness for a moment. 'I promise.'

There was more tapping at a keyboard. 'Okay, your spells are authorised. I'll keep an ear out for the vault alarm and do what I can to slow them down, but do what you have to do quickly. I can't keep them out forever.'

'Thank you,' I said. 'Sometimes I'm not sure I deserve you.'

'You definitely don't. Let me clear that up for you right now.'

I smiled and hung up.

I took a moment to centre myself. If the warlocks wanted to follow in my footsteps, it was time to show them how, and to do that I needed full control of my smug, self-aggrandising arrogance. I had to purge myself of any self-doubt and just remember that I am one powerful bastard behind the Whitehall muzzle. It's an easy thing to convince yourself when you are completely aware of what horrors you are capable.

Confidence pumping through my veins I turned back towards Sophie and her cadre of warlocks. 'Right then. I think it's high time we reminded Whitehall exactly why they are so afraid of us.'

CHAPTER 27

We took a moment before we arrived at the field office to arrange ourselves into that classic 'V' formation you automatically see all superhero teams in when you imagine them. Trying to actually assemble your squad into such an arrangement is a little like herding cats, but it's well worth the effort for the image alone. This was all about image.

As we rounded the corner, the warlocks fanning out behind me like a peculiar cape, I was expecting a scene like that of K's place. Wild and Romsey had a good head start on us, but they had apparently marched at a slower pace than we had, having only just started the assault as we arrived. A few fast-trackers were down already, joined by one or two warlocks, but for the most part it was still very much a scuffle more than anything else.

Wild and Romsey were conspicuous by their absence, and a quick head count told me that perhaps five other warlocks were missing too. It wasn't a stretch to assume they had stormed straight inside, the other warlocks acting as a sort of sentinel to keep the fast-trackers busy.

I stopped, my little squad following suit, and turned to Sophie. 'I say we start small.'

'This is your show, Parker. Whatever you think is best.'

Shaking myself loose, I rolled my shoulders back a few times and felt the muscles in my chest pop gently. Then I clapped my hands together, rubbed them, and planted a small kiss on the knuckles of my left hand. A sign of hope that what I was about to do wouldn't royally screw me up. Or get me killed. I prised my hands apart and began to draw in power.

This wasn't ambient power from my previous spells. I had no need for a pentagram here, this was going to be all me. As the various conduits sprang to life, I held onto the memory of my near implosion a few days back, outside that bar. What I was doing would need a similar level of power, but I had to maintain that wall, I had to stay me. Hopefully Charlie's efforts in Whitehall would give me this spell without any alerts at the vault, but I still needed something to fear to keep me grounded. The lust *needed* to stay bottled up.

And it did. I could feel the pressure building behind the wall in my mind, but I was prepared for it. The temptation to let it trickle through, to ease the tension, was immense, but I plunged that drive into the spell. I let it build in my head, the mental construct of what I was after, channelled it into my left hand specifically, and felt it begin to whirl and crackle in the air around my fingers.

Romsey's men and the fast-trackers hadn't even spotted me. They were fighting amongst themselves, borrowed magic bouncing off enchantments, more or less how I had expected. I was about to make quite an entrance.

The whirling morass of power coalesced in my hand quickly – the whole thing from conception to casting took less than a second – and I flicked my wrist several times to let it loose, sending translucent jets of magic slamming into the asphalt on the approach to the field office. They sat there, like ephemeral runway lights, strobing very gently. When all were placed, I started to walk forwards slowly.

With my right hand, I reached into my pocket and pulled out my phone. A pair of cheap speakers had been wedged onto the headphone port rather haphazardly, but there had only been one electronics shop on the way and we hadn't the time to shop around. I flicked through the options until I found the mp3 player, found the song I was looking for and hit play.

There had been many different options, but I'd gone with *Back in Black* by AC/DC. With the volume cranked as high as it would go, complete with a ready-made enchantment offered from one of Sophie's warlocks to crank it even higher, it spilled out like an atom bomb of rock and roll. Romsey's boys and the fast-trackers couldn't help but hear it.

They stopped fighting and turned to look at me at the exact moment I passed the first landing light, and it exploded in a shower of violet and cerulean flame, launching itself into the air. Each landing light did the same thing, rotating through the more eye-gouging members of the spectrum. By the time I reached the last one, the combatants in front of me were so confused and gobsmacked that they were staring at me in complete and total awe.

I stood there in silence, arms held wide – magic still pooling in the left and the banshee-scream of a guitar emanating from my right – and let them soak me in. A prep-school Jesus, I cut a pretty stark image in front of them, which my pyrotechnics certainly helped to amplify, but now they needed to trigger the next part. Preferably, they would do so soon. It was going to sync up perfectly with the music.

Thankfully, a suit stepped forward. 'Parker? What the hell are you doing?'

I spun in place, a pirouette I had practised in the mirror in my youth. Everyone wants to find a way to make a pirouette look cool in situations that aren't on a stage, and anyone who disagrees is lying to themselves. I had discovered that the best way was to end them with a bang.

At the moment I finished my spin, my left arm shot out towards Romsey's warlocks and the fast-trackers, centred on the suit that had spoken, and I released the energy. A condensed beam of crackling Thorfire erupted from my palm, slammed into the suit and arced off through the entire group. It drove the suit back and cracked his skull on the wall of the building while the rest danced an electric jig beside him, then collapsed.

They smoked gently.

'Cos I'm back in BLAAAAAAAAACK.'

I clicked the music off and surveyed the scene. One warlock was still standing, by design I'll have you know, staring at me with eyes the size of dinner plates. I held myself still and locked my gaze with his for one second, two, three, four, then shrugged my eyebrows at him and flashed my best slasher smile.

He tried to run, but his brain had made the decision so fast that it started acting on it before his legs had received the order. He span and fell on his face, floundered for a moment, scrabbled back to a vertical base and legged it for the field office. There was a scream trapped in his throat, you could feel it, but he was far too scared to breathe.

I flung another bolt of Thorfire his way. He was going to wake up with a monster headache, but when he did I would have a witness that could tell others what he had seen. Not of much use right now, but having someone out there spinning tales of how dangerous you are is rarely a bad thing. Within reason.

I let the chap flop to the ground, then I spun on my heel and directed my smile towards my entourage.

'Boom!' I shouted. 'Now *that* is how you make an entrance!'

There's a good booming laugh that comes with adrenaline, and I wasn't about to deny it its moment in the sun. I guffawed like a good'un as my little soldiers stared at me – some in awe and some in utter confusion, but all of them smiling – and Sophie wrestled with how exactly to think about the whole thing.

Eventually, she facepalmed. 'That was the cheesiest fucking thing I've ever seen.'

'Oh, shut-up. That was *awesome!*' I said. 'Now come along, children. We've got a megalomaniac to set straight.'

I was on an arcane high. The adrenaline was mixing with the magic and pumping around my system so fast that it felt like my thoughts were on fire. It was glorious, and it was catching. The warlocks by my side were glowing with confidence, constrained as they were to what minor magics they could weave from their enchantments, and even Sophie had a glint in her eye.

Despite her apparent dislike of my entrance, I could feel her start to draw in her own power. Gently, slowly, but it was there. Maybe it was even subconscious. She also had free rein with her magic, and although she was showing restraint – or I simply hadn't given her the chance to do anything, which was more likely – I was hoping I had at least galvanised her to enjoy it when an opportunity presented itself. Magic always *looks* better when the caster enjoys it.

There was a definite spring in my step as I strode past and over the smoking, whimpering bodies of the people I had incapacitated. The spell had never been intended to kill them, and I was silently glad that I hadn't over-egged it a little and finished them off. Dark thoughts of the fast-tracker I had crushed were lurking at the periphery of my thoughts, and while I rejected them at the time, the relief that I hadn't repeated the same mistake was still palpable. Although, if I had, I doubt it would have fazed me at the time, excited as I was. I was practically strutting by the time I reached the door.

But I needed them to survive, as much as I might have been able to write off any mistakes at the time. I needed them to see that, even on their best day, they couldn't have taken me. All their magic combined wasn't but a thimbleful of power compared to what I could wield. I needed to educate them quickly, and that seemed the best way. They'd wake up scared of me, of all warlocks of actual meaningful power, and maybe that would be enough to get them to see reason.

It might sound a little grandiose for me to say that I was trying to set myself up as a walking nuclear deterrent. Grandiose, but completely true. After having seen me in action, it wouldn't be a stretch for them to realise that if they were as scared as they were, things would be considerably worse for those without power.

The inside of the field office was considerably more battle-scarred than the outside, although some of it was no doubt a result of my escape the day before. I didn't think I had caused this much damage, however, so I was going to pin the blame on Wild and Romsey. They were the most likely culprits after all.

The impact marks told a story, one that said Wild himself had led the charge. It is my understanding that the fast-tracker doctrine of combat-casting teaches them to rely on pure force magic for prolonged conflicts, and the lack of scorch marks led me to believe Wild had followed this to the letter. That and the bodies of his fellow fast-trackers that looked as though they had been whacked by sledgehammers. A collapsed chest is nasty enough, but you drape one of those over a staved in skull and it's an image that's hard to shift.

Force magic is brutal and easy, which makes it something of a double whammy. You don't have to spark off any real chemical reactions or excite too many molecules, you just move the stuff that's already there. It's not flashy, but it is very effective. Proper magicians like flashy, and flashy is not *hard* to do if you know the theory, but fast-trackers don't.

I could hear screaming in the distance, a helpful beacon to zero in on my targets. There were words trapped in there and trying to get out, but I think only dogs could hear them. Whether they were screams of pain or of fear was hard to say. I would have liked to know, if only to have a better idea of what I was going to blunder into, but you make the best of what you have. Trying to track down Wild in the field office wouldn't have taken too long, but anything to narrow the search was welcome.

Every body we passed was a suit, not a single warlock. The corridors weren't very wide – perhaps enough so you could stand two abreast – so it was likely that Wild had led the charge, similar to myself now, swatting down his comrades one by one. There was no-one left for me to swat, for which I was thankful. The less I had to fight people that weren't affiliated with Wild, the easier the aftermath would be.

I followed the screaming to its source, a room deep inside the building, and put an ear to the door. There was a kerfuffle going on in there, small-scale but deadly enough. It seemed I had the right place. I took a step back and kicked in the door – I was so wired that it didn't even register as a decision, I just had to keep making the best entrances – and there on the other side stood Wild and Romsey, bold as brass.

And Bennett.

And *Kaitlyn*.

They were stood in the centre of the room, back to back, trading spells with Wild while Romsey tried to beat them down. They were mostly on the defensive, focusing on rotating through the various types of wards and shield spells they knew to absorb or deflect the onslaught. The pair of them looked tired, but when one faltered the other was there to pick up the slack, pumping enough power into the shields to keep them functioning.

It was a good plan, but it was a desperate measure. There was little chance they could send out much in the way of offence with that sort of setup, and Wild and Romsey had the room to pace around them, like wolves preparing to pounce. If they could keep up the pressure, Bennett and Kaitlyn would break eventually.

So, really, it was a good thing that I made such a loud entrance. Right?

'Hello, all!' I boomed. 'Sorry I'm late. Parking was a nightmare. It's all disabled and family spaces nearby, did you know that?'

Look, I know that's hardly the most dynamic of entries, but you have to understand I was running on fumes and fairy lights. Most of what was dancing around in my head was the desire to just throw magic at things, so getting actual human words to come out in any sort of coherent order was an achievement. I'd like to see you do better.

Besides, oh ye of little faith and large chortles, it worked. The skirmish halted while everyone in the room turned to look at me, completely bewildered. I like bewilderment. You can get a lot done while a bewildered mind is trying to dislodge the chunk of nonsense you've just jammed into the gears.

'Piss off, Parker,' Wild said. His voice was dry from

exertion, cracking in awkward places. 'This doesn't concern you. We'll get round to you in a minute.'

'I beg to differ, sirrah,' I shot back.

Sophie whispered in my ear. 'Sirrah?'

'I don't know,' I said and shrugged. 'Sounds like a cool word.'

'Try to remember why we're here,' she said.

I nodded and returned my attention to Wild. 'I'm not exactly sure why you're here, but I *am* sure that it probably involves me in some capacity. Everything involves me really. I'm kind of a big deal. Dark Lord of Hampshire, that sort of thing.'

Romsey stepped forward. 'If you were serious about that, we wouldn't *need* to be here! You'd be doing this and we'd be following!'

I strolled into the room a little deeper, letting my posse funnel in behind me. The room was one of the many cubicle farms you'll find tucked away inside anywhere that calls itself an office, and with the cubicles having been blasted to the sides of the room to make way for a nice little fighting arena, there wasn't enough space for everyone to fit in. Not that I needed them to, I just needed them to be seen. Sophie stepped up to my right hand and rubbed hers together, letting a few sparks fly.

'Oh,' I said. 'You mean like this lot? Stand down, gents, you don't have much of a chance.'

I played up the theatricality, although really it was for my own benefit rather than anyone else at this point. The sheer numbers was enough, but having your enemy watch you flick your wrist, bring it up to your temple and pull a spell out of your head, fully formed, is still a glorious thing to do. I let the power dance over my fingers, a completely unfocused and undefined spell, just to show off.

The energy skipped over and around my fingers, the

fairy lights in my head made manifest, so captivating and threatening at the same time. I cocked my head to one side and smiled, ready to graciously accept Wild's surrender.

And then he killed half the people in the room.

CHAPTER 28

I'd never even conceived of that sort of magic before. Combat magic is almost always projectiles, sometimes a sustained beam, but it always has to travel. You harness the power, shape it with your will, then release it. At its very basic level, a spell is just a package of instructions; you still need to deliver it.

All Wild did was raise his left hand towards us, palm forward, and most of my posse just *died*. No fanfare, no pyrotechnics, they just keeled over. It was only after they went down that I even felt the spell wash over me, a thick cloud of coldness and some weird emotions I couldn't place. It stabbed into my hind-brain like a flaming ice pick and just sat there, gently rotating into the pain centres of my mind. An emotion drill.

All sensations other than this melange of emotions just ceased instantly. The outside world was now unimportant, irrelevant, damn-near non-existent. The *pain* was reality now. Not the torturous, bright fire of agony you get from a physical wound, but the cold, smothering anguish of the mental realm. Pressing down on me, a darkness that was all too familiar, drawn from my own thoughts and mined from the very deepest pits of my mind.

There was a face in the darkness. I couldn't see it, but I knew it was out there, watching me. Just a face, not a whole person. It held a realisation, slowly forming around it somehow, an epiphany moulding itself around a memory. Yes, a memory, that's what that was, something I had forgotten in fact. No, had *never known*. Or had I? Was it real?

Then, suddenly, there was another presence. It pushed through the clouds, burning them back everywhere it touched, and I felt myself being dragged back through its wake, out of the smothering anguish and back into the bright agony.

I opened my eyes and found myself staring into the steely frown of Bennett.

'Did it not occur to you that we were hiding behind a shield for a reason?' he said.

I sat up. I was in their shield bubble, Bennett crouching over me and Kaitlyn swearing under her breath as she did her best to hold the thing together without him. 'Yes, but a psychic-death-wave-emotion-drill thing hadn't been my first thought. What happened?'

A bolt of force ricocheted off the shield with a loud noise and Kaitlyn yelped. Bennett leapt to his feet and placed his palms against the inside of the bubble, letting his power shore up the defences again. 'Whatever that spell is, he targeted it at the guys behind you. You and Preston got hit with the wake, for want of a better word. You staggered over to us, Preston just shut down.'

I sprang to my feet, or as best I could in the confined space of the shield, and looked around. Sophie was near the door, surrounded by corpses and not looking particularly well. She was conscious, wrapped in a shield of her own, but her face was white and her eyes heavy. Romsey had all his attention focused on her, trying to smash down her shield with brute force. It wouldn't hold.

'Tell me everything you know about that spell, now,' I said to whichever of the two would listen.

Kaitlyn was the one to reply. 'Blackest of the black,' she said, her voice strained. 'Don't know much about it, only that it snatches the life out of you if you let it. Only seen it once before.'

'How did you counter it?'

She groaned. The shield shifted into a new thread on the magical spectrum. 'Didn't. Shot the bastard with a rifle from three hundred metres. Never saw it coming.'

'Not too helpful here, dear. Anything else?'

Bennett interrupted. 'Shields don't stop it for long. It eats through them. Flipping through the spectrum helps, but not for long.'

'Right, okay, using a spell of that size must eat up a lot of energy. He's got to keep it reserved for the big targets. He didn't use it on the way in, right? That was all your typical fast-tracker combat clout.' I said. 'Okay. I've got an idea.'

I turned towards Wild. He was angry, but he was keeping the rage out of his face. It didn't add up, he had to have been tired by now, running on empty when it came to his magic. Storming the place was all well and good, but this sort of siege should have had him almost completely tapped. Either he was very good at hiding this, or something was amiss.

Another ball of force bounced off the shield. Kaitlyn dropped to one knee and the shield cracked a little.

'Oi, mate,' I shouted at Wild through the shield. 'Can you pack that in for just a minute?'

He didn't look as if he had heard me, just continued drawing in power and hurling it at us with robotic efficiency. He was focused entirely on breaching this shield, which gave me my first piece of good news, at least.

One more spell slammed into the shield, and the moment it was done I stepped forwards and through the membrane, eyes locked on Wild. I could feel him drawing in more power, but as soon as I finished stepping out into the open he stopped. Perhaps my serious face threw him.That was certainly my intention.

'You arrogant shit,' he said. 'Do you honestly think I won't kill you?'

'Hey, you're the one who said this didn't concern me. You go telling a guy that, he's going to think you've gone soft. Besides, you threw your deathpocalypse mind bomb spell thing at my lackeys, not me. You're just giving my ego ammunition at this point, mate.' I played with my collar. I needed to do something with my hands to stop them shaking.

A half-formed force bolt leapt from his fingers but I had expected it and slapped it out of the air with a spell of my own. You don't find too many people willing to parry with their counter-spells nowadays, they're all too caught up on keeping themselves as safe as possible. No style, those guys.

'It's taken me a while, chap, but I think I've finally got a read on you. You like the scales tipped just one percent in your favour, right? Knowing that things are almost, *almost* equal.'

'What are you talking about?'

I ran my tongue over my teeth. 'You were saving that mind bomb for Bennett, I reckon, but I turn up with a small army of warlocks and you figure the scales have tipped against you, so you take them out instead. Now things are a little more even, you try to take me down with a simple combat spell? Either someone loves me very much – and who could blame you – or you've got some weird, twisted sense of honour rattling around in that meat balloon of yours.'

He grinned and flung another brace of spells at me. I

cancelled out the first with a water spell, I think, something that absorbed the force and stopped it dead before it hit me. The second I missed. It slammed into my shoulder and spun me around for a moment. The enchantments in the blazer took most of the damage so my arm stayed attached, but didn't stop the pain.

'You really don't understand how people think,' Wild said. 'You like to think you do, but you're not as clever as you think you are.'

'Hey, I'm still learning. Spent a long time *telling* people what to think. I think I'm doing okay, all things considered,' I replied. The anger might have peeked through a little, but I think I held things together okay.

'If you think I'm driven by honour, you're really not doing very well at all.'

'Well, that's all right,' I said as I spun around. 'I find it easier to deal with the dishonourable.'

Romsey had thought he had been clever, sneaking up on me. Had he not have spent the last minute or so pounding on Sophie's shield, it might actually have worked. The thing is, when such an obvious sound suddenly vanishes, you're going to make people suspicious.

He basically walked right into my fist. I'm not sure how much of the energy of the blow came from me, and how much from the speed at which he was approaching me, but it laid him out cold. Kaitlyn and Bennett started to slowly shuffle towards Sophie like a spectral turtle as I turned back towards Wild.

I should have expected the third force bolt, really. It caught me in the ribs, pushing me back and up into the air, dropping me down hard on my knees and elbows. Another bolt meant to crush my skull but I rolled to one side, splinters of floor peppering my face as I did so. I came up in a crouch and threw a spell of my own.

If Wild was going with the barest basics of combat

casting, I was going to go full on magician. A crackling phoenix of blue-green power shot from my hand and exploded against Wild's snap-conjured shield, splintering into a thousand dancing lights. They dazzled him and, while he tried to blink the spots out of his eyes, I charged him.

I leapt at him with a punch, driving it into his face and sending him off balance. I went for a second and he blocked it, returning one of his own to my already bruised ribs. Before I knew it, we were embroiled in a brawl, with every gap in the punches filled with a wayward spell to try and catch the other party off guard. In my mind's eye, it looks a little like those cartoon dust cloud fights.

At one point I took a hard blow to the chin and fell back, head woozy and vision clouded. I had been so busy dodging his spells that I had lost track of his punches. The only option was to go full defensive, and I managed to get my shield up in time to protect me from a volley of vicious spells. My resolve was starting to waver, and my shield was not up to snuff.

You only get so long before the euphoria wears off and your body has to deal with the effects of pumping so much magic through your system after so long. I could feel the tiredness starting to break through.

Wild's assault stopped and he stared down at me. No tiredness there.

'If I had the option, I would quite enjoy ripping your mind out of your body. Really, it's a shame it didn't work the first time. But I have a job to do. This has to look authentic,' he said.

'What are you talking about?' I said. My voice was raspy and my breathing heavy. Now the wall of euphoria was coming down, every bit of me was suffering, it seemed.

'Why, my dear warlock,' he said, drawing in his

power. 'I'm going to trigger a revolution.'

CHAPTER 29

'Excuse me?'

Wild's face cracked. The cold anger gave way to a colder smile, one that just couldn't resist the chance to gloat. 'There's a massive army of magicians out there, sat on their arses in dank pits, hiding from Whitehall and its warlocks. They think standing up and fighting is impossible, that it would be suicide. Or maybe they just don't care. It's my job to show them that it's not only possible, it's easy and it is *right*.'

'By destroying a field office? That's hardly a particularly bad-ass thing to do,' I said. I needed him to keep talking so I could get some feeling back in, well, my body. People love gloating.

'The field office is secondary, although a nice little beacon. Bennett is the real prize. If I show the free magicians that warlocks, fast-trackers and even sheriffs can be killed, all they'll need is a leader. We start in the North, where the spirit of independence has always resided, and then we'll drag it south.'

'And let me guess. You are going to be their great saviour?'

I've never heard quite so derisive a snort. 'Good god, no. Someone else has called that particular chair, I just want myself a bit more power.'

'The Rider...'

'Turns out some of your kind have a bit more backbone than the others, Parker. When he approached me with his plan, I couldn't deny the logic of it. The tuition, the power, even the money, they're all just bonuses.'

My arm was getting heavy, but I had to keep him talking just a little longer. He'd give me an opening eventually. 'Not to sound like an old meme, but this is madness. Surely you see that? You succeed here and the fallout for warlocks across the country could be incalculable. If you make Whitehall scared –'

Power flared in Wild's eyes. 'He knows that, of course he knows that. But if a hundred, two hundred, ten hundred people have to die to rouse the rest, then that's how it has to be. Don't think this was a decision he made lightly. He had hoped you would understand.'

'People keep saying this,' I said and let out a tired chuckle. 'But I really don't see how. I've never been one for grand ideas.'

'Then maybe The Rider knows you better than you know yourself,' he said and paused. He looked suddenly very pensive. 'He has a way of doing that. But as useful as he reckoned you would be, everyone is expendable. The plan has to come first.'

He blasted me with another bolt, knocking me flat. The shield was barely functional now, more and more of the force bleeding through every time he hit me. That last one felt as though it had dislocated my shoulder, and I could see the spell starting to haemorrhage. Then he hit me again, and I watched my shield evaporate into the air and felt my ribs crack.

Every spell I could think of flashed through my head

at once, which I guess is a little like your life flashing before your eyes. My mind grasped at them, trying to find something I could use to get myself out of this situation, but they all swam around me like silvery fish in a stream. One or two nearly took shape, only to slip through my fingers as the suited bastard stepped in close for the final blow.

I let the spells go. I had chosen to abandon a lot of my youth, as you know, when Whitehall had taken me on. Most of it, when looked back on with a sober mind, was hard to justify. But one thing had always stuck with me. I had decided how I wanted to go out, when it eventually happened. If this was my time to die, I was going to go out staring my killer in the face defiantly. No begging, no squirming, no *fear*.

My eyes locked on his. He nodded at me slowly and started to weave one final bolt of force, the power wrapping around his fingers as a luminescent thread. At least I could take solace in the fact you probably don't really feel your head implode.

He levelled his hand at my head, and got immediately slammed in the back of the head by a violet beam of power.

Wild roared and spun around, firing his spell off randomly at the room behind him while he tried to put out the purple flames that had taken hold in his hair. As he fell to the side, slapping at his own head, he revealed my saviour.

Sophie stood, eyes burning with the same shade of purple, like some figure from a Japanese horror film. Apart from the creepy purple eyes, her complexion was very pallid and it looked as though keeping herself upright was not just difficult but actively painful. Her hands were clenched into fists tight enough to need specialised equipment to unfurl and she was sweating. Apparently punching her way through Wild's mind bomb had done a number on her far worse than my experience. Another strike against the idea that it is always best to do things yourself.

Wild patted out the flames in his hair and immediately started throwing bolt after bolt of force at Sophie. She dodged and danced around them like a ballerina, pirouetting around and flipping over them with such unexpected grace, each beautiful movement followed by a gout of her violet wildfire. Wild's own shield took the brunt of those shots, but alternating between that and his force bolts was strenuous.

This was my time to get a second wind. I couldn't breath, my right arm had gone numb, and my mind was rattling around inside my skull like a loose bolt in a washing machine, but I wasn't dead. That gave me something to hold onto. If I could just ignore the pain, teach my lungs to be obstinate little bastards, I could try and do something about the situation.

'The Rider never briefed me on you, Sophie,' Wild was saying.

Sophie swatted a spell out of the air and rolled with it, sliding under a second. 'If he'd looked further than Parker, he might have had something to say. I wasn't exactly under the radar before they brought me in.'

I looked around for Kaitlyn and Bennett. I found them slumped against the far wall, panting and barely conscious. They had weathered the blows Wild had thrown at them, but the cost had clearly been astronomical. Whatever they had done for Sophie had been the last of their power, and they were out of this fight now. They shot me a glance to tell me as much. Bennett tried to get up, but Kaitlyn put a hand on his shoulder to stop him.

Couldn't fault his dedication, I suppose.

But Sophie couldn't hold out forever, and I needed to get back in the game. She was already starting to get sloppy, Wild's spells getting closer to her with each cast, her dodges becoming less graceful.

I felt for my power and found it erratic and muted, stagnant. Any spell I tried to weave with that would wither and decay before I even had time to cast it, but I had to try. I held up my good hand and willed a spell to form, anything, but apart from a few sickly motes of power there was nothing.

Wild had forsaken magic for the moment now and was moving in for hand-to-hand with Sophie, which was going to be bad for the girl. The closer Wild got, the less room she had to manoeuvre, and there was no way she could beat him in a fist fight. She had speed on her side, but there wasn't much strength behind her strikes in her current state. The best she could hope for was to hold him at bay with irritating and quick blows. But, eventually, he would hit her and he'd do it hard.

To hell with the pain, I thought, *I need to stop this.* I'm not one for belittling the input of a woman, nor am I one of those helplessly chivalrous souls who cannot walk away from a woman in trouble, but I do very much try to be a person who can repay his debts. Sophie had given me a few extra moments of life, and I didn't want that to be at the expense of her own.

One step at a time then. First, up onto my elbows, even the numb one. Next, through the pain, sit forward. The ribs would fight this, screaming at me to just lie still and leave things as they were, but I was going to need to push past this. Then up onto my knees. Then one knee. One deep breath and then up onto my feet. What I'd do once there I could work out when I got to it.

The pain was, to be blunt, a little more vicious than I had expected. I stumbled and fell back a couple of times, but I managed it nonetheless. And I won't lie, it made me feel like a demigod, pushing back that level of pain. It was the sort of thing that made me want to roar, a full on bestial cry of victory. But I'm British, and we're hard-wired to take our victories quietly and with restraint.

As I got to my feet, Sophie was unleashing a spirited assault. Her legs were moving like lightning, striking Wild's upper body and head, although he barely seemed to react. They would knock him off balance a little, but he didn't seem too discouraged or pained by them. She clearly felt she had the advantage, however, as she took a step back to set up for a powerful spin kick. That was when Wild made his move.

A hand shot out as she was mid-spin, catching her by the throat as soon as she completed her rotation. He lifted her up off the ground with a single hand and stared into her eyes.

'That was brave. It'll make for a good story when the revolution kicks off,' he said as she thrashed in his grasp. 'Where'd you learn to fight like that?'

'Public school,' she said, her voice defiant.

'You don't strike me as the public school type.'

'I'll take that as a compliment.'

Sophie was struggling to pry his hand open, and was furiously kicking at what parts of him she could reach all through this seemingly polite dialogue. Wild drove his fist into her diaphragm, taking the wind out of her sails. 'If that'll ease your passing, take it however you like.'

Bennett came in like a shot, throwing himself at Wild's arm, trying to knock Sophie loose. It didn't work. He lacked the strength and the speed to pull it off, and for his trouble he got launched across the room with the magical equivalent of a backhand. There was the sound of cloth tearing and he flew past me and slammed into the far wall. The impact was an unpleasant sound.

But his assault hadn't been entirely in vain. To deliver the arcane bitchslap, Wild had been forced to lower Sophie to the ground momentarily. With her feet on the ground she managed to do some sort of weird, twisty thing and drive her heel straight into Wild's throat. Naturally, he let her go and she followed up with a heel kick, pushing him back.

Then she froze.

'Jesus Christ,' she said, staring at Wild with a mixture of fear and revulsion. I had no idea what it could have been that would have spooked her so until, still sucking air like an overweight vacuum cleaner, Wild turned to face me.

Bennett must have torn his shirt when he was launched across the room, because Wild's chest was now clearly visible through the shreds of his suit. And in the centre, carved into the flesh, was a pentagram. The cuts had begun to scar over on the outskirts, but the centre was still raw and weeping blood. The amount of energy trapped in it had clearly kept those channels from healing properly.

'You stupid bastard,' I said.

Pentagrams draw in and store magic. It's what they do. There's a limit to what they can store, but it's big, in the same way a SCUBA tank can hold an hour or so of air. It compresses it, squeezes as much in as possible and gives magicians a fantastic battery to draw from. But we also have our own, internal batteries.

I've talked about the magic surging through my veins before, and the reason for this is because in a way it truly does. In a very real way blood *is* magic. Thaumaturgy, at its base and most efficient level, is the magic of blood. Any power a magician can draw is dependent on his own blood. It has tolerances, limits built into the very DNA, which is why you get such a range of talent. Some magicians are all out of puff at a magic trick, others – such as myself – could rip the heavens out of the sky and grind them into dust with only a spectre of effort. You can train yourself to improve beyond your natural default, as with most bodily things, but there's still a hard coded limit. The human body is not built for compressed magic.

The pentagram Wild had cut into his body would keep siphoning background magic forever. Every iota of power pulled in and compressed was being shuttled, full force, right into his circulatory system. The power was being jammed in, high pressure thundering around his veins. It explained where he was getting his limitless spell-slinging ability from, but it also spoke wonders for his frame of mind.

It used to be called 'wearing the black'. Think of it as a magical equivalent of the bends, but less life threatening and more sanity obliterating. Leave that sort of thing unchecked, and before you know it you're no longer there. The face is the same, all the motions, but you've been pushed out of your head by the pure chaos of unrepentant creation. The black is in control.

And Wild must have been peering right into that particular abyss.

He looked down and saw his chest was on display. 'You know, when they told me what this would do to me, I wasn't sure I believed them. Seemed too good to be true.'

'That's because it is,' I said. 'Did they even bother to tell you about the creeping insanity? It's the sort of thing that really should be stamped on the box in big black letters.'

The pentagram flared. Flesh shouldn't flare like that. 'They said it was difficult to understand for the layman. It's not insanity, warlock. It's like seeing for the first time.'

'Isn't that what insane people tend to say?'

He snorted. 'I'm not going to argue with you about this. Whether you believe what I see or not, makes no difference. I've got a job to do.'

Wild turned and began to walk to where Bennett had

landed. The sheriff was barely conscious, his head flapping softly from side to side, his eyes unfocused and distant. There was no way he could defend himself now, he was already tapped out by the time I arrived for God's sake. Not that I was a fan of his, but I couldn't just let him get ripped to shreds by a crazy bastard.

But what could I do? My magic was all but exhausted, one of my arms didn't work, by ribs were swearing at me like a gaggle of urban youth, and my allies were either dead or on their way there.

Sophie may have had it in her to kick Wild back, but she was having a hard time standing. Her face was almost skeletal now and her legs were unstable. She was looking at me with an expression that conveyed just how lost she was. Everything she had thrown at him had merely slowed him down, and she was completely burnt out. She wanted me to tell her what to do, and I had nothing. Wild had all the power now, he was going to keep refuelling even as we threw everything we had at him.

Wild had all the power now...

Except he didn't have all of it now, did he?

CHAPTER 30

My veins actually contracted when I reached for my power. I felt it happen. That's a really horrible feeling, just so you know, like trying to suck batter through a straw but with more pain. Magical dry-heaving. There wasn't much to grab, but if I was right I wouldn't need much.

I lurched after Wild. He was a few steps ahead, my current top speed wouldn't be enough to catch him. Sophie tried to fall in beside me, but I signalled her to keep back. This was going to be dangerous enough without her in the blast zone.

'Oi, dickhead,' I shouted. My voice couldn't pick a pitch, wavering all over the place. 'I'm not done with you. If we're going to fight, let's at least do it properly.'

Wild stopped and took a deep breath. 'Enough, Parker.'

'Come on. Bennett isn't going anywhere. And I know you've always wanted to give me a good kicking, Wild. You know how I know that?'

He looked at me over his shoulder. 'How?'

'You've met me.'

His head dropped and he let out a low, rumbling laugh. 'Good point.'

He turned around, a dark grin on his face, and took a two-step run up. He brought his fist back and threw it at me, all his body weight and magical force combined into a single deathblow. I swear to God, he tore the air around his fist as he swung. His other arm came up in a guard, shielding his face from the expected counter – the one I would get before he killed me.

But, naturally, I wasn't going for the expected.

I ducked underneath his punch, swearing at the pain with what little breath my chest was allowing, and drove the shard of mirror into his chest. It cut through the central pentagram easily until it struck bone and I saw the spiderweb cracks crawl back up it from the impact. I unleashed my minute magical charge, breaking the seal.

All the power K had thrown at me back on our first meeting was now, for one brief moment, at my command. All the power stored in that shard, exploding at once into any number of spells, as it had been when I had trapped it. There was no time to think. It wasn't a case of casting a spell, it was one of allowing a spell to cast itself. I gave the spell the perfect conditions to happen, and I just had to hope my subconscious would send some impetus out as a spark.

And I had given it only one place to go.

For one horrible, unending moment, I thought I'd screwed it up.

Then, it happened.

The spell, whatever it was, leaked out of the wound and ran through the channels of the pentagram, a glowing yellow line forcing back the sickly greenish blood. In less than a second, the entire symbol was luminous gold, and it was only getting brighter. I could feel the power growing, building up against itself until the levee finally broke and Wild all but exploded.

The golden light burst out in a blazing corona, throwing me back across the room. I landed on my hip, bounced off something hard and angular, and rolled onto my side, skidding along the floor a few more feet before coming to a stop. I looked up in time to see the thick black spidery power crawl out of Wild's chest in the corona's wake. Tendrils of nothingness, pushing their way out of his chest and creeping out in a weird webby, vein-like way across his body. One climbed upwards, into his nostrils, while two more tried to pry his mouth open. A third slithered behind his left eye. His expression was steadfast.

What had I done? Where had this come from?

I watched in horror as the blackness continued to coat him, forcing its way through every weak point it could. It tightened, sprouting thick barbs that forced their way through his pores, locking the tendrils in place, and still his face didn't change.

Then, with a pop, they turned to mist. The blazing corona and the creeping nothingness it had heralded were gone in a flash, and all Wild had to say about it was one long, relaxed exhalation.

He closed his eyes for a moment. 'That hurt, warlock. That really. Fucking. Hurt.'

Well, that was that. I was a goner.

'Erm, sorry?' I said as I tried to scamper back on my elbows. I managed to scuttle, a low speed scuttle.

'I've had a long time to get used to this magic. You think I couldn't nullify my own power, Parker? You seem to forget that I've actually put the effort in.'

'Honestly, I didn't put much thought into that.'

There was a cold rage building in him now. His hands were forming themselves into claws and all the veins in his neck were popping out. If I was lucky, he'd beat me to death rather than roast me alive or splatter my skull with a bolt of pure magical force. 'You ripped open a conduit to the dreamscape *inside my fucking chest.* They're going to have to invent new words to describe the agony I'm going to bathe you in.'

'Oh, is that what I did?'

He responded by seething, which is both rude and incredibly terrifying. Watching Wild seethe was like watching a bull paw at the ground before it charges, winding up for a world of hurt. When he started moving, my way this time, no amount of scuttling was going to get me to safety.

Sophie tried to position herself between the two of us, but Wild slapped her out the way. There was no strength left in her to fight him, but she had had to try. Noble really. My magnetic personality seems to attract the sort of nobility that gets people punched.

At least I had saved Bennett. For all of an extra minute. Silver lining. Well, it *would* have been a silver lining if I had actually liked him, but what are you going to do.

Wild's first punch knocked my elbows out from under me and laid me flat. The second and third blows had further to travel as a result, and with me having nowhere to go damn near knocked my mind out of my skull. I made the mistake of trying to lift my head before the fourth blow hit, cracking my head back onto the floor for the double whammy.

He was going to beat me to death, and I couldn't stop him.

After a few punches, you stop feeling the pain. Well, not normal punches in a proper fight situation, they're the gift that keeps on giving, but once you're effectively beaten your body realises that pain is pointless. Pain is meant as a warning you can't ignore, something to tell you that things are very wrong in a certain part of your body, but it's not really needed once your face is in the process of being pushed through the back of your own head.

The sixth punch did that, I think, which was around the time I felt my nose break. A cheek bone went on the seventh and, as a last fuck-you, one of Wild's knuckles went on the following punch. That gave him pause, as he stopped punching me to look at his hand for a moment. Then his other hand grabbed me by the scruff of the neck and lifted me up until I was an inch from his face.

'I am going to drag the magicians of this country kicking and screaming into a revolution. I want you to know that,' he said.

Talking would have been agony, but like I said, the pain had shut itself off to prepare for the end. 'You're leading them into a meat grinder.'

'If you think about it, I'm giving them the means to grind themselves. The perfect livestock. The fact is, I don't give a shit about your kind. No-one is going to miss them when they break on the walls of Whitehall. But I'm getting paid to mobilise the masses, so that's what I'm going to do. The Rider wants his smoking gun, his two martyrs,' he shot a glance at Bennett. 'One stone.'

I lifted a hand and draped it over the arm that was holding me, the other hung loosely at my side. 'You're never going to get to spend a crooked penny of that money, Greg.'

He raised an eyebrow. It didn't look natural on him. 'And why is that?'

'Because I've just remembered what's in my pocket.'

He looked down just in time to see me blow his testicles off.

It is a problem that every magician has. You get someone used to throwing fireballs at people, and they are going to forget that the mortal world, oblivious to the wonders of such power, have developed some wonderful bits of technology that work in much the same way. Get too caught up in your own hype, and you'll forget simple things like handguns.

Mine had been sat in my pocket for the entire fight, and not once had I considered going for it. I was running on the power of creation itself, I could summon a supernova in the palm of my hand and launch it at any square foot of land on the planet if I wanted, the pistol didn't even factor into this. Like a pocket knife in a sword fight, it wasn't a weapon to me.

But then I had landed on it. Feeling the metal crunch into my hip, suddenly whatever mental block I had evaporated and I realised I had one very deadly weapon just hiding away in my pocket. The hubris of magic had nearly gotten me killed.

I had fired the gun from inside my pocket, not wanting to have revealed its presence earlier by merit of removing it. In truth, I wasn't sure it would be able to pierce the enchantments on the blazer, but when you're going for a sort of cool one liner, you worry about that sort of thing if and when it occurs. Watching Wild's gonads splatter into a lumpy mist sort of vindicated me, though.

If Wild had screamed, it was drowned out by the portable thunderclap of the gunshot. He looked up from where his balls had been, back into my eyes and I put two more bullets into his chest. His eyes went wide and he keeled over to the side, falling off me as he let out his last breath.

'Thanks for the gun,' I said.

I fell back and lay there, staring at the ceiling. There were a few gooey bits on the ceiling – bloody bits of flesh blown clear of the gunshots, most likely. Unless the cleaners had been woefully bad at their jobs.

Then the pain came back, secure in the knowledge that I wasn't about to die. As if I didn't know some bastard had just been wailing on my face, and my arm, and my god damned ribs. Jesus, the ribs were bad. I let out a pained groan.

Bennett's face popped into view. Lovely. 'You look like hell.'

I would have winced if I could, but I wasn't convinced I even had a face any more, just a gnarled lump of tenderised meat. 'You don't look any better yourself, *boss*. At least I had further to fall down the ugly tree.'

He let out a humourless laugh and offered me a hand. I waved it away and he padded off towards Kaitlyn. I rolled my head to the side to try and watch, but it was out of reach. I could see Sophie though. She looked about as well as I had expected, but she was awake and breathing, which was a good sign.

I gave myself a moment to just breathe. It felt like I hadn't done that for days. It did wonders for the pain, or at least how I perceived it. I didn't have to worry about any new sources of pain cropping up, and seeing as most of me hurt anyway there wasn't exactly room for it. Not that any of it mattered. I could just lie here for a bit now. I'd done my part. Fuck them. I was due a rest. If they wanted a word, they could damn well come to me.

They did. All three of their faces were just coming into view when I blacked out.

CHAPTER 31

I woke up in hospital, which wasn't much of a surprise. Not that I'm a connoisseur of A&E wards or anything, but I was willing to put money on being in the same place as Ania. Why take me anywhere else when they already had an entire ward cleared out and full to the brim with security?

Bennett was sat at the foot of the bed, reading the same paperback he had the first time I saw him. He had bent the spine back on itself, and I wondered if he had done that purely to irk the sort of people who find that repellent – a sure sign I was on the mend. You don't get the time for such pointless thoughts if you're at Death's door.

He looked up at me, smirked and slipped the book back into his jacket. For a man that had taking a magical pounding, and a physical one at that, he looked immaculate. It just wasn't fair.

'Welcome back,' he said. 'You were getting dangerously close to taking the piss, being asleep for so long. Can't have you skiving off work, can we, Warlock Supreme? Not when there's so much to be done.'

I tried to shift my weight around in the bed to get comfortable. The bed *was* comfy, but I was lying on various broken and bruised bones, so I was going to make the most of my right to fidget. 'How did I get here?'

'Ambulance. That's how people normally get to hospital,' he said, deadpan.

'You know what I mean.'

'There's only so long you can throw that sort of mojo around in an enclosed space before people outside start taking note of the racket,' he said and stood up. 'Someone called the police. Whitehall intercepted it, as we do, and sent some backup.'

'Could they not have done that *before* things kicked off?'

He walked around the end of the bed and leant on the foot board. 'I've been asking myself the same thing.'

I'd not seen Bennett like this before. Hell, I'd barely *ever* seen him before, but there's a moment when you first met somewhere where your brain extrapolates how their face works. You deduce what their smile looks like, their frown, their crying face. My mind had done all this for Bennett, but it hadn't once considered him looking harrowed.

'How many casualties?' I asked.

There was the slightest delay in his reply. 'Every fast-track candidate in the building is dead. All the warlocks you brought with you, dead. Some of the clerical staff, most of the custodial staff, one or two passers by, all dead.'

'Jesus.'

'Romsey's lot are okay,' he said. 'Whatever you did to them didn't kill them. Preston and Van Ives are alive, too. Badly burnt out, but alive.'

'I didn't expect to find you working with Kaitlyn,' I said. 'I had figured you'd be at each other's throats.'

'You missed the start,' he said, his eyes twinkling. 'She was in the middle of an escape attempt when Wild and Romsey burst in. 'Priorities shift pretty fast in that sort of situation. To tell you the truth – and I will lie if you ever try to repeat this – I wouldn't be here now if it wasn't for her.'

'She's not the bad guy,' I said.

'Not this time. But she *is* a terrorist. Even if she did save my life.'

'Where are they now, Kaitlyn and Sophie?'

Bennett stood up and stretched. I heard tendons popping with glee all over his body. 'They're here. We've got a lot of spare rooms on offer. We've got Van Ives under heavy guard, of course. Preston is next door. She hasn't woken up yet, but the doctors tell us it's exhaustion, nothing life threatening.'

'Good. Enough people have died today.'

Bennett opened his mouth to reply, then thought better of it and just nodded. We sat in silence for a moment.

'Why did you help us?' he said, eventually.

'Excuse me?'

'I get that Wild was in it for the money or the power, or maybe he actually believed what The Rider was selling, but he was still trying to get the magicians to unify, to mobilise. With a force like that, I'm not sure Whitehall could hold out.'

I thought about it for a moment. 'You mean, why didn't I fight for my freedom?'

'Yes.'

'Because what he was offering wasn't the start of the march to freedom, it was the path to extinction,' I said and leant forward. 'Don't think I'm not aware that the moment any magician uprising is even considered credible, every warlock in the country dies, instantly.' I snapped my fingers for emphasis.

'No, there are rules.'

'Rules are all well and good until a thousand streams of technicolour death are bombarding your inner sanctum. Whitehall would vault everyone it could because, let's face it, you've made us very good at what we do. An army of free magicians led by warlocks would be difficult to beat.'

He frowned. 'Are you saying it was the vault that kept you loyal?'

'No,' I smiled. 'In a proper uprising, we'd find a way around that I should think. How do you think myself and Sophie threw so much magic around today?'

'It never occurred to me at the time.'

'No, I was hoping it wouldn't.'

'There'll be an investigation.'

'I'd appreciate it if there wasn't one.'

He sighed. 'Out of my hands, I'm afraid. It's procedure whenever someone is issued carte blanche. I'm assuming that's what happened?'

I nodded. 'It was never about the vault, anyway.'

'Then what?'

'You saw what Wild did. *How* he did it. You really need to ask that question? He had power and the freedom to use it, and that was some dark shit he pulled. And the worst thing is, in his place I'm not sure I would have acted differently. *That's* why. People never believe me when I tell them that, but it's the truth.'

'I was there, you know,' he said slowly, quietly. 'When you killed her.'

It was a good thirty seconds before I replied. 'I didn't know that.'

'Not many people do. What you did... It has a habit of overwhelming the memory. I doubt you could find a guy on that team who remembers anyone else was there but you and him.' He closed his eyes and took a cleansing breath. I recognised that action, the attempt to clear a mental picture. I'd done that before. 'I believe you.'

I pinched the bridge of my nose. My eyes were starting to hurt, a dull throbbing pain in the dark places behind them. 'What now?'

'You get better, you come back to work. We've got an even more severe warlock shortage now, and not many fast-track candidates to plug the gap. Plus, you know, if it really was The Rider pulling Wild's strings he'll needs to be brought down before he does something like this again. Sounds like an all hands on deck situation is brewing. Time to live up to your title.'

'And what about the investigation into the spells?'

'That should take about a week.'

'That's not what I meant.'

Bennett's face went grave. 'They'll vault you if they find cause. If the authorisation wasn't legitimate...'

'I couldn't possibly comment.'

'Better that way, I would think. I don't tend to give people this advice, but then warlocks don't tend to save my life at the risk of their own, which I think makes me in your debt somewhat.' He looked very awkward at that moment, like a teenager caught by his parents in the aftermath of a house party. 'Perhaps you should consider a holiday. Unofficially.'

I blinked. 'You mean run away?'

'No,' he said firmly. 'I mean a *holiday*. Abroad. Somewhere that might look unkindly upon a thaumaturgical spell going off within its borders. Until, hypothetically, someone who technically owes you a favour has time to smooth this over, seeing as he doesn't relish the prospect of being indebted to a warlock for longer than is necessary. It would be easier for this hypothetical person to do that if you and your unique brand of charm aren't here making things more difficult.'

I'd never considered that. Warlocks never get it into their head to run, largely because they could be tracked down wherever they were through thaumaturgy, or just simply vaulted if it was all too much trouble. But there were countries where a warlock could vanish if he kept his head down, places where the locals had a very suspicious view of magic and the governing bodies took it as a personal slight were it to be used. And these were no flash in the pan, jumped up fiefdoms.

These were the largely in the New World, or the Americas if you want to go by modern nomenclature, a place set up specifically to get away from the magic of the Old World. Granted, you won't find that in the history books, but that doesn't make it any less true. If I could get myself out there, under the auspices of certain new world powers, Whitehall wouldn't dare vault me. It would mean war.

Of course, it was just as likely, if not more, that the locals would track me down and gut me in all sorts of horrible ways anyway. It wasn't as if they would *welcome* me. Nobody wants a warlock in their town. But it had been done before, although not many times. As long as I could keep myself from pushing my luck – no spells, *none*. If I kicked up enough magical menace, Whitehall would vault me regardless of if it would bring a war.

So I guess I had to choose. A long and quiet life of hiding away in the arse crack of the New World, or one last week as the bad-ass in residence, hoping for a last minute reprieve for being such a stud.

Before I could make a decision, an explosion rocked the building. I damn near fell out of bed, the various tubes jacked into my flesh being the only reason I didn't. It was like falling into a latex spider web.

Bennett was on his feet instantly. 'What the hell?'

I untangled myself from the tubes. 'How many guys did you have guarding Kaitlyn?'

His face went white and he bolted for the door,

disappeared through it in a flash. A moment later, his head popped back round. 'Stay. Here. I'll be back.'

I held back a grin and flipped him a salute. 'Be seeing you.'

He was torn for a moment, but then he was gone. I gave him fifteen seconds to return, then I began unhooking myself from the machines.

It hadn't been a hard decision.

My clothes were in a crumpled heap on the floor by the bed, sticky with drying blood and riddled with rips and tears. They'd do. I slipped into them quickly and ducked out the door into the hallway.

It *was* the same hospital Ania had been in, I recognised the corridor. It hadn't been this busy at the time though. The hallway was packed with various suited men, dashing around manically; fast-trackers brought in from Whitehall to help settle things down was my guess. They didn't seem to quite know what to do with themselves, although they were sort of meandering in the direction of the explosion. I purposefully bumped into one and lifted his mobile phone.

Picking a pocket isn't hard. It's made harder by having hands that barely work and a head like a stormed rave, but it's also made easier by the target blundering around in total sensory overload.

Phone in hand, I ducked out into the street and sauntered off away from the hospital. I dialled Charlie.

'Hello, Whitehall,' she said.

I rolled my shoulders. They popped. 'Hello, dear. Care for a holiday?'

EPILOGUE

The east side of the river ain't a place most right-minded people go. You get the uglies down there, them what don't take too kindly to people who ask too many questions. Course, the sort of people what make a home for themselves down there ain't averse to answering a few questions for the right price neither. One of their little quirks. You just gotta know the right way to ask.

The Baron is good at spotting those what know how to ask questions the proper way, which is why he sent me. I'm good. If words ain't getting the job done, I got other means. Most guys only know one or the other.

He wanted to know about some rumour that we had got some wizard in his lands, fresh off the boat from the old world. Them fellas tend to stink of money, which ain't hard to spot, but this one had gone native pretty easy. The Baron didn't like that.

I tracked him to the east side of the river, to some bar what looked like it belonged out in some podunk shit hole in the deep south. No-one there was talking, that very specific way of not talking what says you're lying. No manner of coin was going to loosen them lips. So I grabbed the first shifty guy what I saw and smashed his nose into the bar.

Like I said, I got other methods if I need them.

'Now listen up,' I says. 'The Baron has heard some disturbing rumours that we got ourselves a wizard up in these parts what ain't declared himself. Harbouring such a fella ain't smart. All I'm asking is you point me in his direction.'

They didn't say nothing, of course. But they all looked in the same direction. Don't have to say nothing if your eyes are giving things away now, do you? When you got a score of unwashed uglies all looking at a fella whose hair ain't plastered to his scalp with grease, you figure you've started to make progress.

I pushed my way through the uglies towards this guy. Didn't look rich, but didn't fit in his clothes neither. Filthy clothes like you would expect, but clean face and hair, shiny fingernails and no cuts or coarseness on his hands. Believe they call that probably cause or something.

Pulled my piece on him and he didn't even flinch. Ain't a big one or nothing, not designed to scare but is right good at killing, and most guys still get the message. This one didn't hardly notice. He just kept on drinking something what looked and smelled like sewer water mixed with tree bark.

'You'll be wanting to stand up slowly, fella,' says I.

He puts his drink down and just stares at me with his pearly whites on show. 'There seems to be some mistake, sir,' says he, an old world accent if ever I'd heard one. 'You say you're looking for a wizard?'

'You heard what I said, fella,' says I, cocking my piece.

He smiles one damn crooked smile at me and then leans back and puts his boots on the table. 'No wizard here. Just us warlocks.'

ABOUT THE AUTHOR

You're nosy, why do you want to know things about the author? He writes books, like this one, on a computer that overlooks a garden. It's nice – he can see a tree. He lives with one, sometimes two, cats and from time to time family move in and get in the way.

Also, for what it's worth, he's very much in love with you because you actually took the time to read the book. Unless you didn't, and you just skipped to the end. If that is why you're on this page, well, tsk tsk.

*Anyway, if you want to know more you can find the author knocking about on twitter @**stevetheblack** or on his website **stevekpeacock.com***

Go on, that's your lot.

Nosy.

Printed in Great Britain
by Amazon